THE BOOK OF UR

MARK EVERETT STONE

Black Rose Writing | Texas

ISBN: 978-1-68513-259-0
PUBLISHED BY BLACK ROSE WRITING
www.blackrosewriting.com

Printed in the United States of America
Suggested Retail Price (SRP) $22.95

The Book of Ur is printed in EB Garamond

*As a planet-friendly publisher, Black Rose Writing does its best to eliminate unnecessary waste to reduce paper usage and energy costs, while never compromising the reading experience. As a result, the final word count vs. page count may not meet common expectations.

This one is for my family. Without you I'm just a mad scribbler trying to see in the dark. For Catherine Treadgold, thank you so much for doing that word arranging and punctuation thingie, you're the best. This is also for my cat, Tom, who didn't help with this at all.

Special Thanks to David McDaniel for the encouragement and the pop-up tent.

The Book of Ur

CHAPTER ONE

I found myself on a steel table, one large and sturdy enough to accommodate my size and weight. It felt surprisingly cold, as if taken directly from a morgue. A blue towel descended over my face, soaked through with tepid water that smelled slightly musty and dusty, as if it came from some stagnant forest pool. My arms and legs lay bound with thick plastic straps that dug into my flesh like dull blades, cutting off my circulation. The men who tied those straps obviously did not care about my comfort. Light filtered through the cloth, blue and harsh and I knew what was coming.

Water splashed onto the towel. Despite my somewhat special condition, fear turned like an icy worm in my gut.

I gagged and struggled, the straps cutting great furrows into my limbs as water crept into my nose and mouth. My predicament seemed to delight my captors, who laughed as the ringleader of their little posse kept on pouring water for what seemed like a good part of forever. Blood began to well from beneath the plastic straps, dripping slowly onto the table. I struggled even more so the furrows would not regenerate, I did not want my captors to see me healing.

Somebody spoke in a language that had a lot of harsh sibilants and sounded like there was considerable phlegm at the back of the speaker's throat. Considering the look of the men who had grabbed me, I took it to be Arabic.

The towel moved away and I gagged on a mouthful of the musty water. I managed to clear my nose, flinging snot across my face and chest.

"How do you like that, my man?" the ringleader asked in a curiously high-pitched voice. "I know you are tough, I see your scars, but no one is that tough. Where did you get your scars, my man? They are impressive. You have lot of them." A stubby finger traced the thick worm of tissue that ran from my left temple to my chin.

Cough, cough, choke. My lungs burned and I flailed to no effect. They laughed, much amused. It was like the worst party ever. *Keep laughing, asshole.*

"Sears," I managed once my lungs quit spasming. "Let me buy you some. Chicks dig them."

The laughter died and the towel descended.

Fifteen seconds of water to the face, then a brief respite. Once again, I gasped and spat as the cloth was removed, the harsh light of a 100-watt bulb overhead burning my retinas. Four guys, all of them Middle Eastern, stood above me, laughing and jeering at my discomfort and I made a mental note to kill them all.

"You done with your choking, my man?" The ringleader, a short, fat man with a big, black mole on the side of his ugly beak poked my cheek with a stubby finger. His black hair saw a lot of gray and I estimated him to be in his forties. The mole certainly captured my attention and while ugly, it was a welcome relief from staring at his heroically offensive nose hair.

I spat out some of the awful water. "Yeah, I am fine. In fact, I am going to kill all of you, you know that, right?"

The cluster of sneering faces laughed. Obviously, I was funnier than Dave Chappelle. "Who do you work for?" the ringleader asked.

I reached for a couple of words I had heard on the television last night. "Yo mama."

Ringleader's olive face became mottled with anger and I received some more waterboarding, which went back to sucking the big one.

"What do you know?" short and stubby asked twenty seconds later whilst I gagged. I could not help but stare at that enormous, black mole. It was almost hypnotic. Maybe it would grow a rudimentary intelligence and leap from his face just to get away from that nose hair.

"I know...I know you have a strip outside the city...to the north," I almost wept. Defeat creased my face. *Gag, gag. Whimper, whimper.*

For a moment he looked puzzled, but then his face cleared. "You know this?" he chuckled.

I nodded, feigning exhaustion and despair. "Yeah. That is where you fly the girls out."

His teeth were very white and very even, his most attractive feature. "Who are you, my man? Who do you work for? Are you FBI? ICE? Homeland Security?"

Time for more defiance. "Go screw yourself," I spat.

Out came the blue towel and more water. It was getting tedious, the torture, but I could not let the circle jerk think I was a pushover.

"Who are you, my man?" The ringleader asked again, still smiling his very white smile when the towel departed.

I sobbed and gagged some more. Sure, there was pain, a lot of it in fact, but no real damage thanks my special nature. It was a great performance, though. Someday I will win an award. *And the Oscar goes to...*

"Who are you?"

"ICE," I cried, putting an extra bit of snivel into my voice. "And my guys are going be all over that air strip any second and get the girls."

All four of the men laughed loud and long. "You are misinformed, my man. We use The Spirit of St. Louis." The ringleader slapped my cheek lightly, almost tenderly. "Nothing beats a real American airport for legitimacy. Your men are at the wrong site."

Bingo! I narrowed my eyes. "You have a plane at The Spirit of St. Louis right now?"

He nodded. "Yes, it is waiting for us with all those gorgeous American girls on board. So, you are out of luck...why are you smiling?"

I was not smiling, I was grinning savagely, my lips pulling at my facial scars. "Because I have what I need." Hot fury laced my words. The plastic straps binding my arms and legs to the table parted with a sharp *snap*. More flesh tore and a little blood flew and I did not mind the pain, not one bit. After centuries worth, pain loses its ability to distract.

I drove the stiffened fingers of my left hand into the throat of the biggest man there, a brute who must have been at least six-six. Cartilage gave and crunched and he dropped, gagging and mewling. I jackknifed off the table rising to meet the other three, nasty water dripping from my long, lank hair.

The two to either side of the ringleader went for pistols tucked into the small of their backs. They were fast, but I was faster as I grabbed the table, ripping it free from the brackets holding it to the floor, sending shards of twisted metal and cement flying. With one hand I slammed it into the man on the left, smashing bone and sending him sprawling, while the one on the right stared in shock, dumbfounded at my ability to wield 150 pounds of steel like cheap plastic patio furniture. It delayed him enough that I was able to get right *there*, inside his reach, inside his personal bubble and I grabbed him by the throat and I squeezed *hard*.

Bone and cartilage *popped* and I threw him to the side because he was already dead and a vicious ax kick to the skull drove bone splinters into the brain of the man I had injured with the table as he started to rise and he fell back, lifeless and it was just me and the ringleader, whose eyes were huge with disbelief and fear.

I cursed myself for enjoying his terror. I was supposed to be above such things. These were evil men, but what did it say about me that I was having *fun*? It was enough to add self-loathing to the mixture of emotions swirling in my chest.

"My man," he began. "I can make you rich…I can get you anything you want. Pussy, money, anything." The room was only ten by fifteen and the door to freedom was behind me. He was trapped.

"Do not be vulgar," I said almost conversationally as he flattened against the unpainted cinderblock wall, his stomach fat trembling like a bowl of Jell-O. "Tell me the name of your contacts, where were you flying the girls, and the ID number of the plane."

"I can't tell you that, my man!" he whimpered as I took hold of the collar of his ugly yellow bowling shirt. "Do you know what they'll do to me?"

My face came within an inch of his so he could get a real close look at my scars and I growled like a panther, "If you do not tell me, you will find out what *I* will do and it will much worse than what *they* could ever dream of."

•   •   •

Later, in a black limo, drinking 18-year-old scotch, I gave the man sitting next to me a slip of paper. "It is all there. Plane, location of the Senator's daughter, the other girls, their destination. Everything. The police are on their way to The Spirit of St. Louis airport. An anonymous tip." Hopefully the girls were well, albeit terrified. The kidnappers would not have abused them, preferring to deliver their goods unharmed and unmolested, at least not yet. Although the slave trade promised big money for quality merchandise, it was not unknown for one or two of the kidnapped women to be used poorly before they reached their final destination in Dubai. The slavers wanted the girls to be broken and cowed for their new lives as human chattel and raping a couple to serve as examples certainly kept the others in line. Another reason my conscience never bothered me when I stepped over their kidnappers' corpses.

Marcus Siedell looked at the list and grunted. A big man well into his forties with a blond buzz cut slowly turning gray, he was fit and trim, not an ounce of fat covering his massive frame. A man carved out of flesh-colored granite and twice as hard. He had Devil Dog written all over him, all up and down and squared away carrying a lifetime's worth of marine experience into his civilian job. As Senator Barnes's chief of staff and personal bodyguard, he looked every inch the menacing minder, someone most would have to be crazy to antagonize.

"I am not happy with police involvement," he said quietly, lips hardly moving. Mannequins wore more expressions than this guy. "This was supposed to be handled with the minimum amount of fuss."

A sigh wound past my lips. "I really do not care. Let the police and the news have their day." The scotch was good, top drawer, a brand I had not had in years. "It will only help his re-election campaign to be seen by the public as a concerned father." I stared out into the cold March night. The chill wind tried seep into the car but the heater kept it at bay.

He pursed his lips slightly, considering words as if the Messiah had issued them. Finally, he nodded. "Good point."

From far behind the speeding limo, an orange fireball clawed its way into the sky before mushrooming out and fading into smoke that blended into the night. A moment later the heavy car was rocked slightly by a pressure wave. It was Seidell's turn to sigh.

"Why do that, sir?" he asked softly, his voice the purr of a jungle cat.

I took another sip of scotch and considered the destruction of the drycleaner's that was the source of the explosion and the front for the white slave ring. "Do what? The explosion? A good fire means no trace evidence. I do not care if it looks like arson or not. Besides, those in the know might think twice before setting up shop in St. Louis again."

"Hmmm." Seidell reached into the inside pocket of his black suit jacket and pulled forth a fat envelope. "Here, sir."

Heavy, loaded with more hundreds than I cared to count at the time. "I did not ask for this."

His washed-out blue eyes were devoid of emotion. "A bonus for a job well done."

I speared the big man with my own hard, flat stare. "This does not absolve the favor the senator owes me," I said, hefting the envelope. "When I ask for my favor, he will respond in the affirmative." My voice told him that bad things happened to those who reneged.

"The senator repays he debts, don't worry, sir." Seidell took a deep breath. "How did you do it? Find out it was the drycleaner?"

The scotch burned a trail to my stomach. "Simple really. All three women used the same drycleaner, even though the perps were careful not to leave any evidence."

"Then how did you know, sir? How did you know it was them if there was no evidence?"

"When I interviewed Wendy Hidebrandt's roommate, she said that Wendy had no social life, just school, a trip to the drycleaner once a week, and the library. When I checked her clothes, none of the hangers had drycleaning logos."

"What?"

"You know, those paper sleeves they put on the hangers printed with their logo. They use it as advertisement. What kind of drycleaner fails to do that?"

The minder shook his head. "Smart, sir."

Smart enough. A couple of days of surveillance offered nothing but the ringleader and his men going in and out of the back several times a week at odd hours. While not suspicious in and of itself, it was strange enough for me poke the beehive. I snooped around; asked a lot of obvious questions, let myself be seen as a possible threat. It did not take long for the gang to follow me back to the cheap no-tell motel I stayed at, snatching me from the parking lot using chloroform and a hood that smelled of sweaty armpits. I let the four take me back to the store and begin interrogation.

The best way to obtain the answers you need is for the bad guys to tell you, thinking that you are at their mercy. All the while they were at *mine*.

"Your plane is fueled and ready to go, sir."

I gave Seidell a frosty smile. "Thank you."

Seidell's big, Midwestern face creased into a frown. "May I ask a personal question, sir?"

"Go ahead."

"How did you get into the Personal Security business? You must know we pulled your file, and except for a social security number and date of birth, it was pretty thin. You hardly exist at all, sir, on paper. It's like you appeared out of nowhere and that's strange for a man in your line of business."

I had been expecting the question for quite some time, before I completed the mission, in fact. My name was well known in certain, rarified circles and work was not hard to come by, not in a world where the rich and powerful are more paranoid than the average White Nationalist group.

The only answer I gave Marcus Seidell was an enigmatic smile.

●　　●　　●

Later, after landing at LAX and boarding a private jet to O'ahu, I reclined in my leather seat and pondered Marcus's question. My clients in the

Personal Security business were rich, powerful people whose aid I found myself in greater and greater need. In the digital age, the time of Big Brother, it was becoming harder and harder to remain anonymous.

In the old days I could simply disappear, moving to a different city afforded me the ability to change my name, my history. Back then, the past was a plastic thing, easily stretched and molded to suit a purpose. Nowadays, I found myself seeking hackers and those who roamed the halls of power with impunity to alter records or create new ones.

For the past twelve years I had been Frank Vickers, a Virginian, a humble man risen to riches due to an ability to solve problems. Often by savage means, such as dealing with the kidnappers of Senator Barnes's twenty-year-old daughter, Melanie.

The faces of the slavers flashed across my eyes, each glaring with hate. I felt no remorse at causing the death of evil men. Much like cockroaches, if you saw one, a thousand more would be behind the baseboards. Heaven may find its fill of saints, but Hell always welcomes more sinners. Even on Sundays.

There would come a time, perhaps soon, when it would become necessary to change identities again and change cities, find a new state to live in. Maybe a different country. Although Hawaii was considered laid back by American standards, my distinctive facial scars, my ungainly six-foot six body with overlarge hands and feet, drew much attention. The comforts of city life suited me well, so living in the country, perhaps Wyoming or Montana, would grate like fingernails on a chalkboard.

Perhaps being found out would not be so bad.

No...on second thought it would be horrible. I would become a laboratory experiment, poked and prodded, blood drawn through tubes to fill jars that would be carefully labeled and stored away. Tissue samples harvested without much care or worry about the patient's wellbeing would go on until I was nothing more than a chunks of meat stored in separate facilities in clear plastic, carefully marked containers.

No thank you.

I ordered champagne from an attractive flight attendant with curly auburn hair. She refused to meet my eyes as she handed me the glass of bubbly amber liquid, declining to allow her soft, doe-like orbs settle on my face. After all the years carrying my scars, it still stung to see that reaction.

And I have seen it thousands of times.

Such things no longer surprise me. After all, I am a monster.

CHAPTER TWO

Geneva, June, 1816

I returned at last to the Western World after my long sojourn in China and India. It was strange speaking once again the tongue to which I was born, stranger still returning to the place I once called home.

The dreary day passed as I sat in the carriage, pondering upon what I concluded was the middle of my life (for surely, I could not continue my existence indefinitely, no one lives forever. Not even a damned soul such as myself). Why return? What good could come of it? The answer sprung quickly to mind: before this my life resembled that of a beast rather than a man. Only in the last several decades had rational thought found purchase, snug inside my skull and I wished to see the old world with fresher eyes.

June in Geneva lay cool and rainy, but the city shone in the fading light, seeming both refined and quaint, a marvel of the old and new. When I exited the carriage, the people here did not point or jest at my great size or the deformities that marred my skin, which now, thanks to cosmetics, bore a shade much like that of those afflicted by ginger hair, although I bore no freckles. Perhaps a touch paler than that, although my scars still lay upon my face like fat, purple worms, pulling flesh so the mask I presented the world looked subtly twisted.

My eyes sought refuge behind a pair of spectacles sporting colored glass, which gave me an eccentric appearance, especially when shaded beneath a tall stovepipe hat the color of charcoal. A better solution than baring my orbs for the world to see. While they would no longer cause a fearful reaction, people often would refuse to gaze fully upon them because of their oddity. I did not wish for that. My desire was to pass unremarked as I traveled through the world.

That first night in Geneva bore much adventure and I think I made friends, very possibly my first! It was a concept that both delighted and concerned me because, after all, my time of wandering and avoiding wider humanity meant that finding friends filled me with a modicum of fear. How long will this friendship last? If the truth of my genesis were known, would I be reviled or accepted?

Our meeting occurred after I paid for lodging at the Hotel Comedie and I desired to walk about the town, even though I had just arrived and felt not an inconsiderable fatigue. Excitement at being among a populace into which I could blend gave me a yearning to explore the city which quite overwhelmed my need for sleep.

Nighttime in Geneva...cold, the icy waters of the Rue de Carouge only partially lit by gaslight at the corner of every other block, lending fitful illumination to the dark, dew slick cobbles. The endearing, earthy smell of fresh wet filled the air covering the sour stench of overfull chamber pots. Although darkness covered the streets between gaslight, and my sensitive eyes were nestled behind colored lenses, I could see thanks to my special nature so that even the minutest ray of light rendered the city in shades of the first blush of dawn.

The chill air entered my lungs and I gloried in my return to familiar surroundings, even though much had changed in the years I had been absent. During my travels I found a sort of inner peace, an acceptance of what I was and it braced me like the cold night air. No longer would I wander afraid of what I was. I would now hold my head high and mingle with the masses.

Perhaps it was on the Rue de Sources I found myself, each street seemed like the last. As I passed a tailor's, closed for the night, a shrill scream violently rent the silence and sliced into my ears. For the life of me it sounded like a great cat, enraged and ready for a fight. Without a thought my feet led the way toward the noise, an alley unlit by gaslight but to my eyes a twilight thoroughfare.

Heedless of danger, I sped down the alley and spotted half-a-dozen men, leering and jeering, surrounding a young couple that had their backs to a brick wall grimy with decades of soot. The men were of a rough-and-tumble sort dressed in oft-patched humble clothing, while the couple seemed well turned out, obviously wealthy and thus the target for such depredations.

Perhaps the source of the cat cry was the woman and that hypothesis was confirmed as she once again let loose another fierce wail. A shout of anger absent all fear and it seemed to give the six ruffians pause, as did the knife she pulled forth from the folds of her voluminous dress, a dress so dark a burgundy as to appear black. A lantern lay on the ground, dropped there during the attack, its wick no longer alight. However, a small puddle of burning oil did provide small, yet fitful, illumination that seemed to me a bonfire.

The plight of the two touched me deeply and, without warning, I was among the menacing six. Perhaps if the scoundrels had bothered to keep watch they would have spied my arrival. But that would not have changed the outcome.

One fist hit a man above the ear and I felt the bones of his skull give way to my enormous knuckles with a satisfying crunch and he dropped, lifeless. A sharp kick snapped a shin wetly, the owner of the broken appendage falling to the ground. His shrieks bounced off the grimy walls. My other fist embedded itself in a midriff, doubling the man over, vomiting his internals. All this took less than two seconds while their companions looked at me as if I was a demon from the pit to drag their souls to Hell.

They had no idea how right they were.

As if by magic they turned and fled, carrying their broken-legged comrade with them while the vomiter staggered off, gasping and trailing odorous fluid behind. I bid good riddance to such rubbish, choosing not to pursue in favor of assuring the safety and health of the young couple.

Said couple looked in my direction, the young man attempting to pierce the gloom by force of will. Short of stature and handsome, with hair black as the night that surrounded us, he bore a slight weakness to his chin than marked him an Englishman. "Do not hurt us," he whimpered in the King's. By his accent, I knew him to be from London.

"Don't be silly, John," said the woman in the same tongue, sliding her knife back into her dress. "If he meant us ill, then he would have waited until those ruffians had done us harm." She smiled at me, showing a mouthful of white, even teeth.

It was that smile that struck my heart like a hammerblow. Although young and sharp-featured, that grin transformed the woman's face into something divine and in that instant I was hopelessly, helplessly, smitten. It seemed as if my heart might burst from the cage of my ribs to lay pumping at her feet.

A moment or two later I gathered my lovestruck wits and addressed the pair, although my eyes never left the woman's face. "Allow me the pleasure of an introduction," I said in my smoothest manner, gentling my voice from its normal gravely inflection. Doffing my hat, I performed a credible bow, my shoulder-length dark hair momentarily obscuring my twisted features. It had been years since I spoke the tongue, but my English did not mangle any ears. "I am Victor Franks and I am certainly at your service." Oh, how I wished we would converse in civilized German, or even Rhomansh, but the English rarely bothered to learn any tongue besides French, which was worse.

If anything, her smile became brighter until she practically shone, as if an angel lay beneath her skin. "Our rescuer is a gentleman, John," she said to the man who lifted the lantern and struck a lucifer to relight the wick. "We are blessed indeed."

"Deuced thing has spilt most of its oil." John held up the lantern, its light falling full across my face. He gasped in surprise. "Good lord, man, you are as white as a sheet! Are you well?"

He did not mention the scars, he did not comment on my spectacles or my size. Instead, he inquired as to my health. This raised him much in my estimation. Perhaps there was hope for the English after all.

"John!" the woman scolded. "This is our rescuer. Be polite."

She also failed to mention my scars and my ugliness. For that I loved her even more. "Think nothing of it, my lady," I said with a smile as I donned my hat once again. At least my teeth were even and white, a point of beauty in a field of homeliness. "I suffer from the curse of Albinism. Without the application of cosmetics my skin would resemble snow."

"Be that as it may, it is rude not to offer our names since you have given yours so freely. I am Mary Godwin." A silk-encased hand settled on her breast. By the light of the lantern, I saw she was younger than I had surmised. Perhaps not yet twenty. "And this is Dr. John Polidori."

Dr. Polidori. A young man, perhaps as young as Miss Godwin and quite accomplished for someone of that age. My estimation of him rose again. I offered the worthy a gloved hand, which he shook without hesitation. Another point in his favor "A pleasure, Dr. Polidori." I brought Miss Godwin's offered hand to my lips before reluctantly letting go.

"The pleasure is mine, sir," said Dr. Polidori with much less trepidation than before. "Since without your timely intervention those brutes would have used us ill, I believe. May I ask, is the reason you wear colored spectacles your Albinism?"

"John!" Mary scolded, aghast. I fought back a chuckle.

Polidori blinked. "Right. Quite. I do apologize," he said quickly. "My profession is one where natural curiosity is encouraged, but can be socially awkward at times." He noticed the fallen man for the first time. "Good lord! I believe this man is dead!"

"And I am none the sorrier," Mary sniffed. "That is the scoundrel that lied to us."

I examined the man, although there was no need. A large, fist-shaped concavity marred the side of his head. "What do you mean?"

Mary Godwin kicked the man with a pointed shoe. "Pollydolly and I came into town for a day of shopping and to find something decent to eat. Naturally we became lost, not remembering where we left our cabriolet." Her voice turned ugly with self-recrimination. "This foul beast offered to guide us to the hotel where we left the vehicle."

"I asked you not to call me that, Mary," said Dr. Polidori quietly as he knelt to examine the corpse.

A young couple and naïve indeed to have fallen for such a ruse. More experienced heads would have seen through the sham immediately. "Where did you leave your carriage?" I asked, straightening to my full height.

"The Hotel Comedie."

My eyebrows shot up in surprise and my laughter echoed off the alley walls. "You are indeed fortunate, then. That is my hotel and I was taking the night air, ready to return, when I heard your scream."

Her smile once again took my breath away.

"Good lord, man!" Polidori exclaimed softly from his examination of the corpse. "Not only is this brute's head caved in, but his neck is broken as well." He lifted the lantern as he stood, staring at me in awe. "Such a feat of strength! Surely you have injured your hand with such a mighty blow. Shall I examine it?"

I held up the appendage in question. "No need. As you see, it is fine. A long life of hard labor has made me strong and my bones even stronger. No doubt suffusion of energy brought about by your plight aided my feat of strength."

The young couple stared in amazement at my overlarge hands in their leather sheaths barely covering knuckles the size of walnuts. After a brief moment, Mary tittered. "You know what they say about a man with large hands, Pollydolly?"

"Mary!" gasped the outraged doctor, cheeks flushing.

I knew very well what was said, but I liked the girl's cheek. "What do they say, Miss Godwin?" I asked archly.

She stared at me straightaway and said, "They wear large gloves."

We were still laughing as we exited the alley.

•　•　•

"There you are, Miss Godwin," I grinned as the stable boy brought the cabriolet around. "Have a safe ride to...wherever it is you are staying." It tore at me to say goodbye to the young couple. In the short time we had been together, I had grown quite fond of Mary's fearlessness and Dr. Polidori's sensitive nature. They possessed good hearts and fine characters.

The pair stared at each other a moment before saying in unison, "Come with us."

I was flabbergasted. "What?"

"Oh, please, Victor!" Mary pleaded, laying her dainty hands upon my arm. "Please come with us. My fiancée and I are renting a lovely little villa on the lake and it would make me ever so happy to have you with us, our savior."

At the mention of her fiancée, my heart plummeted, but, in reality, what chance did I have with woman possessed of such fine qualities as Mary Godwin? It should have come as no surprise that such a jewel would be affianced. No doubt the wretch possessed a surfeit of wealth and looks, not to mention charm.

"Can such a small place afford to house a man of my stature?" I joked, standing to my full height, the seams of my greatcoat straining in effort to contain my size.

Mary dimpled prettily and I wanted very much to kiss each concavity. "Of course it can. And my fiancée will want to meet the man who saved the life of his future wife."

"My patron will also want to meet you," Dr. Polidori chimed in with a wide smile. "As he is a good British Lord, he will wish to thank the man who saved the life of his friend and physician."

"It is settled," Mary stated firmly. "You will come and we will not take 'no' for an answer."

Polidori nodded in agreement and I felt had no choice but to acquiesce.

Perhaps Mary Godwin and Dr. John Polidori would not have been so eager for my company had they thought the matter through. A cabriolet is a two-wheeled carriage pulled by a single horse and is often built for only pair of occupants.

They would not let me walk the distance to the villa, so I found myself wedged between them with my travel case upon my lap, my bulk causing no small amount of discomfort for my companions. Although Mary must have felt squeezed in tighter than a robust woman in a corset, she nevertheless graced me with her winning smile, not once voicing a complaint. Although there were uncomfortable grunts and a small groan from Dr. Polidori.

Fortunately, our trip did not take long and we came to Villa Diodati, the residence rented by Mary and her fiancée for the summer. She had named it a 'small villa'. Perhaps she was being modest because it was simply one of the largest houses I had ever seen, three stories of whitewashed masonry. The wall containing the front door held several columns that supported the second story balcony. Lush lawns and tall trees surrounded the structure lending it a sort of grandeur greater than its size would normally allow.

"I thought you said it was small," I breathed in awe. There were more windows that I could easily count in an afternoon.

"Compared to most castles, it is relatively tiny," she said with a grin. "It's true name is Villa Belle Rive, but George named it Diodati after the owners."

"George?"

"My patron," inserted Dr. Polidori proudly. "A true gentleman and a poet of incredible talent, not to mention a fine athlete despite a small limp that hinders him slightly."

At that moment as we drew near, the front door opened pouring warm light out onto the yard, silhouetting a man. He stood there but a moment before dashing toward us and I detected that he favored his right leg, albeit modestly. This informed me the this must be Dr. Polidori's patron, George, and the breadth of his shoulders beneath is white shirt indicated a man of considerable strength.

"Mary, Pollydolly, we have been so worried," shouted the man in a deep, melodic voice. "You should have been back hours ago."

As he neared, I took his measure: a ruggedly handsome with curly black hair receding slightly from a noble brow and one of the biggest chins I had ever beheld. It had a deep cleft and the eye seemed to be drawn to it rather than the full lips or the deep-set dark eyes, eyes that grew wide with alarm as they took in the sight of me.

"It is well, George," said Mary, holding up a hand. "We were set upon by rogues, but for the timely intervention of this good gentleman, we would have been killed."

Dr. Polidori nodded his agreement, not once removing adoring eyes from George's countenance. It was no wonder the good Doctor was so smitten, the man was a good-looking devil, despite the overlarge chin.

Mary's words halted the worthy gentleman in an instant. He gaped at me, as if I sported not one, but two heads, before straightening himself to his full height and executing a bow with flourishes.

"My good sir," he said with all gravity. "I am in your debt."

Extricating myself from the cabriolet involved both Mary and the doctor exiting first and the unfolding of my long legs, but I managed it without falling upon my face and ruining the gravitas of the moment. George's eyes stayed upon me the whole time, amazed. During the exorcise, I noticed another man emerging from the villa, weaving slightly yet despite his obvious inebriation, moving with uncommon grace.

"Let me assure you good sir," I said with a much simpler bow and a flourish of my stovepipe hat. "The pleasure of rescuing such fine people of outstanding character is all mine."

"What an extraordinarily ugly man!" exclaimed the other, emerging into the light of the cabriolets lantern. The words went through me with an electric jolt.

My guts suddenly churned in agony and the familiar anger I had oft been prone to flared briefly. That anger, an old enemy since first I opened my eyes, burned in the hollows of my heart before I ruthlessly stamped it out and I took the time whilst controlling my temper to observe the rude gentleman.

The man possessed curly blond hair, full sensual lips and a pouty face made for rapturous artists to paint. He held a goblet in his right hand, slim form draped in a wine-stained shirt and a bleary look in his blue eyes that indicated his inebriation. But his drunkenness could not hide the intelligence and subtle cruelty of his countenance. He was a rake and a scoundrel for sure and I hated him on sight. I noted that he trod the lawn in bare feet, no doubt we interrupted an evening of debauchery.

"Percy!" shrieked Mary in shocked disgust. "You apologize this instant!"

"Oh, whatever for, my dove? The truth should never be hidden or apologized for."

There came a faint *pop* as my gloves suddenly ripped at the seams as I clenched my fists. The sound floated soft on the air so no one but I heard.

Mary Godwin, no shrinking violet, snatched the goblet from Percy's hand and drained its contents before grabbing his wine spotted white shirt in one hand and pulling him close. "Pollydolly would be dead, as would I, perhaps even abused before being strangled, if it hadn't been for this man coming to our rescue so YOU MIND YOUR FUCKING MANNERS!" This last she finished in a harpy's yell.

I loved her even more at that moment.

Percy blinked rapidly while George and Polidori coughed into their fists. It seemed that this was not the first time Mary had chided Percy in such a manner and her familiarity was such that this man must have been the fiancée she mentioned.

Finally, Percy seemed to find himself and turned to me, executing a passible, if unsteady, bow. "Sir, allow me to escort you into the villa where I will ply you with apologies and wine until you are filled with both." Before I could stop him, he took me by the arm, hooking his around my elbow and staring blearily into my spectacles. "And you can tell me where you obtained such out-of-fashion garments."

I could not help but look at my linen shirt with high collar, loose fitting trousers, and my long-tailed coat, one hand reaching for my tall hat. "Sir, I purchased these at the finest clothiers in all of Russia, where I was assured they were at the height of fashion."

"Oh, my dear man, they were quite fashionable...*ten years ago*! No, no, no...we shall have to see you in a single-breasted tailcoat and a cravat. Yes, and please do grow your sideburns out, you will look so dashing."

Still prattling on about men's fashion and grooming advice, Percy led me, bemused and bewildered, into Villa Diodati.

CHAPTER THREE

Hawaii, the island paradise.

Not quite.

If you have never been to O'ahu, then you are fortunate not to have been stuck in traffic with people who think turn signals are merely a passing fad. Once out of the city there are areas of splendor, but they come with slugs the size of Volkswagens, cockroaches that are big enough to develop language skills, geckos that invade your home to leave little gecko turdlets sticking to the walls and more insects that God ever had in mind when he first created the islands.

Still, the weather is nice.

Instead of heading east toward Diamond Head, or north toward Waialua, I drove my Prius west, then north along the H1 until I hit the 93 where I hugged the coast past Nanakuli until I came to the smallish town of Waianae.

The area was receiving a much-needed face-lift; new houses and businesses popping up while old ones were being torn down. Renovation with an ocean view. Unfortunately, an ocean view only for those who could afford it.

As for me, my house was far back from the 93, up the hill a bit, what the locals call a mountain. Not what I considered a mountain, though. Not near tall enough, not near steep enough and no snow on the crest. True mountains were capped by icy peaks that offered no consolation, only a sudden or cold death for the unwary.

Hawaii proved to be a good place to hide, the people laid back and did not care much what you looked like. The islands are a true melting pot, more so than on the mainland. Filipinos, Chinese, Korean, Portuguese, Hispanic, African-American, Caucasian, Samoan, everything...all ethnicities were well represented, everyone welcomed as long as they respected others.

My home loomed large by island standards, almost 3,000 square feet and isolated, and would normally have attracted the wrong kind of attention, but the look of neglect (cosmetically applied) gave the place a down-on-its-luck air that, along with the state-of-the-art security system, kept it burglar-free. Haunted house chic.

The Prius hummed up the driveway and I parked at the bottom of the stairs leading to the front door. It felt good to be home where I did not have to kill anyone.

My cat, an orange and white tom named Igor, met me at door and gave me a perfunctory meow. Cats are perfect pets...a minor bit of attention, food and water and a place to crap and they are all good. Dogs are too needy and have a nasty habit of shitting in your shoes if neglected.

Once inside I headed toward the kitchen and poured myself a glass of purified water from the fridge, thinking that perhaps my next one should have scotch attached. A long sigh escaped my lips as I set the glass down. Yes, a little scotch should do the trick. I reached in to the cupboard over the microwave and that was when I noticed the intruder.

A man sat in my living room chair clutching a large handgun and drinking a diet cola. One of *my* diet colas. Even though gloom filled the room I could see him well enough.

That was just not right, breaking into a man's house and drinking his sodas. Darn rude, actually. Turned out my state-of-the-art security system was not.

I picked up the glass and took another sip of water. "Somebody has been drinking my soda. Somebody's been sitting in my chair, and he's still here. Somebody's going to be fed his own gun if he does not leave sharpish."

"Forgive me," he said after taking another drink from the can. "But I was thirsty."

"The stereo is pretty good. Probably fetch you at least a grand. The TV is top notch, so that is worth five-hundred."

His laughter sounded like the scraping of dry leaves.

"My safe has about six grand in it," I continued as if he were here to rob me even though I knew different. "I will open it and you can be on your merry."

"You know who I am," he said quietly. The gun was not quite pointed in my direction, but close enough in case I became nervy.

Well...darn. I waited for ten heartbeats. "Not quite."

"But you have ideas."

No reason to lie. "Yes."

"Then look behind you. Slowly."

I heard the sliding glass door open a second before I looked. A woman, pretty in a cold, severe way, short black hair, skintight black pants and black t-shirt stood there, scowling at me, her high cheekbones sharp enough to slice cheese. Twin cylinders gleamed on her back and a hose ran from them to a long slender rod held tight in her hands. Blue flame sputtered at the end of the rod, hissing evilly, the same color as her cold, cold eyes.

Fear, raw naked and immediate shot through me. Memories of flame and pain roared across the landscape of my mind and my testicles shriveled to the size of chickpeas. "A flamethrower?" I asked, showing nothing of the fear that threatened to unman me. "You brought a flamethrower to my house? Do you know what that can do to the property value?" Every particle of me wanted run screaming and not look back. I would probably get about three steps before becoming monster flambé.

The man scratched his chin absently before taking another sip of my soda. "My name is Carter," he said, ignoring my question. Even sitting down Carter radiated menace, a slim stiletto of man with thin features, slicked back brown hair exposing a extreme widow's peak like that of a cartoon villain. "That is Branch." A well-manicured hand indicated the woman. "Obviously we know who you are, hence the flamethrower."

Obviously.

"Tell me," he continued. "We know about the children you saved from the LRA a couple of years ago, and all the money donated to St. Jude's

Children's hospital, enough to fund the facility for two years." His tone was deceptively soft. I ground my teeth, anger warring with fear. That money helped perform miracles for those kids. "Not to mention what you did to Mohammed Farrah Aidid after his surgery, and your handling of the Yemen-based white slave ring that just hit the national news. You have been doing very good deeds and it begs the question: why? Are you trying to buy your way into Heaven?"

Bloody images played across my mind's movie screen: Somalia, Haiti, and Northern Uganda, the Middle Easterners I killed hours earlier. Hard times laced with the evils of the greedy and the vicious. Everything I did, the lives I saved and took, was met with a clear conscience and that was a rarity for most, I believed.

I shook my head. "That money, those things that I have done, have saved a lot of people."

He stared at me for a moment. "Yes, of course. Forgive my impatience, but will you please answer the question."

"No one buys their way into Heaven, that path is not for sale." A brief pause. "But Hell is always free." I gave the woman a pointed look.

"Keep your eyes from me, Abomination," she snarled in a voice like razorblades on glass, lifting the flamethrower a little higher, the hissing blue flame like the devil's pupil in the eye of the nozzle.

I moved my gaze back to the seated man. How he radiated danger while sitting wearing a teal polo and khakis was a trick I wanted to learn. "Look, I am sure you think you know who I am, but I am not who you think. I am not *what* you think."

"Take off your contact lenses," he said mildly after another sip. Almost casually he crushed the aluminum can in his fist.

My heart sank. "I do not understand."

His grey eyes became cold. "Yes. You. Do." Each word bitten off carefully.

Yes, I did. Without another word I reached up and removed my colored scleral lenses, revealing...what they revealed.

The smile Carter threw at me turned diamond hard. "Thank you. I trust there is no more need for dissembling."

Anger and terror in equal parts boiled within. "No. No more need."

Carter stood. The knifelike impression remained. Slim, dark haired, a hint of scars beneath the tight teal polo indicated he had seen combat and the corded muscles along his arms slid under his skin like squirming snakes.

"We are not here for a fight," he said mildly, but with a dangerous edge to his voice. "The flamethrower is to encourage cooperation. We have a job for you and when it is finished, you go your way and we go ours. Fair?"

Too fair. The idea that they would leave me alone felt ridiculous. "I do not suppose this job pays?"

A flash of white through the dark of his beard. "You get to live."

Well, there is that. "That is a good payment," I conceded.

He nodded. "I know. Branch wanted to kill you no matter what."

A low growl sounded from behind. Branch, it seemed, was not one to waste words.

I pointed straight at Carter's chest, at the silver chain that snaked around his throat on which I knew a crucifix dangled. "The Church Militant, correct? The *Manus Dei*." God's Hands, the secret agency of the Vatican that handled all their dirty work, meaning the elimination of supernatural threats and those persons the church dubbed as agents of Satan. Fanatics all, they answered only to the C9, the Council of Cardinal Advisors and the Pope. The fact that the Church sent its agents meant that something big had reared its ugly head. Some rough beast slouching toward Bethlehem, perhaps?

He nodded slowly, confirming.

"The only thing we have to bind us is our word," I remarked. "If you have done any research on me, you will know that once my word is given, it is inviolate. I would rather die than break a trust." I cocked my head to the side. "Given that the Eighth Commandment reads, 'Thou shalt not bear false witness against thy neighbor,' which forbids misrepresentation of the truth, I want you swear under God that you will not try to kill me when this job you want me to do is done."

"Listen, Abomination..." the woman grated through clenched teeth. Her hands tightened upon the rod of the flamethrower.

"No! You listen." I ran over her next words. "Your oath or you might as well pull the trigger right now and get this whole farce over with." Sweat rolled down my back. It was a gamble, but one I had to take.

Carter stretched. "Swear to it, Branch."

"No, I will *not*." A lifetime's worth of hate marred her words.

"Yes you will or this op is done."

"But he is the *Abomination*."

Dry laughter. "That may be...that may be, but the intel says he's never gone back on his word once it's given. Make the oath, then we can continue like civilized people."

There was a long pause, then the words fell from Branch's lips as if they were poison she was trying to spit out. "I swear under Almighty God that if the job we offer you is completed to the satisfaction of all parties, I will not harm you in any way." By the end she was breathing fast, almost panting. That promise must have *hurt*.

"And you have my word on that," Carter said gravely, although I thought I saw a flicker of amusement in his deep eyes. "One professional to another."

Thankfully I am well-read so my next words hit them right between the eyes, "You will not injure or kill me through inaction or allow me to come to harm." *Thank you Isaac Azimov.*

Oh, the fury! Trying not to laugh, I waited patiently until they gave their oaths before offering my own. "And I give my word that I will try my hardest to accomplish the mission you insist I take with no ill intent on my part." That set Carter back on his narrow heels, but he gave a perfunctory nod and even Branch looked somewhat mollified. For a foaming-at-the-mouth fanatic, who thought I was Satan incarnate, that is.

I nodded and walked to the kitchen sink, ran water over my contact lenses and placed them carefully on my eyeballs. They stung for a second. My stomach still felt like it wanted to trade places with my balls, but at least I had hope that I would see the end of this above ground. "Good. Now that that's done, who wants a drink?" I turned to see Branch still at the back door. "You can put the flamethrower down and step inside, I will not hurt you."

Her face became harder. "You are not to be trusted."

"As if I trust you? Stop being silly."

Slowly, she lowered the nozzle of the flamethrower and stepped in, closing the sliding glass door, but she didn't relax one iota. Progress, of a sort.

Two tumblers of scotch later (one for Carter and one for myself. Branch stated flatly she did not drink) and we sat in my living room. The liquor burned smoothly down my throat and settled nicely in my stomach. Possibly the greatest thing ever to come out of Scotland. I stared at the other man blandly, waiting for the request while we savored our drinks. He filled my overstuffed chair with his blade sharp self and I half-lounged on the sofa. If it had been the mainland, the two pieces of furniture would have been leather, but in Hawaii you made due with cloth or (Heaven forbid) wicker.

It did not take long for the slender man to come to the point. "The Book of Ur has been stolen."

My stomach suddenly churned with nausea. *Oh. That's bad.* Very bad indeed. As in 'Four Horsemen of the Apocalypse' bad if it was misused. It took me an instant to realize that whoever stole the book out of the secret Vatican vaults, the ones where they kept ashes of Mary Magdelene and the Spear of Longinus, would know full well how to utilize the book to its most horrific potential.

I swiveled my head until I was staring at Branch, who stood in the kitchen not quite fingering the flamethrower. "How in the Good Lord's name did your boss lose the book? I thought His place was impregnable."

It was Carter who answered. "The details are irrelevant, only the fact that the book is gone is of concern. Someone stole it, caused quite of bit of damage to cover their tracks and we have been tasked to affect its return." He grinned in a way that did not make me feel better. "Of course, the subject of you came up."

"My sources have not told me of any theft in the Vatican, which means His Holiness is scared, and rightly so. I am surprised He did not contact me in Himself. Although, come to think of it, it should have been well-nigh impossible to find me in the first place."

Carter's smile was frost and rue. "He has better things to do, like sending her." A nod to Branch. "And me."

"Why are we wasting time here? Let's go already," Branch said, looking like she needed to commit arson and soon. People like her plagued me as far as I could remember, perpetually irritated and absolutely certain in their moral superiority. It made my skin itch.

"We need him," Carter said irritably. "So let's take it easy, okay?"

When Carter's eyes moved from mine, I unholstered my cell, keeping it out of his sight and carefully began to press buttons. "What do you want from me?"

"Get the book back of course."

Of course. "What makes you think I can find it?"

His smile was glacial. "Call it my faith in your abilities. And the fact that you are the only person walking free in the wide world who has ever seen it up close and personal."

"Swell." There, the last number had been pushed and I waited. Within three seconds, my landline began to ring. "I should get that. Most likely my broker."

Branch gave me a crusty look. "It's still dark out. Sun won't be up for another hour."

I stood and walked slowly to the kitchen, leaving the cell between the couch cushions, out of sight. "It is six hours in later on in the day in New York," I replied as if talking to a child. "It is almost eleven there."

She nodded dubiously and allowed me access to the taupe cordless phone nestled in its cradle affixed to the wall. "Hello?" I kept my voice soft. "Hi Art." My fingers curled over the mouthpiece. "Like I thought, it is my broker," I said to the pair.

Carter nodded once, not taking his eyes from mine while Branch strolled into the living room, carefully avoiding touching the blue flame to anything could combust.

From the cordless, I heard Branch began to speak as my cell picked up their conversation. "Why did you make me promise him?" she whispered furiously.

"What, you're so eager to kill him before he can be of use?" he replied softly. "His Holiness gave us a mandate, we must succeed."

My stomach muscles tightened as I continued to make conversational noises soft enough that they wouldn't emerge from the cell's speakers.

"He's the Abomination. I have sworn before God and now I must let him live." Her voice was raw with hatred and contempt.

"We need him to do the Lord's work. Sometimes evil can be of service to the greater good."

Evil, eh? Go figure. As I glanced over to the pair, their heads together as they held their whispered conversation, I knew that Carter, of the two, was the more dangerous. Branch wore her emotions on her face like tattoos and she no doubt had mad skills, but she also had morals. Carter, well, let's just say he seemed the type to justify wrangling around a sacred oath, which made him the less trustworthy of the duo.

"Okay, Art," I temporized for my small audience. "Sell the Mitsubishi stock, but buy one point five of the Electrum Lux. I have a funny feeling the new electric cars are going to sell better than anyone thinks, regardless of the price."

"Can we trust him?" Branch hissed.

After a moment, Carter nodded. "The file on him states that he keeps his word, plays everything by the book and is as efficient as hell, pardon the expression."

I ground my teeth. A file? Not unexpected at all. His Holiness kept tabs on all the major players from the Sicarii to the Templars, from Jacob's Rule to the Venerable Church of the Unclean Word. The real question, the one that nagged, was how did the Vatican know that I lived on O'ahu? It was not like I advertised and my identity was supposed to be digitally sanitary. It came to me in a flash with a certainty I had learned to trust over the years. I had been sold out and I knew the culprit. *Sonofabitch.*

Senator Barnes. Seemed that he did not like the idea of owing me a favor. Of course, I had no proof, but my instincts never lied, not once. A staunch Catholic, he seemed the type to have connections to the *Manus Dei.*

"Fine, Art. Let me know." I placed the cordless in its cradle, strode back to the living room and sat, palming the cell from between the cushions. It was not first time I had used a cell as a microphone to eavesdrop on a conversation, and I prayed it would not be the last. It let me know that A) I could trust Branch as long as she swore an oath and B) Carter was sneaky as a fox with two tails.

"What makes you think I can locate the Book of Ur?" I asked, grabbing my glass of scotch from the coffee table and emptying the last finger in a gulp.

"No one else has had the book in their possession. No one else has your unique contacts you've built up over a very long and successful career." Carter tried not to look smug. He had me and he knew it. A glance at Branch told me she had not relaxed her vigil with the flamethrower. I could take both of them on and most likely win, but the price would be more than I could bear.

"I have touched it once, a long time ago." Visions of the tome, blackened and crusty with age, greasy and gross still haunted me. "But you are right about the connections. I do have people in mind who could be of help."

Carter smiled wide, revealing a nice and expensive set of veneers. "Wonderful. You have a week to find and deliver the book."

I raised an eyebrow. *A week?* Was this a joke? "No."

"No?" he asked, low and dangerous. Beside him, Branch tensed and I wondered if I could launch out of the couch fast enough to keep her from spraying me with liquid fire. The look in her eye and the set of her shoulders told me 'no'.

"No. Not in a week, not by myself. Whoever took it most likely buried their tracks very well and the book itself is dangerous like you would not believe. Dangerous on a biblical level.

"This job will require more funds than I have available (most of my money is tied up right now, so I am not as liquid as you think) and extra muscle." Not really the truth, but I had no desire to foot the bill for this little bar-b-que. I tossed them my most innocent smile. Children have run screaming from that smile. "Do you even know what the book is?"

They did not answer, which was answer enough. "When Archangel Michael cast Lucifer from Heaven," I began in my best Special Ed school teacher voice. "He tore a large strip of skin from between the falling angel's wings. After Lucifer was locked up in the basement Michael, using his own blood, began to write the story of, well, *everything*, imbuing the skin with divine power, enough so that it took on a sort of life of its own and began to write itself, so to speak. The Book. Upon the Lord's command the angel Raphael placed seven seals upon the book and placed it in what would become the city of Ur located in what is now called Iraq. The book continues to this very day to write itself and it holds all of mankind's secrets, from Kabbalist mysteries to the great words of magic used by mages today. All written in the First Language used before the whole Towel of Babel debacle. Anyone anywhere can read the book and most likely become powerful beyond all imagining. That is the threat of the book. Secrets, magic, and the seals."

This time Branch chimed in; her eyes wide. "You mean the Seven Seals—"

"Yes," I interrupted with a smile that felt like a scream. "The Seven Seals of Revelation adorn the Book of Ur. The same book that John of Patmos saw in his dreams. Whoever breaks those seals brings about the end of days."

CHAPTER FOUR

Geneva, *June, 1816*

"...so you see, galvanism can actually cause even dead tissue to contract. Luigi Galvani called it *animal electricity* in his treatise." Claire Clairmont, Mary Godwin's step-sister, eased back in her chair, sipping her tea, dark eyes alive with merriment. Her full bosom heaved with the fulsomeness of her excitement.

A beautiful creature, voluptuous and sensual with thick ruby lips and long lashes, a far cry from Mary's more austere looks. However, there lay within her a need, perhaps a *gluttonous lust,* for recognition that I found offputting.

George doted on her and she on him, so I believe that satisfied her childish desire. The fact that they lay together at night and did not bother to hide their intimacy felt worrisome at first. No prude I in such matters, but the world at large tended to frown upon relationships that existed beyond the bounds of matrimony.

To quote both Percy and George, 'to hell with the world'. My companions did not care what others, save their friends, thought and freely thumbed their noses at the strictures of social convention. I found this most refreshing and bathed often in the waters of their discourses on 'free love' and 'romanticism'. Although a bit bawdy for my tastes (the four, I took it, were notorious libertines), they possessed intelligence and a zest for life that I had not seen in the common British or European people.

Where Percy seemed soft, unused to physical pursuits, George was a hearty specimen, a competent boxer, a crack shot with a pistol and an extremely strong swimmer. All this great physicality despite being born with a clubfoot! Imagine the rigor and discipline to achieve such things while contending with such a deformity. He gave me hope, that fleeting, fluttery bird I rarely saw, to soldier on and continue my attempts integrate myself into polite society. Even with my pale ugliness, perhaps I could find a measure of acceptance.

How I longed for that day!

Although I was accepted by the residents of Villa Diodati, it was the wider world, the world of the common man that I looked to for approval. Perhaps I shared Claire Clairmont's *gluttonous lust* for recognition.

"What do you think, Victor?" George asked. Ever since our meeting five days ago, George treated me with the respect due a British Lord, not an ugly giant of uncertain provenance. In our discussions, he never once condescended or made an assumption of my ignorance.

"Galvanism?" I rubbed the long, purplish, scar on my cheek. "It is interesting, but serves no real medical purpose that I can see. Perhaps one day, when sufficient advances in the field of medicine are made, but not now."

It was evening and the fire was roaring, warming the large room used for entertaining. The six of us, Mary, Percy, George, Polidori (I could never bring myself to call him Pollydolly like the rest), Claire and myself had finished our supper and took our ease near the fire on chairs and couches sturdy enough to accommodate my weight and plush enough to help alleviate the cool Swiss chill. Of course, Mary and Percy sat together on the couch while George and Claire made use of the chairs with the good doctor. I sat furthest from the blaze, content and relaxed.

Every evening we gathered thus to discuss science, religion, the arts and, of course, England. The news I missed while abroad ranged from the colonies in America successfully rebelling and forming their own government to a growing movement called 'Romanticism', a fad that seemed to rebel against the sciences and focus mainly on the arts. It struck me as unusual a movement that campaigned against the political and aristocratic norm should be so lauded by a British Lord. It took several hours of conversation for me to fully appreciate both the irony and the emotional forces that drove the movement.

Polidori, as well as a fine physician at such a young age, was also of a literary bent. As was Mary. It seemed that the only people who were not poets or writers were Claire and myself. Perhaps it is because of my admiration for my literary friends that I remember them so fondly.

"What about bringing life to dead tissues with the use of Galvanism?" Mary said from her comfortable perch within Percy's arms. "Is that possible?"

"Ah, my dear," Byron said around his wine glass. "I think we have read too much from the *Fantasmagoriana*. Those tales of horror have inspired you to dizzying heights of imagination."

Mary turned to me, face shining. "Victor? What say you?"

I looked into her eyes, glad that mine were hidden behind the dark glass of my spectacles, afraid she would see the love there had I not worn them. "I...think that dead is dead," I said carefully. "People have been struck and killed by lighting and I have never heard of one brought back by its effects."

"Well said!" Percy responded. He was well into his cups. Again. I would have scolded him for his drunkenness, but it was not my place. "I think you are a man of science at heart. Say..." Here he tapped his chin in thought. "If it were possible to bring the dead to life, would they thank us for it, those Lazarai? Or would they curse us to *our* graves?"

Everyone looked at me and I felt a cold chill creep spider-like across my flesh. The conversation had become too close, too personal to what troubled me for my tastes. "I think that, now mind you this is merely conjecture, that if a person were to be reanimated after death, assuming one could keep the flesh from rotting, that they would not be who they were. Hear me out," I said, holding up a hand before Polidori or George could interject. "If we are to believe in the existence of the soul, as most do, then the soul flees after death, bound to whatever fate lies after. If one were to reanimate, bring a person back to life, then how could the soul return after it has been consigned to Heaven or Hell? The Lazarai, as you called them, Percy, would be mindless. Babes once again in need of the most basic education, functioning with no recollection of their former lives. Only by magic, surely a preposterous explanation in these times, could one explain the return of the soul." I poured brandy onto my tongue and swallowed. "And how would this, this...modern Prometheus be perceived should he offer mankind the secret of raising the dead? As a savior or a horror? Someone who seeks to usurp the power of God, perhaps? I think such a learned scientist would be hounded to the ends of the earth and beyond."

There came seconds of silence while the others digested my words with great care. Finally, Mary spoke. "Are you sure you are *not* a man of science, Victor? You seem far too philosophical to be a soldier. Unless you are a Naturalist *and* a soldier."

That was the story I had invented for myself, a former soldier coming home after wandering far abroad in search for life's deepest meaning. It did well to explain my numerous horrid scars.

"I think a man who sees into the very eyes of death is most likely to be philosophical indeed, my dear," said Percy softly, suddenly showing no evidence of inebriation. "Watching the life leave the bodies of men you knew and loved could certainly alter your view on God and Man. Isn't that right, Victor?"

A sudden sea change, indeed. What are you up to, Percy? An ungracious thought, but jealousy makes monsters of us all. "You are right, Percy. More so than you know." Icy fingers trailed along my intestines. I had seen people die. Been the cause of several deaths.

"Incidentally, Victor," Polidori said suddenly. "If I may ask, who sewed the scars on your face? It seems he was more a seamstress than surgeon. No self-respecting doctor would make a hash of such wounds."

"Pollydolly!" Claire scolded, sitting bolt upright.

I held up a hand to forestall any reprimands. "It is all right, Claire. The wounds happened so long ago that I feel no regret." To Polidori, "In the middle of battle, you accept anyone's ministrations, be it a half-trained physician or seamstress. Anything that will keep you alive, no matter the scars, is what is important." I ran my finger down the long scar, then across the short, red one running parallel above my right eyebrow and the thin one that ran like a red vein from beneath my right eye to my right temple. Those were the only visible ones. The rest were hidden beneath my clothes.

"Fortune smiled on me that such hideous wounds did not prove mortal, though it left me a face far less than handsome."

"I apologize if I have offended," Dr. Polidori said gravely, staring at his hands. "Mending war wounds is not my specialty."

"No need for worry, John." I gave him my best smile. The lad seemed to be a caring and kind person at heart. "We are all friends here and can be forgiven mild offenses made out of a surfeit of curiosity."

George lifted his glass. "To friends."

"To friends," we chorused.

After we finished our drinks, Claire stared boldly at my scars. "Tell me, Victor, in what campaigns did you earn such wounds? They do not look like they were made by musket balls."

Here I tread ground I made myself familiar with, having borrowed details from an ex-mercenary I had met during my travels in Russia. "It was during the Irish Rebellion of 1798. My unit was hired by the British Empire to assist with the matter. As for the wounds...it was in County Kildare where a mortar exploded quite near me, shredding me with shrapnel and flinging me a dozen feet in the air. Should you see my body in all its naked horror, you would swear that I had been put together piecemeal by a crazed physician indeed, but I live and that is what counts, fortunate that I did not bleed to death on foreign soil."

Polidori seemed alarmed. "You survived a mortar attack? That is amazing, Victor. Any one of those wounds looks like it could kill."

How could I tell them that they did? That I died and came back, much like Mary's galvanic corpse? "It certainly killed my mercenary career," I replied with a sad smile. "The next months were spent in recovery. After that, thanks to a small inheritance from my father, I traveled the world alone seeking..."

Percy and Mary leaned forward in their seat, fascinated. "Seeking what?" they asked in unison.

"Peace. Seeking peace." And absolution.

"I admire you, Victor," George said suddenly, eyes intent on mine. Lord Byron could burn with life intensely more than any man I ever met, so vigorous was he. "You were not afraid to fight and when near death, you recovered and did the one thing that is more dangerous than fight a war…you traveled the world alone."

"How is travel more dangerous than war, George?" Claire asked, dimpling prettily at her lover.

"Why, my dear, one never knows what awaits in foreign lands. What dangers lurk around the corner or beneath tree. Bandits, bad food, strange fevers that can fell a man in an instant. Sickness has downed more armies in the past than wounds inflicted by the enemy. The world is a harsh place, filled with dangers innumerable and our large friend here, capable rogue that he is, has trod far and wide by himself." He lifted a crystal decanter of brandy and near filled his snifter. "We know he traveled to Russia, that backward kingdom filled with fierce fighters who drink that awful spirit concocted from potatoes. Where else has he been, I wonder?"

My heart lightened; my conscience eased that I could finally tell the truth. "China. China and India."

Those five new friends leaned forward once more, mouths agape as they waited for me to continue. It was a sight so ridiculous that I had to laugh. Mary smiled ruefully while George and Percy chuckled. Claire crossed her arms under her impressive decolletage and Polidori rose to refill his glass from the same decanter George used.

"The Chinese did not accept me at all," I began. "My height, pale skin and fiercesome mien often gave them pause and at times I found myself pummeled by rocks or rotten vegetables. I had to find rest in the forests and in uninhabited places lest I be set upon by superstitious peasants with torches bent on burning me to death."

"You poor man!" exclaimed Mary. "No wonder you left."

I smiled. "Actually, I stayed for five years."

Noises of dismay and disbelief assaulted my ears before I continued. "Nevertheless, I speak truly. It was in the province the locals call Henan that I found shelter with monks. A very peaceful brotherhood of clerics."

"Christian missionaries in China?" asked Polidori, once again seated, his attention no longer fixed upon George.

"Monks of the Buddha," I replied. "Men of peace."

"I have heard of this religion," Mary said happily. "It is said to have originated in the Subcontinent."

I nodded. "That is correct, but it is popular in far Tibet and parts of China. The monks are of a branch of Buddhism called Mahayana, or The Great Voice. I profess not to know much of the subtleties of their beliefs, but they took this wayward soldier in and taught me some of their mysteries and philosophies."

George was rapt. "Such as?"

"Acceptance of who I am, my nature. How to deal with my problems in a nonviolent manner. They taught me *Dyzen,* a sort of meditative state. It is very hard to describe in European terms, but it has much to do with enlightenment of the soul and an insight into oneself and into the teachings of the Buddha."

"So...you are a...Buddhist?" asked Percy, trying the word out and, from his expression, not liking the taste.

I shook my head. "No, I left before I could devote too much time to their teachings. In the main, I worked as a laborer, helping them to maintain their monastery and to fight off bandits."

It was Mary's turn to speak. "You said these 'Buddhists' are people of peace, not warriors."

"Even peaceful people need to protect themselves. These monks, called the Shaolin, have devised a method of combat that focuses on defeating an opponent without killing. A form of hand-to-hand combat and the use of certain, specialized weapons. They deigned not to teach me those martial skills because I am a foreigner and one who harbored no plans to remain. I did, however, learn quite a bit while observing them practice their skills. Yet, despite their standoffish ways, they were kind to this weary traveler."

They took this in with a breathless air, captivated by my account of the Shaolin. However, it was not five years ago when I arrived at the monastery at Song Shan, but almost one hundred. How could I tell my new friends that it was because of me that the Yongzheng Emperor ordered the destruction of the monastery in 1732? I feared so much that if they learned the truth of my past, of my existence, that I would be driven away, or perhaps killed. Although that seemed unlikely because of those assembled, only George had any real physical capability to do me harm.

"Tell us Victor," said Claire. "Tell us of India. I have always wanted to go there. I hear the men all have long black beards and the woman wear jewelry in their noses. I have also heard they have a particular fondness for gold."

My laughter fair shook the room. "All true. Women pierce their noses to wear studs of gold and gems. As for their fondness for gold, for them that metal is more of a religion than a substance. In fact, it seems to be an object of love. It adorns bodies and is passed down through the generations. In fact, if disaster befalls an Indian family, their gold will be sold only as a last resort after all other items of value have been disposed."

Percy smirked. "They sound like Spaniards and Italians."

This, like most of his barbed quips, brought forth a generous round of laughter.

"Tell us more, Victor," Mary urged. "Please! It is so fascinating."

I wiped my lips with a lace kerchief and offered up a small smile. "Further stories are for...another time, perhaps. I feel the need to retire for the evening." Actually, I felt no need for sleep (sleep was a rare occurrence since my rebirth), but it behooved me to act as mortal as possible.

Percy and Mary made sure of my comfort by ensconcing me in a room so large that a dozen people of my size could occupy it and still have room to pace. It was a far cry from the dank little cell the Shaolin monks offered me. That space had been so small that I could stand in the middle and stretch my arms wide and my fingertips would touch the opposite walls. If I stood on one end of the room in the Villa and sneezed, five seconds later an echo would reach my ears. Such comforts achieved the opposite effect on me and I longed to roll up the soft lavender rugs and rest on wooden planks. Living an austere life will strip away any notion that people need luxuries when all a body needs is a safe place to sleep and food enough that the belly forgoes rumbling uncomfortably.

A large dresser with mirror, a basin for washing with soft cloths for drying dominated short wall to the left of the door and it was there I took off my glasses, revealing eyes as yellow as new butter. My skin, once virtually clear as glass showing pink muscle and yellowish sinew, now shone milky white shot through with the blue rivers of my veins. I fair looked like a bleached map of all of England's waterways. Enormous hands with large, gnarled knuckles ran over my torso, wondering how one so muscular could have such narrow shoulders. Lanky, rangy, lean, all good words to describe my physique, although I am particularly fond of odd and unusual. Off-putting, as well.

Mary burst into the room.

"Forgive me Victor, but I *must* hear more of India..." her voice trailed away. "Oh my God," she continued a moment later as I stood frozen, shirt at my feet. "Your *eyes*." Her own dropped to my bared torso. "Your chest..." Dismay colored her voice.

Oh no. My eyes...the spectacles fair mocked me from their perch as I touched my brow in horror. My eyes. Mary.

Oh God, please have mercy.

Quickly I snatched up the spectacles and laid them across the offending orbs, but it was too late. Mary had *seen*.

"My word, Victor, your body, those scars! And your eyes." A soft hand found its way to my arm. "Tell me, please. What...are you?" Tears began to well up between her lids and the sight of it broke my heart. She looked at me and *was not afraid*. The enormity of that nearly sent me to my knees.

"I could tell you," I replied thickly unable to tear my gaze from her troubled face. Such compassion from a relative stranger, it was a situation totally unknown to me. "But you would hate me. I-I cannot bear the thought of that."

She took a deep breath, turned and carefully closed the door. When she turned back around, her face seemed a granite mask of resolve. "You have saved my life and the life of Dr. Polidori, whom I cherish." Casting her gaze about, she chose the writing table chair to sit upon, arranging her burgundy skirts primly. "You will tell me, Victor, *everything* and know that I will not think the less of you."

That voice, that same tone she used on Percy when first I met him (albeit with much less volume). That tone told me she would not leave, not budge without satisfactory answers, so it was with a heavy heart that I made my way to the bed and sat, staring at my overlarge hands.

"My story, Mary, begins so long ago..."

God have mercy on me, I told her. I told her everything.

Later, an hour, perhaps less, my voice ground to a halt, husky and worn from overuse.

I did not look up. I did not want to see the hate in her eyes, the recrimination...it would have destroyed me.

"Oh, you poor man."

How she must hate me.

"You poor, poor man."

It took several moments to digest her words. "What?" I raised my eyes from the floor to see tears streaming down her cheeks. Stunned, I could only watch as she wept, staring at me with shining eyes like liquid diamonds.

"How you must have suffered," she sobbed.

Finally, my lips moved. "I am a monster, Mary. A monster. I have killed and not just those who deserved it." My raspy voice caught. "I have killed the innocent."

She shook her head. "You are a man. A lonely, sad man. But you are no monster."

My cry was the tearing of metal. "Of course I am! I have the blood of innocents on these hands, the blood of a child. There is no deeper, no more heinous sin than killing a child and for that I will *burn* forevermore."

Mary stood, tears dripping from her long face. "You knew not your strength, nor what you had done. In your...state you were as innocent as the child and I think...No! I am positive that you have been forgiven by the Almighty for that transgression."

She came and knelt at my feet, taking my knobbly, large hands into her own. "You are not a monster, no matter your origin. I have seen your heart and in the short time we have known each other, we have become dear friends. Listen to what I say and take comfort."

Dear friends? Oh, how I wish we were so much more! I ached for Mary Godwin like no other woman I had ever met, but Percy, despite his initial obnoxiousness, had become a friend as well. Declaring my feelings would have eased my conscience, but betrayed Percy's friendship.

"My existence disproves your assertion. I *am* a monster, Mary, and always will be." Standing, I gently lifted her to her feet. "Now, I must repair for the night. Please, Mary, can you keep my secret?"

Her face glistened like marble in the rain. "Until my dying day, Victor."

I smiled. "Thank you. Good night." A gentle dismissal.

Mary left with one small, backward glance and by that time my features were set in neutrality.

It was time to put Villa Diodati behind me. Like a thief in the night, I slipped away with only a short note explaining that business concerns required my departure. Perhaps I would see them again.

Perhaps not. Either way, I owed those five people much, for they had supplied me with a modicum of peace and I would never forget their names:

Mary Godwin.

Dr. John Polidori.

George Gordon Byron.

Claire Clairmont

Percy Shelley.

How I miss you all.

CHAPTER FIVE

"You look uncomfortable," I said, cracking open one eye and staring back at the slim agent, who squidged and squirmed in his seat like he suffered a bad case of hemorrhoids. "Big pro tough guy like you? What gives?"

Carter gave me a glare, a good one that I reckoned had lesser men quaking in their boots. "I hate flying when I'm not at the controls," he grunted. "Fucking makes me nervous."

In the seat behind him, Branch rolled her eyes, unaware that I could see her quite well. "What do you do if you have to commit to a HALO?" I asked.

"There are drugs for those occasions."

"Ladies and gentleman, this is your captain. We are making final preparations for our descent into Athens, Greece. The weather is a perfect eighty-two degrees Fahrenheit, or twenty-eight degrees Celsius. Skies are mostly sunny and the local time is 2pm."

"Greece? Why Greece?" Carter had asked when I informed him of our destination.

Branch looked at me as if I'd lost my mind. "It's a trap. Gotta be," she muttered darkly.

"Oh, yeah. I am flying to Greece unarmed with a pair of highly skilled agents who work for possibly the most powerful organization on the planet and who want to see me rendered into a fine slurry and it is a *trap*." I crossed my arms, exasperated at her self-imposed stupidity.

"Don't listen to her," Carter said, setting his drink on the coffee table. I leaned over and set a coaster under the glass. Barbarians, no respect for teak. "Listen to me. Why Greece?"

"Because I have no clue who stole the book and there is only one person in the world who can point us in the right direction."

"He's lying." Branch lifted the nozzle of the flamethrower and I cringed inside.

Carter shook his head. "No, he's not."

"How can you tell?"

The slim man leaned forward; eyes glued to my face. "Because I can. Okay, big man, Greece it is. What do you need?"

"Gold."

"Gold?"

"Yup. And you are paying for this shindig, remember?"

• • •

The King George Palace hotel made the words plush and opulent equate to dismal and small. It resides in the heart of the city of Athens; a stone's throw from the Hellenic Parliament. While its exterior architecture is much like any you'd find in Italy or France, it is interior that smacks the resident in the face with lavish overkill.

The limo (I had ordered one while from the Honolulu Airport, on Carter's dime, of course) glided to a stop in front and the chauffer opened the doors. March in Greece meant that the temperature hung around sixty-one degrees, a bit chilly for most, but almost perfect for me.

"Do not be cheap," I whispered to Carter as I stretched my legs. "Tip him well."

He made a face, but pulled a twenty from the enormous roll tucked into his suit jacket and handed it to the driver who beamed with slightly crooked teeth.

Meanwhile, Branch stood looking sleek and hard in her tight jeans and plain white T-shirt. No sense of style whatsoever, but possessing a clear aura of danger.

As for me, I sported tan cargo slacks, loafers and a salmon-colored Tommy Hilfiger polo, my dark hair slicked back. While not the epitome of chic, I pulled it off rather well.

We stepped through the front doors, my loafers emitting a faint *squeak* as they rubbed against the veined marble floor. The sound carried, echoing throughout the lobby where my eyes beheld soft shades of white and gold, colors that blended and caressed the rods and cones of my retinas, bathing them in visual extravagance. Tables and chairs that would fetch thousands at Sotheby's were artfully arranged across the floor beneath chandeliers dripping crystal tears.

"Ah, Mr. Vickers!" A well-dressed, portly gentleman with a fringe of graying hair on his round head practically leapt out of nowhere to shake my hand vigorously. A plastic room key found its way into my palm. "It is wonderful to see you again. Your room is ready for you and, as always, if there is anything you need, perhaps a vehicle to take you to Missolonghi, do not hesitate to ask."

"Stavros, old friend," I beamed, giving the man a one-armed hug and slipping a wad of bills in his waistcoat. "Thank you so much. As always, your hospitality never fails. However, no vehicle to Missolonghi this time. Itea, that will be my destination. Have it pulled up in twenty minutes and keep the engine running, if you would." I waved a hand and the two agents. "These are my associates, Mr. Carter and Ms. Branch. They will be providing payment for all arrangements. Carter, this is Stavros, the hotel manager."

Carter looked a bit dyspeptic as he fished a credit card out of his wallet and reluctantly handed it over to the smiling Stavros, who fluttered away with assurances of a speedy return.

"Been here before?" he asked dryly.

"Once or twice," I said, heading for the elevators, a bellhop trailing behind with our luggage. "You may have low friends in high places." A barb to let him know I knew about Senator Barnes. "But I have high friends in low places. You can pick the credit card up on our way out."

At the room, the Royal Penthouse Suite, the bellhop carried our bags in and Carter crossed his palm with crinkly American money.

I took a gander about, a large smile on my face as I soaked in the sight of coral paint, softly gleaming wood, and thick cotton. French antiquities decorated the living room. It was a study in understated luxury wrapped in 350 square meters of space. "Dibs on the first room," I said. "Branch can have the second. Looks like you are on the couch, Carter."

"Not while I'm paying."

"Aw, be a gentleman. The lady should have the second bedroom to herself."

The lady in question sniffed and tossed me a sour look. Seemed like no matter what I did her opinion of me would not budge from its nest in the basement.

No pleasing people.

"Hand over the book please." The voice was smooth, cultured, and it sent a shock up my spine like currents of electric ice.

I spun in time to see four men exit the main bedroom. Three wore black polos, tan slacks and had silenced pistols in hand, but were a motley assembly of physical types running from thin to muscular, but all looked to be in peak physical condition. The speaker was a trim Greek in a black suit and sunglasses. He also carried a silenced pistol, which was pointed in the region of my heart.

"Is there a place where you buy identical henchmen," I asked, careful not to make any sudden moves.

The Greek smiled, a twitch of the lips under a thin, black mustache. Without warning, he shot me in the thigh. The bullet tore through skin and muscle before lodging in my femur. The pain was a red-hot sear that ripped along my nerves and slammed into my skull. From far away amid a roaring that crashed in my ears, I heard him say, "I told you to hand over the book."

The area rug tasted terrible, silk and wool...I think. "What book?"

Another shot shattered the bones of my shoulder and sent more agony to the base of my skull.

"Give us the book." The man sounded almost bored.

I am going to kill you, buddy. The thought warmed me and seemed to push away the fire in my flesh somewhat.

"We don't have it with us," said Carter. He sounded cool as a cucumber, as if he discussed the disposition of deadly ancient artifacts on a daily basis under threat of silenced weapons.

"Now, was that so difficult? Your stubborn friend should've been more forthcoming."

My good arm was enough for me to lever myself painfully to my feet, balancing on my good leg. Spots appeared in front of my eyes. "You want forthcoming?" The four other men pointed their weapons at my head.

"Easy men," said the smiling Greek, waving expansively to where I stood unsteadily, blood coloring my clothes. "This is an American tough guy. You may have seen men like this on television. The problem is their innate toughness flees in the face of extreme pain." His pistol hissed and a bullet punched into my abdomen. It did not hurt worse than being slugged by a medium strong man, just enough to double me over.

I coughed blood that sprayed across the flawless oak floorboards. Drops splashed onto the white area rug, harsh red punctuation marks next to the larger stains from my leg and shoulder. "Tough enough." *Who hired these thugs?*

The bespeckled leader cocked his head to the side. "You *are* tough; I will give you that." Rough laughter greeted my declaration. "If John Wayne were alive, tough man, I would have him weeping within ten seconds."

Behind me, I heard a soft growl. Seemed like Carter was a fan of the Duke.

"Who is your boss?" I asked the Bad Guy Number One. Blood coated the back of my tongue.

"None of your business."

"Call it a last request. I have no illusions that I am leaving this room alive."

"What are you doing?" Branch growled.

I ignored the woman, focusing my rage and hate on the bad man. The *evil* man.

He pretended to think about it for a second. "No. Where is the book?"

No more words. I almost made it to the Greek before the others opened fire. Hot lead plowed through muscles and organs and my hands *almost* made it to his neck, but a single round from his weapon entered above my right eye and I dropped at his feet, staining the floor with a large puddle of blood and pink brain.

"Jesus!" Carter, I think. Could not be sure...the voice sounded a little wobbly as the roaring returned, stronger than ever. The world shrank to a bright pinpoint surrounded by an echoing darkness that smelled of death and decay.

As everything began to fade, I heard Branch scream in fury. In moments they would be dead, shot to pieces, because we did not have the Book of Ur and we did not know where it lay, not yet and, although I did not care too much for a snake like Carter, Branch was not so bad once you got past the faith and the Abomination This and Abomination That and I really needed to get up, but the roaring was so loud, it eclipsed everything and the pinpoint of light shrank, folding in on itself as I fought to remain conscious and I felt that maybe I should let go, that it was *time*. I had been alive so long and the shot to the head was not even the worst, not by half...in fact it was pretty small potatoes in a long line of indignities and injuries I had sustained over a very long career as a professional badass and perhaps the world would be a better place without me in it because monsters like me dimmed the light of God's glory.

The roaring became the world, evolving into a voice, a deep, penetrating bass that rumbled from the depths of forever. It was a voice I knew so well and it would come, that voice and it would take over, take all that was me and turn it into a monster the likes the world had not seen and even though I was a monster, a big, bad long-living monster, I was *nothing* compared to what would be if I let go, let the reins slip into other hands and that was not going to happen. I was the cork in the bottle, the finger in the dam and I would not budge.

My eyes opened. There was no one in sight, but I heard the sounds of lazy footfalls behind. The door to the first bedroom a lay couple of feet away, so the bad men, the *evil* men, must be taking care of Carter and Branch somewhere behind me.

I stood, taking forever, my limbs moving in a gooey mass of molasses, the pain of my gut, my shoulder and thigh gone. The only remnant of agony was the swiftly closing hole in my head as the bullet slowly emerged from my skull to fall to the floor. I was a bit wobbly, but good enough to take care of business.

Bad Guy Number One did not know I was upon him until he was airborne; screaming as he flew over the white settee and into the dining room and over the table. The far wall forty feet way interrupted his flight plan. He left a red streak on expensive wallpaper.

That is when Carter and Branch moved into my line of sight, him with a snap kick that broke the nearest henchman's knee, folding the leg backward. Branch's hand flashed and another henchman stared at the gushing stump of his thumb, pistol on the floor next to the severed digit. The woman completed the move with a pirouette that ended with her slim knife buried in another's eye. That man gurgled and dropped in a spray of blood and aqueous fluid as the man with the severed digit took a strike to the throat that crushed his larynx. He died gurgling.

While Carter finished his man with the broken leg, I took the last henchman out with a punch to the back of the neck. Bones popped like firecrackers under my knuckles, shredding the spinal cord into tapioca pudding. He dropped in a lifeless heap, head canted at an unnatural angle.

Bloodied and battered, my wardrobe ruined, I stood swaying slightly as my body finished healing, bullets spitting out of knitting flesh, one after the other to land with a clatter on hardwood flooring.

"Jesus," Carter swore, staring at the bloody and twisted lumps of lead.

"Carter, please." Branch's admonition held no heat. She too was staring, perhaps thinking she did not know what I was after all.

"What are you?" Carter asked.

Branch. "He's the Abomination."

"You two can hold my first ever fan club mixer later," I said, limping slightly as I strode toward the suited man I thrown like a football. A large red dent in the fancy wallpaper covered sheetrock just beyond the table told me of his location, where I had aimed. Pretty good accuracy, if I said so myself.

The man was sprawled awkwardly, barely conscious and his neck felt so damn good in my hands as I raised him to eye level. He was the classic

Greek stereotype: long face, curly black hair, black mustache, swarthy skin and near black eyes, which fluttered in pain. Those dark orbs finally fixed upon my face.

"It's *you*," he breathed painfully, realization dawning almost comically on his face. "I am so sorry; I would have used fire had I known."

Fear ate at me. Another person who knew my identity...it was a scenario I had been avoiding for centuries. *Does everybody know?* "Yes, it's me. Whom do you work for?"

He smiled a bloody smile. "You must understand...I can't say, but know that we will have the book no matter what. We never lose."

My healing wounds throbbed. "Doubt that very much." I drew my face close to his. "Cannot or will not tell me?"

"Take your pick."

A little squeeze to his throat in an effort to hasten cooperation produced zero results. He coughed, he gagged and spat blood, but remained silent as to his employer and I did not have time to screw around.

"Let me have him," growled Carter. "I'll make him talk."

A glance at my two companions showed a hateful look of glee on Carter's face while Branch seemed troubled. She slowly shook her head.

Good for her. Maybe she was not a total waste of space.

Back to the suited man. "I should feed you to Carter here, but I am not that kind of monster."

The Greek spat more blood as he smiled once more exposing reddened teeth. "Monster? You, sir, are *perfection*."

That is an odd thing to say. A bad feeling tingled along my spine.

"Let me have him," urged Carter, infringing on my personal space.

I tossed the man a hard look, and to give him credit, he maintained composure, although he paled a bit. Sighing, I snapped the Greek's neck and dropped him to the floor.

"Why the hell did you do that?" Carter screamed. Branch stared, horrified.

"Because he was not going to talk, no matter what we did to him," I replied tiredly. *Perfection.* Why did he call me that? That was a word I would never use to describe myself and it itched me that he knew of my existence. My healing wounds ached and it left me fatigued. "He is a true believer. Problem is, we do not know what he believes."

"Why did you kill him?" asked Branch.

"Because we cannot have him reporting back to whoever he worked for and he is too dangerous to turn our backs on. True believers never, ever, give up. He would have been back on our necks in no time. This was not a decision I made lightly. If I could have spared his life without risk to ours, I would have taken it without hesitation."

What I did not say, what nagged at me, was one simple question: *how did they know we would be here?* Which led to more questions, like why did they not know *I* would be here, me specifically? What about Branch and Carter? And why did they think we had the book? My head began to hurt and not just from the bullet wound.

"He called you perfection." Branch obviously did not think that word should be associated with the likes of me.

"I do not know why considering I am far from perfect, although I make a mean fratata." *Maybe a perfect monster.* My gut told me that was spot on.

The young woman stared at me for a moment and I was surprised to see that her eyes were a peculiar shade of blue, not a Scandinavian blue like the summer sky, but very light and clear, almost like aquamarines.

"You are not what I expected," she said.

I snorted. "You expected a psychopath?"

She nodded.

"Carter?"

He looked up, still angry. "What?"

"You said you read a file on me, right?"

He nodded.

"Old file?"

Another nod.

"And a new one, I'm sure."

Nod, nod.

"Pretty well detailed, I expect. New information from the Senator mixed with the old."

He scowled. "What are you getting at?"

"Was the old file from your boss at the Vatican?"

His eyes flicked toward her, all the answer I needed.

"Like I thought. Your bosses, or I should say, your Boss, His Holiness, has known about me for a while."

"Impossible!" she almost shrieked. "If He had, you would not be standing here."

I raised an eyebrow. "Really? Then how come the file? How did you find me so easily? I have covered my tracks pretty well over the years, yet I will guess that your boss, note the small B, *told* you what to look for, the politicians to speak to and I will bet my last Buffalo Nickel it was Senator Barnes.

"Sure, I may be a monster, but I am a different kind of monster than what has been bandied about in Rome, different enough that the Church and its *Manus Dei* (yes, I have files, too.) have left me alone for decades. Perhaps they thought I would be of use, like now."

During my speech, her face became more and more troubled, her mouth opening and closing several times. As for Carter, he did not look troubled as much as uncomfortable. At that moment I realized he was senior to Branch and that he had not revealed all he knew about me. Sneaky beggar.

"Another thing you might want to consider, Ms. Branch, is how the Church came into possession of the Book of Ur in the first place."

At this Carter's ears pricked up.

My toothy grin hurt my cheeks and pulled at the scars on my face. "The answer is simple...I gave it to them."

CHAPTER SIX

Greece, *April, 1824*

I found Greece to be a fascinating country. Rich in heritage, the birthplace of our Western Civilization, but yet in several ways provincial, almost backwards in its attitudes and beliefs. This backwardness, however, did not extend to the reception of Europeans, most notably myself.

The people of the small port town of Missolonghi were of the nature standard to the Greek ideal, being short and swarthy with black hair and wide smiles. They seemed curious at my height and fascinated by my scars, but evinced no terror at my ugliness, seeming not the least put off by the giant in their midst. Instead, everywhere my feet led I was greeted generously and with an abundance of warmth. Perhaps it is because they had their hands full with the Turk and they thought me a soldier dedicated to their cause.

Greek independence was the talk of the little port town as well as the heroic British gentleman who attempted to lead the country to its independence from the Ottoman Empire. It was in the tiny market by the docks that I overheard news of the British Lord's sickness, that he had taken to his bed and perhaps never to rise again.

The gossiper proved to be a wine merchant of questionable hygiene and I waited until he concluded business with a tired-looking old man before I stepped to his stall.

"What can you be having from me?" asked the merchant in broken English, smiling with a surfeit of teeth. Perhaps I looked like an Englishman?

Returning his grin, the noonday sun winking off of my spectacles, I laid a silver sceat upon the rough-hewn plank that rested atop two barrels that served as his stall, an impromptu table I saw mirrored at regular intervals around the square. "I could not but help but hear you talking of the British Lord who is ill," I said in flawless Greek. "Pray tell, who is this notable person?"

The sceat disappeared as if Hermes himself snatched it from the wood. "Ah, great sir, you who, by your size, are obviously Herakles reborn. The British lord calls himself Byron and has been ill. It is too bad that his physician is not a Hellene, or he would be up and dancing in no time at all."

"And the location of this lord?"

"He is in the residence of Lukas Mavrodides." A grimy hand pointed in the direction I needed to follow. The little man lowered his voice. "Tell me, large and fearsome hero, can this British lord win independence for our once great nation?"

I thought back to George's vibrancy, his athletic prowess and nodded. "If any man can, it would be George Gordon Byron."

The merchant nodded sagely. "Well, then. I shall pray to Asciepius himself to heal the British lord of his sickness."

From the market, it was not difficult to locate the house of Lukas Mavrodides as the Greeks seemed more than willing to pass this information to me as I was obviously no Turk. In a trice, I came to a small wooden door fronting a squarish house in the heart of the town. By the two stories and fresh whitewash, I took it that Mr. Mavrodides was a man of import in the community.

Knocking produced a short, wide woman in a shapeless dress who took one look at me and gestured me inside. "You are Mr. Franks?" she asked, although by the look she passed to me, she knew full well my identity.

My eyes (firmly ensconced behind their spectacles) took in the tiled floor of the entryway and the polished rail leading to the second floor. Every surface seemed not only clean, they fair gleamed. "Yes."

Without a word, she grabbed my arm and rushed me up the stairs! Imagine my surprise that such a small person could be so forceful. My feet scarce touched the steps.

In a moment, we came to a door from behind which a moaning and a groaning could be heard. The woman stopped, hand on the latch and looked at me with alarm on her wide face.

"You must help him, my lord," she whispered urgently. "He is in a bad way and daily asks for news of your whereabouts. Please, heal him of his sickness."

What could I say? I nodded and indicated that she should open the door.

My heart plummeted at the sight my eyes beheld when the door flew wide. A small room, perhaps ten feet on a side, with a window on the far wall where underneath lay a bed of polished cedar. On that bed writhed George.

I could feel my heart breaking in its bony cage.

In the short time he had been forced into bed, the sickness had eaten the once-vibrant man, rendering him to a skeletal form. Gone were the thick muscles of his arms, the robust set of his shoulders. His flesh looked pale, sallow, with an unhealthy yellowish tinge that bled into his eyes. Only his chin, that great prominence on his face, survived the ravages of illness.

Wearily, the chin pointed my way, the sunken eyes taking in the sight of the large man in the doorway.

"Victor," he breathed, lips lifting in a smile I remembered so well. "At last."

I knelt at his side in an instant. "You know how these modern streets are, George, so much traffic that a body can hardly move."

His laughter sounded like the rattle of dry sticks rubbing together. "Oh, you are a marvel, my friend. I take it you received my summons?"

Summons indeed. A young boy of mixed heritage knocking at my house in Paris asking for me by a name I had not used in years, pressing a sealed letter into my hands before scarpering off like the wind.

"How did you find me?"

A hand, cold and clammy, clasped mine and I almost wept at how frail and bony it felt, like twigs wrapped in rotting velvet. "Victor, I never lost you. I have always known where you were." His eyes burned with the either the fires of his fever or his passion. "Always."

If I had not been so worried for his health, I might have strangled the man. How had he been able to keep me in sight when I had done everything in my power to remain hidden from the gaze of powerful people? It struck me as a thing impossible, but I let the matter rest, too worried for my friend.

"I have done a naughty thing, Victor." George's laughter dissolved into wet, phlegm-y coughing. After it had subsided, he continued, eyes glassy and sweat streaming from his skin. "When you departed so suddenly all those years ago with an excuse so transparent we could use it for a window...well, let us say that it came to me that, with your obvious infatuation with Mary, no...do not look so alarmed, we all knew...it came to me that she might know more than she was willing to reveal."

Once again, his frame became racked with coughs. I grabbed his shoulders, horrified by the hard bluntness of his bones so easily felt through skin worn thin with illness. Eventually the attack ceased and he resumed his narrative.

"Victor, while she and Percy took the boat onto the lake for the afternoon, I crept into her room and read her diary."

A cold knot formed in my midriff and my dismay must have shown because George gripped my hands all his meager strength. "No, do not worry, my friend. She set your story to paper, but showed it to no person. I was a sneak thief, a naughty child willing to risk friendship to satisfy base curiosity.

"What I found startled me. You, the gentle giant with the soul of a warrior poet, were not the man we thought. You are so much more!"

"You know what I am," I said, voice thick with unnamable emotions that churned within my breast. "Perhaps you should have contacted the Vatican."

His drawn face became horrified and he cupped my face with his palms. "And have Rome destroy such a wonderful person like yourself? Never! My friend, you do not know how precious you are, how wonderful."

If there was any more desire for proof of his delirium, he had just given it to me. *Precious indeed*! The thought was absurd and I said so.

"Listen, Victor. When I read Mary's diary and discovered your genesis (for I knew in my very bones it was true, not the ravings of a madwoman), it opened my eyes to a world of wonder, of magic. I have spent years in search of such magics, in Austria, Italy and here, in Greece."

"And have you found the magic you have looked for?" I asked through numb lips.

His eyes grew brighter and he clawed at my arm in excitement. "Yes, yes, I have. I must confess, at first I hoped to find the tome that worked the wonder of you, but you had hidden it far too well, so next I left for Venice where I have seen wondrous things. But it was here, Victor, here in Greece, that I found what I had been looking for."

At the mention of the tome I became alarmed, but hid my consternation out of deference to my friend. "Which was?"

"Prophesy."

"Prophesy?"

"The Oracle at Delphi, Victor. It took years to find, but it is real."

In truth, I could not admit to surprise. Was not my existence proof of magic, of things beyond mortal ken? The world fair thrummed with mysteries that would destroy the minds of mortals.

"What did the Oracle reveal to you, George?"

The sick man licked his lips, staring over my shoulder as if a malign spirit hovered nearby. "The Oracle is the reason I summoned you after all these years. May I have water, please?" George pointed to a small table next to the bed on which rested a crystal decanter of water and a porcelain cup.

His greedy lips found the edge of the cup and drank all that was within, as if it would be his last taste of the sweet fluid.

"Thank you," he said, handing me the empty porcelain. "The throat dries from so much conversation."

"Perhaps I should leave," I remarked, a little alarmed. "Come back later when you are much revived."

Once again that hideous dry laughter. "Victor, there is no revival for me. Listen now for this is important." A thin finger tapped my chest. "Listen to the words of the Oracle: '*George Lord Byron, for you no longer a mortal life...*'

I felt the short hairs on my arms rise as his voice changed, becoming deeper, echoing through the room carrying with it a grave, metallic quality.

"...and much have you done that is evil and little can be done to redress the balance. In one and three years you will die, before you can be a hero to the land of Herakles..."

It went from there, foretelling his fame as a poet, how his name would live centuries after his death. During the recital, George's glassy eyes were fixed to a point on the ceiling, never moving, while the words of prophesy tumbled like pebbles from his lips.

When it was done, he fell in upon himself and I held my friend in my arms as he cried.

"Victor, you must beware," he sobbed. "That was only largest cut of the prophesy. There is more meat to be had."

"What else is there, George?" I asked, stroking his once-fine hair, now limp with sweat.

My friend licked his parched lips and said, "Normally the Oracle would only answer a question directly related to the subject, but I couched my query to include those I felt closest to me. The Oracle gave kind words to Mary and Claire, but for you she did not."

I raised my eyebrows, not at the gender of the seer (that was immaterial), but that George would bother to inquire as to my wellbeing because of our short time together all those years ago. Perhaps he felt racked with guilt over the method of divining my origins. Perhaps he felt, as I did, the strong bonds of true friendship forged quickly.

"What, George? What did the Oracle disclose of my fate?"

"It is fluid, my friend. There are several possible outcomes, but most are grim." Here he clutched my arm with surprising strength. "You are being sought, my friend, sought by forces larger than either of us, more powerful by far. They seek you, one to use, the other to destroy, but those roles will change in time should you avoid their grasp. The Old World can no longer shelter you, my friend, so I tell you that you must travel to the Colonies, to the New World so greedy eyes will, for a time, be blinded."

I rocked back on my heels, slipping from George's fading grasp. "Who are these forces, George? Who seeks me, to do me harm or place me to heel?"

"That is unknown, my friend, the Oracle would not disclose because I used my question and would not receive the answer to any more. However, to hazard a guess, it concerns the tome mentioned in Mary's diary, the artifact that gave you a second life. There are those who would destroy nations to possess the thing and they must believe that you would disclose its location. If you do know, hide it and hide yourself, seek the New World."

In those days I thought myself clever and skilled enough at hiding. "No, I will not do such a thing. I still feel attached to the wide world and have made preparations to visit the land of the Finns and to see Norway as well. I have always wanted to do this and will not be put off by shadowy menaces foretold by mystics."

"You could die!"

"We all die, George. I do not wish to live forever." I closed my eyes. "Sometimes I dream of death, the final comfort in my harsh life and am not afraid. Let these forces attempt what they will, I will not shy from desires."

With a groan, George seemed to shrink under the coverlets and I felt my heart go out to the once virile man. "Victor, for whatever reason you are a subject to forces beyond your comprehension, yet you spit in the face of fate to make your way in this wide world." He smiled, a sickly thing, his chin jutting further. "I respect that. I have fought all my life at what fate has bestowed upon my body and emerged victorious, so how can I begrudge you such struggle? However, promise me that when you are done indulging your desires you will take heed and seek the Americas? It will give you time to marshal forces to fight those that would use or destroy you."

As for me, I felt the fullness of dire forebodings pass through me, a cold wind that fair froze my heart. While I listened with skepticism of things such as clairvoyance and prophesy, George's profound belief withered my doubt.

"Rest, George," I soothed, stroking his hair. "I promise this easy thing because I do wish to see the New World someday. It seems sooner than I planned."

He clutched my coat with desperate strength. "Just be careful, Victor, be wary of those with knowing eyes. For all your might, you lack a certain...ruthlessness that the greedy and venal possess. To warn you of this threat is why I summoned you." He paused. "And to say goodbye."

I nodded, assuring my friend that I would keep a weather eye out for those with 'knowing eyes'.

"Have you heard about Percy?" George asked suddenly.

"Yes." Saddened at the news of the poet's tragic accident at sea, I sent my condolences to Mary via post, a long letter wishing her well and urging her to contact me should she want for anything.

"Our little group is shrinking, Victor. We are down by three?"

"Three, George? I put the count at one so far."

"Ah, you haven't heard then. Pollydolly is dead, passed in '21, bringing the number to two." He gifted me a sad smile. "Soon the number of the departed shall be three."

I had not heard the news of dear, brilliant John Polidori and the pain in my heart became a little sharper, the despair more clearly defined. Such good friends and the total would soon sum up to Mary. *And me, of course.*

"How...how did he die, George?"

"It is said sickness," came the mumbled reply. "But I believe it was poison. Cyanide. He was of ill humor during the end, bitter and in deep debt. Poor Pollydolly, he was too fragile for this harsh world."

Fragile and brilliant. In 1819, I'd read his story, *The Vampyre*. It was published in *The New Monthly Magazine* and had been attributed to George. However, I could hear Polidori's voice in my head as I eagerly flipped the pages. His Lord Ruthven was a frightening aristocrat with the visceral need to drink the blood of others and the character was rendered perfectly by the physician. It was obvious to me, having read George's work, that he was not the hidden hand that guided the pen.

If I were to judge who had written the best horror story, I would have to award the prize to John, whose prose so captivated me, although Mary's work was fine indeed and came a close second. Considering the content of her narrative, perhaps I am biased. Although fictional, it did raise a chill along my flesh for striking so close to the heart.

George soon became exhausted and drank more water from the decanter, which seemed to transform into sweat that broke from his skin like dew and smell sour, like cheese gone to mold. I stayed as long as I dared, but it became evident that he needed his rest.

"Please, come to see me on the morrow, Victor," he whispered as his eyes shut, the lids dark as bruises against his yellowish skin. "We have much more to talk about." He patted my hand affectionately. "You're a good man, my friend."

I am neither good, nor a man. Silence answered George and he seemed content.

Tomorrow, a good day to discuss things, not the least of which was the tome he mentioned. It was of great concern to me and it was necessary for me to learn who else had knowledge of its existence. "On the morrow, George."

I left my friend to his sweaty, uneasy sleep, led away by the plump woman who had greeted me at the door.

The morning sun greeted me to the promise of a brilliant day. That illusion was quickly shattered as I beheld the lifeless body of my friend.

CHAPTER SEVEN

"Why am I driving?" Carter sounded none too amused.

The large white sedan that Stavros had procured looked big enough to satisfy any soccer mom and purred along so quietly I could hardly hear the engine. The only noise was the sound of the A/C, Branch loading her weapon, and Carter's bitching.

Shortly after dispatching the suited man, we exited the hotel, Carter and Branch in the same clothes they had flown in and me in a pair of jeans and a black t-shirt. My other, somewhat perforated, clothes were in stuffed in a small duffel stashed in the trunk of the sedan. The corpses were cooling in the suite behind a DO NOT DISTURB sign while Stavros arranged for a specialized cleaning crew to attend to the mess. All it took was a charge to my Platinum Deluxe card assigned to one of my multitude of identities (this one a Brazilian antiquities dealer named Domingo Betancourt) and our corpse problem would be solved before our return. Nice to have friends in low places.

"Because I hate to drive," I said, examining the suited man's pistol, a Zigana M16. Nine millimeter, seventeen round capacity, chrome with a matte-black grip. The suppressor I stuffed into a front pocket while I wondered if the Greek realized it was a Turkish weapon. Rather odd for a Greek to be sporting such a firearm, even if they were more amenable terms recently. We could not risk bringing weapons into the country, so it proved convenient that we were able to liberate them. If you call getting shot four times convenient. "I would rather ride."

Carter's face settled into a dissatisfied snarl. Maybe he thought he would not have to do any heavy lifting on this job. He was going to find out just how much heavy lifting I had planned.

"What about the bodies? Your buddy Stavros gonna rat us out? If so, I say we head back and stuff him someplace quiet for the rest of his short life."

I shook my head. "Not Stavros. No, he will keep his mouth shut and all records of us will have disappeared from the hotel's computer system. The bodies will not be there if and when we return. It cost a pretty penny, but this one is on me, so you will not have to bother the boss with the expense."

Carter growled and shook his head. "How do you know Stavros is solid?"

"Because he is my friend."

"But why would he help?"

"Because he is my friend."

Carter shook his head. "I have a lot of friends and none of them would stick their necks out like that."

"Then they are not your friends. Besides, I have known Stavros since he was young boy."

"You killed that man," Branch cut in, her voice was cool, almost glacial as she examined her pistol, a Hungarian FEG FP9, a knockoff of the Belgium High Power. Not one of my favorites, I prefer a SIG or the Browning High Power, but beggars cannot be choosers. "That Greek man."

"Is there a question in there somewhere, or do I have to guess?" I asked.

"Why didn't you torture him for information, to find out who's after us, after the book?" she replied.

Ugh. And I thought her opinion of me was low before. "Why do people think that gross physical punishment is a viable interrogation technique? It is messy, brutal, and in most instances not worth the trouble." I checked the clips for the Zigana. Five, all but one full. "Besides, it is wrong."

Out of the corner of my eye I saw her look at me, her crystal blue eyes puzzled. "What?"

"Were you expecting a monster with fangs and a lust for blood? If so, go work with Dracula, not me. I do not like killing people."

"But you kill people anyway," she accused.

"To quote Arnold Schwarzenegger, 'Yeah, but they were all bad.'"

"Not all of them," she said quietly.

A cold lump formed in my chest. An old pain, a familiar one. "Yeah, not all of them." Speaking past the lump in my throat was difficult. "Carter, take the next right, the E962 to Thiva."

He grunted in acknowledgement.

I could *feel* the damn woman's eyes on me. "Spill it, Branch, you are freaking me out."

"Nothing. You're not what I expected. You don't behave like..."

"A monster?"

"Yes."

"What would you call a man who killed a child?"

Her reply was immediate. "A monster."

"There you go."

"So, what happened?" she inquired.

Ah. The Question. I had met people in my travels that knew most of my story and every single one asked The Question. What happened with the child? Or 'How could you?'

"You read the book, Branch?"

"Of course. Required reading before taking this assignment."

Figured. "Most of it is pure fiction. There are a couple of bits that are true. The death of the child is one."

A long silence. Finally. "Well?"

"Well what?" *This hurts every time.* But I had vowed to tell anyone who asked the truth about that time. They deserved to know who they dealt with and I deserved their revulsion. "While traveling, trying to hide from people, starving, cold and alone, I came across a young boy on the outskirts of a small village. He saw me and began to scream, frightened by my...deformity. I tried to quiet him, placing my hands across his mouth and throat." That day came back with a rush...the boy must have been all of seven, dressed in tattered hand-me-downs and dirty as hell to boot, but sweet-looking, like a tiny angel. A cherubic face clothed in rags and dirt. His screams echoed in the chamber of my skull and I could feel heat beating behind my eyeballs. "I accidently broke his neck...it was the first time I ever killed anyone." My vision blurred. "Now I do not want to talk about this anymore. The history lessons are *over*."

An uncomfortable silence gripped the car, thick and pregnant with my remorse. "It will be a couple of hours to our destination," I said after long minutes. "Keep to the speed of traffic."

Once again Carter grunted his acknowledgement. The car was becoming a haven for those short of words.

As we neared Thiva, I decided to break the silence. "Branch, if you do not mind my asking, how does one become an agent of the Catholic Church?"

Those crystal eyes never made it to me as she answered. "What, are we girlfriends now? We sharing?"

Damn, she was in full sulky mode. Not a big stretch for a true believer. "I did, back then. I shared little bit. Now it is your turn." I let that sit for a second. "Call it 'quid pro quo.'"

"Well, we aren't girlfriends and I don't swap stories with monsters."

She's not evil, I will not be forced to kill her. I let that thought run around my brain a hundred times until I almost believed it. I would ask Carter, but I doubted he would tell me as he seemed the type to prefer mayhem to his faith.

Sometime later, still wrapped in silence, the big sedan rolled into Delphi. Our destination and the home of the Oracle.

Modern Delphi looks like any quaint Greek tourist town: narrow, steep streets, whitewashed buildings with red slate roofs older than the U.S. government, and little cars and bicycles zipping hither and yon, screeching around corners and somehow narrowly missing pedestrians. Despite the modern touches, the place carried with it a sense of antiquity, as if, at any moment, warriors in bronze clamshell armor carrying spears and shields were going to pop out of the alleyways to declare war on the unwary European traveler.

I directed Carter to stay to the north side of town, out of the narrow inner streets the large sedan might become wedged in. Minutes later we stopped in front of one of the square, whitewashed homes. What made this residence different was the complete lack of vehicles parked along the street.

"You two stay here," I said, shoving the Zigana into my waistband and pulling the T-shirt over the telltale bulge.

The two exited with me, clearly in no mood to take orders. No matter. I knocked at a plain wooden door darkened with a patina of antiquity. It opened to reveal a short, fat man, grossly ugly, wearing a stained wife beater T-shirt and boxers of dubious cleanliness.

"Whaddaya want?" he asked in Greek.

"May Helios shine upon all who dwell here," I said smoothly the same language. "And may Golden Apollo cast his favor on the priestess who dwells within."

He blinked rapidly. "Nice to see that there are those who still remember the old ways. What of these two?" His tone indicated that he found my companions less than worthy.

"What did he say?" Carter bristled. He may not have understood Greek, but he understood tones damn well. By the look on Branch's face, she did, too.

I grinned. "He says you cannot come in."

The slim man drew his own confiscated pistol and was about to shove it in the little man's belly when there came a blur of motion, almost too fast to see. Carter blinked, gasped, then stared at the stub of broken iron in his hand that used to be a weapon. The remainder was in the fat Greek's hand, in several pieces. They tinkled merrily off the sidewalk as he dropped them.

"How the hell did he do that?" Carter breathed, eyes wide, the mangled lump of metal dropping from his numbed hand. Branch looked impressed. And a little scared.

"Who is this man?" asked the Greek, no longer seeming the picture of a fat, lazy slob.

"An agent of Rome. They both are," I said.

"American?"

I nodded.

"Figures."

"He says you two should stay outside with the car," I told them drily.

My companions quickly nodded, looking like a pair of bobble-heads.

"Do you have an offering?" asked the Greek when the two re-entered the vehicle.

I dug into my pants pocket and pulled out a small gold coin, which he took with reverence.

"It has been a long time since I've heard the old greeting, or seen a proper offering."

My smile was ear-to-ear as I watched him fondle the coin Carter had procured at my request. "Call me old-fashioned."

The man grinned (this did not improve his looks) and moved from the doorway, indicating that I should enter. "This will get you an answer to one question and one only. Unless it doesn't."

Cute. Inside I was treated to the sight of a slovenly living room. Fast-food containers and half empty bottles of local beer graced every surface. The room smelled like stale fries and spilt beer long gone sour. Litter covered a dirty avocado green carpeting. In one corner an old TV was blaring, an episode of *Justified*. Timothy Olyphant gave a steely-eyed speech to Walton Goggins, who stared back blandly before replying in a suitably convoluted manner. A modern western dubbed in Greek.

"Like what you haven't done to the place," I said, stepping over something I did not care to identify.

"Protective camouflage," came the reply. Immediately, the television vanished, along with all the clutter, leaving us in a dark space illuminated by a single candle.

Said candle was held by a large man dressed in what was, back in the day, called an *exomis*, a cylinder of cloth that resembled a short toga. A gold belt cinched it tight at the waist and the garment had been opened at the right to allow the right arm pass through.

"Have not seen one of those in a while," I remarked, pointing at his gold trimmed *exomis*.

The man, no longer ugly and fat, grinned through a bushy black beard, a slice of white in the darkness. "I like keeping to the old ways, as you can tell." Although shorter than me, his shoulders were broader, as was his chest and his muscles bugled impressively beneath bronzed skin. He had chosen a form designed to astound. "Follow me," he said, heading off into the darkness.

With only the pale, yellow light of the candle to light the way, I walked into the darkness. Before taking more than a dozen steps, I noticed the floor had gone from the nasty avocado green cut-pile carpet to carefully laid stones, planed flat and polished to a high gloss that shone a faint rose in color. I half expected to hear my sneakers echo into the distance, but the soft dark swallowed all noise in its cottony embrace. There was a sense of infinite distance coupled with horrific danger. It suddenly came to me with uncanny clarity that if I strayed, or lagged behind that flickering flame, I would be lost forever. Or at least until I met something much meaner and nastier than myself.

Step, step, step, the soft squeak of my sneakers a ridiculous counterpoint to the gentle slaps of my guide's kidskin sandals. With each passing minute, my sense of foreboding grew. Something was out there in the dark. Something big and hungry, infinitely hungry, something that waited for the fluttering flame to snuff out so it would have its chance. Then it would rend and tear and shred flesh, crush and splinter bones while we screamed and screamed as blood began to clog our throats and...

All right...enough of that! What was wrong with me? I was hardly the kind to succumb to panic and flights of alarmed fancy. Taking a deep breath, stuffing the corners of my lungs with every iota of air, I continued following the candle. I let my breath out slowly through my nose, imagining that I was exhaling my fear. Soon my heart was beating normally and I did not feel the need to run screaming.

"Where are we?" The dark grabbed my voice and nearly smothered it.

"In between," came the calm reply.

"That is not much of an answer."

"It's the one that fits."

After several centuries, I spotted a dot of light, which slowly grew into a doorway. Sunlight, a warm and inviting point in the darkness. I quickened my pace and when I started to pass the large man, a hand the size of a dinner plate stopped me.

"Do not," he warned. "Stay close until you are through the door."

"What happens if I make a break for the door?" I inquired.

A flash of teeth answered me, a warning more visceral than mere words. *Mental note, stay with the candle holder.*

Soon enough we were through, the light blinding me for a moment. When my eyes adjusted, I found myself standing on...a rough flagstone patio.

The large man stood at my side, smoke curling from the candle wick, the flame blown out. We stood in a meadow and behind us the doorway we'd just passed through led to a small hut with a thatched roof. The flagstone patio was a rough oval shape, one end at the doorway, while at the far end, fifteen feet away, lay a small, rough-hewn table of unpainted pine. Two chairs carved from tree stumps sat next to the table. Russet bark still clung to the backs.

Above us soft clouds scudded through a sky so blue it almost hurt to look at and when I looked down, a riot of color met my eyes from the wildflowers dotting a meadow strewn with white boulders. Unfamiliar mountains lay in the distance, their tops piercing clouds that didn't seem to move. The air smelled of springtime, growing things, the sweetness of flowers and hope.

"What is this place?" I asked, sure that the answer would not satisfy.

"Delphi," came the lilting reply. A young girl exited the hut from behind us, clad in a floral print peasant dress. She had hair so black it seemed to suck up the light and a spray of freckles under her soft brown eyes.

I was right...the answer did not satisfy at all.

"Oracle," the large man said, smiling softly. "Here is one who knows the old ways, who brings yellow gold as an offering to Apollo."

The girl cocked her head to the side and smiled. "It has been a long while since a proper greeting and offering has been made. I thank you."

"Forgive me, but *you* are the Oracle at Delphi?" I did not want to sound condescending, but the girl was barely old enough to start forming breasts, much less be a conduit for Apollo.

She took my hand and her skin felt like velvet. "Of course, silly. My name is Monica."

I shook my head. "Monica?"

"Yes."

"Really?"

"It's my mother's name. She's from Cardiff. That's in Wales. Father was Greek, a descendant of the Oracles of Delphi."

"I think I need to sit down," I murmured unsteadily. *The Oracle Monica of Delphi? George would have a such a fit if he heard that.*

Wordlessly, she tugged at me until we reached the table and chairs and I sat heavily. The chair creaked, but held my weight.

Monica the Oracle, possibly one of the most powerful people on Earth, sat down opposite and dimpled prettily. "I know you're a little confused about where we are, who I am and such, but don't worry."

"How about—?"

"Shhhh," she interrupted, placing a small finger against my lips. I smelled strawberry and jasmine. "There are things that should remain a mystery, don't you think?"

I nodded.

"Good. Now that that's settled, why don't you ask your question? You may ask more than one, but an offering is required for each answer. However, Apollo often chooses to answer only one question, so make it the correct one. If he does choose to answer more than one, the offerings for the answers become quite dear." Her face clouded. "You could wind up paying far more than you bargained. Understand?"

Again, I nodded.

"Cool. Ask your question, but think about it and make sure it's a question you want to ask."

I wanted to ask a host of questions, but at what cost? George told me he asked only one convoluted question, but did he ask another and was afraid to pay the price? This life felt precious to me, with more and more wonders to be discovered every year. Imagine *watching* the evolution of flight from December 17, 1903, to the present and knowing that humanity had just scratched the surface. The advent of the computer age, the first man on the moon and the iPhone.

Life was far too interesting to give up for information.

So, what to ask? Who were those idiots at the hotel? Who did they work for? How could I keep myself safe from the Vatican and its agents? As interesting as those questions were, it was moot if I could not complete the mission.

In the end, there was only one question that really mattered. "Where can I recover the Book of Ur?" *There, that should do it.*

Monica's face slowly became slack; her mouth dropping open and the hands that gripped mine became papery and dry. The meadow, which had been still and placid save for birdsong and insects, fell absolutely silent, not a whisper, not a buzz. The kind of absence of sound that, in itself, was louder than any noise. A cold dread gripped my heart.

"In three days and one the First Book shall come to rest," came the voice from Monica's open mouth. Her jaw and lips remained still, however, and the deep, metallic voice belonged to nothing that could be considered human. It was the same voice that once flowed from George's mouth all those years ago. No longer a pubescent teen, Monica looked serene and indescribably old, as if what lay beneath her skin should have been long fossilized.

From Monica's hand came a current of power, flowing into mine and pulsing with every syllable that poured from her mouth. It was like sticking your finger into a light socket, but there was no pain, just a steady thrum of energy that burned the Oracle's words into my brain.

"Travel to the far wild west where to find the Book shall usher in your greatest test, but beware the Dead, and the Cursed, for they oppose you and can end your eternal quest.'

My stomach churned. *Of course, it had to be verse.*

Monica's hands tightened on mine, so hard, in fact, her nails dug into my skin and blood began to well from the cuts.

"At every turn there is a great chance of death," the cold, metallic voice sounded almost...desperate. *"What lays inside the Tome can still mankind's*

breath. Only when the book reaches the start is there hope you can do your part."

Okay, that was somewhat vague. As I considered the words that were branded into my mind and understood what had to be done, although the reference to the Cursed and the Dead were too opaque for me to parse at the time. However, the part about my death definitely needed no interpretation. The hairs on my arms were standing straight up, as were the small ones on the nape of my neck.

What lays inside the Tome can still mankind's breath. That one looked to be fairly obvious.

As quickly as it began the energy cut off and the Oracle let go of my hands, once again a young girl named Monica who blinked rapidly as the sounds from the normal world came crashing back.

"I-I hope I was able to help," Monica said unsteadily. She licked her lips and the Greek warrior was there with a tin cup of water from which she drank greedily.

My lips formed a tight tragedy of a smile as I nodded.

CHAPTER EIGHT

London, November, 1850

I did not like London.

The Britons would revile me for such a remark, but it was how I felt.

The trip from Calais was blessedly brief and I found myself more than willing to take shank's mare in order to locate Mary's residence. Who knew that the city would be so large and complex in its thoroughfares? It was my first time there and the noise and bustle fair burst my ears, far more strident than cities in France such as Paris.

The only thing London had in common with its French counterparts was the smell. God above the stench! I felt like I would never become used to a culture that does not bathe on a regular basis. The odor that wafted from the men and women fair stung my eyes and I realized that olfactory overload was one of the reasons I made my residence in the countryside, away from the hustle and bustle and smell of modern life. I thought my time in Greece would accustom me to such harsh assaults, but London raised the bar for offensive odors, combining sweat, rotten vegetation, feces, dead fish, and the thick wafts of coal smoke into one hideous miasmic cloud that corroded the sinuses. Even the Thames smelled like a leper's piss pot. It was no wonder that upon disembarking from the ship urchins and women tried to sell me flowers, bright blooms called 'nosegays', at an exorbitant price. I fervently wished I had purchased one.

People scarce looked at me, however, which gave me much relief. I found myself not to be the tallest man as I had passed several on the streets who equaled my length.

For hours and hours, I traveled the busy streets of the metropolis and while crowded and damp, the Londoners were more than willing to point the way to Chester Square, located in what I found was called the Belgravia District.

Coal smoke irritated my lungs and my eyes watered behind colored spectacles, but as the sun began to hide behind the tall buildings, I found myself close to Mary's house.

Mary! My heart raced at the thought of my mortal love. Over the years I had written her perhaps a dozen times. Each letter I sent gave clue to as my current residence in the case that she desired to make contact. In all that time, she wrote but twice: once shortly after Percy's death, the second not more than two months ago urging me to London for 'one last gathering'. I found that phrasing ominous.

"Excuse me, lad," I said to a young, shabbily dressed boy of perhaps ten. He stared at me as though I would spring at him with claws and pointed teeth bared. "I am looking for the house of Mary Shelley." A silver penny made its way to my fingertips. "Perhaps you can tell me where?"

The lad's eyes never left the penny. "Ain't no Mary Shelley I know of 'round here, sir," he said. "But I delivers packages for the people hereabouts and there's a Percy Shelley house right over there." A grubby finger pointed at a doorway not more than twenty paces away. My heart thudded laboriously. So close!

A silver penny richer, the boy scampered off while I stared at the doorway. Percy Florence Shelley, Mary's son. Of course, I knew of her only surviving child, an unremarkable, ordinary boy of mild and jovial temperament. Nothing like the rake of his father, but that was just as well. It seemed that people of ordinary disposition lived longer lives. Happier as well.

At first my legs rebelled against my will and my heart continued pounding as if I had just completed great physical labor. Now that my destination lay close, my trepidation overcame desire. Scolding myself for a coward, I forced my feet to find the last paces to the front door of Percy Florence's house and I knocked.

A young woman answered, pale and plump with flaxen hair parted down the middle and gathered into a bun at the back of her head. Her eyes lit at the sight of me. "Victor!" she exclaimed.

I was thoroughly at a loss. Had I met this young woman on occasion and lost the memory? Her pale blue dress with skirts made full with a bevy of flounces struck no recognition and I cudgeled my mind, searching for a seed of memory that would bloom into an answer.

Seeing my confusion, the woman smiled, showing slightly crooked teeth. "Mary has told us all about you," she clarified, urging me to enter. "I feel as if we've been friends forever. Please, do come in."

"You have the better of me, my lady," I said, passing through the threshold.

"Oh my goodness!" The woman placed a slim hand across her mouth. "Please forgive me, I am Jane Gibson Shelley. Percy's wife." She extended her hand, bold as you please.

Percy. For a moment a score and more years were stripped away. The longer I traveled, the more roads I took, the more my mind slipped through the years at the mention of familiar names and places. Percy. Briefly, I felt the pang of his loss. The news of his drowning when his schooner sank sailing from Leghorn gave me a moment of visceral misery, but I hastily put such thoughts away and took the proffered hand.

"Victor Franks," I said, bowing over the appendage. "It is my honor to meet you."

"Oh my, your manners are flawless. Just as Mary said."

My heart beat faster. "And is Mary in residence?" I looked around. Narrow, clean hallways with oaken floors stained dark. An archway to the left led to a hallway while to right led to a richly appointed rooms and a staircase dead ahead ran to the second story.

"Of course, she lives with us. Currently she is ensconced in the library." Jane dimpled prettily. "Allow me." So saying, she hooked her arm through mine and led me to the archway to the left.

She led me down a short hallway decorated with paintings of the Godwins: William, Mary's father, a philosopher journalist, smiled benevolently at the viewer. Mary Wollstonecraft, my Mary's mother, a woman of stern expression and even sterner beauty. If I remembered correctly, she was an advocate of women's rights and novelist of no mean repute. There were others, people I did not recognize, but who bore a strong family resemblance to William.

At the end of the hall we encountered a door on which Jane rapped gently before opening, not waiting for an answer. Warm light flooded the hall and I found myself staring into what could only be the Godwin family library: a large room on which all four walls were surfaced with shelves and the books they held. More books that I had ever seen at one time, tomes of varying sizes and width on what appeared to be every subject known to man. A writing desk was tucked into the far corner, a worn and battered thing, an object better used for firewood than scholarship.

My heart leapt, for standing in front of the desk, facing us, stood Mary.

Time had done little to erase the signs of beauty from her long face. Oh, lines marred the soft planes of her flesh where before there were none, but they only served to enhance the strength of her features. Instead of youthful innocence, there was mature grace and experience. Her hair still maintained its luminous, fulsome quality and was styled in the same manner as Jane's, parted down the middle and drawn into a bun at the nape of the neck.

Her dress, also heavily flounced like Jane's, was black in color, a color that could mean either sorrow or contemplation. Knowing Mary's nature, I took it to mean both. However, her smile, that same smile that so captivated me a generation ago, still held its power to grasp my heart.

Mary, oh my Mary. I loved you still.

"Victor," she smiled, bringing the sun to my life. "I am so glad you came."

"He is just as you said, Mother," said Jane in a voice full of affection. "Except his skin is not so pale."

Mary cocked her head to the side, regarding my features. "Yes, Victor, you are subtly darker than I remember." Her smile was turned to her daughter-by-marriage. There was love in her eyes as she spoke to Jane. "Will you please bring us tea, dear?"

Jane dimpled and nodded, bestowing a knowing look, and closed the door behind her.

Immediately I was assaulted by a veritable storm of feminine affection. I grunted as Mary's body collided with mine and twin snakes wrapped around my waist to hug me tight. By damn, she was strong for a middle-aged woman!

"Dear Victor," she sobbed into my chest. "How I have missed you so."

My arms encircled her thin shoulders. "You could have sent for me sooner. You have always known where to find me," I rasped. Surely my heart, that vast and mighty muscle, could not be beating in my throat?

Mary pulled free, wiping her eyes. "My friend, I could not set such a burden on your shoulders."

"It is no burden, Mary."

She shook her head. "Of course it is, Victor, because I am a mortal woman and I am dying."

I felt the room tilt and turn beneath my feet as the news assailed my senses. My head fair filled with a muted roaring, as if the world decided to end and I heard the tearing of the earth dimly across a vast distance. Did I hear right? *Dying*?

The back of my legs hit something hard and I found myself falling backward into a chair that creaked alarmingly.

"Dying?" I asked faintly as the world stabilized somewhat.

Through the water of my eyes, I saw my beloved nod tersely, as if the focus of her will was to maintain her composure. "Yes, Victor. I have had days when I have woken to find one or more of my appendages unresponsive. Twice in as many months I have been struck blind without warning, only to have my sight return in a day or two."

Such illnesses were known to me, whether products of unbalanced humors or, as people were wont to say, demons attacking the flesh from within (this I doubted very much). I did not know where the truth lay, only at that moment my sanity teetered on the edge of a precipice, but the threat of what lay coiled asleep within me kept me from plunging into madness.

"And you brought me here to bear witness to your demise?" I asked without heat. Creeping numbness slid its way across my skin like freezing oil.

Mary shook her head and made to answer, but there came a knock at the door and Jane entered, bearing a tray brimming with a fine silver tea service. Smiling she set the tray upon the writing desk and poured three cups. Mary may have been annoyed, but I felt nothing but relief in the comfort of silence while sipping tea.

It was obvious that Mary wished Jane would depart and leave us to our conversation, but I was glad of her presence and reveled in the small talk she provided. For several minutes I swam in the seas of banality while my mind attempted to wrestle with the concept of Mary impending death.

Far too soon for my taste, Jane rose and bid us adieu, eyeing Mary quite forcefully. This caused me no end of speculation. Did she know of my...affection toward Percy Florence's mother? My true nature as I related it to Mary long years ago? I shook my head, the answers did not matter, what mattered was why my love summoned me to London. When Jane left, I broached that very subject over a cup of fine tea, my curiosity too much to tolerate the social niceties of chitchat.

"I invited you here not to have you witness my death, but to ask a favor," she said simply.

"Anything." Why not? There was little that I could not do given time.

Mary sipped her tea thoughtfully before continuing. "What do you know of my children?"

Children? "I know Percy Florence is the only child of four who lived to become an adult."

She seemed surprised. "You are remarkably well informed, Victor."

I performed a slight shrug. "After all these years I have amassed enough wealth to live modestly and well. My hobbies include knowing much of my friends, traveling the wide world, aiding the innocent, and not being known to others, keeping my secrets close."

"Hmm." She pondered this. "As well informed as you are, dear Victor, Percy Florence is *not* my only child who survived to adulthood."

Long ago I realized that information equals power and I prided myself on the quality gleaned from various sources. Mary had been my one obsession, the only person from whom I could not divorce deep emotion.

To think that my sources missed such a salacious tidbit bothered me more than a little.

"Do tell," I said quietly.

"It was in Italy, at the Villa Magni, that I had my fifth and final child."

I set down my cup and steepled my fingers, furrowing my brow in thought. Her account would put the date at 1822 when she and Percy stayed at the villa with Jane and Edward Williams. Reports concluded that Mary had a miscarriage and nearly died, having been saved by a quick-thinking Percy. Apparently, she had been bleeding to death from the trauma and her husband had immersed her in an ice bath to slow the loss of blood. The local doctor (a man easily swayed by coin and who divulged all secrets to me at the sight of gold) said that the treatment had saved her life.

"You did not miscarry, then?" It seemed the doctor was not as forthcoming as seemed.

Her gaze was level and contained a measure of steel. "No. I gave birth to a baby girl who I named Victoria in honor of...a friend."

The lump in my throat threatened to cut off the air to my lungs. It was with great difficulty that I swallowed it back. "Victoria?"

"Yes."

"She lives still?" If she did, I would find her. A great need to see my namesake overcame me and I felt such a protective urge flow over me that I felt I would drown under the tide of emotion.

Mary took a deep breath, face troubled. "Yes, and that is what I would like to talk to you about, but first I have a confession to make."

I nodded at her to continue. *Anything for you, love.*

She bit her lip. "That time in June at Villa Diodati I fear I did you a great disservice." There came a long sigh full of regret. "During the first two or three days it became painfully obvious that you were smitten with me and this fact was noted by everyone. It was the source of amusement to Percy and Polidori, who viewed it as a mockery of that emotion. How could a 'grotesque giant', as they put it, feel such for a proper British lady. What good could come of it?

"I must confess, Victor, that as a silly girl so overwhelmed by Percy's charm that I made sport of you. It was while you were chatting with George about horses or somesuch that I called you 'a misshapen beast' and other horrible, horrible things." She shook her head violent in self-recrimination while my insides became lumps of frozen flesh. "I was so stupid! It was all in an attempt to prove myself clever, to hold myself above an obviously well-traveled warrior as I believed you to be." Mary dabbed at her eyes. "It was terrible of me to abuse our friendship and it was Claire who scolded me quite firmly. My step-sister took me by the chin and treated me to the sharp side of her tongue for what felt like hours. Percy and Polidori tried to intervene, but Claire would not let them speak, so livid was she, so consumed by her shame of my behavior and disgust at our words."

Misshapen Beast? My frozen heart failed to beat. As Mary talked, her words became fainter, being drowned by the roaring of my shame and anger. Often I had been reviled for my appearance and size. People had run screaming at the sight of my countenance. How could I have thought that Mary would be any different from all the simple folk who feared me in the past? Despair opened her maw to swallow me whole while an icy anger filled my breast.

"You made...sport of me?" I ground out through the millstone in my throat.

Tears formed in Mary's eyes. "Yes," she whispered. "And I know how much of a dreadful person I was, speaking of my savior in such terms, making light of your scars, your pale skin." My shoulders slumped as she spoke, burdened by the betrayal I felt. "But know this, Victor," she pleaded. "Claire did set me a more honorable path and I was truly chastised! Her words made me realize the sort of foolish, self-involved girl I was becoming and I am so very sorry." Leaning over, she grasped my hands, each of my enormous digits as long as her hand. It looked as if she clutched a parcel of flesh-colored sausages.

What could I say? No words came to my lips; no crass collection of consonants and vowels strung together could describe the sheer monstrousness of what I felt. It came to me then that I could snap her bones with the slightest twitch of my arms and break her neck as easily as I would a bird's. The old madness simmering inside since my creation bubbled to the surface of my thoughts, coloring my vision in shades of scarlet and rue. It would be so easy, it would take no effort whatsoever to tear the entire house apart and destroy everything that was associated with Mary Shelley, including her family.

Family. That word rocked me back in my chair, bringing with it a measure of calming sanity. Family. Family was the reason for my being. Without family, there would be no Abomination, no Monster. Flashes of my first awareness rose from memory, the face of a horrified man who bore a striking resemblance to me, albeit without scars. I knew this man bore relation to me, a brother or father, I knew not which.

Did I regret being? Was my monstrous genesis reason enough to cast myself in a horrid, volcanic pit to put an end to an unnatural existence? The emotions I felt, both dark and bright, would cease and the wonders I had seen flicker out as I left this pale clay to burn. *Do I want to live and feel such things?*

As for the hatred, how can I describe its clever seduction? I longed to give into its embrace and fully let loose the power that resided within because I knew it would be sweeter than wine, more fulfilling than any ambrosia. With the madness flowing through my veins, I would be complete and the reason for my being would finally be realized and all before me would be laid waste.

Such sweet temptation. Such horrid results.

Those thoughts swirled through my mind as I stared at Mary's anguished face, so thin and drawn. For the first time I noticed how bony her countenance had become, the blades of her cheeks pressing against her skin as if to free them from the prison of her flesh. Her eyes were fever bright not just with tears, but with the kind of intense passions usually found in fanatics and martyrs.

"Oh please forgive me, Victor," she pleaded through her tears. "I couldn't stand it if you didn't."

"Of course I forgive you." The words were forced through numb lips. It was the first and last time I lied to Mary Wollstonecraft Shelley.

Her relief washed over me, a gelid flood that threatened to clog my throat. "Thank you, Victor."

I spared a brief nod, unable or unwilling to speak further.

Now that she received a measure of forgiveness (false as it was), Mary settled back into her chair, letting go of my hands. She looked around, as if bewildered, and reached for her tea.

"Did you know that George read your diary?" I said, desperate to fill the void between us.

Her mouth opened, a circle of shock.

"Yes," I affirmed. "After I left Geneva. He knew."

"Oh my God, Victor," she breathed. "I am so sorry." Her hands covered her thin face. "It seems I will be apologizing to you even after God takes my last breath."

"No need to apologize. I ask only that you destroy your diary, or that part that includes any mention of me." My eyes, safe behind their lenses, pierced her and did not move until she nodded. "I understand if you cannot and if the desire to keep that volume intact is the greater part of your will, then gift it to your daughter Victoria with the instruction to show it to no one outside the family."

"Of course."

"Thank you." Somehow, I think that my request hurt her, as if the deletion of any aspect of her life would be a bleeding wound. I might have felt more concern, but her recent confession left me numb to regret or shame. I thought it most likely she would not destroy the diary. Slowly I raised the teacup and the flavorful liquid became ashes in my mouth.

The uncomfortable silence hung thick and stifling about us and it was minutes before Mary spoke, her voice harsh with regret. "My Victoria is married now to a fine gentleman name Arthur. She is twenty-seven years old and has two children of her own and it comforts me that no one knows of her lineage, with the exception of herself, of course.

"The deaths of my other children, William, Clara, and the girl I lost shortly before we met, have weighed upon my mind these past decades. So much so that I began to see a sort of *conspiracy* in what I now believe is their murders."

I had been only half-listening, somewhat lost in the darkness of my thoughts, but at the mention of murder and my attention became completely captured.

Mary noted the force of my gaze. "I assure you, dear Victor, I am *not* mad. Three years after our meeting in Geneva, my son William passed away from what the doctors deduced as malaria." Here her gaze became fierce. "But it was not so. Malaria victims do not die from exsanguination."

I was aghast. "What?"

That fierce gaze pinned me to my seat and I remembered the forceful woman who berated Percy thirty-four years ago. "Yes, Victor. Poor William was found dead in his bed, cold and unmoving. We were in Rome when he died and Percy would not let me see our son's body, fearing for my sanity. I knew our son had been sick, but he was on the mend. When I last saw him before retiring for the evening, there was good color in his cheeks and his forehead was cool and dry. How could he be dead by morning? It was a question that plagued me for years, but when I confronted Percy about it, he bade me to pay it no heed, that illness strikes not at the whim of man.

"Mind you, this was our second child to die in Italy, for my good daughter Clara died in Venice almost a year earlier. Dysentery was the cause.

"Or so I thought."

"Exsanguination?" I asked.

She nodded. "So I believe."

"And what of Percy?"

"He would not speak of it," she murmured. "He would not let me see Clara's body as well, fearing my 'delicate' woman's nature."

My mind began to tumble with thoughts that splintered and broke, unable to stand the light of reason. Finally, after perhaps two minutes of contemplation while Mary sipped her tea, I came to a conclusion. "Percy knew something was amok, as well as the doctor who diagnosed Clara's sickness. If my guess is correct, he was the same doctor who attended William."

She nodded. "That is so and you know this man, this doctor whom we trusted with our lives."

The name hit me with force enough to stun. "Polidori."

"Yes, dear Pollydolly."

"What were Percy and John trying to hide?"

Mary shook her head. "I know not, Victor, save that before Percy's death, he met his doppelgänger."

That word sent a chill straight through my heart. A doppelgänger (or 'double walker') had long been considered the harbinger of ill fortune. Although the existence of magic (or forces so far beyond our ken it would seem to be magic) was a given, I had never given credence to that particular legend. To hear Mary claim that Percy actually *encountered* a doppelgänger sent me reeling.

"Can it be true?" I breathed.

She nodded. "He sent me a letter filled with words of fear and foreboding. I have no doubt now it was that legendary monster."

"So, Mary, not to be indelicate, but what does that have to do with your summons?"

Her thin mouth became thinner as she chose her next words carefully. "In 1813, Percy was attacked by a mysterious stranger while residing in Plas Tan-Yr-Allt, a house he rented in north-west Wales. He barely escaped with his life and bore the scars, two parallel marks, on his left shoulder for the rest of his days. Since then, he never stayed in the same place for any extended length of time, sure he was pursued by inimical forces." Here her face became drawn and angry, as if she had bitten bitter fruit. "And he chose *not* to tell me why or who pursued. I could forgive him much, his philandering, his spendthrift ways, but that silence on the subject I will *never* forgive, for I think it led to the death of my children.

"I do not know if I could have prevented their deaths, but, as their mother, I deserved to know. Now, Percy Florence is a good man, a gentle, amiable soul without artistic bent, but Victoria is the spitting image of her father, with her father's creative ability. I can think of no other reason than his keen mind that he was singled out by the forces that sent the doppelgänger."

The logic was convoluted, but I followed the knotted thread to the best of my ability. "You think she is in danger, or could become a danger?"

She nodded.

"You want me to protect her." It was not a question. I knew to the core of my being that this was the reason for my summoning.

"Yes," she replied, the word emerging hesitantly, as if frightened by the possibility of a negative response.

I sighed heavily, a sudden gush of air and regret and sorrow. Her trepidation beat against my conscience and clipped my desire to have her squirm. Yes, I still stung from her earlier confession and considered hurting her as she hurt me, but the despair and regret on her face moved my cold heart. In the end, she was still my first love and nothing could change that. "Yes, I will safeguard your family."

The chair cracked beneath me as it took Mary's extra weight, her body pressing me into the seat while she enveloped me in a crushing embrace.

"Oh, thank you Victor," she said, kissing my forehead. "Thank you so much!"

We spent several long moments holding each other while my chair creaked ominously and what started as an embrace between two friends began to evolve. A burning flush came to my skin, starting at my scalp and traveling down past my cold scars, my throat, the jagged mess of tissue on my torso and my navel before flowing into my groin.

Mary must have felt my reaction because she pulled away slightly, a grin suddenly appearing, causing her face to lose decades. "Come, Victor," she purred. "My dear sweet Victor, let me show you how much I value your friendship." She stood and held out a slim hand.

There was no one to be seen as Mary led me down the hall and up the stairs to her room and for the first and last time I took my love to bed.

CHAPTER NINE

Back in the dark, following the warrior in his gold-edged exomis and the dancing flame atop the candle and this time I felt no dread, no foreshadowing of ravenous *things* lurking just out of sight ready to rend and tear. That was a huge relief because I spent most of my concentration on trying to decipher the prophesy given by the Oracle and only fifty percent made any sense, the rest being typical mummer's gibberish.

But I knew better. The Oracle was the real deal and every word, every line, had to be carefully examined for meaning. Whether I could find those meanings before dying was the $64,000 question.

Who were the Cursed and the Dead? I did not think curses were *real*, which proved to be pretty damn silly considering what I knew of magic and my very existence. Goes to show you that even an old man like me can be wrong.

As for the book, I had a sneaking suspicion of where it might lie, although the Oracle failed to pinpoint its location. Artifacts, especially the Book of Ur, had a way of remaining lost or extremely difficult to find, otherwise countries would be using the Ark of the Covenant as a biblical version of a nuclear deterrent.

The bar in the King George Palace hotel sported the same luxury as the suites, which is to say an overabundance. So much so that I kept my eyes on the tumbler of eighteen-year-old Macallan so to give them a rest from such opulence. The two agents availed themselves of a nearby restaurant (recommended by Stavros, of course) while I sat and drank. Carter really did not want me out of sight, but once I handed him my passport and told him of my desire to sit and think, he let his objections slide.

Magic permeates this world, from Divine to Hellish and all manner in-between. One merely had to look with open eyes and heart to see it all around. In the past I fought creatures both human and not so much, so I felt in my bones that this time I would face more of both. Someone sent those assassins to our room, someone who knew we would be at the hotel, someone a step ahead, yet behind enough to think I possessed the book. Obviously, this mystery person or persons thought I was the one who stole it from the Vatican. Since the assassins shed their mortal coils, it felt safe to say there would be more to come.

With these lovely thoughts rattling around my cranium, I sat oblivious to the man who approached until he sat at the bar next to me.

"Hello, *mon ami*," he said in a French accent thick enough to cut. It reminded me of Peter Sellers' Inspector Clouseau. "Let me buy you a drink, from one professional to another."

I tossed back the Macallan and swirled it around my mouth for a bit, savoring the flavor before swallowing. "Another," I said to the bartender in Greek. "On his dime."

Frenchy ordered a double shot of chilled vodka. "I would order wine," he said in French. "But these barbarians drink the equivalent of horse piss."

Sitting there in his fine, off-white suit with a pale blue shirt starched so thick it looked practically bulletproof, he looked the epitome of the classic French man. Black hair slicked back, piercing blue eyes, pencil thin mustache and a nose so proud it could have doubled as an eagle's beak. Despite the heroic nose being in the way, I saw his broad shoulders and trim waist, the obscenely thick and yellowed callouses on his palms and surmised that he was probably a very dangerous individual. Of course, I disliked him on the spot.

"So, Frenchy," I said after another sip of scotch. "Go ahead and give me the pitch, I have a plane to catch."

He leaned in close, whispering, "I like that, *mon ami*, a man of spare words and to the point. How very American." A grin split his narrow face. His teeth looked impossibly white and his canines looked far too pointy. I felt a shiver of unease. "The rumor is you have the book. No, no, do not bother to pretend innocence. We are professionals, you and I, so let us dispense with any games and be honest. My employer wishes to have the book and will pay quite handsomely to possess such an artifact. All you have to do is give me the book and you will find yourself a hundred million dollars richer."

One hundred million? Someone possessed deep pockets, which begged the question...who? Things looked to be getting far out of hand, so I tried for the truth. "I do not have it. I am looking for it, but it is not in my possession."

Frenchy lifted his chin and gave a peculiar little sniff, the nostrils on his proud beak flaring. "You speak the truth, *mon ami*. That is of concern since rumor has it that a large, scarred man such as you stole the book."

"No, I did not. Thank you, have a good evening."

After a sip of his vodka, Frenchy placed a hand on my bicep. The knuckles were carpeted in thick, black hair. "Ah, because you knew of what I spoke, that means you *are* looking for the book. I suggest we join forces and split a handsome reward, yes?"

"No."

"*Oui.*"

"Nope, nein, nyet, pal. I have things to do, places to go."

"Such as visiting the Oracle of Delphi, *oui*?"

Good thing for me that at my advanced age nothing much surprises me anymore, but this came close. Somewhere someone possessed a set of loose lips and I felt the need to glue them shut. "Believe what you wish."

"I believe you should take my rather generous offer."

My hand enclosed his where it lay upon my bicep and I gave a tiny squeeze, not quite enough to powder bone. He took it without a flinch, but he let go. There were hidden depths to Frenchy that tickled my curiosity bump. No time to indulge my interest, though. "No. Thank, you, but fuck off."

"Americans," he sniffed. "Since you are a very capable man, I shall offer you one million dollars, right here, right now, to cease your quest for the book."

"Fuck off twice. Let me drink in peace." People just do not get the hint.

As silently as he arrived, Frenchy departed leaving only an empty tumbler to indicate he had actually been there. I knew I would see him again. My palms itched for his soft throat.

The bartender, a rolly-polly older gent with a white mustache, poured me most of the bottle before the epiphany hit. The sad thing was it should have hit much sooner.

An epiphany is usually defined as a sudden manifestation or perception of the essential nature or meaning of something. So technically what I had could not be called that because what happened to me should be defined as: coming to my bloody senses.

Only one person could have set me up. Only one, but me facing that fact meant that someone I loved slipped a dagger in my back and stabbed my heart. Tears tried to come to the fore but I dashed them away as I dropped a three-hundred euros on the bar (yes, Macallan is *that* expensive) and made my way with a battered soul toward the lobby.

A night clerk tried to stop me as I walked wearily toward the back offices, but a good glare from my scarred face had him quailing and he let me pass. Sometimes my ugliness is helpful.

In Stavros' office I found his body slumped over his desk, white fluid leaking from his mouth onto the blotter and eyes staring off into the distance. A sheet of cream white paper lay beneath his head and I teased it out, stomach churning.

Uncle: I am so sorry. They forced me to help them. My wife and children were used as hostages for my cooperation, but they went back on their word and killed them all, letting me live to suffer loss and betrayal. I don't know who they are, but they seem to think you have something they want. Forgive me my treachery and don't think too unkindly of me. I love you. —Stavros

The smell of death, voided bowels and vomit made my eyes water. Everything went blurry for a moment before I caught sight of an empty prescription bottle on the floor. Sleeping pills, fifty of them if the label was to be trusted. I tucked the note in a pocket.

Poor Stavros. Rage began to replace remorse in my heart and I slowly turned away, closing the door behind me, my heart once again a frozen lump lying inert in the cage of my ribs.

"Call the police," I told the night clerk when I emerged into the lobby. I left without a word.

Carter and Branch were not hard to find and my obvious poor demeanor had them reaching for weapons secreted on their persons. I raised a hand and said, "We have to go."

•   •   •

At thirty thousand feet and several hours later on a private jet obtained on the Vatican's dime, I finally began to relax. Gentleman Jack in a tumbler and a slow fire in my gut, I lounged in an obscenely plush leather chair taking in the comfort of the humming engines.

After napping and a refuel in Great Britain we continued our voyage west in silence, the agents not sure what to make of the trip to Greece and not wanting to disturb my funk. Meanwhile, I did not give a damn about starting a conversation, the loss of Stavros a fresh wound on my scar laden spirit. I had known the man since he was in short pants and counted him among my most trusted allies and all it took for him to betray me was a direct threat to his family.

I really cannot blame him. Still, it hurt.

The two agents sat a couple feet away across the aisle sipping a rather nice cabernet while trying their best not to stare. Surprisingly, it was somewhere over the states when Branch finally broke the silence. "What happened?" she asked, not meeting my eyes. "And where are we going."

The *Manus Dei* deserved answers, so answers I gave. "Those men in the suite. Stavros let them in. Apparently they held his family hostage in order to turn him." Talking past the lump in my throat hurt. "He had two boys and a girl. Her name was Thea and she was six. She liked horses and Thomas the Tank Engine. His wife was named Lia and she cooked the best spanakopita in all of Greece, it alone was enough to make one believe in a higher power. She had a smile that could light up a room and make you feel like you were home. Like you were safe." I took a sip of Gentleman Jack. The smooth burn made it past the lump and hit my stomach like a bomb. "Stavros...Stavros was a good friend and he called me uncle." A tear slipped down my face. "In his suicide note he told me he loved me." I sniffed. "As for where we are heading, I know a guy who can probably help. He lives in Colorado so we should land in Denver in a couple of hours." *Travel to far wild west* the Oracle said.

. I usually spent my time helping those innocents unable to help themselves, but that had to be put on the back burner because after I returned the book, I was going to kill every last man jack of them. *Damn them. Damn them all to Hell*

"You weep for a traitor?" Branch asked, facing me full now.

"Do you have children, a husband?"

She shook her head. "We're not nuns or priests, but no, I have no one in my life like that."

"Then you have no fucking clue what you would do to save your children, your spouse, when the pistols are pointed at their skulls and only a half-pound of pressure is needed to blow their brains out. I think when and if that time comes you will move Heaven and earth to save their lives and damn anyone who gets in your way." There I went and got all preachy, so I stopped because the look on Branch's face told me my words were bouncing off of her skull like ping-pong balls.

I turned to Carter. "Her I have figured out. She's a fanatic, true believer who will not part with a notion once it is firmly rooted in her skull, but you Carter, you are something else. Sure, you are *Manus Dei*, but you are no fanatic. You are far to pragmatic, too easy going to be the usual agent for His Holiness. Why are *you* here?"

A predatory smile accompanied the answer. "Why for you, of course. A chance to meet the man who inspired Shelly's book. I wanted to meet Frankenstein himself." His grin became something almost ugly and his eyes looked as cold as the space between stars.

Branch chimed in, "The Abomination."

Damn, what a one-track mind. "Frankenstein was the man, not the monster. The monster referred to himself as 'the Adam of your labors', which was as close to a name as he ever gave. You would know this if you actually read the book instead of watched all those dreadful movies." I almost shuddered. Talk about grotesque, the creature played by Boris Karloff turned out to be a macabre parody of the one of which my Mary wrote. When I saw the movie for the first time all those years ago, I walked straight out of the theater, sickened by how the screen writers twisted the tale and how poorly the creature was portrayed. Although Karloff did add a sense of pathos, it was too little too late for my taste. "Really, that was your motivation? To meet The Monster?" I put the capitals right there for them to hear. "You need a hobby."

"What I need to know," Carter said, still smiling. "Is how come you are? I mean, how did you become like this? Was it science? Black magic? What?"

Nausea gripped me as old wounds burst open, poisoning my mind with its familiar sting. Not many people knew my story and, in fact, much of it lay secret from me. The Vatican knew a good portion of my story and it begged the question as to why His Holiness did not bother to tell his agents.

Did I even care? Did I believe him? Fuck it, I turned my attention back to Branch and asked, "What is your take on the Book of Ur, agent?"

Her pale blue eyes finally met mine, loaded with her fervent belief. "It is the book that writes itself made from the skin of an angel and the blood of another, which makes it the most powerful divine artifact in the world, more so than the Holy Grail or the Ark of the Covenant. Like you said, it bears the Seven Seals and breaking even one them brings about the End of Days."

I nodded. "Sure, that is true, but remember what I said about secrets and mysteries?"

She nodded doubtfully, obviously not sure where this was heading.

"Every magic spell created by man, every ritual to summon demons, angels and beings from beyond the pale lie within that book. It is the ultimate repository of knowledge, so if it is so holy, how is it that the Book of Ur can create an abomination such as myself? It brought me to life."

That set the both of them back on their heels as the private jet flew ever west over America.

CHAPTER TEN

New York City, February, 1859

If London proved to be a smelly sewer of a city, then New York was the effluvium that flowed from its bowels, bearing all manner of vermin and foul stenches best left unnamed. Despite the grime and soot, the entire city fair buzzed with energy, as if an unnamable, deep river of power flowed through its roots, infecting rich and poor alike.

I found the people rude, the food tolerable only to goats, and the smell offensive enough to bring tears to the eyes of God himself. Paris and London shone as springtime bouquets compared to the streets I found myself treading. My promise had been kept to George...the New World was now under my feet, albeit sooner than expected.

For three days I had been tracking my prey, if what you call spending far too much silver for information and my hard-earned coin led me to the worst part of the Island of Manhattan: The Five Points.

For nearly a year I lived in this raging beehive of a city and never found need, nor desire, to visit the Points. I served as head of security to the notable Samuel L. Barlow, an attorney with a penchant for luxury and a need for safety. That need was intensified after the Great Police Riot in June of 1857, just short months before my arrival.

My great height and strength were finally of an advantage to me because New York proved to be a city besieged by fear, where not even the members of law enforcement could be counted on to keep the peace. It turned out that the those of the Municipal and Metropolitan Police departments were the ones at war and it inspired the Dead Rabbits Riot in July. Once I learned of these events, it was only logical that I represent myself as a retired mercenary fresh from the Crimean War, easily believed thanks to my horrific scarring.

For the first time in my existence my deformities worked in my favor and soon I began to take the odd job or two, protecting those who could afford my services. It was not long before those with even more money and influence noticed my efforts. Before five months passed, I was attending events where the influential gathered. Perhaps 'attended' is true strong a word...I was relegated to waiting with the other bodyguards and security types outside the servant's entrance. Although a rough-and-tumble lot, I found them to be both affable and genuine, much more so than those I safeguarded.

It was at one of those affairs, hosted by Mr. George Brinton McClellan, the Vice President of Illinois Central Railroad and Chief Engineer, that I caught Mr. Barlow's eye. Three interviews, and much bartering over the cost of my services, saw me employed by the millionaire.

The cold night air stung my eyes, the winter wind bitter iron against exposed skin, sending those who would be outside keeping watch against rival gangs into the comfort of their homes. The Points seemed empty, but as the most crime-ridden, gang infested neighborhood in New York, but there would be those who braved the weather to keep an eye out for trouble.

And, as if to prove my point, "What brings ya here?" asked a young voice full of mean and nasty. "This be a dangerous place to set yer feet, big man, it being our soil and all."

I turned slowly and saw a youth in a black stovepipe hat, flared trousers and calfskin boots. Between the folds of his buttonless rag-tag coat I caught sight of a black vest over a red shirt and I knew him to be a member of one of the most feared gangs in the city...The Bowery Boys. Three more young men, all in similar garb with similar snarls on their dirty faces, stood behind him, two carrying lanterns.

"Business brings me here," I replied, hands in plain view. "Business with the Dead Rabbits."

At the mention of their Irish rivals, the youths tensed, the night air filling with incipient violence. "That's a name we don' like to hear," the spokesman said, lips curled in an angry frown. The one Bowery Boy behind him reached into his coat.

Before the gang member could produce a weapon, I had a revolver in hand and aimed at the Boy with his hand in his coat. The bore of the .44 Remmington yawned like a portal to Hell, ready to swallow souls with one bite. It was a new model, fresh produced for Mr. Barlow's security detail, and I saw the Boys eyeing the weapon fearfully and covetously. Unfortunately for them they would have to wait another year before the revolvers were available to the public.

"I would seriously consider removing your hand from your coat," I told the Boy, who had frozen in fear. His large, green eyes were glazed as he stared at the pistol. The other three licked their lips nervously.

"No need to get nervy there, mister," said the ringleader. "We'll leave ya to yer business."

"Your name, boy," I demanded. "Give me your name."

For the briefest of moments, he considered lying, but decided that the road to truth would be the better route. "Rawlins. Damian Rawlins."

With a flourish, I disappeared the Remmington into the folds of my coat. It cost Mr. Barlow a pretty penny, but the benefits of such a lethal device outweighed its cost. I'd drawn it twice since purchase and had yet to shoot anyone.

Yet.

"You Bowery Boys have no reason to fret yourselves," I said. "The Dead Rabbits have something of mine and I intend to get it back. You go on your merry way and let me deal with hard business."

Rawlins squinted. "Ya sayin' you mean the Dead Rabbits no good?" He sounded hopeful.

"I mean to get what's mine and if the Rabbits refuse to cooperate, then God have mercy on their souls."

That made him smile through his dirt-crusted face and gave him an even more youthful cast. He could not have been more than fifteen. "Well why didn' ya say so in the first place?" He took a step forward, suddenly full of good will and camaraderie. "Ya see that building over there?" He pointed to a dark, three-story, brick and wood squarish affair couple blocks away that looked more a firetrap than serviceable abode. Still, it seemed it could house at least a fifty people in a small amount of comfort. "Inside there be Rabbits, but be careful, they burrow. There are levels under as over."

"Good to know." I nodded. More than a hundred, then. This would be much more difficult than I expected. After brief consideration, I asked, "You know a Rabbit by the name of Templeton Reid?"

"You mean Tenbuster Reid?" Rawlins asked. "Never heard no 'Templeton', but the leader of the Dead Rabbits is Tenbuster, on account he busted up ten men in one fight. If yer business is with him, ya gotta lot of Rabbits to get through first and liable rightwise to get fur in your teeth." This was met with quiet laughter. "And mister, that's fine with the Bowery Boys. Ya kill enough Rabbits, we be happy men, indeed. So let me give ya a little advice, ya get up top of that building over there if ya can." He indicated a taller, four-story building of red stone separated from the Rabbit's warren by a sizeable gap. "Then jump over, if ya can. Most likely Tenbuster is up top, but if he ain't he'll be at the bottom, underground."

My heart sank further and further with each sentence. *Of course. Fate has never given thought to making things easy for me.*

Before I could thank him, he stepped closer and I tensed, ready for a hint of violence.

"Mister," he whispered. "Ya be crazier than a back alley dog, that's for sure, but if ya don' wanna be filled with lead balls, ya best get to it, before light hits the sky because not many be wakeful now."

"What are you four doing out here on a night as cold as I've ever felt?" I asked, staring at the young man. So far, he acted as if a large man traipsing around past midnight in the most crime-ridden shitheap of a city on a night so cold most men would cup their privates to keep them from freezing off was a sight common to these parts.

Rawlins spat and I thought I could hear his spittle crack and freeze before it hit the ground. "The Bowery Boys patrol our soil against the

Rabbits, even the far edges like this. It's an honor to be on patrol and keep our gang safe. Them Rabbits is too soft to be out on a night like this."

I cocked an eyebrow. For a criminal and thug, there was something almost likeable about the lad. "So, what you are saying is you pissed off the boss and now you and your friends have the shit detail, is that correct?"

He grinned ruefully, showing gaps where teeth once resided. "Somethin' like that, yeah."

Well, I had to admit they were good. They managed to sneak up on me and that was no mean feat. Considering the Rawlins and his hatred of the Dead Rabbits, the threads of a plan began to weave together in my mind.

The Bowery Boy stepped back. "Mister, I don' like that smile on your face."

That smile grew wide and far more sinister as a plan began to form. "How would you and yours like to earn five dollars apiece?"

It took a moment, but his smile soon matched mine.

•　　•　　•

The four-story next to the Rabbit warren stood on Orange Street, almost to the junction where it met Cross and Anthony. The streets formed a triangular block, creating the fifth 'point'. The building was constructed of red brick and mortar, one of the sturdiest structures around considering the rest of the neighborhood looked ready to collapse or burst into flames.

To the average eye, it looked a smooth rise to the top, an imposing monster that would let no one reach the summit. To an experienced climber, however, it was a gentle staircase allowing access to the apex. Ledges, decorative carvings, and big, bold windows provided all the hand and footholds needed. But the Rabbit's building was barely scalable, with handholds that were half-rotted or non-existent. Although I could easily survive a three-story fall, I did not want to take any chances. Heading up from the inside might cause alarm if the building housed Rabbits, so outside and up looked to be the prudent course if I did not want to leave a long trail of bodies behind me.

The windows were shuttered close against the cold, not a ray of light to shine between rough-hewn boards. Standing in the alley, I gazed up and steeled my nerves, readying for the climb. One, two, and three breaths later I jumped, hands catching a jutting brick and *heaved*. Although treated poorly by harsh weather and neglect, the brick proved to be sturdy enough.

As I climbed, the flesh of my fingers split, the cold and rough surfacing tearing at my fingernails while my booted feet found precarious purchase. Blood froze against brick as I grabbed on tight. My hands began to itch with healing power as flesh knit, then tore again, over and over while the cold robbed my skin of feeling.

Second story and my right boot split at the seam. I had pushed far too hard, my strength too much for the oiled leather and it tore against unforgiving brickwork. Halfway to the third and the left began to tear as well. No matter. The Rabbits had something of mine and I would not allow damaged footwear to impede my mission. At the third story ledge, I shook the boots off, then my socks. The icy wind ate ate the soles of my feet, burrowing into flesh and I had to console myself that at least it was not fire. *Anything but fire.*

Each inch froze more skin, left more blood and flesh to decorate icy bricks, each inch a razors bite into my healing fingertips. Skin regrew, only to freeze and tear away against the rough surface and I bit my lower lip hard to steel myself against the relentless pain. In the past I suffered greater injuries, greater insults to my durable flesh, but this was an incremental assault to my mind as well as body, taxing my patience and discipline. I wanted to scream and jump about, anything to stop the damned itching, but stopping would be worse and cursing would only draw attention to those who were awake guarding their territory. Nothing to do but grit my teeth and carry on with cautious haste.

A last push and I was on the roof, panting, fingernails and toenails split and bloody. It had taken less than ten minutes and now the only thing to do was wait.

● ● ●

"What do mean five dollars apiece?" Rawlins had asked, his compatriots leaning in close at the mention of money.

My grin wouldn't go away. It felt too good. I was finally close to my objective and could almost smell the completion of my task. "I mean to give every Bowery Boy five dollars *apiece* to come down here and cause trouble for the Dead Rabbits."

Rawlin's smile seemed a hungry, ugly thing. "So, we're to be yer stalking horse, is that it?" There was an edge to his voice that could cut.

I shook my head. "A distraction. You don't have to fight, but I need you to be bothersome. Can you be bothersome?"

"Oh, the Bowery Boys can be as bothersome as ya need, mister, but I ain't doing anything unless I see folding money."

"Don't have script." As anger clouded his face as I held up a hand. Cupped in my palm were five $10 Double Eagles. A look of wonder, the lust of gold, transformed their faces as the small pile of coins glinted in the lantern light. "These have three brothers, that's eighty dollars total. You think you can get me twelve more volunteers."

"Mister," said Rawlins, reaching for the gold. "For this much, I can get the whole gang."

I snatched my hand back, the gold coins disappearing into my coat. "After. Not now."

He nodded. "Give me fifteen minutes."

•   •   •

Forty Bowery Boys ran down the street, coats whipping to and fro. They bore bottles to which rags were tied. As they drew close to the Rabbit warren, they all stopped, lit the rags using lanterns and threw the bottles at the street fronting the building.

Immediately balls of fire roared skyward as glass broke and oil caught. Greasy smoke touched my nostrils and I took that as my signal to proceed.

The alley gap was fifteen feet and the difference in height of one story and that was enough to break an ankle or leg. Nothing for it but get it over with.

At least it is not fire.

I made a running start, half-a-dozen long strides that had the tarred roof booming and my right foot hit the lip, a vertical protrusion of brick that served as a launching point and then I flew through the air, the frozen wind biting at my face, feet and hands.

The alley flashed below me, lit by the burning oil splashed along the street. Whoops and catcalls slid through the wind rushing past my ears and my leather hat tried to fly from my head, but I grabbed the brim before the wind did.

Over the alley and down and I could see the tarred roof of the smaller building coming at me fast, almost too fast and I knew it would hurt. My feet hit and I bent my knees, but not before hearing a loud *crack* and I felt a sickening jolt of writhing fire from my left ankle. The roof hit me in the face. Very hard.

I fell *through*. Tar-covered wood parted all around me with a horrendous crash while splinters and nails punched through my clothes. Skin parted with a sound like tearing paper and blood flew. I tumbled head over heels as what felt like a six-inch dagger punched through my gut as things unseen broke beneath and inside of me and my headlong tumble into darkness finally came to a halt with my body hitting a floor that was substantially more durable than the roof.

There came a splintering *pop* as the small bones in my neck shattered and I lost all feeling below my skull, although my face still hurt madly.

Shouts and screams, very close, muffled by falling wood and the hellishly loud ringing in my head. There came a scraping sound and sparks flew, bright flashes that I caught out of the corner of my eye. Slowly sensation returned to my neck as bones realigned, squirming like maggots beneath the skin and with that squirming came daggers of pain stabbing at the flesh of my neck.

A soft glow illuminated the floor as a lantern was lit and a voice exclaimed I know not what because my ears still did not function to full capacity, but my flesh started to become my own again and that pain, that old familiar friend that had been with me for so long that to be without was unthinkable because pain defined me, it was my world, whether physical, emotional or spiritual, pain was a constant friend and its absence would unman me and I didn't think I could function without its hot and cold presence.

A rough voice crashed through the ringing in my ears. "Who the fuck are ye, boyo?" A pair of large, dirty feet came into view.

I thought it best to play dead, happy that my heavy coat hid the snake-like sliding of bones under my skin.

Then came a familiar, feminine voice, one I thought I might never hear again. "Uncle?"

"This fuckin' bastard yer Uncle?" A hard kick to my side. "He's a big 'un. Why haven't ye told me about him b'fore?"

"He's an old friend of the family, a former soldier. Mum must have sent him."

"Well, yer mum has sent a dead man, she has."

My bones continued their writhing and I felt pieces of wood slowly extrude from my skin as the itching of regeneration continued its relentless course.

The feet disappeared and I heard the gruff voice of a man speaking to several others who apparently arrived on the scene, while the girl knelt at my side. "Oh, Uncle, why? Why? I was perfectly happy with Templeton."

A rib snapped into place wetly and I felt good enough to quit the charade. "Because, Elizabeth," I said over the winter wind and the shouting of the Bowery Boys blowing in from the hole in the roof. "Your mother is worried sick." Rising to my feet was difficult at first, but I managed, swaying slightly.

Elizabeth, clad in only a blanket, blonde hair in disarray, shrieked and jumped back, fist to her mouth. I took a brief opportunity to look around.

A big room, rectangular with a large bed a couple feet away. A small, ratty desk, chairs and a claw-footed tub in the corner separated from the rest of the room by a folding screen. The tub was the nicest object in the place, enameled and clean, a pearl in the midden of the Rabbit warren, perhaps the spoils of the '57 riots. On the far wall was an open doorway through which several angry voices emerged.

As for Elizabeth, Victoria's only daughter, she sat on the bed, cringing from me, which broke my heart. I had learned to love the impulsive girl since Mary first introduced me nine years ago. Victoria and her husband Arthur (a polite, quiet man) knew of my identity, but their children did not. Assuming I would survive the night, she had hard truths to face.

"Come on, Elizabeth," I said softly, holding out a large, gnarled hand. "Let's go home."

"Who the fuck are ye and how the fuck are ye walkin'?" asked a hard voice.

I lifted my eyes to see the broad form of Templeton Reid stride into the room clad only in a pair of well-worn trousers. Muscles gleamed impressively under his fair skin and his dirty blond hair was tousled, messy. He had lively green eyes, a straight nose and full lips. All and all a handsome man whose looks were marred by the cruelty that etched his face like acid.

"This woman is coming with me." My voice rose from my gut flat and emotionless. I reached for my gun, but found it missing and I realized it must have been lost during the fall.

Reid laughed, walking slowly and confidently to stand at Elizabeth's side. He laid a large, possessive hand on her slender shoulder. "She's mine, boyo."

I narrowed my eyes as Elizabeth blurted. "I love him, Uncle."

"God's truth, man," Reid cut in. "But ye're ugly. I ain't ever seen such large, purple-y scars like that before."

Enough was enough. I was in no mood for games. "Come with me, Elizabeth. This piece of trash doesn't love you."

"Yes he does," she yelled, suddenly furious. "He's going to marry me."

Nothing surprised me more than when Reid laughed.

CHAPTER ELEVEN

Branch stared openmouthed, startled by my reluctant revelation.

"Son of a bitch!" Carter swore, moving up from his seat to sit at my elbow. "What the fuck do you mean you were brought to fucking life by the fucking Book of fucking Ur." His face was flushed and his eyes were wide, as if he'd just run screaming from King Kong.

"You heard me," I answered blithely, sipping my whiskey. "And mind your mouth, young man, it is not very Vatican-y to use the word fuck so prolifically."

Carter stared at me a moment, mouth agape. With a grimace, I lifted the bottle of Gentleman Jack and gulped down at least six shots worth in one go.

Branch bit her lip. "How is that possible?" she asked, eyes on a faraway place.

"You really don't know, do you?" I asked, startled.

Her crystal eyes narrowed. "Know what?"

"The book is pure knowledge and contains all the spells known to humanity. There are secrets within its pages that can unmake a mind, turn lead into gold and bring the dead back to life. Really, I thought His Holiness would have told you."

"It isn't like His Holiness and I are on a first name basis," she snarled. "It wasn't his decision—"

I held up a hand. "Yeah, I know. It was the C9 who gave you this mission and they are the ones who pointed you in my direction."

She merely glowered.

A muffled shot rang through the plane, a barking noise that emanated from somewhere at the nose and a second later I found myself staring down at the front of the plane at a sixty-degree angle. My stomach tried to switch places with my throat as I found myself falling slowly past Carter's startled face. For him and Branch, both facing the rear, the sudden shift of perception must have been startling as gravity performed a little flip flop. For me, it was an opportunity to fall past my companions to land on the door to the cockpit, although my arms cushioned the blow.

The heavily reinforced door creaked alarmingly, but held. Unfortunately, despite the 'reduced gravity' of the nose-dive, my left arm (which was held at an awkward angle) gave way, snapping with a wet, crunching sound as my body folded on top of it. My weight might have been reduced, but not my mass and the pain was an electric wave behind my eyes and for precious seconds the world faded from my sight as darkness crept around the edges of my vision.

Reality came snapping back with Carter's slide down the aisle, feet first and his ugly little 9mm drawn. "Move, goddammit!" he yelled, aiming the pistol.

There was just enough oomph left for me to push off with my good arm, rolling to my left and sliding to the floor. Carter's big boots hit the door a fraction of a second later, narrowly missing my skull. During my life I regenerated a lot of damage, but I had no idea if my head could heal up from being pounded flat by a pair of size twelves.

Before I could curse at his laces, the FP9 barked several times, shredding the door latch and lock and sending shards of steel flying. Grunting, Carter gathered himself and kicked with both feet and the cockpit door exploded inward.

Everything became moments of time, images taken together to make a cohesive whole out of a chaotic jumble.

One second:

The pilot, the top of his head a crater, lay on the floor, blue eyes staring through me into the abyss.

Two seconds:

The co-pilot, grinning through the wild tangle of his russet beard, on his knees, aimed his pistol at my head, finger tightening on the trigger.

Three seconds:

Through the window a dense gray mixed with smatterings of black. We were still at a high altitude, but at the angle of our descent it would not be long before we become one with the earth.

Next to my ear, the 9mm roared twice, the noise tearing through my eardrums. Twin holes appeared on the co-pilot's forehead and gouts of gore erupted from the back of his skull, decorating the roof the cockpit. The bullets failed to pierce the durable fuselage. The co-pilot slumped to floor as I attempted to fight through the agony in my arm and stand.

"Fuck me," Carter swore. The agent shoved past the co-pilot and sat in the pilot's chair, hands gripping the yoke.

"Get your ass in the other chair!" he shouted.

Already the pins-and-needles itch of regeneration flooded through my left arm, damping the pain as I managed to lever my bulk in the co-pilot's chair.

"What's going on?" Branch yelled over the roar of the engines and the hammering of my heart.

"Pull, goddammit, pull!"

Grabbing hold of the yoke with my right arm I hauled, bracing my feet against the floor. The plane shuddered and shook, fighting my efforts and the damn yoke felt cemented in place. Grimacing, I set my feet and hauled again, grunting and straining, but no joy, the thing didn't budge and we were still heading down, down, down.

In front of me the clouds parted and I saw the earth, still blissfully far away, rushing toward us, the ridges and humps of mountains reached their stony fingers for the plummeting plane. Night gathered all around but I could see my impending doom well enough My stomach gave a tiny lurch.

"Come on, you sonofawhore," Carter chanted, sweat slicking his forehead. "Come on, come on, comeoncomeoncomeon..." After a couple of sweating seconds, he grunted and let go of his yoke, "We're fucked," he panted.

The thought of the plane hitting the ground at six hundred miles an hour and exploding in a ball of fire was enough to get the juices flowing, prompting me to place my left hand on the yoke even though that arm felt far from healed. Snarling, I heaved.

My old friend agony came for another visit as the regenerating bones of my arm popped, sending slithering heat across my nerves. I did not let that deter me as I continued to pull, back straining, sweat popping from my skin, and it hurt so much I thought I would pass out and I could not feel my left hand, but I knew it was there, I could *see* it grasping, holding the yoke as I struggled to bring the plane shuddering out of its dive and I heard a high-pitched whining that drove spikes through my ears into my brain, the plane was screaming in outrage and I was screaming, my throat raw and bleeding and still I pulled because I did not want to *burn*.

Howling, the nose of the plane began to rise, but the mountains were so close now and I could see snow whipping past the windshield, thick and heavy. I dimly noted it looked like the dry, powdery stuff skiers loved and I filed that away as irrelevant because I was about to die and why did I think of the damndest things in situations like this? Before my arm could finally give out and turn into a lump of dead meat hanging from my shoulder, the plane leveled and I let go, shaking and sweating, cursing under my breath.

From the corner of my eye, I saw Carter staring, hands limply holding the yoke. "How did you do that?" he asked in wonderment.

"Luck," I answered, trying not to pass out.

A second later, Branch entered the cockpit. "What happened?" she repeated.

"The co-pilot fucked us," the slim agent snarled, checking the gauges.

I met her eyes. "We're okay. I managed to level the plane out." Outside, mountaintops fled below, disturbingly close while white flakes sped by in a blur.

"Hate to break it to you two, but we're still fucked." Carter tapped a gauge twice. "That asshole opened the fuel dump. Right now, we have about maybe five to ten minutes before this crate drops like a brick and we become one with Patsy Cline and the Audie Murphy."

Not good. My eyes couldn't seem to focus and my left arm burned like mad, but I tried to make sense of the multitude of buttons, bells and whistles the plane had to offer. My brain refused to cooperate. "Where are we?"

Branch pointed to a monitor mounted above our heads. She stretched and tapped the touch screen. "The West Canada Lake Wilderness, wherever that is." Despite her brave face, I could sense she was terrified.

Oh damn We were supposed be much farther south approaching Albany. Yeah, we are fucked all right. "Expand the view there." I pointed

Branch nodded and obliged.

"What's that?" I asked.

She looked closer. "Black spot. Dunno."

Carter grunted. "That's a lake."

"That isn't a lake," Branch said, peering close, expanding the NAV image even further. "That's a couple of hundred feet of shallow wet in the middle of a big nowhere."

"Carter, how far away is that?"

"Hmmm...three, maybe five minutes."

I shook my head. "Then it is our only shot, unless you like the thought of kissing a mountain, besides, with fuel we can control our descent. Once it is out, we drop like a rock." The plane shook. "Especially in these winds."

"Gonna have to fly south, then turn around north so we can use the long axis of the lake," Carter said, staring at the NAV screen. "The lake is too narrow to attempt an east-west landing, so it has to be from south to north or visa versa. I figure we slow to almost a stall and attempt a landing that way."

"How much time is that going to eat?"

"Minute, minute and a half. Gonna be close."

"Can you fly this thing?"

There was a hint of madness in the look he gave me. "I can fly just about any crate that made by man. Never deliberately landed one in the middle of winter on a frozen lake, though. If it's frozen solid, we'll have a better chance. Let us pray that the ice is at least fourteen inches thick."

"Yeah?"

"Yeah, because if the crash doesn't kill us, we'll probably drown."

To Branch he said, "Buckle up."

Hard blue eyes regarded me for a bare second before she disappeared into the back. I heard her begin the Lord's Prayer and silently followed along. It could not hurt.

"Getting ready for the turn." Carter had his eyes glued to the Nav.

I looked out the window, but the snow was too thick for me to see anything clearly. "What do you need me to do?"

"Shut the fuck up and strap in," Carter growled. "Unless you can fly a plane, you ain't of any use to me."

Good point. I shut up rather quickly and strapped myself in, left arm a mass of itchy, squirmy feelings.

The plane banked hard. "Fuck, there's not a lot of room to maneuver in this valley," Carter said, teeth clenched. "Okay, slowing. Better pray there's no wind shear."

As we slowed, the plane bucked and shuddered as if in the grip of a seizure. Carter kept up a continuous stream of swearing, face red with exertion. Looking out, I saw through the gray haze of snow a blackness that was approaching far too swiftly. There came a *thump* as the landing gear locked into place.

Carter screamed, "This is it!"

The belly of the plane plunged suddenly into the blackness and my vision went white.

• • •

Cold...harsh and unrelenting. It sandblasted my cheeks with tiny chunks of ice and my lips felt numb with its urgent kisses. My ass and thighs were icy as well while my hands felt...nothing. The cold interfered with the peaceful, cushioning dark I found myself in, an enveloping blackness that took away pain, anger and loss and wrapped me in a soft embrace I never wanted to leave, but that blackness was receding, driven off by the cold. I tried to return to the comfort of that darkness like a child who nestled into his blankets to snatch more precious moments of sleep, but the cold would not relent its pull.

As ice tore at me, another sensation ate at the edge of my consciousness...heat. I did not know where it came from, then I did...my hands, which before felt nothing, now radiated warmth. That felt good, yes, I could get used to the blessed warmth that caressed my hands except...they started to burn.

Burn? Fire?

FIRE!

The beast inside lashed out and I was propelled into the waking world, screaming my denial at any and all.

My eyes opened to the sight of flames eating at my hands, a piece of burning stuffing from one of the jet's seats that was torn open like sacrificial goat. I ripped my hands away from the melting, burning plastic and plunged it into the snow that lay thick all around while my eyes watered at acrid smoke from the burning insulation and foam rubber. While frozen tears dotted my cheeks, kept my burned hands in the snow to cool them, I blinked rapidly to clear my eyes and assessed the situation.

Darkness all around crowded the feeble fire, but to my eyes it became a mixture of grays and blacks and I noticed my sunglasses, an integral component of my ensemble, were missing, so my vision was unimpeded by colored lenses. Directly behind me lay the lake half hidden by snow carried on the bitter wind and instead of nice, soft water, there was a long strip of shattered ice a couple hundred feet long with razor shards sticking up at odd angles. It seemed that the landing gear tore into ice that was far less than fourteen inches thick before reaching the water beneath. From the spotty wreckage still burning out on the frozen lake, it must have flipped and rolled several times before hitting the shore where it burst open like a rotted corpse. It came to rest on an upslope to the mountain looming above, massive, gray and brooding.

The night was barely lit by fire, electrical, chemical and otherwise. To one side lay an engine...a twisted, gutted wreck that dripped streams of flame, what was left of the fuel. On the slope, the fuselage lay like a child's broken toy, massive holes where the wings used to be.

"Carter!" I bellowed, standing, pulling my regenerating hands from the snow. I knew that there would be gnarled, melted-wax looking scar marring the skin forevermore, but it was just one more to add to the list.

Damn, but I felt *exhausted* and cold. A bitter chill that leached the energy from my bones and had my head spinning. Looking down I saw the shreds of my shirt and realized that I had just finished regenerating a horrible wound and my body started to pay the price in a terrible hunger that tugged at me hard. "Branch!"

"In here!" came the reply, rendered faint by the wind.

My uncanny eyes pierced the gloom and I made my way through the wreckage to what remained of the fuselage, which also was dotted with sputtering flames. Climbing inside, I brushed the edge of the wreck and a dagger sharp shred of metal sliced through the shirt and deep into my shoulder.

"Son of a *bitch*!" I swore. *This is becoming tiresome!* The thought spun through my head as I looked for the source of the voice.

"About time," Branch yelled. Her exposed skin looked startlingly white, as if her body had been drained of blood.

She hung from the ceiling, still strapped into her seat. Directly below the fuselage had buckled inward where sharp rock had slashed through and knives of metal pointed up toward her head. It was clear why she had not unbuckled, becoming a shish-ke-Branch probably not high on her 'to do' list.

Despite the wind whipping outside, the burst fuselage provided a break. The lateral gouge I climbed through faced the lake, away from the mountain, the direction of the icy wind. The two ends of the plane were filled with debris and scree, effectively sealing each so what we had was a gashed cylinder with shattered portholes.

"You okay?" I asked. She looked fine, albeit cold.

"Get me down." The words emerged mushy through blue lips.

Nodding, I reached up and tore her seatbelt from its mooring, catching her before she impaled herself on the jagged spikes of metal. Branch gave a little squeal and held on tight as I maneuvered her away from danger.

"You scared the heck out of me," she scolded as I put her down, pulling away from my embrace. I guessed her gratitude did not extend prolonged contact with the Abomination.

"Less complaining, more surviving and watch your language," I grumped. "In case you haven't noticed, it is freezing and we are not dressed for it."

"Where's Carter?"

Good question. "I do not know. Woke up a several minutes ago. Listen, I would love to organize a search, but if we do not find clothing and prepare a proper fire, we are done."

A quick search of the plane yielded a pair of pilot's blazers, too big for her, too small for me, but it was something. By the time we were through we had found a dozen candy bars, a plastic quart bottle of milk, four slightly damaged steaks and a half a loaf of bread that did not look dodgy after the jumble around during the crash. By the time we were finished, we had ripped the interior apart. We had just started peeling the leather from the seats to use as makeshift blankets when a familiar form ducked inside.

"Good to see you both are alive." Carter grinned. In his arms were bundles of torn fabric. "Found what's left of our suitcases." The agent grinned from the layers of clothing that swaddled him. He looked ridiculous. Ridiculous and *warm*.

"Where have you been?" Branch asked while I just looked askance, tearing seat leather into strips.

Carter dropped his load of ripped clothing and started stacking the meager pile of wood he'd accumulated just inside the fuselage to the left of the hole. By the way his fingers moved, his hands were near useless with cold, the lack of gloves showing hard. "I woke up shortly after the crash, still harnessed in the pilot's seat, which was out on the ice, 'bout froze my dick off, let me tell you. When we touched down, the landing gear must have hit a thick spot because the nose became one with the ice." He set a twig into a still fluttering flame that was eating chair stuffing and, once lit, moved it carefully to the teepee of sticks. "Followed the flames and found tall, dark, and scarred there out next to lake, guts all over the place from a hole in his stomach. I stuffed his intestines back in and found you unconscious hanging in your seat, so I figured you were okay for a while and went to look for our luggage. Most of it survived. American Tourister...always buy the best." He rubbed chapped hands over the fire. "They were scattered all over the place and I decided to pile on the layers right then and there so I could hunt for wood. If we can hold out to daylight, we might have a chance."

"Good thinking," I said, winding strips of supple leather around my shoes and tying them off. "Take these strips, our shoes are not going to last long. Patent leather is not good for strenuous hiking."

"Strenuous hiking?" asked Branch, picking up the strips and commencing to reinforce her sensible flats.

"I know where we are."

From the fire, Carter raised an eyebrow.

"From the Nav, I saw we were fairly close to civilization, but way the hell off course from our destination, our pilots deliberately flew north and west of Albany to crash us into the mountains, trying to make it look like an accident. I should have paid better attention while we were flying, but I was too busy woolgathering. As for civilization, while close, we may find small houses here and there, we'll have to walk through the mountains and heavy snowfall. So, best thing we can do is lay up until this storm passes then head on out. If we do not find people soon, we have enough food to last a several days if we start rationing."

"We should just wait." Branch sounded tired, as if her very bones could hardly stand the process of existing. "The plane's transponder will let the FAA know where we are."

I shook my head. "Bet you anything the co-pilot disabled the transponder."

"But maybe he didn't."

"Do you want to bet your life on that?"

Branch looked down at the fire, shaking her head, hard lines bracketing her mouth.

"Any idea how long this blizzard will last?" asked Carter.

"Best guess... no more than a day."

Silence met that revelation and we hunkered down for the night, the moaning wind a poignant counterpoint to our shivering misery.

CHAPTER TWELVE

New York City, February 1859

Elizabeth and I stared while Tenbuster laughed as if he had heard the funniest joke in the world. His mouth grew wide with mirth, exposing a multitude of slightly crooked teeth and his hand lay flat against his stomach, as if he were preventing his entrails from bursting forth in a torrent of gore.

"Oy, Jesus, that is precious," he gasped, wiping tears from his eyes. "Sorry, luv, but ye ain't Irish and it would crack me sainted mother's heart not to marry a lass from the homeland."

My large hands curled into fists, the oversized knuckles cracking as tears welled in Elizabeth's cornflower eyes. "But, Templeton, you said you loved me! You said you wanted to be with me."

"And I was with you, wasn't I?" he replied with a sneer. "We was with each other for three days, and what fine time of it we had."

Enough. "Boy, just walk away and I will take her home." The cold wind of death slithered out of my mouth, coloring my words in hoarfrost. Elizabeth caught my intent and her eyes opened wide in fear. This was a side of me she had never seen, the dangerous, violent side that could snuff out a life like a weak flame.

"Ugly man," said the gang leader. "I ain't done with this one yet. She's going to be a top earner, she is."

Finally, a little fire came to the girl's eyes, just a hint of the roaring flames that I saw in Mary so long ago. "Top earner?"

"Aye, girlie," he said, chucking her under the chin. "I brought ye here to teach you the ways of earning on yer back, I did. And ye learned just fine. I am going to make a pile of silver off yer sweet honey pot."

Elizabeth stared at the man she thought loved her. Two months ago they had met at the funeral of Matthew Calbraith Perry, the famous naval man who successfully negotiated trade agreements with isolationist Japan. Tenbuster had posed as the son of a rich haberdasher who did business with the Perry s and caught the very impressionable Elizabeth's eye.

The two started meeting clandestinely, the excuse he used was that his father would never condone the courting of a mere accountant's daughter. Although Arthur had proven to be a man of industry, working hard to provide for Victoria and the children, he had yet to climb far in social circles.

Clever though Elizabeth was, her parent's caught her out and forbade her to have any more dealings with the haberdasher's son, citing that that such surreptitious meetings spoke ill of the young man. The girl acquiesced, but disappeared the next night.

That's where I came in.

Straightaway, Victoria came to see me, bleeding tears and misery and I went to Mr. Barlow, informing my employer that a family crisis had emerged and that I would be leaving for an unspecified amount of time. Although a hard, practical man, Mr. Barlow was learned enough in the nuances of human expression to see my well-contained anxiety and steely resolve. He politely granted me leave, but said that if I took more than two weeks I should seek employment elsewhere. The smile I showed him caused the blood to drain from his face.

"Not to worry, sir," I said softly. "If I cannot conclude this business in the aforementioned time, then I do not deserve to be in your employ."

I did not think twice about draining my hard-won savings, nor about visiting the haberdasher whose son Reid claimed to be. When I found out the man possessed no children, it was only a matter of time and well-spent coin to find out that her paramour was Templeton Reid, a member of the infamous Irish gang, the Dead Rabbits.

Snarling, Elizabeth lunged at her lover, fingers curled into claws, but he was faster. Almost contemptuously he backhanded her onto the bed where she began to sob uncontrollably. Two things happened next.

One: I charged the man who hurt Elizabeth, rage forming a black haze across my vision. My hands reached for his throat. I was going to kill him and, God help me, I knew I would enjoy it.

Second: Faster than I thought possible, Tenbuster drew a tiny pistol from small of his back and shot me in the head and I fell near insensate at the feet of my enemy. I lay stricken, white noise plugging my ears and a clattering gray shrouding my sight.

Soon after everything resolved in a kaleidoscope of sensations, colors clashing like broken cymbals inside the chamber of my skull, resounding painfully. I saw various shades of brown and black that tasted like licorice and melons, with a bitter aftertaste like burnt herbs. I smelled words, acidic and flowery at the same time and they did not seem to register, their meaning lost on me.

"Waltrwegrdwhmmm?" The voice smelled like pepper, deep and musty and with a hint of gold.

Another voice, pewter and brass, smelling like offal, answered. "Irknwbrnhm."

Time, folding in on itself in a display of plasticity, sped up, then slowed to a gray trickle, never letting me in sync with its rhythms. The world filled with a yellow and red cadence that clogged my veins with fire and lye and I felt, deep within me, in the secret place I dared not go, a great stirring began like a leviathan sluggishly rolling in the lightless depths of the ocean.

No! Spirit flailing wildly, I swam hastily to the surface of my mind.

My eyes opened and I saw my colored spectacles were gone and that rough worked stone greeted my uncovered orbs. It was hot, almost unbearably so and voices bounced strangely around my skull.

"What're we ta do wit 'im?" asked one high, warbling voice.

"Tenbuster wants us ta cut 'im up and dump 'im in da river," answered another. "Gonna be a handful o' work, though. He's a big bastard, dat's for sure."

"We oughta strip him right and proper, he looks like he might have coin. That's a nice coat he be wearin', although da hat be a crime against fashion."

It dawned suddenly that they were talking about me, which lent a certain urgency to my muscles, propelling me to my feet in a rush. There came squeaks of surprise as blood rushed from my skull leaving me dizzy so I flailed, finding hard stone to support my considerable weight.

I found myself in a tunnel roughly carved out of the living rock beneath the city, cramped and hot, lit by flickering flames of crude lanterns burning noxious oils. Off to my left I saw a widening, while to the right the tunnel split in two. At the junction of the split, five feet away, two harridans stared, virtually toothless jaws gaping, gray hair puffed in stringy clouds upon their heads, shapeless dresses a mishmash of faded colors. They both gobbled like plucked turkeys.

"Ladies," I said, trying my best to sound nonchalant. "Insulting a man's hat is quite offensive." One hand swept the garment from my head and I executed a passible bow without falling over. "Pray, can you inform me where I might find Mr. Tenbuster?"

One crone, eyes bleached by cataracts, wordlessly pointed toward the tunnel ceiling, while the other, sporting more wrinkles than a well-used saddlebag, dropped the cleaver she carried.

"By the Good Lord," she said, voice a-quiver. "Yer eyes, mister...they be yellow." Tears began to drip from hers. "Are ye Satan, come ta take us ta Hell?" The cataract-ridden crone fell to her knees and began pray in what I assumed was Gaelic.

My eyes. It had been a long while since another saw them. Daffodil yellow, they fairly shone in even the faintest light. "Madame, trust me when I say that if I were indeed Satan, there would be no doubt. You would already be in Hell."

"Then, then...what be ya?" The other crone continued her praying, saliva dribbling from the corners of her mouth.

That was a very good question. "I am something you do not wish to annoy."

She nodded hastily.

"How did I come to be here?" I asked.

"Tenbuster's men brought ya, they did. Told us to disappear yer body an clothes."

"Where are these people now?" I looked around. The tunnels were very quiet considering they were the Rabbit's warren. The silence was broken only by the flickering flames and the rhythmic chant of prayer.

"They be outside, brouhaha with the Bowery Boys, I hear."

Bless those bought and paid for scoundrels, I thought, happy that my money had been put to good use, although I reasoned that the Bowery Boys needed very little incentive to tangle with the Dead Rabbits. "Good, how do I exit these tunnels?"

The woman pointed toward the widening behind me.

I nodded. "Now, behave or I will come back." Even making a veiled threat to a woman brought bile to my throat. It was not gentlemanly, but it ensured that the alarm would not be raised. I hoped.

Back at the widening I found a sturdy wooden ladder affixed to the rough tunnel wall that led to a wooden trap door on the ceiling. I climbed the ladder and pushed the door. It lifted easily and I peered through the crack into a small, dark room. Empty.

Smiling, I climbed into what I found was a large closet or pantry. Sounds of fighting came from outside, screams of pain and rage and curses so vile it caused the hair on my arms to stand up straight.

I opened to door to the closet to find a Rabbit, a smallish man, standing with his back to me. The door creaked just enough to alert him and as he turned my fist shot forward, slamming hard against his jaw, which gave with a harsh *crack*.

Stepping over his unconscious body, I walked down a hallway that ended in a lobby with double doors leading outside where the two gangs fought like crazed dervishes. To my left, stairs led up.

"Oy, who da fuck you be?" a Rabbit yelled, bounding down the stairs two at a time. He wore a stovepipe hat canted at a jaunty angle on his head.

Instead of answering, I met the charge and lifted him screaming into the air before slamming his body hard down onto the dirty wooden floor. The boards shook violently and I left him moaning and retching.

The building proved to be a maze of improvised hastily constructed walls, hallways that led nowhere and doors cobbled out of whatever material lay at hand, but I finally managed to find my way to the third floor. The entire area was empty of detritus as the first two were full. Obviously Tenbuster wanted his personal space clear of debris and he ruled over the Rabbits like a British lord. Finding his room was simple, seeing what lay inside nearly drove me insane.

Elizabeth lay beneath Tenbuster, who was frantically pumping in and out of her like an out-of-control machine in a frenzy of enthusiastic rape. Her mouth was open, slack, with drool oozing from a corner. Eyes that once held blue fire now stared sightlessly at the ceiling. It appeared that Tenbuster did not care that his minions fought without his guidance.

Despite his lustful frenzy, Tenbuster still managed to catch sight of me as I entered and was on his feet in an instant.

"That's not possible!" he cried, not bothering to pull on his trousers. "That can't be!"

I fancied that the grin I gave him would have scared lesser men shitless.

His small, single shot pistol lay on the bedside table and he went for it with all the speed of the terrified, but I was there as well, fury erupting in my breast. One large hand engulfed his as he raised the weapon and I *squeezed*.

Flesh and bone became pulp and joined with wood and iron as I crushed the hand and pistol together and Tenbuster screamed and screamed and screamed, mouth opened wide in a rictus of terror and pain and he knew he was going to die because the look on my face told him I would take my sweet time in the killing and I would enjoy it very, very much.

His ever-rising screams of agony were suddenly cut off and a look of puzzlement descended upon his features. One, then two seconds passed while I held him upright by his mangled hand before he vomited forth a copious amount of blood, staining the floorboards black.

Tenbuster's body went slack, held up only by a grip that oozed blood, crushed flesh and iron particles. I stared at his lifeless, staring eyes for moments before letting go and wiping my hands on my coat. Elizabeth stood, naked and unafraid, the blazing light of madness shining from her face, a long, bloody knife grasped in one hand.

"He kept this under his pillow," she hissed, spittle flying from her mouth.

"Good girl."

•   •   •

Boot met doors and doors lost, cracking open wide like a portal to a different world. Noise flowed past, but I paid no heed. Visions of fighting assaulted my eyes, struggling, biting, scratching, kicking, stabbing, blood flowing, flesh tearing, a glimpse of a bloody smile with an ear dangling from the corner like a shred of half-consumed beef. All this cascaded over and around me, but I stood fast, a rock in the torrent, holding my precious cargo fast to my chest.

There were two steps to take to reach the ground, now churned to bloody mud, and as I took them, I freed one arm, the burden of Elizabeth nothing to my great strength, and fired the Remmington (found in the corner of Tenbuster's room) into the air. The report was the trumpeting announcement of my arrival.

"Make way," I grated into the sudden silence, my voice promising more violence than humans could imagine. Bowery Boys and Dead Rabbits stood side-by-side, bloodied and battered men and women staring at my yellow-eyed gaze. They crossed themselves while and performed the gesture for warding off the evil eye. I did not care, all that was necessary was to take Elizabeth home.

"'e's got Tenbuster's girl, he does," said one Rabbit, a largish man missing two front teeth. "That's Lizzy, an' she belongs to us."

The Remmington barked a second time and the Rabbit pitched back and collapsed, sporting a brand-new hole in his forehead. "This is Elizabeth Riggins," I barked savagely, nodding at the blanket draped woman in my arms. "She and hers are under *my* protection and belong to no one but themselves. Anyone have a problem with that?"

No Rabbit spoke or moved.

"Good. Now...I hear of any harm coming to Riggins family and I will find those responsible and I will make them *pay*. This I swear by Almighty God and the angels above."

Rawlins, bearing a trio of scratches down his face and a black eye, came forward out of the crowd. "So this is what ya come for, eh?" he asked, eyes refusing to settle on my face.

"Yes." Holstering the Remmington, I drew forth a fat wallet. "Here," I said, tossing it to him. "A little extra in there. You and yours went above and beyond."

Looking inside the wallet, Rawlins whistled appreciatively. "Mister, ya can call on the Bowery Boys anytime ya want."

I tipped him a nod. "Good to know."

Before the Rabbits could comment on our obvious business relationship, I strode forward casting my gaze all around, the force of which parted the crowd. Wordlessly, I strode down the aisle, back straight, my burden clutching tightly at my shoulders.

●   ●   ●

"Oh my!" Victoria's face drained of all color when she opened the door to find me standing there, Elizabeth virtually unconscious in my arms, wrapped in a soiled blanket.

"Uncle," she cried. "What happened to my baby?" From inside the town home, Arthur Riggins, Victoria's husband, emerged, lantern in hand. "Come in, Uncle," he said grimly. "Put her on the settee."

A small man with the wide shoulders of a bricklayer, Arthur was a man whose life was defined by practicality. Practical shoes, clothing, haircut, and demeanor, this man with sharpish features like that of a ferret never struck anyone as a dreamer, but a powerful dreamer he was. Hampered by the class system of England, he dreamt of a place where, by dint of hard work and brains, his children could grow to become people of worth and note. America was that place and Elizabeth and James those children whom he believed with all his heart would become both powerful and compassionate.

Victoria, with Mary's blood strong in her veins, took to the idea of my bizarre existence with a will, accepting a world filled with magic and wonder. One would have thought Arthur more inflexible in his thought processes, not one to take such things to heart, but he surprised even me with his calm acceptance of both my existence and my role as family protector.

"What happened, Uncle?" he asked when Elizabeth was placed upon the small couch. His eyes never left her face and the depth of his love was plain to see.

"That is a story she must tell when she is able." The flickering lantern light cast odd shadows throughout the room. "Let us say that she has had a sore trial."

Victoria knelt at her youngest child's side and took her hands, kissing them tenderly.

"What is happening?" James, the eldest at twenty-one, entered the room in his nightclothes, rubbing the sleep from his eyes. "Uncle! You're back." His eyes landed on his sister. "Wonderful, you brought Elizabeth home. I knew you could do it." Face full of hero worship, he treated me to a hard hug, arms iron bars around my waist.

Once again, I marveled at how much he had grown in the past nine years. At only six-inches shorter than my own prodigious height, with dark blond hair and lively brown eyes, he was the spitting image of his grandfather, although a taller and stronger version of the poet Shelley.

I kissed the top of the boy's head and returned the hug. It pained me to say that he was always my favorite, the one closest to my heart, though I did love his sister dearly. "It is good to see you again, James."

"Uncle, where are your glasses?" he asked upon disengaging.

My hands went involuntarily to my face and I gave a shuddering sigh. My heart plummeted at thought of what I had to tell my adoptive family. "Let us all sit, please."

As they stared up at me, I said, "The time has come for me to leave New York."

Arthur and Victoria nodded, lips slightly pursed while James jumped to his feet, alarmed. "But Uncle—!" he began.

"Enough," I interrupted, raising a hand. "People saw my eyes tonight and by morning it will be the talk of the town. Staying would be too dangerous for me and draw attention to you. This I cannot allow."

James sat slowly, absently pulling at his longish hair. "Where will you go?"

My eyes went to the window, seeing the cloud-filled sky reflecting sickly, yellow light back to the ground, a jaundiced, a diseased look that I would not miss at all. There was only one place to go, a place where I could lose myself for a while. A place where individuality and privacy were still valued. A place where wild things still roamed.

"West."

CHAPTER THIRTEEN

"Can you tell what you know about the Book of Ur?"

Carter's voice broke the silence with almost sledgehammer force. During the sleepless hours of huddling around our meager fire, before the first rays of dawn could penetrate the dense cloud cover, my companions began to grunt and groan. Abused muscles and bones were making themselves known in no uncertain terms now that adrenalin had worn off. No one wanted to talk, we were all pretty damn miserable and lost in ourselves.

We looked like hobo mummies wrapped in the abundance of our clothes, but it kept us warm and the fire, supplemented by what I could find out on the mountain slope, made sure we stood a chance.

Almost without thinking, I answered. "It's the first book."

Branch stared at the fire; her disturbing eyes locked on things I could not see. Carter, meanwhile, scratched his head in confusion. "I thought the first real book was the Epic of Gilgamesh."

My estimation of the man's education rose a notch.

"No," Branch said. "I think it was the five books of the Torah."

Sighing, I poked the fire with a small stick. The little pile collapsed inward and I added more bits of wood. The wind was dying, but the snow still fell and a goodly drift had formed at the jagged opening of the fuselage. "It is, of course, the Book of Ur. It is the first book, given to man by the Archangel Raphael to safeguard and to use as needed. Did not your *Primus* brief you?"

She shook her head. "How do you know about the *Primus*?"

"I think what you are really saying is 'how can the Abomination know so much?' right?" I countered. "Listen, I have been around a long time and the Church did not always consider me an abomination. There was a time when the Church and I were allies."

"You lie!" she protested, tensing.

I shook my head. "What are you, a *Tertius*?" There were eight levels of *Manus Dei*, starting with *Octavus*, or most junior agent, to *Primus*, the head of the agency. I did not pretend to understand its intricacies, but there was a definite and understandable hierarchy.

The muscles at the corners of Branch's jaws bunched, looking like walnuts under the skin. "*Quartus*," she said finally.

Quartus? I hid my surprise. *Not the lowest level of Vatican agent, but with something like the Book of Ur, you would think they would send a Secundus or least a Tertius.* Filing the tidbit away to chew on later, I continued. "You've been almost terminally underbriefed, young lady. The Book was written on the skin of a fallen angel and it placed in a golden box and given to man to use and safeguard. That gold box was the pattern from which the Ark of the Covenant was created."

"Why would the angel Raphael give the Book to men?" Carter asked. "And what was its purpose?"

"Not to be rude, Carter, but go fuck yourself, you ignorant wretch."

The slim man gaped. Branch gawped. It was small of me, but I was enjoying myself far too much.

He was fast; I'll give him that. Most people would have been caught unawares, but I was not most people and I was prepared. Like a silent predator, he leapt, hands extended, grasping at my throat ready to rend and tear, but my hands were faster and I caught him mid-flight, my fingers bunching in the layers of clothing and I stood, lifting him overhead and his mouth made an 'o' of surprise and fear as I held him there, helpless and before he could react I had him to my chest, my arm around his throat and I squeezed, cutting off his air, the blood supply to his brain as smoothly as any MMA fighter and within seconds he slumped unconscious in my arms.

I placed him gently on the floor and turned to find the muzzle of a 9mm in my face. "Don't you move," growled Branch, eyes hooded in rage. "This may not kill you, but it will slow you down enough for me to burn you to ashes."

Dry laughter found its way past my lips as I sat, warming my hands. Time not to show any fear. "Carter is an untrustworthy ass and you know, although I expected better self-control from what I suspect is a *Tertius* or *Secundus*. Ever since I found you two in my home I knew he outranked you. The cold and fatigue must have sapped his discipline." The flames kissed my fingers and in the back of my mind the leviathan stirred in its sleep. "I wanted to tell you about the Book, but such knowledge is not for *him*. At least not yet, despite his rank within your agency." I shrugged. "That means I can only trust him about as far as I can shot-put this mountain. Maybe I will tell him more when he earns my trust."

The muzzle lowered a fraction. "You set him up," she accused.

Smiling took too much effort and I was so damn tired. "Yeah."

The gun disappeared. "That was just to stuff his ears full of sleep."

I nodded. "Even us abominations have standards."

She said nothing, merely stared at our sad little fire and shivered.

"You seemed puzzled at who I am, or what I appear to be."

"Don't know what you are. You seem to change your nature every time I look."

I shook my head. "But I am different than what you imagined, not at all the baby-eating fiend with flames in his eyes."

Those blue crystal eyes hit me hard. "I will reserve judgment for now. What do you want to tell me about the book?"

I rubbed my hands together. "Your *Primus* should have told you, should have kept you in the loop about the book so you'd know exactly how dangerous it is. It is the most dangerous thing on the planet."

"Tell me."

Breathe, just breathe. "Thousands and thousands of years ago, the Archangel Michael created the Book at God's behest using the skin a certain fallen angel who shall remain nameless, and his own blood for ink. Horrible, eh? But the flesh and blood of angels are the only media that could hold the power that God poured into to the book because of its dual purpose."

"Dual purpose?" she asked.

"It was originally called The Book of Forgiveness. In it were crafted Words and Incantations that would allow the Fallen, the angels who rebelled against God, a second chance. If a Fallen is truly repentant, the book grants forgiveness so they may re-enter Heaven. This is its greatest power. Shortly after the founding of the ancient Sumerian city of Ur, Archangel Raphael gave the book to an order of holy men called Atu Anna Anunnaki, which roughly translates to 'Gatekeeper Unto Heaven'. It was placed in a gold covered wooden box about yea big." I held my hands apart to indicate a container about two feet on a side. "The Atu Anna Anunnaki were separate from the regular Enki and Inanna worshipping Sumerians and persecuted because of their monotheistic view of the heavens. They absolutely believed in a single God and the angels and held the book and the box in sacred trust for thousands of years, through the Great Flood and well past the birth and resurrection of Christ. That is until the year 1099 AD."

"The First Crusade," said Branch, rapt.

"You know your history."

She nodded. "It's a requirement for agents to learn Church history."

Go figure. "July 1099, the Franks invaded Jerusalem with the intent on liberating the city from the Jews and Muslims. They wound up creating what were called the Crusader States, independent kingdoms run by French speaking Christians: The County of Edessa, the Principality of Antioch, the County of Tripoli and, of course, the Kingdom of Jerusalem. Another side effect of the invasion was the death of the Atu Anna Anunnaki as a whole at the hands of the Sicarri, an ancient order of assassins dedicated to the overthrow of the Church." There was more to the Sicarri than that. Founded as guerilla warriors against the Romans in ancient Judea, their leader, Judas Iscariot, had gone on to become the most infamous man in history. At the mention of the Sicarri, Branch's face tightened, becoming a mask of uncompromising granite.

"The assassins were part of the invasion, sent there by their master to undermine the Crusade, or to help organize a Muslim uprising should their primary mission fail. Instead, they found the Atu Anna Anunnaki and the book and the box before the Franks could. They wiped that holy order from the face of the earth once they realized the book's true worth. Four of their best warriors were assigned to take the book to Switzerland, to their headquarters near Geneva. The four sailed to Italy and began their overland trek. They had just crossed the Alps when they were ambushed by bandits and there the book was lost to history for several hundred years."

Branch let out an explosive breath. "What do you mean 'lost to history'? And why would God give the book to Man in the first place?"

"If you do not mind, I work better without interruptions."

She had the grace to look a little embarrassed. "Sorry."

"Quite alright. I will chalk it up to an overabundance of enthusiasm. Now, as to your questions...Lucifer led the rebellion against Heaven because God placed His grace upon Man, something the rebels felt was undeserved, so I think it was with a sense of irony that God gave Man the power to forgive the Fallen. To any angel or Fallen, it is merely a collection of bound pages, unreadable, unknowable, but in the hands of a human being, it is the gateway to Heaven. Any of the Fallen who are truly repentant could petition the holder of the book for forgiveness, and if the holder of the book so desired, upon reading certain Words, the angel could once again rejoin Heaven's ranks.

"You see, the human who holds the book invokes the Summoning, which brings the repentant Fallen to the holder. If the holder of the book feels that the angel is worthy, then he invokes the Forgiveness, and if God wills it, the angel may re-enter heaven. Perhaps that's what Christ meant when he said 'the meek shall inherit the earth'.

I rubbed my face, exhausted and afraid. Talking about the book have me the itchies and I'd revealed more in the last minutes than I had...ever, but I needed Branch on my side. I needed her to understand about the book because there were dark things coming and for the first time in a long time, I felt mortal.

"The book is split into three parts: The History, The Grimoire and the Seven. The Grimoire is just that, a spell book containing fractions of the Word of Creation that God used when forming the universe. With those Words, a person can do great and terrible things such as forgive the Fallen.

There are other Words, such as Binding, and Summoning, and so forth and so on. The History is just that, a history of the Book of Ur, pages that are being written even as we speak because the book *writes itself.*

"As for the Seven—"

A soft moan interrupted my narrative. Carter was coming round and I set myself for action in case he woke up...unhappy.

"What the fuck?" he grumbled, eyes glazed as he came to.

"Wakey, wakey," I said, feigning unconcern. There was every confidence that I could take him out, but you do not live to be several centuries old by taking unnecessary risks.

"You choked me!" he accused, levering himself upright.

"You attacked me."

As he rubbed his neck, I caught Branch hiding a smile. A real honest-to-goodness smile! I almost fainted with surprise because I could have sworn she had those facial muscles removed at birth.

"Why did you do that?" The slim man sat up, keeping his hands well clear of the pistol tucked underneath his armpit.

"Because you're a liar and an opportunist and I needed to talk to Branch and I knew you would not give us any privacy, so I made my own."

We stared at each other for seconds before he nodded carefully and reached for the fire, rubbing his hands. He finally knew down to his bones how much I did not trust him and I wanted it that way because he might think twice before stabbing me in the back.

Outside the wind howled.

"What's that?" Branch's eyes were bright and puzzled.

"Just the wind," replied Carter. "Wait. No, that's a helicopter."

The Vatican agent jumped to her feet. "What are you waiting for? Let's go!"

I shook my head. "Whoever is flying that helo will not see us at night." My finger stabbed at the fire. "We do not know who that is, it could be part of the group that killed Stavros's family. Besides, there are still a couple of fires outside that could catch attention." Earlier I had piled a lot of seat stuffing on a fuel fire outside and had kept feeding the blaze during my intermittent scrounging efforts. It was a long shot, hoping that someone would see the fire, but *not* doing anything was a guarantee of failure. "Let us wait until daylight before heading outside."

Carter lifted his head, eyes narrowing. After a moment I caught wind of what he had noticed. The helo was circling back, the rotor wash coming closer and closer, then moving away before moving closer again.

"All we have to do is stay put now," said Carter, a smile flashing through his beard. "We've been spotted. Now all they have to do is alert the authorities."

Nodding, I added more wood to our fire and sat back, crossing my arms and letting the yellow light wash over me. We had survived the unsurvivable and now it looked like we might be rescued. Branch seemed so happy that she actually tossed me a grim little smile, a look that spoke volumes for the taciturn woman.

Carter interrupted us before I could tell her of the Seven, but the story could wait a bit until we reached civilization and a little more privacy. My only hope was that I would not have to put a bullet in the Carter's head, but I had a niggling suspicion that I would not be offered a choice. Sooner or later, he would figure a way around the oath he took and then it would come down to him or me and I knew which outcome I favored.

Minutes later an eerie howl pierced the night, cutting through the freezing wind like a knife. The sound sliced through my eardrums like an icicle, raising goosebumps across my skin in a wave. The wolf sounded like a lost, damned thing tossing its cry into the sky in hopes of an answer. Loneliness and fear, loss and betrayal, all contained in a single howl.

And people think that animals do not *feel*.

Within seconds that haunting howl was joined by another and another and another until the little valley rang with the demented cries of what sounded like hundreds of wolves.

"Damn, that's creepy," muttered Carter, fingering his pistol. "I didn't know there were wolves in this area."

"Extinct for a while, but they have been slowly repopulating the area," I replied, licking my lips. Peering out into the night, I could not see a damn thing, the snow still fell thick and fast. "There should not be this many."

Carter grunted. "I don't think they give a shit."

Branch stepped forward and joined me at the tear in the fuselage. "You know, I think he's right...they don't give a shit."

Hearing her swear scared me more than the wolves and before I could say anything a noise slithered out of the storm, a guttural, feral cry that made the howling of the wolves' sound like a baby's giggle.

It started low, an almost subsonic vibration that was felt more than heard, a subtle pressure against the skin that vibrated flesh all the way to bone, setting blood a-dancing in the veins. The noise grew from there, rising in volume and pitch, blasting though the wind with tsunami like force until I could feel the cry ripple my hair. It was a yowl that was all anger and hate, rage and lust.

Unfortunately, I knew exactly what yelled out there in the night, thirsting for our blood, aching to rend us limb from limb. And being ripped apart was something I was sure I couldn't regenerate.

Hustling back inside, I turned to my companions. "Silver. Give me silver, anything you have. Now!"

"What the fuck is that?" Carter's eyes were wild while Branch was more pale than usual. "I've never heard anything like *that*."

"Silver, dammit! Get me silver." It wouldn't be long. The thing coming for us was beyond my current state, stronger and faster. At least I had my answer to the question of the Cursed mentioned in the prophecy, faint comfort that it was.

Carter tried to pull off a snarl, but was too scared to be successful. "What do I look like, a pawn shop? I don't have any silver."

A five-inch-long cross was slapped into my hand, Branch's strong, slender fingers holding tight to my own with the holy symbol trapped between. "Here you go," she said, eyes a little wild. "What's out there? Why do you need silver?"

My own eyes were just as wide. "Get your guns ready because there is going to be a storm of wolves coming for you while I fight their leader."

"Their leader?"

I nodded. "Yeah. A wolfman."

CHAPTER FOURTEEN

Deadwood, Nov. 1877

Deadwood. What a fucking shithole.

I rode into town on old Tom, the only horse I had ever known who could put up with me. The first thing I noticed as Tom's hooves churned mud was the smell of horseshit, piss and vomit. It was enough to make God turn away and puke.

We drew the eye, old Tom and I, as we plodded down the muddy main street, the locals giving us a wide berth, both of us being so big and all. The place was busy as hell; the gold rush there in full swing and the diversity and bustle of the population was an assault on my senses.

Men and women clad in fine Sunday best rubbed elbows with those dressed more in mud than cloth. Rough cut miners, if I was any judge. Impromptu stalls selling wares littered the street, reminding me of Greece all those years ago, but whereas the good people of Missolonghi tried for cleanliness, it seemed the citizens of Deadwood reveled in filth and their makeshift stalls were as covered in crap as the people. There were half-frozen puddles of water everywhere as the unusually mild Dakota winter tried to grab hold of the town. Personally, I think it was the piss that kept the ground from freezing solid.

Like I said...what a fucking shithole.

I steered Tom to what looked like a hardware shop, a wide spot on the filthy road, and dismounted, sending a spray of muddy water everywhere. Tom stood placidly, relieved that I removed my bulk from his strong back. At twenty hands, he was probably the biggest horse in the whole territory.

"You are a mess," said a familiar voice.

My smile stretched the scars on my face. "Seth." I looked up to see a medium tall man dressed all clean and dapper-like in a black suit, sporting a handlebar mustache and carrying a cavalry Colt slung low on his hip. He stood on a wooden sidewalk a little above the mud of the main street, a big grin on his handsome face. Eyes as gray as winter stared at me from beneath a wide-brimmed black hat.

"You look like you rode through Hell and back," he observed with a smile. "I have never seen you so dirty."

"That is five hundred miles of road grime," I replied, shedding my canvas coat revealing a worn brown shirt and a pair of trousers more patches than whole cloth, taking a step onto the sidewalk. Seth and I exchanged a hard hug and from the lean strength I felt in his arms, he was as healthy as ever. "You look good, boy."

"And you look like a bad road, Uncle."

At the familiarity, I smiled even wider. Last time I saw Seth he was sheriff of Lewis and Clark County in the Montana territory. He'd gone from a bad situation at home where violence wore the face of his father, to a mild speaking man of justice. I was proud to know the man and to be the recipient of his affection.

"Long, hard roads, long hard times. Good thing I have a fine horse." I patted Tom between the ears. "I need to find the sheriff. Care to point me in the right direction?"

Thin lips under a bushy mustache parted, revealing white, but slightly crooked, teeth. Moving his coat and suit jacket aside, Seth revealed a shiny star pinned to his vest.

"You are the sheriff?" I asked, shocked. "Thought you swore off the law after Montana?"

"Didn't take. This town needed a lawman after Hickok got himself shot dead by that nitwit Jack McCall."

"Heard about that, shooting a man in the back. Bad business. Heard he was found innocent for a silly reason."

Seth shook his head. "No worries there, Uncle. He got himself in a tangle in Wyoming and I hear they're fit to retry him for the murder, saying double jeopardy doesn't apply because he wasn't tried the first time under a legally constituted court system. Mark my words, he'll get his."

At the mention of comeuppance, I sighed and pulled a folded sheet from my coat pocket. Careful not to tear the paper, I spread it for Seth to see...a wanted poster with a crude likeness underneath a bold headline. The reward was posted at five-hundred dollars.

"See this man before, Seth? Goes by the name of Two-Shot Higgs," I said.

He took the paper and examined it closely. "Can't say that I have. Just a second." Turning his head to the hardware store behind him, he bellowed. "Sol!"

Moments later a slightly smaller man with black, slicked back hair and bushy mustache just like Seth's exited the store, apron around his waist and a soiled rag in hand. Unlike Seth, his face held a note of worry that I reckoned was a permanent fixture.

"What the livin' daylights are you hollering ab—" His tirade cut short as he caught sight of me. "I'll be dipped in shit," he whispered in awe, stretching a hand my way. "You must be the legendary Uncle I've been hearing so much about, colored glasses and all. An honor, a real honor."

I stared at the hand a moment before giving it a good shake. Even though he looked skinny as a malnourished mule, his grip had starch. "All about me, eh?"

"Not all," Seth said dryly.

Good, I thought. "I cannot say the same thing, Mr...."

"Star. Solomon Star," the smaller man replied. "Seth's business partner."

I raised an eyebrow.

"Sol is good with numbers," explained Seth, handing Sol the wanted poster. "You ever see this fella, Sol? Goes by the name Two-Shot or somesuch."

The other man examined the poster carefully, squinting. Finally, he nodded. "Yeah, I think this guy frequents the Gem."

I blinked. *Close...finally.* It had been long months chasing rumors and trying to separate fact from fiction. A lot of money had been spent, a lot of arms twisted to the breaking point and now there might actually be a result.

My hands clenched into fists and I felt a sudden sweat on my upper lip despite the chill November air. Both Seth and Sol took a couple steps back.

"What did he do?' Seth inquired. He knew me, he knew I would not get this worked up about any old villain.

Eyes scanning the street to finally alight on a building a hundred feet away, the words THE GEM VARIETY THEATER painted in garish colors over the double doors. The building took up half a block and was two stories of brick and mortar with a third story (what I supposed were offices) over one third of its length. Several women dressed in low cut bright clothes stood on the second-floor balcony waving at passerby. It was not hard to figure out what kind of place it was.

I pointed with a trembling hand. "There?"

"What did he do?" Iron had crept into Seth's voice, part and parcel of his lawman persona.

His voice may have been cold, but his eyes were warm and troubled as I faced him once again. "He killed one of mine."

Seth blew a great sigh out from beneath that huge mustache of his and removed his hat, staring at a cloudy sky pregnant with snow or rain. "Then you won't have any trouble with me," he said quietly and closed his eyes. "But stay away from the Gem's owner, Al Swearengen. He's meaner than a rabid dog and liable to slit your throat as to look at you."

I nodded, not really listening; my boots were already making a beeline to the theater, which dominated the corner of Wall and Main like a carbuncle on the butt of the town. The whores saw me coming and started to wave and pitch their wares, but once they caught sight of my face, they stopped and stepped back, perhaps afraid that my horrific scars were catching.

The thing that hit me first was the noise...an almost physical blow to my ears. Drunks singing and yelling, card players hollering and whores screeching like rabid cats. The second was the smell: the sharp tang of old booze, bad booze, harsh cigars that reeked more of mildew than tobacco, stale farts, rancid lamp oil and the dank musk unwashed bodies. A *lot* of unwashed bodies. The place smelled like a sweaty, smoking, fat man took a shit on the floor and rolled around in it. My nose wanted to jump from my face and head toward the edge of town, but I took hold of my disgust and rammed it down into a deep dark place and shut the lid. I had work to do.

As I walked, I eyed the crowd. Rough trade...miners and hired guns, a few not so rough such as well-dressed dandies coming to get their ashes hauled by women that had not been Frenchified yet. The prostitutes looked meaner and leaner than the miners, all fake smiles and dead, empty eyes and scars here and there where someone entertained themselves with a blade.

No Two-Shot Higgs, though.

"What's yer poison?" yelled the bartender as I bellied up. He was a fat man with large forearms and a beard that looked part cactus.

I bellowed back. "Whiskey. Hey, you seen a fella called Two-Shot?"

"He ain't here," came the reply as he poured me a small glass of amber fluid. "Haven't seen him in a couple of days, not since his horse threw a shoe at Del Talvern's camp." He took my coin and sauntered off.

The whiskey tasted like it was made in a chamber pot that morning and watered down with piss and vinegar. Still, it was wet and I was thirsty.

"Want your cock sucked, handsome?"

Eyes watering from the shitty whiskey, I looked for the source of the voice and saw a slender woman at my elbow, cheeks red with rouge with a smile as fake as a three-dollar bill. "I do it better than anyone here. Big boy like you needs attention, I'll wager."

A shake of my head was my only answer.

The whore became insistent. "C'mon, mister, I'll take really good care of you. That is, unless, you're one of the fellas that likes the boys."

My eyes seemed to close of their own accord as I sighed. *It is always something.*

"Hey mister," continued the talkative prostitute. "What the fuck happened to your face? Them's the ugliest scars I ever seen, all purple and twisty."

"Cut myself shaving." I signaled the bartender for another. "You know a guy named Two-Shot?" A stab in the dark, but I learned long ago to leave no stone unturned.

"Higgs? Yeah, he ain't been around for a while. Mister, you want me to suck you off or not?"

"Not."

The girl disappeared faster than I would have imagined, as if she'd never been.

"Any idea where Two-Shot could be?" I asked the bartender as he poured me another drink. A fat ten-dollar gold piece appeared on the counter, glinting in the wan light. Squinting, he shook his head, a small frown appearing through the mange of his beard and he scooted off as if I lit a fire under his ass.

More piss whiskey passed my lips and I knew attention had been brought. It was only a matter of time before something happened. As the warmth of the whiskey radiated outward from my belly, I wished for the millionth time that I could get drunk. Not tipsy, not slightly off, but falling down, piss-in-your-pants, vomit explosively, out-of-your-damn mind drunk. There had to be a reason why people did it and I wanted to find it because maybe it made things a little more bearable. Maybe a nice haze of booze colored the world something else besides shit nasty brown and gray and kept madness at bay for just a little while. Time enough to adapt to the quickly changing world and the fucking assholes that seemed to crawl out of the woodwork like greasy termites intent on ruining it for the rest of us.

"You're asking a lot of questions around here. You a lawman?" asked a harsh, grating voice, deep and powerful with a natural air of command and it quickly snapped me out of my reverie. I had a very good idea to whom that voice belonged.

"No, not a lawman," I replied, not bothering to look at the speaker. "Just someone who needs to talk to a certain fella, that is all." Another glass of whiskey had appeared and I downed it quick before the taste could make me vomit.

"You know what we do 'round these parts when a fucking cocksucker starts asking questions?"

I couldn't help myself. "Serve them this pisswater whiskey?"

Rough, sandpapery laughter scraped against my ears. At least the speaker had a sense of humor.

"Finish up your drinking, mister, then git on out." Despite the noisome crowd, I heard heels tapping away.

"Can you tell me where to find Two-Shot." I waited a heartbeat. "Please."

The steps halted and so did the noise. From the corner of my eyes I saw the bartender's hands disappear beneath the counter and I knew they would be caressing a scattergun.

"Mister, unless you plan on spending money on cunny or drinks, git the fuck out of my sight."

A small smile crept onto my face like an insect. Turning, I caught sight of the speaker, a thirty something year old man with hair as black as a demon's soul and slightly foxy features. Mid-tall, he had broad shoulders and large forearms, a man used to his strength and the will to use it well. His mustache was pencil thin and black as his hair while his skin had the slightly windburnt quality you would find on a sailor. This was a man used to getting his way and not giving a shit about what people thought of him.

I took in the scars on his knuckles and the casual cruelty of his face. A genuine hard ass, if I was not mistaken.

Just the man I need to see.

Slowly, I held my hands out to the side so the bartender would not get all nervy like and try to separate my head from shoulders with that cannon of his. One step, slow and easy, then two, moving closer and closer to the infamous Al Swearengen, approaching him like he was a half-mad mutt.

"What's your fucking problem, besides your face?" he growled, going for maximum intimidation.

My fingers brushed the ever-present spectacles perched on my face and pulled them off, exposing my eyes.

"Sweet fucking Jesus," he moaned, taking a step back. He stumbled slightly, not used to the action.

"Heard of him, but never met the man," I said with a terrible smile.

My hands stayed well away from my Colt, but the bartender still brought the scattergun up from behind the bar, taking aim. I was perpendicular to the him, watching out of the corner of my eye and it was about fifty-fifty I would be able to turn and draw before he cut me down with enough buckshot to fell a moose.

Click.

From my peripheral vision I saw a revolver appear. A big Colt, just like mine. "Put it down," said a deep voice.

Seth.

"Sheriff Bullock," the bartender said in a trembling voice. "That man is fixing to kill Al."

A dry chuckle greeted that statement. "If he was, Charlie, Al would be dead already, leaking out onto the floor. Now put the shotgun away."

With a quick nod, the bartender did just that and I went to keeping my yellow gaze on Al. "Yeah, Jesus was big on forgiveness and all that. A real sweetheart." Another step forward for me, another back for Al. "But me, I am cut from a different kind of cloth altogether."

"What are you?" A tinny note crept into Al's voice.

I leaned forward and down until I was nose to nose with the Gem owner, my eyes an amber glow from gates of Hell. "Reckoning. I am a reckoning that is owed to Two-Shot and you are going tell me where I might find him." He was going to tell me. Oh yes, he *was.*

Swearengen fell backward into a chair and people scattered, yelling, catching a glimpse of my horrid eyes and the Gem cleared out quicker than a house a-fire. I caught a whiff of something both musty and acrid and looked to see a growing stain on Al's crotch.

Moaning, he pointed toward the door. "Down by the Chinee, where they pitch camp, that's where the blacksmith has his shop and that's where you'll find your sonfawhore Two-Shot. He's gotta pick up a new shoe for his horse. Hell, he mighta picked it up already."

I wrinkled my nose and practically fled the Gem, my dun canvas coat swirling about my ankles and Colt in hand. Dead or alive, Two-Shot was coming with me.

Finding the camp at the edge of town where the Chinese hung their hats did not prove difficult, all I had to do follow the smell of roasting pork and the billowing clouds of steam. Men and women in black clothes strolled purposefully in a camp that looked unusually clean and tidy. By that time my spectacles were firmly affixed to the bridge of my nose, but my height and terrible scars sent the immigrants fleeing.

The blacksmith was only slightly less hard to find considering the 350-pound anvil under an awning in front of the shop, not to mention the blacksmith himself. A giant of man, taller than myself, who worked a glowing red strip of metal with a hammer the size of a country ham. He was clean-shaven with a round, kindly face, bulging biceps and huge hands.

"Excuse me, sir." I kept my voice polite. It was a rare day I met a bigger man and a little courtesy went a long way.

He glanced my way, a brief flicker of his eyes, and kept pounding away. "What kin I do for you, Stranger?" he asked between beats of that massive hammer.

"Looking for Two-Shot. You seen him?"

"And why would I tell you?"

I placed a $10 gold coin on the step of the anvil right above the horn. "Because of this and because he is wanted for murder in New York City."

The blacksmith said nothing for minutes, just kept pounding and shaping that strip of iron until he was ready whereby he carefully dunked it in a pail of water. I watched as steam hissed up into his face. "That true, Stranger?" He held the tongs up, the strip of iron in the jaws and examined it closely.

"Yes. Yes it is." I held up the creased and stained wanted poster.

He picked up the gold coin and tossed it to me. "Then I don't want no truck with the man. He'll be by directly for a horseshoe, I expect. You can wait for him or come back, all the same to me."

I placed the coin back on the anvil. "For your time, sir."

A small smile appeared on that round face and he tucked the coin into the pocket of his worn leather apron. "Thankee kindly...oh, shit..."

My two least favorite words, especially since I heard the bootsteps from behind accompanied by a sneering voice. "I heard you been looking for me."

Fucking Al Swearengen. Must have sent one of his men looking for Two-Shot while I dallied with the blacksmith. A flood of curses quietly left my mouth as I leaned against the anvil, one hand resting on the face over a square opening called the Hardy hole.

"Been running for six months, David Higgs," I said tiredly, not bothering to turn around. It was a sure bet he had a pistol leveled at the back of my head.

"Thought I lost you in Kentucky," he said angrily. "Never knew a bounty hunter could be so persistent for something like five-hundred dollars."

My fingers tightened on the anvil. "It is not the money, it is the man you shot in the back, James Riggins. He meant something to me, so do the three children and the widow you left grieving over the body." I could feel my pulse in my throat and there was a peculiar roaring in my ears.

"Well, I'm tired of running, mister whatever-your-name-is, so I reckon it's gotta end now." *Click,* the sound of a hammer drawing into firing position.

The smile on my face had nothing to do with good humor, not at all. "You know, David Higgs, you are right."

Three-hundred fifty pounds of cold iron. I calculated my odds in a fraction of a second, faster than Two-Shot finger could squeeze the trigger, faster than the beat of a hummingbirds wing. It was possible, I reasoned, if just barely.

Time became taffy as my body swung around, the anvil a weight at the end of a pendulum, arcing toward the gunman who was pulling the trigger to an enormous Smith and Wesson Schofield revolver. The same gun that had belonged to my dear James, stolen from his cooling corpse and that fueled me, gave me the rage to complete the swing as Two-Shot fired, the bullet striking the anvil and breaking into flinders and I let the weight go as something gave inside my arm and torso, snapping like high-tension wire, but the anvil was loose and flying toward the target. The anvil horn caught

Two-Shot on the forehead, crushing inward, tearing through bone and brain as its weight bore down on the murderer, flinging him back half out of his boots, body airborne for a split second.

The world resumed its normal pace as Two-Shot hit ground, the anvil crushing his head flat into the mud, sending a bloody and brainy shower across the street.

Silence, as if the world were encased in thick layers of cotton that absorbed all sound. I stood panting over the corpse, a sense of a job well done coursing through me along with the pain in my arm and torso and I noticed the Chinese staring, mouths agape, pedestrians (who must have scattered at the sight of Two-Shot leveling his gun) with wide eyes full of fear and wonder and Al Swearengen, his own weapon, a revolver that had seen better times, forgotten his hand.

"Jesus God," he swore as sound came rushing back hard enough to hurt my ears. "Oh Jesusjesusjesus."

"What did you just do, Stranger?" asked the blacksmith in a voice choked with awe. "What did you just do?"

"Mr. Swearengen," I said, ignoring the blacksmith. Once again, I came nose to nose with the brothel owner and I removed my spectacles, giving him a good glare. "Figured you could shoot me in the back when distracted?"

Mouth slack, he nodded.

"That is not nice, but, then again, I reckon you are not such a nice man, are you?"

His voice emerged a tinny rasp. "You better kill me now because I'm gonna kill you, mister, if'n I see you again. I'm gonna put a bullet in your brain."

I took his pistol from nerveless fingers and replaced my spectacles. "Then I best take this, then." With that, I walked back to Tom who watched me placidly from the hitching post, the crowd parting before me. Seth stood in front of the store; eyes all squinted shut as if he'd been watching the sun.

"Never a dull moment, eh Uncle?" he asked tersely.

"Prayed for a lot of dull moments, Seth," I said, stroking Tom's gray neck. He whickered appreciatively. "Unfortunately, my life seems to attract excitement. At least everything went quicker than I expected." An itch began in my torso and arm as the healing took over torn muscles and ligaments. As the pain drained, I sighed with relief.

Seth gestured to Tom. "That's one of them French horses, the Percherons, isn't it?"

I nodded, stepping up to the sidewalk. Wordlessly, I gave Seth a hug, which he returned mightily. "I must go, boy. Already attracted too much attention."

"Should be easy enough. Was it just about vengeance, Uncle, killing Two-Shot?" he asked from the comfort of my shoulder, reminding me of the sixteen-year-old boy he used to be, covered in the bruises of his father's anger and hate. A lump formed in my throat at the thought of outliving the good man he'd become.

"I was not planning on killing him," I husked. "But I'm not shedding any tears over the man. Sorry about the mess, though."

"It'll be taken care of. What about the reward money?"

"Do not care in the slightest." I didn't follow Two-Shot all over creation for a reward and accepting money for something eagerly done felt...wrong.

I left town amid an ocean of stares and muttering, Tom's big hooves squelching through the stinking mud.

Deadwood. What a fucking shithole.

CHAPTER FIFTEEN

My lips felt dust dry as I stared out into the snow-screened dark, eyes piercing dimly the harsh storm. Four inches of silver cross stuck through my fingers, a poor man's dagger. Practically useless, but it was all I had.

"Please tell me you're not serious!" Carter shouted into the wind, squinting against the cold.

"Oh, I am plenty serious," I replied.

"You mean like 'even a man who is pure in heart and says his prayers by night, may become a wolf when the wolfbane blooms and the autumn moon is bright'?"

I nodded. "Good to see you know the classics."

"That's not fucking possible." A note of hysteria crept into his voice.

My laughter was lost in the wind. "You are standing in the middle of the Adirondacks with the man who was the inspiration for *Frankenstein* after surviving a plane crash relatively unscathed. All this while on a mission to retrieve the most dangerous magical artifact the world has never heard of and you think the fucking *wolfman* is impossible?" It was rich, so rich that mirth threatened to unhinge my mind right then and there.

Got to hand it to Carter, though, he took it like a man and joined me in a moment of rare camaraderie. "Okay, I get you, big man, but you and I are going to talk about that little choke hold of yours. My throat still hurts."

"Get inside the plane," I hollered. "And guard that precious throat of yours so it does not get torn out."

Branch grabbed hold of the man and practically dragged him inside where at least they would have protection against what was coming. I did not know the number of rounds they carried for their weapons, but every shot would have to count and I threw a glance over my shoulder to see the *Manus Dei* standing in the ragged gash, pistols in one hand and knives in the other. If death came for them, at least they had no plans to sell their life cheap. The blades looked to be about six inches long with handles of antler and brass butt-caps, the type of knife the Finns liked to use called *puukko*, sturdy, good steel and sharp as hell.

I turned back to see a flash of ivory, a blur really, arrowing toward my throat and my own pistol barked, a dagger of flame lighting the night and a wolf, a big bastard with pale fur almost indistinguishable from snow fell at my feet in a spray of blood and shattered teeth.

A pulse of fear mixed with anger flared through my body and I raised my arms in defiance. "Is that all you got, you bloody great bastard?" I screamed, the sound torn from my mouth and scattered by the ferocious wind.

Through the veil of snow, I saw another shape lope toward me, a great beast of a wolf, possibly the alpha of the pack. Its glaring yellow eyes reminded me of my own and I leaned forward, holstering the 9mm beneath my layers of clothing in one fluid motion, the cold bite of the metal spurring me forward as I charged the beast.

This I could do, fight a fair fight, challenge that which would rend and tear with what tools God gave me and I felt my smile stretch wide, twisting my scars and my muscles felt good, *I* felt good and the cold was nothing, only we two possessed meaning, wolf and monster, the only two things in existence and all was right in the universe.

We collided in an eruption of fur and flannel, ripping and hammering. The great beast had fangs three inches long that flashed toward my throat, but I shoved a well-padded arm in the way and it bit down *hard*. Twin snaps sounded through the night as both bones of my forearm broke explosively under the pressure of steel-like jaws and the pain was shard of icy hot agony ripping through my nerves, searing tissue and I howled like a maddened, damned thing myself, screaming into the jaws of the wolf.

It tore at my arm in an effort to rip it from my body as its hind legs curled forward and raked at my thighs, half-inch claws ripping through fabric and scoring flesh and my other hand, the hand with the silver cross, came down hard on its skull, the full force of my terrible strength focused on one singular point.

My fist with its great knobby knuckles punched the wolf from my savaged arm, feeling bone give like wet cardboard, and hurled it to the ice where it bounced and lay, hind legs twitching spastically and I grabbed the beast by its greasy long fur, ignoring the itchy pain throb of my arm and I hoisted it high above my head, screaming my defiance.

Dark loping shapes flowed around, dozens of wolves with flashing eyes of green, gold and brown passed by without looking at my grisly burden or me. Instead, they headed toward the bright, flickering point of light behind, two people encased in a shell of steel. Popcorn noises came from the fuselage and wolves dropped or howled in pain and I threw my trophy to the ice, rubbing my forearm as flesh and bone knitted.

A blast of noise like the bone trumpets of Hell washed over my ears and I looked out, eyes piercing the darkness and I *saw*.

Green eyes. Baleful, glowing and full of malice, brimming with all manner of evil, bouncing up and down as the creature that owned them bounded toward me in great, graceful strides. Long arms ending in three-inch talons tore furrows in the ice, propelling the wolfman, its oddly jointed legs bunching and flexing with clockwork precision, the muscles beneath its short, dense fur writhing in effort to move its great mass. Standing, it would be taller than me, well over seven feet, in fact, but on all fours, arms as long as its powerful legs, it came to my navel and I knew, with an odd sort of clarity, that it was stronger than me and faster by far.

Its features were vaguely human, with short hair protecting a slightly protruding muzzle filled chock full of gleaming razor teeth. A shaggy mop of black hair rested on its skull, a tribute to what humanity remained and filled with styling gel, a wolfman with a pompadour. It wore pants that ended at the top of its calves and I was reminded of the Incredible Hulk's purple pants, the only part of his outfit to ever survive his transformation from Bruce Banner and I nearly laughed.

Thirty meters. Its grace stunned enough to humble the finest gymnast or ballerina.

Twenty meters. So fast, covering thirty feet with each sinuous lope. Terrifying, beautiful, and deadly.

Ten meters. I tensed, readying myself. *Here we go...*

My left arm blurred forward as massive claws reached for my face. The thin spike of silver protruding between my fingers traveled slowly, oh so slowly, toward the wolfman's right eye, a gleaming spike of poisonous death. I felt my mouth stretch wide with the joy of battle, and the cold went away, replaced by a feeling of righteousness.

I missed. Or, more correctly, it easily avoided the punch. Claws flashed and my right arm was gripped in steely bands tipped with daggers that sent me flying as the creature sailed overhead, dragging me with. The world became a black and white blur and I tumbled ass over teakettle across the snow-covered ice and I dimly heard the steady *pop pop pop* of pistol fire before all sound, all sense, was knocked from my body as I landed *hard*. My lungs seized and my heart skipped a couple of beats while I slid, back scored by jagged ice where the plane had torn great rents in the lake and I had a brief moment of happiness for the several layers of clothing draped around my abused body.

Get up, you idiot. But I did not want to...the urge to lie there and let my depleted lungs recover was almost too much to bear, but a niggling survival instinct kicked in before my mind had a chance to evaluate the situation and I moved. Just in time, too, because a great, hairy foot, elongated with inch-long nails, slammed into the space my head had just vacated, sending cracked and broken ice flying.

I made it upright in time to take four claws across the chest, the nails shredding the layers of clothing and drawing parallel lines of blood. The other claw made a play for my face, attempting to add to the scars already there, but I flinched back as they whistled by.

It lunged, teeth flashing and I dodged, going low and rising with an uppercut that had the strength of my entire length behind it and it connected hard to a furry jaw, lifting the wolfman two feet into the air.

I readied myself for its fall onto the ice, but the werewolf turned a fall into a backward somersault before landing on its clawed feet, facing me with a snarl. Normally, a punch like with that serious amount of sauce on it would have ripped the head off of a human, but the werewolf shrugged it off like a mosquito bite.

We stared at each other for a moment, its eyes almost hypnotic in their intensity along with its sinuous, muscular grace. The wolfman continued to catch my eyes, swaying slightly in the frigid wind, upright, yet hunched, it matched my height and was half again as broad in the shoulders.

What's it waiting for? I shook my head slightly, breaking eye contact yet maintaining my hyper awareness. Why did it hesitate its attack? It was becoming unnerving, the slight swaying to and fro of its body.

Wolf...wolf! What do wolves do?

The answer hit so suddenly I almost stumbled.

They distract.

• • •

Ever watch a documentary where a group of wolves surrounds a bear, or a deer, or a moose? One of the wolves will charge the prey, lunging, going for a forelimb, taunting their food so it will be distracted, so it will not notice the wolf coming from behind for the hamstringing bite that will signify the end of the hunt and the beginning of dinner time.

From behind. I lashed out with one large foot...backward. My size eighteen connected hard against bone and the wolf lost that argument sharpish, neck cracking with a loud report and eliciting a pained howl that sent shivers up my spine.

While I was off balance for that brief moment, the wolfman struck in a flurry of teeth and claws, shredding cloth and flesh, sending searing waves of pain throughout my body, but my mind was on one thing and one thing only: getting inside his reach and grapple, putting it within reach of the silver spike in my hand.

Needle sharp teeth punched into my shoulder and the wolfman's jaws locked on tight, crushing muscle and bone, sending blood flying and my right arm went numb while curved nails tore into my back as it pulled me close and the smell of it was *incredible*, a rank mix of animal musk, sweat, and wet dog. Oh well, I wanted to grapple, now I had to survive the event.

Snarling through my blood, the wolfman leapt high in the air and if I did not blanket my sense of wonder I would have been amazed it could jump so high carrying so many pounds of flailing monster.

My stomach tried for an emergency ejection procedure via my throat as we hit the top of the arc. It became a moot point as gravity, deceleration trauma, and severe compression nearly shot the organ out through my nose, the creature's massive body almost crushing me flat as we hit the ice with it on top.

Vertebrae shattered, popped and cracked and I would have screamed, but my teeth were firmly parked in my tongue and blood flooded my throat in sticky waves and it all hurt so much, but the big bastard was *biting* me, savaging my shoulder and neck, trying to rip into my throat and that was not going to happen, no way José, because I was the best chance at retrieving the book, and God my shoulder *hurt so fucking much* and the temptation to just lay back and let the wolfman shred me into little bits was so fucking strong because I was so fucking tired and why, why, fucking *why*?

I could hear the creature swallow chunks of my flesh, hear his tongue lap at my blood and it was sick, foul and terrible and I had had enough. A horrid big creature of legend it was, but I was the big boy on the block and time to let the bastard know that fact. Anger, pure, white and hot surged through me and my left arm, the one with the silver spike, flailed at the beast and where the argent metal met hairy flesh, the flesh parted like butter, greasy black smoke whipping away in the wind and that lent me strength I did not know I possessed, so I flailed with the spike and the beast bellowed. Like a ships klaxon, resounding, penetrating, the howl of Satan in pain and that just spurred me on and I stabbed the thing in the neck, the shoulder, the side, the skull, everywhere I could reach and it was my turn to hold onto it, to keep it close despite the rank smell, the stewing and rotten vegetable reek of it, and I kept at it until the greasy smoke was all around, a heavy cloud the wind couldn't penetrate and it was in my eyes, my nose, choking me...

Cold began to numb my back as my spine writhed with healing power and dark forms, large, hairy forms rushed about past where I lay under my unmoving burden. Flesh knit, bones realigned slowly, painfully and the pack flowed past into the lonely embrace of the dark and I caught my breath in a great *whoosh!* as my lungs began to function again.

The weight on my chest moaned, a human sound full of pain and regret, startling me, but in my current state of healing, all I could do was lie there and stare.

A man...a very familiar one, one that I had shared a drink with in Greece. "Dude," I grunted. "You are way too heavy."

The man lifted his head and startling green eyes met mine. Bloody drool spilled from his lips as his emerald eyes bored into mine.

"*Mon ami*, you are a tough man to kill." He said with his thick French accent. "I have underestimated you. I am sorry I never introduced myself, I am Mr. Talbot." More blood drooled from his mouth as he smiled, revealing red-stained, even teeth. Ragged, jagged, burned-looking rents covered his neck, shoulder and back, each deep hole smoking gently as if he smoldered from the inside.

From all around came the baying of wolves and the dozens of animals that ran past before bounded away, their numbers greatly reduced. Whatever magic the wolfman used to bind them was gone.

"Mr. Talbot," I said as sudden realization cut through the pain in my everywhere. "The cursed character from *The Wolfman*."

"I am so sorry, *mon ami*." A wet cough shook the man. "I didn't know it was *you*. Had I known I would never accepted this job. You are the best of us, the suffering immortal and know that I hold you in the highest regard."

A wolfman fanboy. Swell. "Who is your employer, the one offering a hundred mil?"

Through the haze of pain glazing his eyes like cataracts, he nodded. "*Oui*, why not. It is not like they can kill me now. It is Jacob's Rule."

Jacob's Rule. Of all the nefarious organizations that litter the world like discarded candy wrappers it happened to be those morons. Named for Jacob Carnegar who believed that if you could grab it, then was yours. Survival of the fittest, the strongest and damn everyone else for losers. Sort of like the Mafia if it was run by corporate businessmen mixed with white supremacists. "They never would have paid you."

A bloody smile answered me and I understood the meaning. When, not if, those pinheads in Jacob's Rule betrayed him it would have resulted in their rather messy demise. "I know that, *mon ami,* now." Talbot coughed up blood through his gargoyle smile and I held him until the spasm passed. "You are a legend, you know, the who walks forever. A man who loves deeply, who became the protector of the Shelley lineage."

"How did—?"

"Everyone knows, *mon ami.* Everyone who counts, that is. You are a hero to those of the cursed and the lost."

The cursed. The Cursed. Part of the Monica's prophecy clicked into place again but it offered no comfort. In another life this man, Talbot, and I could have been friends. Now that future died, shriveled like his remaining breaths.

"Jacob's Rule thought *I* stole the book?"

"Yes."

"Did they say why?"

A wet caught splattered blooded into my eyes and I blinked rapidly to clear them. "Only that they had information that a fixer, well known in certain circles, named Franklin Vickers was involved somehow in the theft. The file they had on you was thin, but enough for me locate you and attempt to retrieve the book When I told my employer you did not have the book, that you searched for it as well, they asked me to eliminate you lest you succeed." He grimaced. "Oh, what they didn't know was that I had no intention of giving them the book, that it would be like giving a nuclear weapon to a toddler. You see, even though I took some of their money the book is a prize that belongs in a deep, dark hole in the bottom of the ocean so the rest of the world can be safe."

Amen, brother. "So, the pilots..."

"Jacob's Rule fanatics. They believe that their families will be provided for."

My snort of disgust carried blood back to Talbot, who grinned. His employer would pinch a penny until Lincoln screamed before providing for those who were gullible enough to spend their lives so cheaply.

"*Mon ami*, may I ask that you consign my body to the depths?"

I looked into Talbot's verdant gaze as my bones finally mended enough for me to wriggle out from beneath and I nodded.

"Ah, thank..." His next words were a rattle of dice in the bottom of a plastic cup and he lay still, his last breath frosting the air.

Damnit. My flesh felt new, but the same old grief welled up in my breast. I held no animosity toward Talbot, not really. He would have either given the book back to the Vatican (not likely) or found a remote, virtually inaccessible place to bury it (much more likely). Either way, he was a fellow monster and that gave him a special place in my heart.

Knees cracking, I stood and stared around. The fire still burned in the fuselage and I could see two outlines in the rent. Good to know Carter and Branch survived the wolves.

I raised a foot and stamped. Hard. Then again and again, each fall sending a deep thrum across the ice. Again and again until the ice cracked and the bones of my foot shattered, so then I used the other foot and damned the pain, it kept me going, kept me sane and I stamped until my foot burst through nine inches of ice and sent cold water all the way to my knee. Seconds of windmilling my arms kept me from falling in and I dragged Talbot to the hole and sent him in headfirst. He sank without a bubble and I limped away, a skim of ice already forming on the water.

"Good to see you won," said Carter as I walked wearily up to the fuselage. I took a seat next to the fire to melt the chill from my flesh.

"You saw that dude turn from werewolf to human, didn't you?" he asked.

I nodded.

Branch took a step closer, coming into my field of vision. She looked like shit, clothes half-torn from her body, bloody gashes on her hands dripping onto the floor.

"Don't you get it? *Frankenstein vs. The Wolfman*, only this time in real life." Carter's laughter brayed across the ice.

Oh, Lord, save me from idiots.

Branch shook her head, black semi-circles beneath her eyes. "You are such a moron, Carter."

He continued to laugh.

Before I could make a sarcastic comment, Branch walked over and held out a candy bar, a move so shocking and out of character that I gaped for a moment before I accepted and swallowed it all in two bites.

"Nice," I said after a jaw-cracking yawn. "Thank you."

Those blue crystal eyes fixed on me as she holstered her sidearm. "Don't thank me, we still need what's in your head, so don't take this as a great show of solidarity or sentimentality."

Of course.

Carter stared at the blood on my clothing. "It bit you, right?"

I nodded.

"Does that mean you're going to turn into a wolfman? Be cursed and stuff?"

"No." I shook my head. "I'm already cursed. And by the way, Carter," I slurred, bone tired. "Let me remind you *once again*, Frankenstein was the man, not the monster."

CHAPTER SIXTEEN

Scottsbluff, Nebraska, October 1901

If Deadwood was a shithole, then Scottsbluff was what emerged from said hole. Founded just a couple of years ago and named for the fur trader Hiram Scott and the bluff that stood tall nearby, it looked barely put together, not a proper town at all, really. Although the buildings looked fairly new, they seemed to be constructed in such a haphazard manner as to be considered a failure of architecture. Sure, maybe there stood three or four buildings in decent repair, but they occupied a minority status and the streets seemed to be comprised more of mud than cobble, which could change years later, but I did not hold out hope.

I had taken the rail out west from Omaha after my man in New York telegraphed me a message received from Ellis Riggins, Mary's direct descendant (Victoria's last son), a man who took his family out west to settle the hard lands of Western Nebraska. A smart boy, he made a good living as a trader/shopkeeper and provided for his family despite living on the edge of civilization.

At Fort Niobrara I exited the train along with good old Jed, who fared well on the trip thanks to an attendant who had never seen a Percheron before. Established over twenty years ago, the fort's main function was to monitor and deal with the Lakota Sioux. I took the term monitor to mean oppress and control and from the looks of the Sioux at the fort buying supplies, it seemed to be dead accurate. I had seen dogs treated better.

It came to me that I preferred to rub elbows with the 25th infantry, a segregated black troop of as fine a group of men as I had ever met, instead of mingling with the white officers and soldiers. It raised my hackles to see such 'gentlemen' treat others so just because of skin tone. It took a while for the 25th to chum up to me, but bottles of whiskey cemented friendships.

All and all, I felt happy to put the fort behind me and head toward Scottsbluff.

The farms around this neck of the Nebraska had houses of sod, which withstood the brutal winters and the dry as dust summers and if it was not for the aquifer (a couple of scant feet under the topsoil in places) this area would be considered a desert. As it was, the grass looked a sallow green, the rats hopped around on their back legs almost like frogs and rattlers lay almost everywhere.

Nebraska sure was a strange place, fit only for bison and those crazy enough to try eke out a living from this sandy soil.

Jed plodded placidly through the mud, the huge horse undisturbed by the smell of manure, urine and other things best left unidentified. Old Tom passed away a years ago and Jed served as a solid replacement, another Percheron to handle my bulk. A dapple gray, he stood nineteen hands and allowed me an almost bird's eye view of the town as we entered.

I kept my canvas coat snug around my body and hat slung low over my face despite the unseasonably warm winter day. In this part of the country the weather could change faster than a jackrabbit could jump.

"Howdy stranger." The voice seemed friendly, but the speaker sure did not.

A tall bearded man, so thin he almost seemed gaunt, stood to my left on a wooden sidewalk clear of churned mud. He wore a nice suit the same color as Jed with a silver star attached to the lapel. His left hand rested on the butt of a Colt. His eyes peeked between squinted lids and I knew he sized me up pretty well.

"Howdy, sheriff," I replied, doffing my hat slowly. No sudden movements. "Pleasant day."

If he felt any startlement at my scars it did not show. "Pleasant day, stranger. What brings to our fair town?"

Fair town? The man needs bifocals. I smiled. "Seeking relatives of mine. The Riggins family. Perhaps you know them?"

"Sure do. Fine upstanding folk, they are. What's your business with them if'n you don't mind me saying?"

And you do not give a shit if I do. "They are family. I am Ellis's uncle Frank."

The squint disappeared revealing eyes as gray as his suit. A smile pushed through the forest of his beard and the hand disappeared from the butt of the Colt. "So, you're the famous uncle Frank I've heard tell of. Well, the stories don't do you a lick of justice. Ellis said you'd be a-coming." The smile disappeared. "You better git on over to the Riggins house then, they'll be needing you. A half mile down the way toward the bluff, white house with yellow shutters." With solemn gravity the sheriff tipped his hat and I nodded back, my stomach clenching. Something in the sheriff's tone and manner told me good news lay far, far away.

I passed storefronts and saloons looking worse for the wear, paint chipping and peeling, the wood weathered. The people, however, looked fit and happy, not a limp or disfigurement in sight, which lay at odds on most frontier towns. Indians I took to be of the Sioux tribe stood in front of a general goods store fiercely negotiating trade for a roll of pelts while four of their brethren stood around as if acting as an honor guard. All of them had the lean physique and the wary eyes of warriors and their eyes met mine boldly. I gave them a nod and continued on, their gazes burning against my back.

The mud of the town became the mud of a cart track that led out and sure as a politician will take a bribe the house that came into view a half mile later, not more than a twenty-minute ride to the bluff, turned out to be Ellis's. Two stories, painted white with yellow shutters, just like the sheriff said. A large barn stood to the back and right of the main house with a hitching post out front. I tied old Jed off and strapped on a feed bag for a well-earned treat of dry oats.

Before I reached the door it opened and I found myself with an armful of Ellis's plump but pretty wife, Thelma.

"Oh, uncle," she sobbed into my chest. "Thank the Lord you received our telegraph."

My big hands stroked her blonde hair which lay in a bun at the nape of her neck. "Of course I did, Thel," I whispered down to her. "Uncle is here."

"Uncle." Ellis came into view, a medium-sized man with tousled blond hair that reminded me so much of Percy. "Thank you. You are a Godsend."

I moved one arm from around Thelma and pulled the lad into a strong embrace which he returned with spice. Hard life on the frontier put muscles on him and from the feel of his bones beneath his shirt I reckoned he lost a good forty pounds. "Good to see you, son," I murmured into his ear as I squeezed gently. They both groaned a bit, but did not let go.

When we had our fill of embraces, the led me into the house and up the stairs so quickly I did not have a chance to see what the first floor looked like. I had an impression of clean, wood and fresh paint, but that was all.

Within moments I found myself in a modest bedroom where the only touch of luxury proved to be a buffalo hide rug on which stood a child's bed. The child in question lay beneath a quilt, face sallow and drawn. A young boy about ten with tousled blond hair and high cheekbones that reminded me so much of my Mary that it set me back on my heels for a moment. I knew this was Arlis, Ellis's only child.

"It started a month ago and I knew it was something different." Ellis spoke mechanically, as if he had been hollowed out and clockwork parts replaced his innards. "One night Arlis snuck out of the house to go playing in a pond near the bluff with his friends from town. They're thicker than thieves that bunch." Ellis wiped a tear from his impassive face, eyes glistening. "He said they met a boy that looked just like him, so much so they thought he might be related."

I felt a chill start at my guts and worm its way up to my chest. A twin. A doppelganger. The old story of Percy meeting his double came back to hit me hard, causing me to kneel at the boy's side. I remember Mary telling me of the twin scars n Percy's shoulder. "What happened then?"

Ellis shrugged. "I gave him a good talking to. He knows better than to go out at night, this part of the country isn't that civilized just yet. Could be any sort of wild animal who wouldn't think twice about attacking a child. It's the devil's land out there at night."

That might be truer than you know. "And then?"

"Like I said in the telegraph, he got himself sick, then sicker. Now he barely wakes and doesn't want to eat anything. Thelma has to threaten him with a stropping just to get him to down meat broth." He shuddered, finally showing emotion as the tears began to run freely. "I didn't think you'd be able to make it here before...before..."

He dies, I finished silently. What did Mary say all those years ago? Exsanguination. Yes, that was it. Somehow her children were murdered, bled dry. Where the icy worm of fear once roamed now came the thread of an old familiar anger heating up my bones until my skin felt stretched tight like a bladder fixing to burst. I pulled the covers away revealing the boy in his night clothes, a plain cotton pullover that covered him from neck to ankles. "I just finished business in Omaha when I received your telegraph." Said business involved a gang of wanted men running a brothel featuring a bevy of young girls no more than twelve years old. I collected a goodly bounty and none of the men saw daylight again. "Sam in Des Moines knew where I set my boots and sent me your plea." I rode Jed like demons of Hell were after me to make it to Scottsbluff in time.

The boy's limbs looked like twigs beneath his night clothes, all bone and rawhide. I could see he could ill afford to lose another ounce of flesh so thin was he. My eyes and hands commenced examining the child, my knobby fingers sliding over flesh cool enough to belong to a corpse. It took only a minute or two for me to find something, something that explained everything...at least to me. Two small puncture wounds on the backside of the boy's left knee, barely big enough to notice except the marks looked slightly inflamed.

"Shit," I muttered. *Vampire.* Telling Ellis and Thelma would only bring undue stress to already frayed nerves, so I decided to keep my own counsel on the matter.

Exsanguination. Of course. I would have to be a damn fool not to believe in the supernatural, myself being a prime example of such. That and the Book of Ur. I heard tell of vampires and their eyes made of precious stones. The older the vampire, the clearer the gems, the oldest having diamond eyes, faceted and clear as a pure ice, a legend I learned of out in China during my travels. The monks knew of them and so did the wise men of India, all of them feeding me the stories of the blood drinkers with gemmy eyes. It sure looked like the Riggins family had one gunning for young Arlis.

I felt it in my bones when Mary told me of her children's deaths, but what could I do but stick around in case it struck again. Now, so much time later, I finally had the chance to put the fucker to earth. Permanently.

Thelma saw the set of my shoulders, the sudden stiffness and the creases around my scars that became canyons on my face. "What?"

What to say? "Keep force feeding him that broth, Thelma and keep your doors locked. Ellis, you stay up tonight in this room. You have a shotgun?"

He nodded, face cracking with concern, but he was a good boy and kept his mouth shut, trusting me completely. It was time to really earn that trust.

"No one in this room except you, Ellis, until sunup. Anyone comes in then you shoot them without hesitation, even if it is me or Thelma. No one."

"Got it."

Thelma muttered a prayer under her breath.

"Good, once the sun goes down in a couple of hours the real work commences."

•　　•　　•

Each minute until sundown ticked against my nerves until my hands began to shake something awful. I sat drinking coffee alone in the kitchen with a 1901 Mauser C96, a German made pistol given to me by a friend in Navy Command who briefly considered the weapon for the American Armed Forces. It used 7.63x25 boxed ammunition I needed to custom order because no one in the States produced it in mass quantities. I heard British officers loved the weapon and purchased them privately from Mauser in Germany, but I liked it because it was easy to reload and proved as accurate as any revolver I used. Big and a little bulky, it nevertheless fit my big right hand almost perfectly.

When my hands began to shake, I closed my yellow eyes behind their colored lenses and inhaled and exhaled slowly, trying to reach a meditative state taught to me by the monks in China. It did not work.

Fuck it. I left the house before sundown, setting my boots to walking to the little pond on the Riggins property. It was time to collect a pair of gemmy eyes.

CHAPTER SEVENTEEN

We crashed into the Adirondaks and survived. Had I been normal I would not have, but what can you do? All things considering, I do not blame any of us for missing the obvious and it turned out to be Carter who provided the final clue.

Sleep avoided us for most of the night, our adrenalin levels and the cold kept it away. We sat around the smoldering remains of the fire, eyes crusted, exposed skin white as the snow the blew into the fuselage.

"How the fucking hell did Talbot find us?" Carter asked as we prepped for departure.

Branch rolled her beautiful eyes at his vulgarity. "An electronic tracker?"

"Yeah, but we were only down for three hours or so before he attacked. I mean, look around, it's not like we landed near a Wal-Mart or anything." Carter shook his head. "We're in the middle of the fucking wilderness. How did he *get* here? Even running as fast as a wolf he couldn't get here so quickly. And that helo must've been a spotter because it never landed, at least not nearby."

Well...shit and fried eggs. I almost smacked myself on the forehead. "Damn, Carter, way to go," I blurted, feeling like five kinds of prize idiot. "There is no way he arrived on foot. Sure, he might have come a few miles picking up his lupine comrades, but not initially. No, he arrived here by other means. Perhaps the helicopter and Carter is right, it did not land nearby." My head felt ready to pop off my shoulders so massive was my embarrassment for having missed this detail, although, to be reasonable, I had been busy fighting a supernatural man/wolf hybrid. Not to mention healing from the plane crash.

Branch looked out at the first rays of dawn, frowning. "The wolves came from across the lake, from the west."

"Then west is where we will go."

We commenced trekking, the mountains here were pretty gentle with easy slopes so there we held no worry about having to go Donner Party on each other and within three miles or so we came to a little flat-bottomed valley. At the bottom rested something that made my heart soar like an eagle. For a moment.

A helicopter. Perhaps *the* helicopter. I did not know how to fly one, but by Carter's excited whoops of glee that bounced around the little vale I knew he did. He began an awkward loping run down the slope, hampered by the layers of clothing keeping him warm.

"Hot damn and pass the potatoes," he breathed as the doors opened to a touch. "This is a Bell 430! I can fly this!"

Now my heart really began to race.

Carter scrambled into the pilot seat and began to flip switches and push buttons. "Okay, everything looks good. Someone really loved this baby, gave it a spare fuel reserve. Hmmm...looks like, if I'm reading this right, we have another three hundred miles left in this sucker." He turned to me with a smile so wide I could see the entirety of his expensive dental work. "Welcome to Carter Airlines, please buckle your seat belts and put your trays and seat backs in their full upright and locked positions, kiddies. We are gonesville."

Branch gave with a brilliant smile that almost blinded me and shocked me a little. *Dear diary, today I witnessed a miracle...*

We took off without a backward glance.

Not wanting to attract attention, we landed the Bell a while later a couple miles outside of a little town called Speculator, NY and rode shank's mare the rest of the way, shedding excess layers so we would not attract too much attention. Once in town we hit the nearest golden arches where the morning crowd gave us plenty of looks as we downed enough McGriddles to feed a battalion. We did not care and I helped myself to a second and third portion. Regeneration took it out of a body.

As soon as 9 AM rolled around we hit the Speculator Department Store (creativity did not exist there, it seemed) and we purchased new outfits, leaving our old ones in the fitting room.

During this time, I thought long and hard about how Talbot and Jacob's Rule managed to plant agents aboard our plane and how they tracked us. I came to a conclusion, the only one I could make. "Damn me for a fool again. I must be losing my touch."

That garnered me looks.

"Look," I said. "Jacob's rule has been on our necks from day one and the only way they could is if someone fed them intelligence. Not blaming you two, but it was the Church who paid for everything, the flight, the hotel. Everything."

"Now wait a minute!" Branch grew red in face and her eyes blazed. "Are you blaming the Catholic *Church*?"

Before I could answer Carter held up a hand, his face troubled. "No, he's saying that someone in the Church fed them intel and the only way they could have got our itinerary was that someone tipped them off." He dug into a pocket and pulled out a black Amex card. "Or they could be monitoring our cards."

"Give the man a cookie."

"So what now?"

I held up one of my own credit cards, one that I never used. "The next plane ride is on me."

Actually, it turned out to be the next plane ride and pretty much everything else. I racked up a lot of debt on that card, but I did not tell the others I could easily afford it.

• • •

Early the next day after a redeye out of Albany we landed in Denver International and rented a car. A new Nissan Xterra, a tough SUV that ate gas like a fat man chowing down at a buffet. Carter and Branch felt more than comfortable for me to drive as the next destination was up to me and I did not really clue them in except to tell them it was needed to help complete the mission.

Before we headed toward our destination, I stopped at a Wells Fargo bank. The two agents followed me in, but I stopped them from accompanying me to the vault where the safety deposit boxes were held.

"Wait here you two," I said.

Branch crossed her arms. "Why?"

I waved my arms around. "A bit of privacy would be nice. I am merely retrieving items of value to aid in our quest. Be patient and trust me if you can."

She looked unconvinced but relented.

From around my neck I removed a silver chain to which a key dangled and opened box number 236 to retrieve something I had stored there years ago for such an occasion. Glittering wealth met my eyes when I lifted the lid and I could not help but smile.

In a lifetime that spanned centuries I learned patience and it looked like that patience would pay off, assuming the man we traveled to meet did not kill me first. I left the bank with a jaunty whistle that irked Carter to no end, which only made my mood brighter.

We tooled up the 70 to the Rockies, taking in the view of the rugged mountains and although the traffic annoyed me, we made good time. Past Idaho Springs and on until we approached Glenwood Springs, made famous as the site where Doc Holliday died of consumption. There I turned off a seldom used road, which was a generous term considering it consisted of two overgrown ruts, rocks and enough tall grass to scrape the undercarriage.

"Your friend sure lives in the boonies," Carter commented while munching on a Lara Bar. He chewed with his mouth open, the philistine.

"A sort of friend," I replied. "Someone I worked with once." The Xterra jounced over good sized rocks, almost approaching boulders in size, but the sturdy SUV took them like a champ. My companions' teeth rattled and my butt hurt something awful, but that is just the perils of off-roading.

"Your not-friend needs a better road," Branch said after a hard jounce.

"He really does not like visitors," I replied.

Branch grunted. "Reminds me of you."

My smile grew from ear to ear. "Oh, I love visitors. When they are not bearing flamethrowers. And I know they are coming."

She merely stared back at me in the rear view with her customary flatness, as if I told a joke in poor taste. People are never happy, it seems.

Before the day grew late we came upon a pair of boulders the SUV could not tackle. At least four feet tall and almost twice as wide, they stood one to a rut, one behind the other, an effective barricade for those who would travel beyond.

"Okay, Mr. Smartypants, what now?" Carter asked as I stopped the vehicle. We all exited and stared that the blockage that defied us with the inevitability of time, their gray presence a reminder of how little we were in the grand scheme of things.

"Damn, now I have to do this the hard way," I muttered. To left a cliff that threatened more boulders, to the right a drop off down the side of the mountain.

Branch stared down the mountain where it joined another that stood tall and proud. "Your acquaintance did this?"

I shrugged. "Maybe."

"If we used the jack and all of us push we can roll them down the mountain." Carter said doubtfully.

"No need."

After stretching and deep breaths, I placed my gnarled, knobby hands on the nearest one and *pushed*.

Branch gasped. "What in the Lord's name are you doing?"

I grunted, strained, the tendons tenting the flesh on the backs of my great hands. My lungs burned with the fires of my effort and my face became suffused with blood, my vision becoming dark.

"What do you think you're doing?" Carter's voice came from distant place, my ears thundering with my pulse. *Move, damn you! Move!*

The boulder budged. Only a centimeter at first, then two, three. There came a sharp *pop* and a stab of pain from my right elbow as my arm gave way, slamming my shoulder against the stone with bone numbing force that sent stars to my eyes. Pain suffused me, an old friend, one experience taught me to tolerate, so I set to with renewed vigor that some might call stubbornness. All right, most would.

A deep grinding sound tore through the blood thunder in my ears and I found myself suddenly free of the burden and moving forward at speed as the boulder disappeared. Four hands gripped my shoulders, sending renewed agony through my bones, tendons and muscles.

"Jesus, God," I heard as my ass met the ground with a resounding *thump*. "How the fuck did you do that?"

"Don't take the Lord's name in vain, Carter."

"Shut up, Branch. Did you see what he did?"

"Of course I did. Not like I could miss it."

Bones creaked and sinew popped as regeneration kicked in, but I felt myself lost in an effort to supply enough oxygen to my starved lungs in that thin atmosphere. In and out my lungs filling like a bellows and expelling CO_2, the blood thunder in my ears.

"I didn't know you could do that." Carter's voice held a reverential awe. "I mean, I knew you were strong, you beat Talbot, but damn, man, that was next level shit."

I opened my eyes to see Branch staring deep into them. "He's right, that was next level...stuff."

"That thing must've weight at least four tons or more." Carter looked down the mountain, fingers ruffling through his beard. Suddenly he turned to me. "You could have killed us at any time, right?"

I nodded.

"Why didn't you?"

With my head clearing I nodded again, saying, "I am not an indiscriminate killer. I only kill those who prey on the innocent." Getting to my feet took a bit of doing, but the pair of agents helped me up. "We need each other to retrieve the Book of Ur and hand it back to His Holiness. After that we go on our separate ways, right?"

They nodded, still in awe at my feat of strength and regarding me like one would a pit bull who suddenly growled menacingly. *Good, a little fear keeps people honest.*

"Relax, if I wanted you dead, you would have never left my house in Hawaii. By the way, thanks for keeping me from falling down the mountain. It would have been a bitch to climb at night."

That did not ease the tension any, not that it was meant to.

Things proceeded pretty much the same with the second boulder, including the torn ligaments, tendons and bones broken from the strain. It hurt. A lot.

The things I do for humanity.

Once the road was clear there were no more obstacles for the Xterra to navigate, in fact the road (being generous here) became relatively smooth. 'Bout time something went right. Which usually means it will go drastically wrong. And soon.

Carter piped up. "I've been thinking."

Uh-oh. "And thus is true danger born." I tried to keep my tone airy, light, but Branch's face in the rear-view told me that the effort of levity slid off her like oil on porcelain.

Back in the '20s I knew a young man named Raine just like her, inscrutable, stubborn and disciplined. He would get an idea stuck in his head and pursue it come hell or high water, no matter the cost, but he always kept an open mind. I surely hoped she shared that trait.

Carter continued. "We've been following you this entire time, following your leads." The world passed by outside at 25 mph, not fast but to go any faster risked us plunging down the mountainside ass over teakettle. I might survive, but not so much my companions. "You've been leading us all the way and we've come along quietly."

Not so quiet. I kept my mouth shut wondering what came next.

"This isn't something that we're used to as agents. As Americans, given our citizens natural distrust to authority. We've done all this virtually without complaint." He glanced at Branch who merely *hrummphed.* "But I think it's time you start being a little more up front with us, we need more information. You asked us to believe in the Oracle of Delphi, and I believe you, but Branch has her doubts."

"So you have expressed from the start." During the drive the sky began to turn dark, now it was a couple of shades before midnight so I turned on the lights, which bathed the world in stark, contrasting images. Bright gray grass, gray ruts and the shadows pools of midnight.

Branch kicked her two cents in. "I still doubt you, but I don't think of you as the Abomination anymore."

My foot mashed on the brake and the Xterra skidded to a stop. I turned to Banch. "You serious? You are not joking?"

She nodded.

Carter looked impressed. "Wow, man."

"Dead serious." Branch affirmed.

"Wow, indeed." I sat for a minute, my thoughts awhirl until finally, "Okay, Agent Branch of the *Manus Dei*. Information you want, information you will have. We are going to meet a man named Biltmore. Do not ask me his full name for that is what he is known by and that alone. He is a rabbi who once held the Book of Ur for a couple of years and has been transformed by it, and by that he has gained great knowledge of magic. To the best of my knowledge, he is over a hundred years old and time has not softened him one bit. If anyone can help us find the book and make sense of the Oracle's prophecy, it is him." I raised a finger, pointing between the two. "Just understand he is a bit crusty and dislikes authority more than I, however he values good manners and respect, so do not, under any circumstances, piss him off. He is liable to turn you two into newts."

Carter raised an eyebrow. He was good at it. "Newts."

"If he does, you will get better. Now let us shove off and pray he does not shoot us on sight." I put the SUV back into gear and commenced our drive. "It will not be long now."

A couple of minutes later Carter said, "Speaking of joking, I have one for you."

Carter making jokes? This I had to hear. "Go on."

"Okay," he began, "Christ is on the cross—"

"Carter!" Branch practically yelled.

"Easy, partner. Jokes lighten the mood. Not everyone likes the subject matter but that doesn't mean they're not funny. Where was I? Oh yeah...Christ is on the cross atop Golgatha and he yells 'Peter!

"Now Peter, being a good disciple, tries to approach but the Roman guards won't let him, but he's insistent so they cut his arm off as a warning. He goes running back into the crowd who commences binding his wounds.

"'Peter!' yells Christ. Peter comes a running, but the soldiers, tired of the dealing with the guy, cuts a leg off with one sweep of a sword. Peter hops back into the crowd who bind his wound.

"Once again Christ yells for his disciple and, sure enough, Peter hops out. Swoosh! Off comes the other leg, but he keeps dragging himself forward using his remaining arm. 'Ah, let the poor guy go,' says one Roman guard, 'he's not long for the world.' So Peter laboriously drags himself up Golgatha, head swimming in pain, half-dead.

"'Peter!' shouts Christ.

"'I'm here, my Lord,' says Peter, one hand on the base of the cross, finally at his destination. 'Give to me your words of wisdom.'

"Christ looks down seeing Peter bloody and mostly dismembered and says, 'Peter, I can see your house from here.'"

It started slowly with a chuckle from yours truly, a tiny expression of mirth, but Carter laid his head back and *laughed* great big bellows of laughter and Lord help me I joined him. In the rear-view Branch's lips twitched, then she tittered, finally giving way to heaping big belly laughs that nearly shook the Xterra.

We laughed the rest of the way to our destination like madmen.

CHAPTER EIGHTEEN

Scottsbluff, Nebraska, October 1901

Finding the little pond, more of a glorified mudhole, proved easy. It lay exactly where Ellis said and the half moon and stars above transformed night into day for my amber eyes. Limber pine, oak, cottonwood and ash dotted the landscape, becoming more and more dense as one drew closer to the North Platte River. Even though the soil remained sandy, the aquifer lay high enough that trees took well to the area, which supplied the wood to build the town and more wealthy surrounding farmsteads and ranches.

An oak whose best days lay behind it shrouded the pond, sticking its branches over the water allowing children to climb up and jump in to the water. I could see why the local kids loved to play there. And why this monster would prey there.

I found a stump of another oak Ellis must have used for his fine house and I had a seat, grunting with fatigue.

Peaceful, that is the word to describe the scene with the blanket of stars overhead and the partial moon shining down. I could rest here for a bit, stay with Ellis and Thelma and try my hand at doing whatever it was they did, even though it might bore me to tears.

What a nice dream. That was all it was, a dream of peace. The need that drove would not let me do anything like settle down, live a comfortable life in Nowhere Nebraska. Everyone I loved grew old and died while I stayed virtually the same. Sure, my skin darkened over time so I looked more human, but inside I was still the immortal monster and monsters are not entitled to happy endings.

I sighed, feeling all the years pile up like bricks on my shoulders. Fortunately, my shoulders felt broad enough to take the load, but I felt it was only a matter of time before it crushed me to paste.

I feel old. So fucking old. How long can I stand it? Suicide was not the answer. If I possessed a soul, killing myself would damn me to Hell and I knew for fact Heaven existed, so there must be a Hell and that did not sound like a trip I wanted to take, even on Christmas.

To give the creature credit, it made very little noise, just enough for me to place a hand under my canvas coat to grab the butt of the Mauser.

"No time for playing about," I said to the darkness, my eyes roaming over the landscape. "We are above such things, you and I."

The voice that came from the direction of the oak slithered through the air like silk, breathy, deep and cultured. "But I do like to play, oh Immortal One. It's the only thing the decently passes the time and I have so much of it."

Where are you, you sonofabitch? Out here on the frontier everyone carried so it knew I had a weapon to decorate it's body with a multitude of tiny holes that bled a lot. "Try taking up a hobby. Whittling, for example."

"I need to feed and I can't drink wood. Blood is my game, you handsome man and theirs is so sweet."

Cold enveloped my guts like a fog. "Whose blood?" I asked in an attempt to buy time.

"Those with Shelley's blood. When I met him all those years ago, I took a bite and it was better than I could *imagine*. Wine and chocolate mixed with the attar of roses. It was if I found what Ponce de Leon could not, the Fountain of Youth, but much better."

My hand tightened on the butt of the Mauser until wood splintered and it took a bit doing to unclench my hand. This was the one, the one who killed my darling Mary's children, the bane of her family.

Was this the doppelganger that haunted Percy? A vampire who found the poet's blood so nourishing that he preyed upon Mary's family for centuries? It all fell in place, neat and tidy. That put me on edge. Nothing was ever neat and tidy. "You are stalking Percy Shelley's descendants because he *tasted* good?"

"Beyond good. They're sublime. Don't worry, I have no intention of killing the boy because he needs to breed, create more delicacies for me."

Nausea replaced the cold in my stomach and everything became shades of red, but I held on to my fury like an old lover, not willing it to guide my actions. Hard fought discipline stuffed that ball of anger deep into the back of my mind to use later, to provide me strength of purpose. "Let us discuss this like gentlemen, no chicanery."

"Doubt you want to be gentlemanly considering your hand is on that pistol." At my start amused laughter hung in the air. "Yes, I can see you very well, good sir."

"If both our cards are showing, then let us end this."

"I have given you enough respite. Why not?" Like a wraith, a shadow disconnected from the oak to reveal a man, the shock of which kept me in my seat. Tall, bony, with narrow shoulders covered in a canvas coat and a wide-brimmed hat held low over his face. But I knew the visage it would reveal to me as I watched a large, gnobbly hand sweep the hat away to reveal a face disfigured by familiar scars. "Do you like my guise?" asked the doppelganger with an insincere smile that was all teeth and gleeful malice. It's eyes glittered with jade evil. "Allow me to introduce myself, I am Darius."

Bam! The first shot hit the vampire high in the chest before I realized I fired. The second and third striking low in the gut and before I knew it the pistol clanked empty. Before the smoke had a chance to dissipate in the soft, chill breeze I was already half way around the pond and accelerating.

The vampire straightened then crouched in anticipation of my attack.

A train hit me from the side, a punishing blow that launched me five feet in the air and ten across the pond, shattering the ribs on my left flank. I landed in frigid water with a resounding splash that sent a wave of agony through me as bones ground together. Soft mud squelched between my fingers as I flailed, ribs searing. Water entered my nose, stinging, and then my lungs. I coughed and gagged, blinded by pain and liquid as fear warred with the agony in my ribs.

Another splash. Twin steel pythons wrapped around my skull and then a dull *wrench* as they twisted my head around my neck.

The light of my consciousness went out.

•   •   •

When I came to it was with a sudden clarity, no transition from sleep to awake. One second out, the next alert as my body reacted to imminent danger.

"Good, you're awake." The voice, that hated smooth silk that so offended me by the pond.

Yellow eyes wide, no spectacles, I looked around. Sandstone walls, a musty smell like a bevy of snakes and the flickering of sputtering torchlight. The vampire crouched in front of me and I leaped for it's throat. Or tried to. I lay propped against a sandstone wall, hat gone, grit in my hair, heavy chains wrapped around my body. The vampire grinned with my face, fangs jutting over it's lower lip, scars twisting and squirming on the skin like purple worms. It's eyes glittered a frosted jade instead of my own carious yellow.

"Comfy?" it asked.

My snarl replied that I was far from it.

Another vampire appeared in my line of sight, crouching next to the first. It's eyes were the color of rubies dipped in blood. "Dinner looks irritated."

"Relax," chided the first one. "He is understandably upset."

"We should drain him now. He is dangerous."

"Who are you?" I burst. "Take off that face."

It's head cocked to one side like a rooster examining a worm. "Fair enough." The smile it bestowed told me it felt no real empathy, then it's skin rippled like water when a stone is dropped in and seconds later I beheld Percy. But it was not him. Percy could never grin like that and I doubted anything human could. "Better?"

"Not much."

"No pleasing people," it said.

Of all the pickles I found myself in the past, this one topped them all. For the first time I felt I might actually die. A small, sad part of me looked forward to the prospect. "What now?"

Again with the curious bird-like head tilt. "We want to drink you, of course."

"It took you this long to finally be in the position?" I asked, trying to buy time.

"I wasn't strong enough before." It patted the other vampire affectionately, like one would a dog. "And I have mouths to feed. Say hello to my offspring."

"Hello to my offspring," I said

"Cute."

"I try."

It happened so quickly. Faster than a rattler's strike, swifter than a hummingbird's wing the vampire went from the wall to my neck, fangs slashing. There came the sound of paper ripping and the sting of rent flesh. Blood flowed and lips colder than a miser's heart clamped hard down upon the junction of my neck and shoulder. I felt and heard an obscene sucking sound and my skin crawled. Nausea gripped me as I tried to pull away but icy hands stronger than bronze held me steady as those wormy lips sucked my blood down a greedy maw.

Fifty years ago I swam in warm waters of the coast of the newly made state of California just because I could. There was nothing like the gentle waves of salt water buoying you softly up and down with nothing but more water beneath your toes. It is a feeling of freedom if you are not afraid of the ocean, of the monsters that lurk within swimming lazily for prey to fill their gullets.

The noon day summer sun shone down bright in a sky devoid of clouds backed by a sky so brilliantly blue it hurt my eyes to look at it. Everything about that moment, bobbing up and down like a man-shaped cork, the slight kiss of a breeze, the aquamarine sky, renewed my faith in a higher power. It renewed my faith in God for only the Almighty could create something so heart-stoppingly beautiful, so perfect.

At first it felt like a sharp tug, as if a tree branch snagged my foot and my head suddenly disappeared under the soft waves. Then came another tug, sharp, stinging and I found myself in surrounded by clouds of billowing red. I felt myself twisted around and around by the foot, shaken like a rat in a dog's jaws. Water shot up my nose, stinging my sinuses.

Even though I could see in the dark, peering through seawater was another thing entirely, but I did catch a glimpse of long barrel shaped *thing* that worried my leg, violently shaking back and forth. I saw the dorsal fin and knew fear. Shark.

With a final tug that produced more of the billowing red the shark spun away, disappearing from sight. Fear gave me strength and I swam up and up until fresh air caressed my lungs. I gagged and coughed out water.

I do not know if the shark did not like the taste of monster, but it never came back so I swam toward shore trailing blood. Salt stung my wound and I felt momentary surprise that my leg did not hurt more. It was not until I reached shallow water and tried to stand that I realized that the shark had taken my foot with it. I dragged myself to the shoreline and stared at the stump of my leg where it ended abruptly at the ankle.

The feeling that came over me then as I stared at the stump was the same horrified fascination that overwhelmed me as the vampire drank my blood. Nausea, terror and pain rolled into a barbed wire ball of misery that slashed my insides.

With a wrench and a gobbet of blood the vampire fell back, mouth agape, two-inch fangs glistening redly. Great lungfuls of air whooshed in and out of that horrible mouth, past those wormy lips, head back and gemmy jade eyes wide.

"What is it father?" asked the other vampire with a steadying hand on Darius's shoulder.

"I never imagined," Darius breathed. "I never dreamed it could be like this."

What happened next nearly unzipped my mind.

Darius sat there against the cave wall and stared at me as if I was the second coming, gem eyes so wide his eyelids disappeared. As I watched the jade coloring of his eyes began to fade, the color leaching from them like water down a drain until all that remained were faceted twin orbs of the utmost clarity. Twin diamonds that split the torchlight into rainbows and I knew deep in my heart, as blood pumped sluggishly from my shoulder, that it had grown stronger.

The reality of those crystalline orbs floored me as much as a solid thump to the skull. The older the vampire, the clearer the eyes. Diamond eyes were worn by the eldest of bloodsuckers, the strongest and the meanest. One good drink of my blood turned Darius into a Vampire Master, one who could control dozens, if not hundreds, of lesser vampires. What would happen if he drank more? Drain me dry?

I did not want to find out.

"Father! Father! Your eyes!"

Darius grinned, a twisting of his worm lips that had nothing to do with humor or good will. "Ah, yes my child. I feel it. The power...intoxicating."

The vampire cub grinned, showing its dagger fangs. Almost as quick as it's sire it was upon me with those teeth lunging toward my throat. I braced myself for death because it sure did not look as if this thing would hold back. It would slice my arteries wide open and drain me dry and I did not think even my regenerative powers could bring me back from complete exsanguination.

Those hideous teeth never made it.

Feet dangling inches from the floor, the vampire cub howled like a scalded cat, thrashing in the grip of Darius's fist clamped firmly in his greasy brown hair. "No, child, this treat is not for you," purred the master vampire.

It turned it's diamond eyes toward me as I sat there panting, dizzy from blood loss, my head filled with bees and trying not to pass clean out. "You, my dear friend, are the answer to a prayer," said the newly minted Master Vampire.

"If you were praying for a slow, miserable death," I gasped. "Then I am more than willing to comply."

More smiling. Still very unnerving. "Cute."

CHAPTER NINETEEN

Just as the sun kissed the mountaintops, we came upon a nice little two-story red brick house fronted by a bright red door with a wrought iron knocker shaped like clenched fist. I parked the SUV and sauntered up, my guts tightening in anticipation.

"Your friend lives in a nice house in the middle of nowhere," said Branch, pointing to a satellite dish. "With modern conveniences."

"He's not a savage, just likes his privacy."

Carter raised an eyebrow. "Something wrong? You look like a man headed toward a firing squad."

I almost laughed by my nerves were too on edge. "Funny you should say that." We stopped at the door and I turned to my companions. "Listen, you have to be careful of Biltmore, he knows things...call it a gift from the book when he had it in his possession and he will use it to fuck with you both. You cannot let him get to you. Keep your cool and focus on the mission."

"Knows things?" scoffed Carter with a lopsided grin that split his beard. "C'mon, man, we're *agents*. We can hold our own."

Branch merely nodded.

"Okay. Do not say I did not warn you. And whatever you do, do not draw your weapons. Agreed?" They agreed and I turned to the door, slamming the knocker against oak. *Thwack! Thwack! Thwack!*

"Oh, come on in, you bloody great bastard," called a voice from the other side.

"Thought he was a friend of yours," said Carter, eyebrow raised.

"It could be possible I overstated the relationship." I took a deep breath and turned the knob. *This is really going to hurt*, I thought as I opened the door.

Bang!

It felt like a good-sized man just punched me hard in the stomach. The shot took me in the belly leaving silver dollar-sized hole which began to gout spurt blood in hideously copious amounts, practically jetting from between my fingertips. A solid wave of agony swept from my gut and my balls felt like they would shrivel up and depart for whereabouts unknown.

"Take that, you bloody great oaf!"

"Ah, fuck!" I cried, bent over in pain. Moments later I managed to draw enough air to curse. "This really fucking hurts, Bilt!"

A short, slightly rotund man with an oiled beard hanging down in ringlets to his waist grinned, showing a fortune's worth of gold dental work in his nut-brown face, and motioned the two agents in while telling me to wait outside. The shotgun in his hands ensured politeness. While his back was turned my companions started in surprise seeing the yarmulka perched on the back of his head. "I don't want blood on my bamboo flooring. Heal up first," he remarked in a Cockney accent.

"You're from England?" Branch asked as she carefully crossed the threshold into a lavishly appointed living room complete with a leather sectional and a coffee table that looked like it would be at home at a Sotheby's auction house.

"London. Cheapside, what you Yanks would call the East End. "C'mon you two, let's have a cuppa while that bloody great omadhaun regenerates."

"I cannot believe you used omahaun in a sentence, Bilt," I gasped.

"And I can't believe you still sound like stuck-arse Oxford professor, Vince."

Carter did the eyebrow thing again.

I shrugged. "Vince is the name I used when I first met Biltmore years and years ago."

"Yah," said Bilt as he laid the shotgun on a mantle over a fireplace that looked like it could accommodate an entire ox. "Years, indeed. Back in a mo."

"Damn you, Bilt," I cried. "You ruined a perfectly good shirt." The wound in my gut began to heal, popping out pellets that clattered against the front step.

"It looks like you shopped at Wal-Mart, you great idiot," he hollered back from deep within the house. My companions sat on the sectional enjoying the buttery soft brown leather. "I did you a bloody great favor, I did, you wanker." Biltmore emerged from the kitchen with a tray containing porcelain tea cups, a pot and a creamer. "Drink up, my lovelies, it'll be a moment while that bloody bastard heals. Sugar?"

When the last pellet *plunked* down upon concrete, I straightened my shirt (now soaked in blood and bearing a hole the size of my fist (goodbye Spectator Department Store special buy for only $9.99). Inside Bilt poured me a cup of tea and I tossed in four sugars and a dollop of cream. Without blowing on it I took a sip of the scalding liquid and savored the flavor. "Aw, Bilt, the good stuff. You always know how to treat a friend."

"*Oy gevalt,* you *schmuck,* I'm not your friend, you great twat," said Bilt around his cup which bore a cute floral design around the rim. "You still owe me."

Carter, of course, could not keep his mouth shut. "You're Jewish!" Any wider and his eyelids would disappear into his skull.

"And you're a feygehleh, but who am I to judge?"

"Feygala?" he asked, butchering the word.

Well, dip me in shit. "It's Feygehleh," I said, pronouncing the word slowly. "It means gay. A homosexual."

Now it was Branch's turn to do the wide-eyed thing.

Carter dropped his cup, which of course shattered into a thousand pieces on the bamboo floor. "But—but—how?"

"Like I said, Carter, he knows things. It is his gift." Okay, a small, mean part of me enjoyed his discomfiture a little too much. Later I would pray for forgiveness, but now I just leaned back and enjoyed the show.

Branch: "You can't be Catholic and be gay, Carter."

Carter: "Who says?"

Branch: "The Church, dummy!"

Carter: "Fuck that, I'm a believer and an agent. What the Church doesn't know won't hurt 'em."

All I needed was popcorn.

Branch: "I'll have to tell the *Primus*."

Carter: (voice rising to a squeak) "The fuck you will! I'm the senior agent here and you'll keep your damn mouth shut!" I could see the fear climb all over him like a rash.

"QUIET!" Bilt thundered. Silenced reigned. I silently bid goodbye to the popcorn.

Carter and Branch both shut their traps, awed by the volume of Bilt's voice which was almost loud enough to shatter the lovely tea set. *I bet that was expensive.*

A stubby finger pointed toward Branch. "You want to quote Leviticus, right? Verses 18:22 and 20:13, 'If a man lieth with a man, as he lieth with a woman, both have committed an abomination', right?"

Branch reluctantly nodded.

"Well, miss hoity-toity, since you're *Manus Dei* and all New Testament-like, if you'd really studied, the apostle Paul taught that you Christians are no longer under the Old Law. You're not supposed to follow the Old Testament. Galatians 3:13 states that '*Christ redeemed us from the curse of the Law by becoming a curse for us.*' It was Jesus's death on the cross that saved you Christians from the curse of the Law. Therefore, quoting Leviticus as an excuse for hating gays is in itself morally wrong." Bilt gave with a golden toothy grin. "But since I'm Jewish and follow the Torah, my views are a little different, although I do like a good BLT from time to time. Call it my little sin, won't you."

"Says the Indian Jew."

Bilt looked askance at Carter. If he felt offended, it did not show. "Judaism is a religion, you *meshuggah* child. Haven't you ever heard of Sammy Davis, Jr? Rod Carew? It's not a race, no matter what those *schleps* in the Aryan Nation might say. So, I'm an Indian? So what? You're white and obviously entitled, *boychik*."

For the first time I saw Carter at a loss for words. I cannot tell you how satisfying that felt. *Who needs popcorn?*

As for Branch, she merely nodded, a little taken aback, but not too much, bending down to pick up the pieces of Carter's tea cup.

Clap, clap, clap. The sound of my great hands filled the living room. "Now that we have had our theology lesson, let us get back on track, shall we?"

"True, true, you great oaf." Bilt began helping Branch. "You came to find the Book of Ur and you need my help, don'tcha? "

I nodded.

"Well, you bloody big lout, let's get to work, shall we? And if you try that stunt like you did the last time, I'm gonna shoot you again, I will."

"What is it with you two?" asked Branch, placing little white shards on the tray.

Bilt pointed at me. "Ask that bloody big idiot."

I shrugged. "Biltmore had the book and I took it from him and gave it to the Vatican."

"It was mine!" he shouted.

"No one should have that power!" I countered.

"I made things better!"

"You bettered yourself."

"Arrgh!" Bilt flung up his hands. "Enough of this. We could 'round all day and never get anything done, but let me tell you, you're gonna have to regenerate an awful lot of bits if you betray me again, won'tcha?" He stood and smoothed his beard. "Now, it's late and I haveta make supper. You're all welcome to join. Jobs don't get done on an empty stomach, do they?"

Best thing I heard all day. I hoped he had popcorn.

Dinner turned out to be oven roasted chicken, BLT's, mashed potatoes, gravy, salad, potato latkes, and PB bacon and banana sandwiches (I had two. If they were good enough for the king of rock-n-roll, they were good enough for me). Except to eat, the two agents kept their mouths shut, perhaps still shaken by the conversation with Bilt. I could not blame them, Bilt was enough to give Satan the heebee-jeebies.

We all tucked in with a will, eating the entire lot in less than a half hour while Bilt stared at use in amazement. "You all didn't have much time to eat, didya?" he asked.

"Been a long day, Bilt," Carter mumbled around a mouthful of mashed potatoes.

When we were done and our bellies bulged, I looked to our host. "Have any popcorn?"

That earned me a massive stink-eye, but I got my popcorn. Extra butter.

Later. "So, you went to see that *fakata* oracle, right?" he asked.

I nodded with a mouth full of buttery goodness. I used my shirt to wipe my fingers because what else was I to do with the infernal thing? It was destined for the rubbish bin.

"What did the oracle say?" Bilt said slowly as if I was a child. Normally that would get under my skin but I was far too fat and happy to care, so I relayed the prophecy.

"*Oy*, verse."

I nodded. "That's what I thought. See, great minds think alike."

Bilt gave me his own version of the hairy eyeball before continuing. "Well, the Cursed is easy considering that wolfman you killed, what was his name?"

"Talbott."

"Can't people be original anymore? I swear, their love of cinema is going to give me *schpilkes*. So, you have the Dead to worry about, which brings to mind zombies. Now there's a tired old trope, let me tell you."

The two agents leaned back on the sectional, obviously fascinated. Probably better than reality TV. Then again, most things are.

"But to get back to the main," continued the tubby man. "The oracle said when the book reaches the start there is hope you can do something, do your part, didn't' she?"

"Yes."

"You must go to the start."

"That is the part that perplexes me. I reckoned the undead, ghosts or whatnot, will encounter us soon, but the entire start business has me scratching my head."

"Well, *boychik*, where do you think everything started?"

"'Let there be light.'" Branch crossed her arms and smiled. That was the second time. If she kept that up her face might break.

Silence reigned for a while until Carter said, "What?"

"'Let there be light', Book of Genesis."

"Good!" Bilt enthused. "Excellent, but not quite."

"Not quite?" asked Branch.

"Think a little farther down history's road, my dear lady."

It hit me and I wanted to smack my head in frustration. *How can I be so dim?* "He means Eden, Branch. The Garden of Eden."

That sure captured their attention, sharpish. "Eden?" Carter looked skeptical.

Branch chimed in. "Eden has been lost. It's guarded by the flaming sword of Heaven, entrusted to the Cherubim by God to guard the Garden."

"Ooo-hoo! Look who's so knowledgeable." Bilt's golden dentate reflected the rooms light. "When your Christ was crucified, the sword was removed from the entrance of the Garden so mankind could search out the perfect paradise. At least that's the rumor, innit? All you have to do is find the Garden."

"That's Eastern Orthodox belief, Mr. Biltmore," said Carter, scratching his chin. "Not really in line with Catholic dogma now."

"Ooo! Look, now we have two smarty pants. Who woulda thought?" Bilt's chubby face still bore the same gold encrusted smile. "Within every religion there's a kernel of truth, innit? Just so happens this is one of those kernels, *boychik*." He spread his hands wide in glee. "All you have to do is find the Garden of Eden and wait there for the book."

He spoke as if finding the garden was as easy as walking down to the corner market, but something hidden for millennia tends to remain hidden. If it was so easy, everyone would walk in toot-sweet, not to mention nations would start wars to see who would control the greatest discovery in in the history of mankind. I spoke up. "Great, we will leave in the morning. Pack your bags, Bilt, it is time for an adventure."

"Oh, no, no, no! I'm going nowhere with you, am I? People tend to die around you."

I pointed to the *Manus Dei*. "These two did not."

"Well, goodie for them. Give them a biscuit and send them on their way, they'll live longer."

"Come on, Bilt, do you not want to see the book again? Hold in your hands? Perhaps study it for an hour or two? Besides, we have no clue how to find the garden and we need your help."

Like a balloon with a pinhole leak, Bilt began to deflate until his shoulders slumped and I could not see the gold of his teeth anymore. "I can help you find the garden from here, thank you very much. As for me going...nope, as much as it pains me, my lad, not even to hold the Book of Ur again. Nope, never."

I studied him for a moment. Bilt could move giant boulders with his magic, call afrits with a spell, but faced with the possibility of danger seemed to unman him. It confused me, I thought he would jump at the chance to hold the book again.

We had a complex history, him and I, one based on respect if not trust and I felt in my bones, like a deep ache, that his participation gave us the best chance at success. "Do you want to see Jacob's Rule with the book, Bilt?"

"*Pfft*," he scoffed, waving a hand. "Jacob's Rule are a bunch of morons, which is the kindest thing I can say about them. They have money, but no brains. Children playing in the pen with lions not knowing when they're about to be eaten. I'm not afraid of white supremacists or their money. As for the Sicarii, they're distracted by other enemies and the Venerable

Church of the Unclean Word, well, let's just say they had a run-in with the Templars and find themselves in need of recruitment."

"What, or who, are you really afraid of, Bilt?" I asked.

"I'm afraid of nothing, ain't I?"

"Everyone is afraid of something, even me."

"Not me, I have everything I need, everything I could want." Bilt waved his arms around. "I am the premier magician on this planet, very little can actually harm me so I don't need to fear, do I?"

"Bullshit."

For the first time since he shot me, Bilt showed real anger. His eyes narrowed until only slices of brown and white showed and his normally placid face became scarred with a feral snarl. "Damn you, you asshole. I already told—"

"You are afraid of finding the book."

Bilt's golden jaws snapped shut and I spoke quickly before he could interrupt. "You are afraid that if we find the book, you will not be able to resist its call because of its addictive nature. Like a junkie who has given up heroin, the seductive call of the book will overcome your reason and you will try something incredibly stupid to try to steal it back." I crossed my arms. "It is the power; the ultimate drug and you are the ultimate junkie and God save anyone who tries to keep you from the book because you know you will do *anything* to keep it. Face it, Bilt, there is nothing you fear more."

"Damn you."

Score one for me. Why did it feel like I just kicked a puppy?

"Damn you to hell, Frank Vickers, Vincent Franks, Fredrick Valley and all the other names you've used. Damn you for looking into my soul and being right." Bilt sat there, slumped, defeated, looking like a man at the end of his rope. "Thanks to the book I've lived over a hundred years and haven't changed an inch. It offered me the secrets of the universe and took them like a baby to a mama's tit. I suckled on that knowledge and used to extend my life, to play with the fundamental forces of existence. That kind of power is worse than heroin or oxy, so yes...I'm a junkie, which is why I should thank you for taking it away from me."

"Then why did you shoot me, Bilt?"

A shrug. "For grins. Loved the look on your face, I did."

"So come with us. Help us."

"There's nothing you can offer me that would make me change my mind."

I kept a grin from my face, merely reaching into my front pocket to retrieve that which I took from the safety deposit box at Wells and held it out for Bilt to see.

My companions stared. Bilt's eyes bugged. "Well, I'll be damned. I guess I was wrong."

CHAPTER TWENTY

Scotssbluff, Nebraska, October 1901

I think days passed, at least two or three, tied up in that damned cave with no company except for vampires and a small hoard of Daddy Longleg spiders. When Darius let me recover from a daily draining of blood, the spiders crawled over me with careless abandon and I let them, they proved harmless.

I tried to break the shackles the bound my body but Darius's feeding kept me weak and I could hardly feel my fingers anymore. My toes as well. Another thing on a very long list to hold against the vampires.

In the time between draining my mind drifted in a fog of memory, reliving moments from my past like watching moving pictures from a French cinematographie, but played at ridiculous speeds. *One second I sip tea in a village outside of Munich, the next I kill a mugger with one blow of my mighty hand, feeling the crack a bones throughout my flesh. A monk lashes out and I dodge to the side only to receive a kick to the groin. I double up and drop, the monk standing over me shaking his head.*

Over and over these little pictures flashed through my mind as I lay in a spider-laden daze within that sandstone cave set so far back the light of day did not penetrate the gloom. The constant draining of my blood keeping me within that stupor and even my heroic regeneration could not cope, not without food to sustain it, which was denied to me by my captors. They only provided spare cups of water.

No matter how much it whined, Darius would not let his offspring drink from the chalice of my flesh, saving me only for himself. His wormy lips touched my skin and I felt the kiss of razor teeth, he sucked and sucked until his belly lay gorged with my blood. Every time he would shudder and shake as with obscene sexual pleasure. Every time he seemed to grow stronger, although his diamond eyes never grew clearer or evidenced change.

"Wake up, morsel."

The crooning voice broke me from my torpor and I opened my eyes to see the ruby ones of Darius' offspring. A knot of fear balled in my gut.

"Father is gone a-hunting," it said with a leering smile. "He loves your blood, but he loves the thrill of the kill even more."

"Go...eat...shit," I managed, shaking loose spiders.

"It's a shame to hear such an erudite man speak in such callous terms."

"Pardon...me." I cleared my throat in an effort to clear my thoughts. "Remove yourself...and consume...vast quantities of...fecal matter."

That earned me a smiled dominated by two-inch fangs, a smile that would have most men shit their drawers. "My, defiant. I like that."

I stared into those dark ruby eyes and knew what he was about to do. I struggled against my bonds, but the chains bound me well.

It lunged forward and those needle teeth punctured my throat while cold lips clamped tight with the ruthlessness of a lamprey, sucking, sucking, sucking.

My mind flew back, sent to the distant past by blood loss and I knew then I would die from this draining and that small, mean part of me actually wished for this end, to be relieved from the burden of life. I breathed a last sigh as my heart slowed, its normal staccato rhythm becoming labored and turgid.

I traveled back years and years to a time when I looked upon the world with new eyes:

Stumbling through broken fields of shattered rock and tattered bodies, limbs strewn about with careless abandon as if torn from trunks by a cruel, malevolent child. I do not know what they are, only that the smell of blood and the acrid odor gunpowder stings my nose, although at that point I have no name for the stench. Only that it hurts my watering eyes.

A man emerges from the evening fog bare-headed, long hair flowing past his shoulders over a chainmail hauberk. The sword he carries is curved; steely death held in one hand. His bearded faces opens in a scream as he lunges toward me, but he stops as he nears, clearly startled.

"Shaitan!" he breathes just before lunging at me.

I stumble back, confused, not knowing the word he uses or the garbling gabble that I later realized was a prayer.

The blade whistles as he oversteps and anger floods me. I charge and swing a meaty fist that punches through his face and deep into his skull. He drops as shattered bone cuts my knuckles, which are heavily coated in blood and brain. I stare at my fist and note the transparent skin and the blue tracery of vessels beneath that float above pink muscle.

The bloodied ground flashes by as I run and keep running, naked and afraid into this strange land for which I have no definition. I am without context or knowledge, a tabula rasa given monstrous form. Torn metal cuts my feet, but I pay no attention for I am as an animal, surviving on instinct alone. Away I run, away from others because I know they will try to kill me for I know now I am different and to them different means they will want me dead.

Trees suddenly surround me, sheltering me from the stars, but I keep running despite the fire in my lungs and the hitch in my side because fear gives me strength. Bushes and branches scrape my skin, drawing blood, their sting goes unnoticed because the fear propels me, forces me to ignore these slights. I run and run until my body fails and I fall to the forest floor, cushioned by leaves. For a long time I know no more.

Wetness on my face. A slow, drawn-out warbling sound that cuts through the ringing in my ears. I tasted salty copper, familiar.

More warbling.

"Glagh." Best I could do, my throat so dry it felt as if it was packed with brittle leaves.

"Uncle? Uncle!"

Me. Uncle? Uncle. "Elllsss?"

"Yeah, me Ellis. You remember?"

Of course I did, but Ellis lay abed in his nice comfy house, not here with the spiders. That honor was mine. I tried again. "Ellsss?"

"Here." Cool water trickled into my mouth. My God, Heaven! "Slowly, Uncle, slowly or you'll throw it up."

Slowly? How could I? My greedy lips wanted more...more...more. Then that fabulous elixir disappeared. "No!"

"Easy, there. Open your eyes.

Were they shut? Interesting. Although it felt as if twin boulders perched upon my lids, I gathered what will remained and forced them open. Soft lantern light met my eyes along with a visage that lifted my heart.

Ellis. Smiling. *How nice.*

"Good to see you lad." My throat managed to produce the words past the dried leaves. The water worked its miracle and though I felt logy and listless I became more aware than I had in days. I tested the manacles around my wrists but they still held. I was far too weak to affect an escape. Grunting and straining, I sat up, spilling spiders off of my body. "Can you pick the lock?"

"Aren't you wondering why you're all wet?"

That took me aback and I looked about. At my feet knelt Ellis holding the lantern while at my side lay the vampire child of Darius's, minus the top ten percent of his body, the stump leaking blood onto thirsty sandstone. "It appears to be missing the space between its ears."

Ellis grinned, lifting a shotgun. "Amazing what will happen at close range."

Amazing indeed. "I did not think a vampire could be killed by a shotgun to the skull. We learn something new every day. Still, it does not remove the shackles."

That earned me another grin from his wide face. "Just so happens, Uncle, I may have a solution to our dilemma." Ellis set the shotgun down and pulled out a rucksack, pouring out the contents onto my lap. Dried meat, apples, candy, a cornucopia of tasties for yours truly. "When you didn't come back in the morning, I reckoned you found yourself in a bad spot, so I decided to go a-hunting. Took me a couple of days, but I spied with my little eye a small cave a couple hundred feet up Scott's Bluff and I thought to myself, 'self, if I were keeping a lion captive where it would be difficult to for him to escape, wouldn't a cave up the side of a steep drop be perfect?' and I answered, 'self, that's a brilliant idea, let's go give it a look, shall we?' Well, that's what I did, although it took a couple of days to get the gear and supplies so I could make a good rescue attempt."

Elllis began feeding me food one piece at a time and I greedily consumed it all with abandon, hardly chewing at all. The candy disappeared the quickest. "You know Uncle, you should have let me come with you in the first place."

"Then you would be dead," I managed around a mouthful of beef jerky. I asked for more water.

"Be that as it may, you took a foolish risk with the monster."

"Monsters."

"Come again?"

"Plural. Monsters. More candy." I could feel strength returning to my limbs. After a couple more minutes of gorging, I tested my bonds, flexing with all my burgeoning strength and the snap of metal rewarded me.

"Thank the Lord," I muttered, grabbing at an apple. It fell through numb fingers.

Ellis smiled grimly. "I guess we'll have to wait until your hands recover."

"Damn."

Pins and needles began at my fingertips, slowly building toward the palms, a sensation not unlike acidic cobwebs sliding across my skin. Within moments my hands were afire with agony, but I kept my focus on consuming more food fed to me by my companion. "I am lucky you did not take my ear off with that scattergun," I said before another gulp of water.

"You kidding, Uncle, I can practically shave with this thing." Ellis grinned wide, happier than I had seen him since his wedding, which made it worse when suddenly his head separated from his body. The lantern fell and cracked, spilling flaming oil onto sandstone.

Darius grinned around the bloodied blade of a fourteen-inch bowie knife. "I hated his voice *so* much."

Ellis.

Perhaps the vampire desired witty repartee, but I was fresh out. Only the rage remained. That and the black hole in my heart that used to house Ellis's presence. I leapt at Darius, hands outstretched. The tip of the bowie entered my left palm as if it was gossamer and slid out back of my hand, the pain a shock that traveled up my arm like lightning, but pain and I were old friends. I ignored it, making a fist and yanking the knife from the vampire's hand.

Suddenly I found myself in the middle of a whirlwind, one formed of claws, teeth and unimaginable hate that spun me around and around in storm of blood. Bear-like claws raked my forearms drawing great welters of blood that splashed the cave while my good hand stayed firmly wrapped around an icy throat. I slammed my hand against its skull, my palm sliding down the blade to give me fresh pain. The knife popped free and the beast *screamed*, a high, piercing shriek that slid into my ears like an ice pick.

Snarling, I placed both hands on the side of the thing's head and dug my thumbs into its eyes as it raked my shoulders with it's bear claws, shredding my flesh to the bone. That did not affect my forearms, though, and my thumbs pushed into those diamond eyes *hard*, so hard, hard enough to push them back deep into it's skull until my thumbs were knuckle-deep into it's head.

If I thought it screamed before, then I was sorely mistaken because what came out of it's mouth sounded like a cross between the Trumps of Doom and the tortured rip of tearing metal, but I did not care, not one bit and I kept pushing until it's head came apart in my big hands with a hellish crack leaving them covered in blood and brains.

As I shook the flesh from my hands the body began to wither, crumbling into dust with the sound of crackling leaves until nothing remained but it's eyes. Moments later I was left with two bodies, handfuls of dust and a pair of diamond orbs.

"Aww, Ellis," I mourned, cradling his headless body. "Not you, too."

Later, with a face full of tears, I dropped Ellis's head and body down the side of bluff where they rolled to a stop a couple hundred feet away. I could see where he had cut hand and footholds into the soft sandstone and marveled at the effort he must have made. It was a tribute to his determination and love and fresh tears leaked from my yellow eyes. I knew that those shallow grooves would not hold my great weight, so I did the logical thing...I jumped.

CHAPTER TWENTY-ONE

"What I can't get through my head is why horses?" Carter sat on the back of his bay mare like sack of grain, obviously feeling a goodly amount of discomfort in his hind parts that rested in the saddle.

It took discipline, but I kept the smile from stealing onto my face. "Bilt says it is necessary and I do not cotton to go against the sweet end of his wisdom."

Branch had no reservation and grinned like she found out she won the lottery, which in a manner of speaking seemed to be the case considering her enjoyment. This did not endear her to her fellow agent.

"Keep your heels down so that nag don't unseat you, *boychik*," said Bilt, riding up on a dapple gelding with a spark in its eye.

Carter glared, but did as he was told, riding his bay in a circle so he could get a better feel for the animal. At one time I reckoned he might have argued a bit, but the time of his natural argumentativeness had long since passed, which I guessed was good thing. Life is the best teacher and those that listen to those lessens tend to live longer than those who do not.

Two days since the evening in the Rockies, three days of Bilt keeping his silence except for terse words here and there after agreeing to accompany us. By my reckoning we were late by a perhaps at most a day, perhaps as little as a few hours. Late, but maybe we had time enough to complete the job.

At the cabin Bilt looked at what I held in the palm of my hand, his face turning white, and exclaimed, "How the hell did you get those?"

"How do you think?" I replied.

With fingers trembling as if palsied, he stretched out his hand and I dropped the two diamonds in his palm.

"Gems?" Carter asked with a frown. "You're bribing him with diamonds the size of ping-pong balls? Why not give him money instead?"

"These aren't just ordinary diamonds, are they?" Bilt held them to the light. "They're *eyes*."

"Eyes?" Branch shook her head. "They're diamonds. Big diamonds, but diamonds nonetheless."

"No." Bilt's breathing was ragged, as if his breath struggled mightily to escape. "They're the eyes of a vampire. A *master* vampire."

I felt my scars stretch as I smiled. "You see, my young friends, vampires have gemstones for eyes. The older the vampire, the lighter they become until the vampire reaches the height of its power...then those eyes become diamonds. I took those from a master vampire in Scottsbluff, Nebraska over a hundred years ago. It turned into dust upon its death, but the eyes remained." Fond memories. Except for Ellis. "It had an offspring who was too young to become dust, instead shriveling to a mummified state. I have it's eyes, too."

That grabbed Bilt's attention, but he kept his attention on the diamonds. "You have them now?"

I held out a pair of dark, dark rubies that glittered in the light. "Yes."

"Gimme!" exclaimed the tubby little man.

My fingers curled around the orbs. "Only when you agree to guide us to Eden."

"Anything!"

"Done."

Bilt gave a golden grin. "Then we'll need horses, rugged clothing, small gold ingots, and travel rations for a couple of days."

The two agents looked dumbfounded. "Horses?"

My laughter shook the room. "I can help with that."

Cordelia, New Mexico, thirty miles outside of Taos. A large spread of land filled with scrub grass, pinon pine, juniper, white fir and a creek or two for good measure. It served as a preserve for rescue animals. Dozens of horses, goats, dogs, cats, cows, llamas, ostrich, chickens, and the occasional tortoise, among others. My pet project (pardon the pun) that I financed through one of shell companies. I had a soft spot for children, but the abuses animals suffered at the hands of their owners would turn your hair white and they needed a place to feel safe. Just like everybody.

Carter's mount was a sturdy Morgan, while Branch sat astride a Quarter Horse/Arab cross and Bilt set his fundament on an old Thoroughbred I saved from becoming glue. As for myself, I rode a Percheron (named him Jed, of course), a breed I had grown familiar with during my long stint in the Wild West. Black as sin and headstrong, it held my weight as if I was a toddler. Every now and then I would come to the preserve to ride and check the animals, most of whom were grateful to have a little peace and quiet and a regular meal. It always calmed my nerves and put a smile on my face, a sensation I needed more and more often as the world tumbled into the future with great violence and hate. Things are simpler when surrounded by animals that look to you with love rather than fear, it eases the mind and smooths out bad feelings.

"You have been keeping your cards close to your vest, Bilt. Do you mind letting us know what comes next?" I asked.

We all wore tough denim trousers, canvas dusters, and rucks attached to the back of the saddles. Except for Bilt, our saddles also held rifles, mine a Lee Enfield while the two agents opted for Ruger American Ranch that shot 5.56 NATO rounds and between us there were enough bullets to start a small Latin American war. My collection of weapons back at the ranch house included more powerful weapons, but Bilt told us they would not be needed, that we would travel light.

I pulled my Stetson down over my eyes to shield them from the midday sun while my companions found shade with baseball caps. Go figure that Carter was a Yankees fan. No accounting for taste.

"What comes next, you great big bastard, is we ride for Eden," he answered.

Carter looked surprised. "Eden is in the US?"

Bilt looked askance at Carter. "Are you daft, *boychik*? This trip's a metaphysical one as much as physical. There's only one way to Eden and the book let me know how it's done, it did. You best pray to your Catholic god that we do this right or we ain't coming back no matter how hard we ride." He looked to the sky. "Our shadows are getting long, aren't they? Magic time, a sacred time, time to get a ride one. You all stay close to me, no more than a couple of feet. Follow me exactly, do what I say or you'll be lost. Forever."

"The things I do for the Church." Carter spat on the dry and dusty ground.

"Could be worse," said Branch with a smile.

"How? How could this be worse?"

"Could be raining."

I'm really starting to like her. I grinned and Bilt let loose a belly laugh that shook the air all around and urged us to follow as he put his Thoroughbred into a trot. We rode close like he instructed, Carter bouncing like a novice sure to earn his rear end bruises.

Bilt held up one of the diamonds to the fading light and in his palm they glowed with a faint, fey light. "Umph. Good. We're on the right track, my hearties."

Carter leaned over to whisper to Branch. "Did he say 'my hearties'?"

"Yup."

"Good. Thought so. For a second I thought I was hallucinating."

For a time Bilt led us around in a wide circle, muttering and gesticulating. Every now and then I caught a snippet of words I had not heard in years. Ancient Hebrew mixed with ancient Egyptian. The agents asked and I replied, startled that I recognized the language. I merely shrugged and said, "I read a lot." Call it the benefit of a classical education.

Minutes later Bilt called a halt. He dismounted and took a large swig out of his canteen, water dripping into his luxurious black beard. "Glad I waited for Wednesday. Wotan's Day. Auspicious time for magical doings, it is. Now Monday, Moon's Day, would be straight out unless it was a full moon and Thursday, Thor's Day, well, let's just say I wasn't in the mood to sacrifice a goat or three."

At the agents' mystified looks he continued, "Every day has a certain magical aspect, a certain time for great magical doings. For example, on Sunday, Sun's Day, we would have had to wait until noon when our shadows lay directly under our feet and strip naked so's the sun could shine on skin." He rubbed his belly fondly. "I really don't think you need to see my colorful, egg-shaped body or my pride and joy waving about, do you?"

Branch made a face.

"Thought not," Bilt said dryly. "It was an auspicious turn that we started on Wotan's Day. Now, dismount and wait a spell, this will be the short trip, it will. The next leg will be much longer."

We did as he bid and I took a sip from my own canteen. Lemon-flavored Gatorade. Never did much take to the taste of water from a metal canteen. Too tinny.

"What are we waiting for?" asked Branch.

Bilt pointed up. We followed his fingers and we all gave out gasps of wonder.

The sky still shone a bright blue like a robin's egg, pristine and pure with not a cloud to mar its beauty. It was the kind of sky that motion pictures tried to capture, but failed. You could stare at it forever and be lost in wonder for ages except for one small fact.

The sun was gone.

Light remained, but the source proved to be a mystery, only the blue sky remained above. Everything seemed the same, only the absent sun marked the strangeness of the moment like a turd in a punch bowl.

"Still looks like New Mexico," said Carter pointing all around at the scrub grass and pinon pine. "Damn, lost my hat somewhere..."

"Well, maybe it is, maybe it isn't and as we travel your lost hat will be the least of your problems." Bilt stretched and gave with a yawn that stretched wide revealing enough gold to pay for a Cadillac. "You never know with these things, do you? Magic isn't an exact science, *boychik*. In other words, you have to ride this coaster until the end. Where we'll end up, I can only guess."

Carter sighed. "Are you ever going to give a straight answer?"

"Oh, hell no. I deliberately keep things vague for a reason. Take a page from your big friend there, he's willing to wing it until the mission is done, he is. He trusts me if only that I'll not act against my own self-interest." He grinned. "Which is true for most of us, if you think about it. Well, it won't be long now."

As if the universe heard his pronouncement and complied we suddenly found ourselves beneath a sun a hand's breath from the horizon and a familiar mountain range to the northeast. "Well, that is Mt. Wheeler. We are still in New Mexico." I remarked. It took me a moment to realize I no longer wore my colored contact lenses. Instead I found a pair of old-fashioned wire-rimmed sunglasses perched on my nose. *Strange.*

"I thought this was going to be a journey," said Branch, mounting her Arab cross.

"It is a journey, darling," said Bilt from the top of the Thoroughbred. "We might still be in New Mexico, but the journey's begun. Now don't be giving me the stink eye, young lady. You'll find out soon enough and don't ask. I wouldn't spoil the surprise for all the tea in China."

I sniffed the air, smelling only dust and a familiar purity I had long forgotten. My grin stretched my scars. "Bilt, you old scoundrel. If I knew what kind of chicanery you were up to, I would not have believed it at all."

"It's good to be a wizard, you big omadhaun."

Branch saved the stink eye for me. "You know what he's up to?"

"I surely do and trust me; the surprise is well worth it. Come on, let us ride to Taos." Setting heels to Jed's barrel, I trotted away toward the night.

Dark came fully by the time the first faint light of the town came into sight, the heavens above opening itself up in all its glory. Stars beyond counting, nebulae and planets shining down to illuminate our way. It had been a powerful spell since such a sight greeted my eyes. The modern world filled the sky with light pollution, blotting out the wonders of the universe and seeing them so exposed brought exaltation to my tired and jaded heart. My companions, Bilt included, stared upward in constant, total amazement while I led them to glittering lantern light.

What at first you might think to be a one of those man-made Old West studio towns used for filming movies turned out to be the real deal. I knew it like I knew the back of my own gnarled hands. Taos in the 19th century sure as I was riding a damn fine horse.

"What is this?" whispered Branch.

"Taos. In the 1870s if I am not mistaken," I answered.

"We're in the *past*?"

"Yup. I have been here before."

Bilt laughed. "How the fuck did you think we were going to get to Eden, young lady? A road seldom traveled, it is."

For a moment I thought she would, as people say, lose her shit, but she screwed her mouth shut and nodded once."

Carter sighed. "The things I do for the fucking Church."

I added to Bilt's laughter with my own. "Come on, I know where we can get a drink and a decent meal."

We tethered our horses in front of a place called the Jericho Jewel, a lively looking little joint where laughter and music spilled out of the windows along with warm firelight that lit the wooden sidewalk. Without hesitation I pushed my way through the saloon doors followed by my companions and I couldn't stop a grin from appearing.

"Jericho Watkins, you old scoundrel," I hollered. "Give me a bottle of bond and four glasses. Something to eat would be fine as well."

Behind the bar stood a stout man in a white shirt and vest, bushy brown beard turning to gray, with impressively large forearms and spectacles on a pug nose. His apple cheeks and smile lines beside his eyes informed all of his good humor.

"Fred?" said the bartender. "Is that you?"

"You know anyone else that looks like me, Jericho?" I picked a table and sat, enduring the stares of the whores and the card players. In the corner a black man played a lively tune on a piano, long fingers dancing along the keys like a spider on a hot plate. I knew him just like I knew Jericho and the names of half the soiled doves that led customers upstairs to their bedrooms.

A big smile plastered itself onto Jericho's round face, but it faded quickly. "Now, Fred, you know we don't serve their kind here." He pointed a stubby finger Bilt's way.

The music stopped as the player sensed unwelcome violence might ensue. My companion merely smiled his golden smile and leaned back in his chair.

"Now, Jericho, he is with me." I nodded to the agents. "They all are, even the woman dressed as a man, so you get Juan to stable and feed our horses and I will forgive your lapse in manners." My glare cut through the bartender. "Or do we have a problem?"

"N-no puh-problem, Fred," he stammered. He shouted for his livery boy and in short order we found ourselves in possession of a bottle of bonded, four glasses and assurances that a meal was forthcoming.

The whiskey burned all the way down and set up fiery shop in my stomach. My companions partook as well. Soon enough we had plates of beans and a bowl of beef stew so good the smell qualified as a meal in and of itself. It did not take long for us to wolf down the entire thing and let me tell you it felt like coming home.

Before we finished, the music started back up and the ladies went back to plying their age-old commerce while Jericho still tossed Bilt the old side-eye whilst pouring drinks.

I forgot how much I loved this era of human history, warts and all. The days of westward expansion toward the Pacific. Sure, growth like this came at a steep cost: the ill treatment of the natives and the Chinese, smallpox, horrible weather and the slaughter of the buffalo. It was a hard, desperate time filled with terror, but also moments of unbelievable beauty and grace. It was time of myth and legend, Paul Bunyan and Pecos Bill, Wyatt Earp and Doc Holliday. God, I did not realize how much I missed those days.

"Ya big galoot, you don't even have the moral courtesy of calling on an old friend." The speaker pulled up a chair and sat down, placing his hat on the table. He was a lean man weathered by sun and wind with a long handlebar moustache and sporting a fine black three-piece suit and a tin star.

"I reckoned you'd show up eventually, Klaus," I said drily, downing another shot of bonded whiskey. *One thing I can say about the 20th Century...better booze.* "Lady and gentlemen, allow me to make introductions, this is sheriff Klaus Bischoff, formerly a professor of mathematics in Germany, the good law in this flyspeck town."

Klaus gave with a big smile that showed a missing front tooth. "It is a genuine pleasure to meet you all," he said with slight touch of a German accent. "If I am not mistaken, this gentleman is from the famed sub-continent."

"Sheriff, let me introduce you to my companions. Mr. Carter and Miss Branch from the Pinkerton Detective Agency and the esteemed professor of anthropology in New York City, Dr. Biltmore."

"Charmed, I am sure." To me. "I knew you kept interesting company, Fred, but a professor from India and Pinkerton agents, one a member of the fairer sex at that, well, you have outdone yourself."

"Miss Branch can out-drink and outfight most men I know, Klaus, and Dr. Biltmore is the most learned you will ever meet. As for Mr. Carter, let us just say that while he does not look like much, most men cannot handle themselves better."

Branch. "Pleasure to meet you, Sheriff."

Carter. "Same goes for me."

Bilt. "How do you know this great ape of a man? I'd think you'd have better taste in friends, I do."

Klaus laughed. "I'll allow he does nothing for the ladies in the looks department, but he is a dab hand with helping out an old man with miscreants bent on mayhem."

"Sheriff, if you do not mind, would you mind providing me with the date?"

That earned me a look. "Well, Fred, it's been only three weeks since you rode out."

"July, 1877, correct?"

"What are you up to, Fred?"

A gunshot rang out. "Sheriff, I would have words!" The voice came from outside the Jewel.

"Aw, hellfire," said Klaus, rising and drawing his pistol.

CHAPTER TWENTY-TWO

Denver, November 1904

"What did you do then?" the fat man asked, drinking his shot of cloudy rum.

"Well, I told the girls there was plenty of me to go around and bought them *both* for the night!"

The Buckhorn Exchange squatted toad-like on Osage street in the heart of the city, two thin stories of bar/restaurant that catered to everyone from miners, silver barons, to red Indians. It served decent food and plenty of it and every kind of liquor a man could ask for, both of which suited me down to my toes.

The fat man, one Arliss Townsey, roared loud and long, his laughter bouncing off the wooden walls and shaking the stuffed animals that decorated every square inch of the restaurant. "You are a pip," he wheezed, taking a sip of his cloudy rum. "A real pip, mister."

I tipped him a nod and tore into my buffalo steak. It was lean, charred nicely and tasted like heaven after a fair passel of time on a train from Washington D.C. eating the pig slop they called food in the dining car.

Townsey dressed nice, the only nice thing about the man. He talked too loud, his hair had too much oil and his greedy, piggy brown eyes had sick sort of lustful cheer. Just looking at his smug face made me want to bury my fist down his throat.

"Thanks, Townsey," I said around one last big bite of buffalo. "But I have to go. People to see, whores to fuck." All bullshit, of course. Townsey was my business. That and putting paid to *his* business, but I needed to dangle the hook and see if he would go for the bait.

Weeks earlier, while in my New York office, a slender man dressed in a dove gray suit walked in unannounced. He was tall, with light brown hair, high, hard cheekbones and piercing blue eyes that spoke of a sharp mind. I noticed a gold pinkie ring as he extended his hand.

"Guy Virtanen," he said simply.

"Welcome, sir," I returned, shaking his hand gently. "Have we met?" My business was on a referral basis only and the office had no sign. Everything was kept quite hush-hush, just how I preferred.

"You were recommended by Representative Hearst." He pulled a cream-colored envelope from his jacket pocket. "This is a letter from the worthy gentleman. He said it was the only way you would accept my case was by referral."

I nodded, took the envelope and indicated he should sit. The famous newspaperman had employed me on several occasions, the last to thwart a very real threat against his life. With a small smile, I read the terse letter of introduction finalized with the Representative's cramped, near illegible, scrawl. "Mr. Hearst is too kind," I said after I sat. "What can I do for you?"

He studied me for a moment. "I trust I have your complete discretion?"

"You already know this, or Mr. Hearst would not have sent you, sir." The fear it would be another case of blackmail against a rich philanderer bloomed inside me and I moved to the wet bar to pour a drink. "Bourbon? Wait...Virtanen...you're a Finn, so you would probably prefer vodka."

"Not a Finn," he said in surprise. "Estonian, but close enough. Yes, vodka would be wonderful."

I poured our drinks and sat down, savoring the fine taste of Spear's bourbon as it rolled across my tongue. "Mr. Virtanen, because of who I am and the things I do you are here to engage my service on behalf of either a politician or a very rich person, or perhaps they are one and the same." His eyes lit up in appreciation of the vodka as he took a sip and I smiled. "Therefore, in the parlance of the man on the street, let us cut the foreplay and get down to it. What do you want?" Crude, but I had an appointment with my barber and I hated to be late.

"Mr. Hearst said you are a blunt man."

"Mr. Hearst *is* a blunt man," I countered.

"Very true, although he is a very good friend of my patron, Mr. Samuel Riverwood. Have you heard of him?"

Ah, a rich man, then, not a politician. "Of course. He is a famous oil and sugar man out of St. Louis, if I am not mistaken. Makes Hearst look like a beggar."

"Indeed. Did you know he had a young son, a Charles Riverwood?"

A cold wind blew across my soul and I knew what Virtanen was there for. "Had? Past tense. The boy is dead?" My voice dropped nearly an octave and I felt my hands start to clench. It took a considerable portion of my will not to crush the tumbler of bourbon.

Virtanen nodded.

Of course. "Recently?"

"He was discovered a month ago," he said, his handsome face became frosty with dire emotions and I realized he knew the boy, perhaps even loved him. My estimation of the man began to rise. "His body washed up on shore just shy of Memphis."

"Long way from St. Louis."

Again, he nodded.

I folded my hands in front of me and took a deep breath. "Start from the beginning."

The vodka disappeared down Virtanen's throat. "Five months ago, Charles went missing from a day trip with his nanny and a bodyguard, a man named Welsh. Mr. Riverwood contacted the authorities and a search was conducted. Three days later, they found the bodies of the nanny and Welsh buried in shallow graves near Lake Madison. Of Charles, nothing was found until his body washed up on shore four months later. From the conclusions of the private physician hired by Mr. Riverwood, the boy appears to have been strangled and his body thrown into the river. But that seems to have been done months *after* the kidnapping.

"Sir, I ask you in your investigative capacity, if this was an ordinary kidnapping, why was there no ransom demand? If it was an act of revenge, and Mr. Riverwood, like most rich men, has a plethora of enemies, why wasn't the boy killed immediately?" He sat there and waited for my response.

I leaned back and closed my eyes, thinking hard. The rich can afford rewards, although charlatans and confidence men appear as if by magic when one is offered. No, Riverwood wanted to deal with this swiftly and quietly, which was my specialty. No feast for the newspaper gore crows to pick at, no horrifying details to shock the populace. It only took a minute for me to come to a conclusion "There is more that you have not said."

"Indeed."

"It will be ugly, yes?" I asked.

A heavy sigh filled with simmering anger. "Indeed."

"Tell me."

"The boy was...used poorly. And often."

"I will take the case." No hesitation. There are worse monsters than me out there and I aimed to trim their numbers down a fair bit.

Virtanen's eyebrows shot up. "No negotiations on your fee?"

I shook my head. "None. You will give me $10,000 for expenses, no ifs ands, or buts. Upon the conclusion of this case, Mr. Riverwood will owe me a favor which he will grant, when asked for, with no qualms or equivocations, no matter the legality."

With a grim smile, Virtanen pulled from his copious pockets three more envelopes. "Fifteen thousand dollars, sir. Keep what you don't use, just as long as you catch the person or persons responsible. As for the favor, consider it granted."

Hearst must have informed Riverwood about my peculiar method of remuneration. I dealt in cash, of course, but my primary compensation was favors, which was the greater currency. "I am not to be interfered with in any way, but from time to time I may need information vital to the case and said information will be offered with no hesitation."

"Done. Although I would like to be part of this investigation. However, your secrets and methods I will take to my grave, sir."

I opened my eyes and stared at Virtanen from behind my colored spectacles. His face was flushed and his nostrils flared. The big muscles at the corners of his jaw were clenched so hard they seemed ready to burst from his skin in a shower of blood. "What was he to you?"

He blinked in surprise. "What?"

"The boy. What was he to you?"

"My employer's son," he said evenly.

"Bullshit. Do not lie to me, it insults my intelligence."

Virtanen's fair skin colored and he answered, the words forced out of his mouth as if with fishhooks. "I've been Mr. Riverwood's valet, assistant, bodyguard, and all-around dogsbody for twelve years now and I've never been happier. From the first, he treated me with respect and like a member of the family. I was there when the boy was born, waiting with his father in the downstairs drawing room as his mother screamed and bled. I was there watching when his father held him for the first time, squalling and purple, still dripping with birth slime. When he took his first steps, I watched and his first word to me was Uncle." Virtanen's voice cracked and naked grief suffused his face, raw and hurting. He was in such pain that I made to stand, my mouth opening to let loose inane words of comfort, but he waved me back. Seconds of struggle brought composure and he continued in a dry, dead voice. "I watched him grow, sir, from an infant to a young boy any man would be proud to call 'son' and I loved him so much. I loved him from the moment he opened his brilliant blue eyes to the moment we set him into the cold, stony soil of Missouri and now my heart is barren, sir, barren because he was, in a very real sense, mine as well. Can you fathom that, sir, loving the child of another man, someone you look up to and admire beyond words? Someone you love and would kill or die for?"

All too well. I let the words die before they reached my lips.

By the end of his speech, tears tracked down the Virtanen's cheeks and in seconds he aged years. I could only nod, unable to trust my own voice while tears beaded up behind my spectacles.

"One last thing, sir," Virtanen said, standing and primly adjusting his splendid jacket. "This is from me, not Mr. Riverwood, mind you. When you find the culprits, I want you to kill the motherfuckers."

That was an agreement I could easily make and I shook his hand to seal the deal.

Most people would talk to the coppers or spread word of a reward. I went to those who could help the most: criminals.

Usually those on the other side of the law would not flap their lips my way save to curse me up one side and down the other, but even to the most hardened, nasty criminal a child killer is beyond the pale. After spending nearly $8,000 and twisting arms, I finally caught wind of something useful.

"You think he knows anything?" Virtanen asked later, smoking a hand rolled and adjusting his derby. The wind rolled harsh and wet down Broadway St. in Columbia, Missouri. The remaining shoppers and students were abandoning the evening for the comfort of indoors.

I nodded. "Blue-Eyes said he was the man who knows all about the criminal underground in the Midwest. Patience, young man. Patience is the key to everything."

Blue-Eyes was a St. Louis pimp of renown, a big Norseman built like a blond bear, and he informed us that if anyone could help me in my endeavors, it would be a man named Fisk, a confidence man and pickpocket living in Columbia. I thanked the big pimp, paid him $2,000, but did not apologize for the dislocated shoulder. I would not have dislocated it if he had been a little more forthcoming.

Having another body while chasing down a slippery weasel like Fisk, the type that possessed a sixth sense when it came to danger, would be useful. If not handled correctly, the man could disappear for a long time. I contacted Virtanen and found him more than willing to join the hunt.

We stood in front of a ladies' clothier, hunched under the overhang just out of the rain. The owner had been giving us the evil eye, but one look at my face quelled any desire to ask us to leave. Virtanen looked the gentleman, but not me. Dressed in my oiled canvas coat, riding boots, thick canvas pants and shapeless hat, I looked the part of a shabby cowboy down on his luck, just two steps away from committing robbery to keep from starving.

I thrust my chin at an approaching man. "There he is."

Virtanen grunted and puffed his foul-smelling cigarette.

Out of the rain came a copper, slicked jacket dribbling water and looking like a drowned hound dog with his drooping, soaked mustache.

"Your man is in a rough-and-tumble two blocks from here named Shandy's," he said. "He's been drinking powerful, so I don't think he'll be much trouble." The copper, a middle-aged florid-faced Irish type, sneezed explosively and blew snot onto the slick cobbles. Without preamble he held out a large hand, which I crossed with several hundred dollars.

"Nice doing business with you, gentlemen," he said with a gap-toothed smile. "Just remember not to kill him."

Virtanen scowled. "No promises."

"Then you get rid of the body," the copper snapped, turning away back into the rain.

"Not very polite," I observed.

"Men like him are a blight," he said.

"Men like him make my job easier."

"That buys him forgiveness, then. Let's get that asshole."

We traveled downs Broadway keeping to overhangs and awnings to the 'rough-and-tumble' called Shandy's, a dive bar and brothel that we found catered to the university students that lived in town. Once there, I laid a hand on Virtanen's shoulder, keeping him from crossing the street and entering the bar.

"What are you waiting for?" he snapped, eager as a hound at the leash.

I grinned. "Let the man drink his fill and carouse a bit. A drunk man puts up less of a fight and will more likely succumb to pressure."

He considered this then nodded. "Patience?"

"Patience," I affirmed with a smile. So, we waited in an alley, cold and miserable, while our prey drank and fucked until the midnight hour. It was tedious, boring work, but necessary.

"Is that him? I can't tell, it's too dark," Virtanen whispered, elbowing me in the gut while I half-dozed. It had been his turn at watch.

I peered into the street, the darkness giving way to my enhanced sight. "Skinny, mustache trimmed thin, and big mole on his cheek. Yep, that is him."

"Damn, your eyes are better than mine."

"Let us go."

We ambled across the street toward where the weaving Fisk stood swaying slightly and lighting a fat cigar. Thin was too kind a description, he was gaunt, almost emaciated, his pants loose around his waist and held up with a pair of suspenders. His cheeks were sallow and his skin chalky and although he was a man in his mid-twenties, hard living had aged him a couple of decades, adding gray to the hair flowing out from beneath a battered bowler hat.

Ten steps to go, a couple of long strides from wringing answers from that lowlife.

Then Virtanen fucked it all up.

"Harry Fisk," he hollered, sounding tough and pissed off.

Skinny and drunk he might have been, but Harry Fisk took off quick as a jackrabbit, bounding along wooden sidewalks and down the nearest alley. He moved so fast most athletes would have been put to shame.

Growling, I gave chase with Virtanen fast on my heels. My boots were not made for running, but I made do, slipping and sliding through mud and slop and other dubious bits of matter best left undescribed as I hit the alley at speed.

My eyes were filled with rage at my temporary partner, his foolishness for alerting our prey and my stupidity for including him in the first place. I made a mental note to work alone from then on. *Amateurs.*

Fisk's splashing footfalls, plus my untrammeled vision, gave me plenty of clues as to his location and my long strides had me ahead of Virtanen, who huffed and puffed so hard that I thought his lungs might leap out of his mouth in protest. At the next street, I caught sight of Fisk leaping to his feet after colliding with a pedestrian, a woman in bright petticoats who shrieked loud enough to wake the dead while holding an obviously broken forearm. I added that to the growing list of things the little weasel had done to piss me off.

Next alley I was running full steam, my legs flashing and pumping with machine-like precision. It was not a fast sprint, but I could keep it up for a long damn time. I need not have worried...Fisk lay face down in a puddle of what I assumed was water, half conscious after tripping over the mounds of garbage that littered the tiny thoroughfare.

"Well, thanks for being stumbling drunk," I huffed, picking the dazed man up. "Let us get you squared away." Turning to see Virtanen enter the alley, I frowned. "Next time you get a wild hair, *do not*. Follow me, keep your mouth shut and do *exactly* as I say. Got me?"

He nodded, shamefaced and we proceeded to escort Mr. Fisk to more amenable accommodation. Amenable to us, that is.

Outside of town, far enough away to do business but close enough to see the gas lights. I brought my covered wagon to a halt and hobbled the horses, slipping the pair feed bags to enforce their docile nature. In the back, Virtanen sat in the dim light of a single lantern with the bound and gagged Fisk who lay uncomfortably on the floor of the wagon. The Estonian stared at the criminal with a catlike intensity that I found disturbing and Fisk, by his popping eyes and muffled grunts, thought of as terrifying.

"Hello, Mr. Fisk," I said as I climbed aboard, squeezing my bulk underneath the canvas covering. The rain made little *thumpity thump* sounds as it beat against the oiled material. "Glad to see you are awake. Now, I am going to remove that gag. You will be quiet. Grunt twice if you understand."

Grunt, grunt, went our captive. Good, he was sober enough to follow directions.

"Excellent!" I removed the gag and Fisk bit his lip, staring fearfully at Virtanen. "Now Mr. Fisk, pay attention." I slapped his cheek gently and his frightened eyes traveled to me, wincing slightly at the sight of my scars. "You have heard of Mr. Samuel Riverwood, yes? You may speak...quietly."

"Y-yes," he whispered and there was a catch in his voice, a subtle flutter that made my heart race. He knew of Riverwood, all right and I was willing to bet my last dollar that he knew why we were here.

"Wonderful," I purred. "His son went missing a while back."

"I-I heard something 'bout that," he stammered.

"Everyone I...persuaded to talk have pointed me in your direction as a man to deal with when dastardly deeds are performed in the Show-Me State." Let him infer what 'persuaded' meant. Sometimes the imagination provides more horror than reality. "Why is that, Mr. Fisk? Why would hardened criminals who would slit their grandmother's throats for two bits tell me *you* are the man to go to? Why is that?"

"I dunno!" he whispered. Big, salty tears tracked down his temples to wet his greasy hair.

Grabbing his left arm, I clenched tightly and broke the bones of his forearm. Now he understood how the poor lady in the street felt. Judging by his shriek, he did not like it very much.

I shook my head sadly as the man's shrieks became whimpers became muffled sobs. "Tsk, tsk, tsk, Mr. Fisk," I said minutes later. "It pains me, yes...deeply pains me that you cannot be forthcoming and that I must perform such heinous deeds. It occurs to me that you might indeed know why such bad men point in your direction and it also occurs to me that you know *exactly* what happened to young Master Riverwood." At that Virtanen growled, a soft, dangerous noise reminiscent of a hungry cougar. Fisk's eyes tracked to Riverwood's man and he flinched, the agony of his arm momentarily forgotten.

Yeah, he *knew*. I could feel it in my water.

"Have you a knife?" I asked Virtanen

Wordlessly, he pulled a short, sharp blade from a sheath in the small of his back and held it up. I looked as if it could cut the breath exiting your nostrils and leave it bleeding.

"Now, if he does not answer my next question, cut his left eye out."

Fisk whimpered and Virtanen looked at me questioningly.

"You bet your ass," I growled at the man, dead serious.

Nodding, the Estonian laid the tip of the blade under Fisk's left eye and pressed ever so lightly. A thin drop of blood oozed out.

"Now, Mr. Fisk, do you know what happened to young Master Riverwood?"

He nodded miserably and Virtanen tensed, his entire body now thrumming with violence, but the knife remained rock steady in his hand.

"Excellent. Tell me."

"I can't!" he wailed. "They'll kill me."

The first rule of interrogation is *always* carry through on a threat. If you back down, you might as well kill the victim. I hate torture, detest it with a passion that often startled me, but I would use it on evil men if absolutely necessary. The ends justifying the means and whatnot. "Take the eye."

Virtanen went to with a will and Fisk screamed long and hard, a sobbing cry that rode up and down, carrying tones of pain and despair. While the Estonian worked with the knife, I held our thrashing captive still while bile rose to burn the back of my throat. *What good is a monster with a conscience?*

When Fisk's cries tapered off into gentle moans, I continued. "There, Mr. Fisk, you can see that you will be killed if you do not tell and believe me, I have lived long enough to know how to make a man *hurt*. Doing this does not please me, but I will not shy from my responsibilities." For emphasis, Virtanen wiped the blade on Fisk's torn and stained shirt.

Fisk blubbered, he moaned and cried while snot drooled from his nose and down his cheeks and I felt like a shitheel, but I thought of that little boy fished up from the river and held my resolve. We waited while Fisk, the red hole in his face leaking blood, finally came to the only recourse available to him.

He talked.

"It wasn't me what took the boy," he blubbered. "You must believe me, I had nothin' to do with it."

"Shhh...there, there," I soothed. "I do believe you Mr. Fisk. And believe you me, talking will ensure that I will not harm you in any way, nor will you suffer further abuse at my hands."

That seemed to pacify him. "It were the Traveling Show, they took the boy."

A chill rippled down my spine and my stomach roiled in dismay. I exchanged a hard look with Virtanen. We had heard of the Show, of course, a story spoken in hushed tones throughout America, a brothel so secretive, whose owners were so ruthless, that the mere *thought* of betraying their existence brought swift and final punishment. The Show traveled the country peddling their wares, offering delights both mundane and depraved. It was also rumored to have temptations so forbidden, so sinful as to make Satan himself blush. Part rumor, part conjecture, and a smattering of fact, the Show had been the boil on the ass of America and at least three different Presidents had tried to find and eradicate the brothel, all with zero success.

"Are you sure, Mr. Fisk?" I asked, fearing the answer, hoping against hope that the Show was merely smoke and mirrors. "The Show is like the boogeyman of stories, a phantom, an amusing and titillating anecdote for the gullible."

"They's real, I shill for them, scaring up rich clientele like. You know, people what can afford it."

That sharper than sharp blade plunged into the wood next to Fisk's ear. "Why would they kidnap Riverwood's son!" screamed Virtanen, face red, the cords of his neck standing out in stark relief. "Why?"

Fisk began to blubber, the crimson hole in his head an accusation pointed at my heart. I had seen tough men, those who could take punishment after punishment and still keep smiling through the blood on their teeth and Fisk was not one of them. He was a terrified little man who wholly believed what he was telling us.

And I believed Fisk. The Show was real and the look on Virtanen's face told me he believed him too. With a heart full of dread, I waited until Fisk had his fill of crying then posed the question Virtanen needed answered so badly. "Why, Fisk? Why Charles Riverwood?"

"Because...because someone paid for him."

Virtanen and I traded a look of shock. "What?"

"When the Show started settin' up in St. Louis, someone paid a ton o' cash for the chance to use the boy, so the Show had him kidnapped, kept him well fed and rested until the Show started up. Only the guy what bought him for the night got all crazy and kilt him after using him." Fisk face was a mirror to the horror I felt in my heart. "The Show done paid me well to get rid of the body and I put him in the river."

Through the thickness in my throat, I asked, "Who paid for the boy?"

Fisk shook his head miserably. "Dunno."

"I have an idea," growled Virtanen. Death hung about him like a cloak. "A good idea."

His ideas be damned. I was more interested in further details. "This happens often?"

The skinny criminal nodded. "Every city they go to there's always a market for...young people. There are always orphanages willin' to sell kids, and what we can't buy, we steal. Those that do the kidnappin' are called Snatchers and they fill the ranks for them that have been...worn out."

Worn out? I puzzled over that term for a little bit. *Worn out...worn out.* A pressure was building under my skin, as if my veins contained too much blood, as if my bones were growing, but my hide remained the same size and it *hurt*. There was a dull thudding inside my skull and I realized that Fisk was talking, but I couldn't *hear* him, all I heard was those two words over and over and over again and my universe compressed into a hot spot of anger, diamond hard, and that sleeping beast, the leviathan beneath my mind stirred, disturbed by my growing ire.

"Hey, are you all right?" A hard hand gripped my shoulder. I looked at the fingers of that hand considered snapping them off, but it was Virtanen's hand, the hand of a man who lost a child he loved more than life. The rising, bubbling anger flattened out and faded just like *that*, and the world was the world again because that man was a good man, he was not a monster.

Like me.

"You will be wanting to leave the wagon," I said, my tone brooking no argument. He nodded and climbed past and it was just the two of us, the monster and the skinny criminal.

"Mr. Fisk," I began, slowly removing my spectacles, the flickering lantern light running across the thin metal frames. "You are going to tell me where the Show is now, who their Snatchers are, and who else shills for them." I turned the full force of my yellow gaze on his single eye, watching it grow wide in horror. "Believe me, the alternative will be worse than you can imagine."

Of course, he talked.

Spectacles once again firmly planted on my face, I left the crying man in the wagon, joining Virtanen outside in the cool air. He held out a lucifer and a hand rolled which I took and lit, inhaling deeply. The harsh paper and tobacco scraped along my lungs and I felt my heart beat a little faster.

It was a rare thing for me, indulging like this, but I needed something to take the edge off.

"You said earlier you had an idea."

Virtanen nodded.

"Who?"

"Melvin Ambrose."

"Never heard of him."

"Mr. Ravenwood's biggest rival in the oil business and a known sodomite, although no one talks about it." He spat out a shred of tobacco from between his lips. "A Texas man, Dallas, but he was in St. Louis at the time of the kidnapping. Should have seen it sooner."

"No. Do not blame yourself. Blame Ambrose, blame Fisk, blame the Show, but not yourself."

Virtanen let out a smoky sigh and held out a hand. "You earned your money, sir. Thank you."

I shook his hand gently. "Not done yet."

"The Show?"

"The Show," I affirmed.

"What about Fisk?" he asked, nodding toward the wagon.

"Made a promise I would not kill him," I said, turning toward the horses. "Did not say anything about *you*."

●　　●　　●

That was how I learned that the Show was scheduled for Colorado in November. I learned of Townsey, the Show's shill in Denver and his love for the Buckhorn Exchange, cheap rum and expensive clothes. Fisk had met the man and was able to provide a description.

It was not hard to catch his eye; all I had to do was flash a fat wad of cash and play the happy whore chaser, spreading tales and buying drinks. I wore tailored suits, a gold pocket watch and my hair was nicely coiffed. Gold rings inset with precious gems decorated my fingers and my shoes shone as if they glowed. All in all, I dripped money and the desire to spend it.

Two days of dining and drinking, two more just making his acquaintance all nice and easy like and by the fifth he figured me for a potential customer started making subtle overtures. When he inquired as to my line of work, I merely raised an eyebrow and grinned, letting him read into that what he would. An air of mystery always lends people the idea you are up to something the law might not approve of.

"If you're looking for whores, sir," said Townsey with a greedy grin, lips shiny with spit. "Then maybe I can help you out."

I looked into his greasy face and resisted the urge to punch through his eyes and crush his brain in my fist. "I do not think you can help me with my needs." It was not hard to play the whore chaser, one look at my face and people thought it was the only way I could have a woman.

He leaned in close, his breath smelling of cheap rum and mint. "You would be surprised my friend," he whispered. "I know of a place where you can get anything you desire. *Anything*."

Silence. I let him eat as much quiet as he could handle until his mouth opened to try his pitch again, but I cut him off. "My desires are most likely unknown to you, Townsey," I said quietly, my happy-go-lucky smile slipping from my face. "They are far from pedestrian, rather exotic, if you catch my meaning."

He caught my meaning straightaway. "Oh, sir, let me tell you that I know of a place that any desires you may have can be satiated." Piggy eyes stared at my spectacles. A pink worm of a tongue licked his fat lips. "Provided you have the wherewithal, if you get *my* meaning."

You fucking shill, I thought, keeping it from my face, I produced a fist full of folded bills and smiled. It felt false and wrong on my face and my scars hurt like hell, but the fat man had eyes only for the cash.

CHAPTER TWENTY-THREE

"Would you mind, Fred?" Klaus asked.

I stood. "After you, Sheriff, but I have to ask about your deputy."

"Clark's wife Sarah gave birth last night so he's at his spread outside of town. Doubt he'll get here in time."

"Fair enough." To my companions, "Stay here, if you do not mind."

We exited the saloon with guns drawn and I felt more than a little surprise that the Browning Hi-Power that once graced my holster now looked to be a Navy Colt. *What the everlasting fuck?*

Six men on horseback waited for us, guns at the ready. An older man with a pot belly and fine clothes sat astride a chestnut mare of fine quality. The others rode a mixture of sorry animals that looked worse for the wear.

"Henry Pembry," said Klaus. "Mind putting your irons down so's we can conversate a bit without resorting to uncomfortable mayhem?"

"Drop your weapons, you two," replied Pembry with an upper crust British accent. "I've come for my second favorite son which you have put in your jail. Bring him out forthwith."

"He's in jail for putting unwanted hands on Bill Tomlinson's daughter Hazel. Your second favorite son is a miserable drunken wretch."

"The smith will answer for sticking his hand in the forge. Doc Griffith tells me it looks like melted candle wax and he might not gain the full use of it. That won't stand, Klaus Bischoff."

"That is *Sheriff Bischoff*, Henry Penbry." I made sure my gun hand held steady.

"And who might you be, stranger?" asked Penbry. "You realize this isn't any of your business."

"Uh, Boss," cut in one of Penbry's men in a quavering voice, a skinny fellow with a deep scar bisecting his left eyebrow. "That there is Scar Face Fred Vaughn."

"The bounty hunter?" asked Pembry.

"Yes, Boss."

"We have the numbers and if they shoot, he'll die like any other."

My smile contained nothing of mirth. "If I start shooting, Penbry, you will die first." The long barrel of the Colt centered on his face. "Believe that."

One of the men, a big lout with a brown hat, fired his revolver. I felt my coat twitch as the bullet passed through and between my arm and side, exiting cleanly. Suddenly the air became thick with lead.

Despite the fact that I felt pretty sure that I would survive any gunshot, that did not mean I stood still. My Stetson flew off as a bullet skimmed above my scalp and my return fire took the man in the eye, blowing out the back of his skull.

Klaus fired with calm precision, gut-shooting Pembry and killing another with a round that tore his jaw off. The sheriff then grunted, the pistol falling from his hand followed by his own self. Immediately lead starting coming my way and I felt the sting of several shots as I spun behind a post.

More shots ensued and the post became riddled with holes. I shot back, killing another man just as the last three sprouted blood as their bodies became home to several holes. Bodies fell in a heap and I looked up to see Branch and Carter standing just inside the open saloon doors, guns dribbling acrid smoke. All but two of the horses bolted, heading out of town.

Stillness gripped the small town as the bodies of Pembry and his men lay in the hard dirt, soaking it with their lives.

Branch stepped out. "It turns out, *Fred*, we actually do mind staying inside."

"Fine by me," I replied. "Let's get the sheriff to the jail. Carter, down the road a block is a sign that reads 'Doc Griffiths', mind bringing him to the jail. Klaus requires stitching if I am not mistaken. I will take care of the bodies."

The sheriff cursed up a storm as Doc Griffith sewed up his thigh. "Quick your whining, Sheriff," said the young and handsome doctor, a man with a full head of shaggy blond hair. "The bullet went straight through the meat and didn't hit any arteries. You'll be fine in a couple of weeks."

I stood staring at Pembry's second favorite son, Anton, who lay passed out in the jail cell, a thick bandage wrapped around his hand. Even at rest I could see the pouty lines of a spoiled child. Motioning to my companions, I led them to a corner. "Bilt, when can we leave, continue our journey?"

"And do you mind telling us why our weapons changed?" Branch held her Colt up for inspection.

Bilt grinned through his oiled beard. "Notice that your clothes now have wooden buttons, your boots leather soles. These items have no power, so they change to conform to the time in which they exist, so your pistols become revolvers. This will happen when we travel back in time to search for Eden."

"Why do we have to go back in time?" Carter asked in a careful whisper.

"Because it's the only way, isn't it? You lot have to realize that we just have to go back far enough to reach the thin spot in the world where we can transition to Eden's location. It doesn't exist in our modern world, does it?"

Carter scratched his beard. "I thought you said Eden was accessible after Christ's death."

"It is. That's what the book was for. Well, one of its uses. Fortunately for us I memorized the spell,"

"What are you lot going on about?" said Klaus through gritted teeth.

"Personal business," I replied. "We must leave soon."

"Not too soon, my friend. We killed Pembry and five of his men, but there are at least a dozen or two more that might feel put off that we shot their livelihood. They'll know something went wrong when those horses return without riders. I reckon they'll ride in to practice chicanery once they realize that they're out of work. I suspect they'll take no prisoners. Especially his eldest boy, Gregory."

Carter spat to the side. "Can we get out of here?"

"We are not leaving." I stood to my full height and I could feel my scars pulsing to the beat of my heart. "If Pembry's men are coming, we will be here waiting."

The two agents checked their weapons. "Then it looks like there's going to be a fight," Branch growled and right then I pitied the men who would face her down.

Sunlight kissed the mountains when we first heard the thundering of hooves on hard packed earth and Klaus began to hand out weapons. Two rifles and shotgun. "When it happens, aim careful and don't miss," he said, limping to the window with a quiet hiss of pain.

Near two dozen men on horseback thundered into to town and arranged themselves in front of the jail. A big man in a derby hat carrying a Remmington rifle and a shit-eating grin reined in his horse at the front of the jail. "Sheriff, we wanna have words," he shouted.

"Walter Huntington, you reprobate," Klaus answered back. "Words or bullets?"

"The boss is dead, Sheriff and you're to blame. We mean to show you that the law doesn't get to get away with such things."

"Then he shouldn't have come for trouble."

"Get out here right now, surrender yourself to the hangman's rope and the good folk of Taos don't need to be harmed none." Walter spat a wad of tobacco onto the ground.

Klaus looked over. "Miss Branch, you any good with that rifle?"

"Good enough Mr. Sheriff."

"Would you mind, then?"

A shot rang out, the bullet bursting through glass to hit Walter square between the eyes. He fell in in puddle of his own brains and the men scattered like rats in cornfield.

The jail windows exploded inward and we ducked just in time to avoid being perforated, although I heard a squawk from Branch and Klaus used choice words not meant for polite company.

Both agents rose, taking advantage of a brief hesitation to return fire, the room filling with the acrid stench of gunpowder. During this Anton kept to his slumber, snoring and drooling on himself.

Lucky bastard.

More shots. A ricochet tugged at the heel of my boot. "Carter, Branch, cover me. Klaus, keep your head down and kill anything that comes through that door." I hefted the shotgun. Two rounds. Had to make them count.

Carter: "Got it, Boss."

Branch: "Heard."

Klaus: "Fred you can't!"

"Shut it, Klaus, and keep your head down!" With at I ran at the door, blowing it apart in a shower of splinters. Time slowed as multiple rounds tore into my gut. The shotgun roared and an advancing man dropped like a wet sack of laundry.

I ran, boots thudding on the wooden sidewalk as splinters chased me down the street, the sting of bullets taking chunks from my flesh and ruining my wardrobe. The hits, little needles of heat, were not debilitating, but it slowed me...enough that I lost more flesh and blood before I made it a muddy little alley between the jail and the general store.

A shotgun roared and a giant fist slammed me in the back, white light eclipsed my vision and I fell, legs lifeless, spinning in screeching agony. A ball of fire churned in my guts and I curled around my useless legs trying not to whimper.

No stranger to pain, I managed to lie still and keep my mouth shut, playing possum until I healed. I had been shot more times than I have had hot breakfasts, but you never get used to the gut-wrenching pain, you can only build a tolerance, like callouses on your soul, and hope for the best.

More gun shots, more screaming. It seemed my companions gave a good account of themselves as I lay in the dust of the alley waiting to heal. By the time I felt the first tingle in my legs, a pins-and-needle sensation that set my teeth on edge, the gunfire slowed to an occasional shot. I guessed our attackers felt the need to regroup. Minutes later the pain faded as pellets were slowly extruded from my tissues and I managed to sit up, then stand.

A man came pelting around the alley corner, shotgun hugged tight to his chest and he skidded to a stop when he saw me. "But you're dead!" he screamed, eyes wide and round.

I drew my Navy Colt and fired. "No, you are." It gave me no pleasure, but I admit to s certain satisfaction. We cannot all be perfect.

My boots thudded against hard pack as I ran to the back of the jail in time to see a couple of men readying a bottles with flaming rags stuffed into the necks. There was no back door so it seemed like they felt able to burn themselves an entrance. My first shot broke a bottle and flaming liquid covered one man. His screams shattered the air while my second took the other man in the gut. He dropped his bottle, which broke, creating a puddle of fire. Him falling into that puddle was a merely a side effect of him being dead and all.

Did I feel sad for those men? No, not at all. They chose the path of evil and it was my duty to oppose the will of the wicked, but that did not mean I reveled in their demise. It was a lot like putting down a rabid dog. Unpleasant, but necessary.

No windows on this wall. Good. I trotted along the back of the buildings, my newly healed skin stretching tight.

At the blacksmith's I climbed to the roof, the cold smell of the forge in my nostrils as I took position. Most of the gunfire came from Jewel, which stood near opposite to the jail. Bodies littered the street, testament to the shooting ability of the agents. I counted seven dead with two writhing in agony and trying to crawl to safety, leaving their blood to soak into the dirt. Bullets still screamed toward the jail.

Three men pushed a table out the door, using the sturdy wood as a shield. Several shots slammed into it, but the men took no damage as they began to cross the street.

Bang, bang! I fired twice and two of the men fell as my shoots took them in the feet. The table fell and the third man died with a half-dozen rounds in his chest. The other two died shortly after, filled with holes from my companion's guns.

"Give up and you can ride out of here." Two or three horses bolted, but others did not mind the sound of gunshots and they milled around at the end of the street.

"Yer gonna shoot us if'n we do!" came the shout from the Jewel. "We just want Anton and the sheriff, that's all. Ya'll kin go about yer business."

"The only deal you are going to get is the one I offered. You can trust me, my name is Fred Vaughn and I keep my word, so go now so I do not have to end your lives."

Shouts from inside and I heard my name mentioned in panicked tones. Sometimes it is good to have a fearsome reputation.

Bullets crashed against the Blacksmith's. *I guess that is a 'no'.* Time for something drastic.

Twelve feet to the ground, not too great a drop. I considered my options and none of them were palatable. This needed to be done quickly before they organized a serious attack and overwhelmed the jail.

My boots hit the dirt a second after I jumped. I flexed my knees and rolled, springing to my feet in an instant and ran straight for the saloon doors, the Colt cocked and ready to go. Bullets whizzed past, but none hit and I was through to the inside quick as a wink.

The first shot took a man in the knee right before return fire hit me in the gut and smoke and flame erupted from my Colt, dropping a man behind the bar. Blood flew as fire tore into my hip with the power of a mule kick. Two bullets into a man raising a shotgun and another who stood over the dead body of Jericho. My last round killed a man only a couple feet away, blowing through his cheek out the back of his head, gore splatting against the wall.

No use trying to reload, I would be shot to pieces before the first bullet entered the chamber, so I drew a K-bar, which now looked like a bowie knife and set to, leaping toward the next man as I took another round to the gut. The razors edge of the knife kissed a throat, opening a second mouth. The man gargled and drowned in his own blood.

I ran across the saloon toward gunfire, more bullets finding my torso, but I was in a state of berserker rage, my vision a tunnel of red. Blood gushed from my body as I gutted another man, then I grabbed a chair, braining a cowboy who shot me in the chest.

"He's the devil! He cain't be kilt!"

"Run!"

"Lookit that face!"

Shouting, general confusion and mayhem as I laid about with the bowie, spilling blood and slicing flesh, lost in my fury, cutting, cutting, cutting. Boots clattered across wood and guns roared and moments later I was left standing amid bodies and gore.

A chair caught my butt as I near collapsed in pain and fatigue.

Carter's hand clasped my shoulder and I looked up to see his grave face, beard coated with dust. "You chased them out and we cut them down."

I nodded, then near jumped as a soft moan came from behind the bar. "Carter, can you go see who that is? I would but I am too damn tired." *And too damned hurt.*

Carter nodded and jumped over the bar, revolver at the read. "Young guy. Gut shot."

"Find out who he is."

The agent disappeared and after a moment he called out, "A guy named Gregory."

Branch walked through the door, face a study in anger.

"Klaus?" I asked.

She shook her head.

Fuck. No the time for sadness, but I shed a lone tear anyway. He was a good man. The best.

"That must be Pembry's oldest." I raised my voice, "Will he live?"

Carter shook his head. "Doubt it."

"They should have taken the deal."

Bilt walked through the door, shoulders slumped. "You scared them out, Fred. These two shot them to pieces as they tried to run, they did."

One, two, three bullets popped out of my body. There was no one to see me heal, the ladies hiding upstairs and would not come out until we left. "Can we leave today?"

A shrug. "It's Thursday, isn't it? I guess as long as we have a couple goats to sacrifice, we can."

I looked around. "Does it have to be goats?"

CHAPTER TWENTY-FOUR

Denver, November 1904

Three others sat with me inside the carriage: a fat man in a striped waistcoat and sporting muttonchops whom I dubbed Pig, an older man with a white mustache, thin, dressed in a stovepipe hat and a black suit twenty years out of style. I named him Grandfather. Last, but in no way least, was a middle-aged, good-looking successful type sporting a tasteful charcoal suit and silk cravat. He reeked of inherited wealth and privilege and the slightly distasteful look he gave me spoke of a lifetime of plenty without want and an overinflated notion of self-worth.

I dubbed him Asshole.

Pig sat with Grandfather while Asshole and I sat opposite, the rich man scooting far from me as possible as if my scars were catching. Grandfather looked bored and tired while Pig's erection threatened to burst from his trousers. I made sure not to stare lest he took it for interest.

There were heavy curtains covering the carriage windows, thick and stapled tight to their frames and the only illumination was a tiny lantern bolted to one wall. Obviously our shill, Townsey, did not want us to know the location of the Show. Our instructions were clear: wait at the Brown Palace Hotel until a driver came to transport us to our destination, ask no questions, do not attempt to look outside of the carriage once underway, and never, ever speak of the Show. Cooperation, Townsey leered, fat lips quivering with conspiratorial lust, and would ensure a night of pleasure never to be forgotten. If things went according to my shirttail plan, the pleasure would be all mine.

"Is this your first time?"

It took a moment for me to realize the question was directed my way. "Excuse me?"

Pig grinned, the expression contorting his fat face. And they called *me* ugly. "I said, good sir, is this your first time? To the...our destination." His eyes were fever bright and I resisted the urge to throw him out the carriage headfirst.

I made do with a nod.

"Splendid! Splendid! This is my second time, and let me say this...you are in for quite a treat. Quite a treat, indeed."

My smile was a ghastly thing and Pig recoiled slightly. Even Grandfather seemed a tad disturbed.

"I say, good sir," the old man said, squinting through the dim light. "Where did you receive those fabulous scars? Quite impressive, I must say."

Fabulous? Those scars had been called several things, but fabulous was not one. Thick and purple-y, my scars, the ones people could see, had frightened even grown men. "Cuba."

Grandfather seemed amazed and Pig regarded me closely. "The Spanish-American War?"

I nodded.

The old man leaned forward; eyes bright. "Do you know President Roosevelt? Did you fight with him at Kettle Hill? At San Juan Hill?"

Oh yeah, I was at San Juan and Kettle Hill. I wanted to tell the old guy that yes, I knew the President when he was just a Colonel fighting an ugly battle that had blood running in streams down a dusty slope. I wanted to tell him that the Colonel and the Rough Riders were as tough and fearsome as their growing legend. Hell, I wanted to tell him that Theodore Roosevelt was the bravest, toughest, stubbornest, most honest sonofabitch I had ever met in all my living life. My guts ached at the desire to tell him, but I swore to the Colonel those long years ago that I would not reveal anything about the true nature of the battle in Cuba and our quest for the Spear of Longinus that was ultimately a failure. However, for my efforts, the

Colonel let my name be well known among the politicos of the day, bolstering my growing security firm quite well.

"Not with him, per se," I said mildly. "But under him."

"You were a Rough Rider then?"

"No, I was an attaché assigned to General Wood. I did fight a little at Kettle Hill, but was wounded."

"Is that where you received your scars, sir?"

I nodded.

"Deucedly poor stitching job, that. They should sack their surgeon."

Further conversation was thwarted by the carriage coming to a jouncing stop. "We are here," exclaimed the Pig, his rising lust even more evident.

There came the scrape of wood on wood and a section of ceiling above my head slid aside to reveal Townsey's fat face. He could have been Pig's long-lost sibling. "Here you go," he said, lowering black cloth, which turned out to be four blindfolds. "Put 'em on, gentlemen. Your night of satiation is about to begin."

Swiftly removing my spectacles and keeping my eyes shut, I donned the blindfold and shortly I was led from the carriage into what I could only assume was a large building because my kidskin boots echoed loudly across marble. We were then led into a small space that proved to be a lift by the stomach-dropping sensation as we rose. Within a matter of a minute we were instructed to remove our blindfolds.

Spectacles back in place, I noted Townsey standing before us, a shit-eating grin stretching his slug-like lips wide. They were wet with either anticipation or lust. Perhaps both. Behind him was a plain wooden door with a glass knob set in wall papered in a gold and burgundy *fleur de lis* pattern. The carpet I found myself on was burgundy as well, very expensive, very plush. Although the room seemed devoid of furniture I could tell by the carpet and wallpaper that we were in a place used to the smell of money.

Townsey clapped his hands. "Gentlemen, may I have your attention. Behind me is the door to your dreams, the door to your fondest appetites. Once inside, take your ease, take whatever victuals or libations you desire. Someone will come to inquire what it is that brought you to the Show then escort you to your destination. You may stay as long as you wish. However, what you may *not* do is breathe word of the Show to any other living soul. Penalties for such indiscretions are severe. Do you understand?'

All four of us nodded.

"Wonderful. Not to be crass, but I believe you kind gentlemen have a donation you wish to make at this point. Please, if you would." One wide hand was held out, palm up.

We unlimbered our wallets and money clips, placing large amounts of cash into his waiting hand. When the pile grew too large, he brought forth his other hand to steady the stack of bills. With all due haste, the money disappeared into his black suit and he bowed. With a smile, the fat man opened the door.

And we entered a palace of sin and depravity

How to describe a sultan's seraglio combined with the most decadent brothel in New Orleans and a Chinese opium den? Couches and cushions of every color, shimmering, translucent drapes of fabric hanging from the ceiling giving the long room we found ourselves in a hypnotic, hazy quality. Strangely scented smoke floated near the ceiling and even a cautious sniff made my head feel light and somehow disconnected from the rest of my body. Women in bangles, women in scarves, in exotic gold chains, in tight leather outfits that beggared description, and in nothing but smiles. All heavily made up and perfumed, lounging with men on those couches and cushions in indolence. Some couples merely talked gaily, others kissed and petted each other heavily. Women fed the men grapes and figs and little triangular pastries called baklava, placing each delicacy on the tongue. A number of customers on the couches were also female, women of high station and wealth ranging from very young to a ripe grandmotherly type who had to have been at least ninety.

Blonde, brunette, redhead, the Show had them all, in every size and shape. There were Indians, Negroes, Chinese, Japanese, dusky ladies from India and one I believed was an Eskimo with long black hair that hung to her ankles. More than one woman sported dark tattoos of strange and eye bending designs that confused even my heightened powers of perception.

The walls of the room were covered in fine paintings, most of an erotic theme, as well as silken tapestries depicting hunting scenes, bacchanalias, and acts of fornication I'd only seen in certain works during my stay in India. I felt my cheeks begin to flame and was certain that their color overshadowed my scars.

Strange music I floated in the air...sharp dissonant notes that blended together to form unusual yet soothing harmonies that twittered pleasantly across my skin.

A young woman wearing nothing but diaphanous scarves and a coronet of feathers appeared from behind on of the shimmering fabric panels and hooked her arm through mine. "Hello, I am Fatima." She batted her huge dark eyes and an intoxicating, musky scent wafted from her dusky skin. "I am your pleasure guide for the evening. Anything you desire you may tell me and I will see that you are satisfied."

Several notions came to mind, but I was in town for business, not pleasure. I smiled and she flinched slightly, just the tiniest motion of her mouth and eyes. If I had not been looking, I would not have seen it, but it was enough to sour my disposition right quick.

I nodded and let her lead me to a vacant couch. She attempted to remove my brown canvass coat (freshly laundered and waxed for the occasion), but I refused with a small shake of my head, sitting down and pretending to relax.

Slender fingers twined through my long, black hair. "Shall I fetch you refreshment?"

"Absinthe."

"Ahh, a traveled man who knows the lure of the Green Fairy. Coming up." Watching her leave was almost as enjoyable as watching her arrive.

As I sat there, vaguely uncomfortable, listening to the discordant music, which I took to be from a stringed instrument, my eyes darted this way and that behind my spectacles. The walls were heavily wallpapered in a gold and yellow floral pattern yet I could detect small imperfections here and there at roughly the same height and evenly spaced. Spyholes? Murderholes? Perhaps both. The Show didn't last as long as it had by not applying equal parts caution and paranoia.

It had been a long road to reach this place and I was almost surprised at how easy it was to attend. Then again, money does open doors and it was my intention to kick this one shut forever. The thought of kidnapped children given to those with the wherewithal to buy them brought an ugly heat to my eyes and once again, deep down in the secret places of my soul, the leviathan stirred.

A sherry glass filled with greenish liquid appeared out of nowhere. "Here you go, handsome," Fatima said, all red smiles and white teeth.

I took a sip of absinthe and let it slide across my tongue before slithering down my throat. Bourbon suited me better.

Warm, sweet breath brushed my ear. "What is your desire, sir?" Fatima rubbed against my arm and snuggled close, letting me know that her services were available.

Without looking at her, I answered. "Young."

A brief hesitation. "Beg your pardon?"

I turned my head slowly, keeping my voice soft and low. "I like them young."

"Of course, handsome," she said with the barest hint of relief. Standing, her scarves moving suggestively, she held out a slender hand while removing the empty sherry glass with the other. "Come with me."

Warm and soft, not a callous to mark that sweet, supple skin. I wanted to hold that velvet hand forever. As she led me down the room past the couches and the cushions, the men and women in the middle of elaborate foreplay, I could feel hidden eyes upon my flesh, tracking my movement; my every stride and I began to feel an itch at the center of my back.

I tried not to sneeze the dizzying, narcotic smoke that hung from the ceiling out of my nose and the music, that weird, clang-y music, seemed to ring round and round in the chamber of my skull and my eyes began to cross, my vision blurring in and out in and out to the beat of my thudding heart and the blood in my veins wanted to explode, to shoot out of its sheath and decorate the walls with coppery, crimson paint and I held on, I tried to hold on, but the leviathan inside was stirring, more so than normal and it would wake and I had no clue what would happen if the sleeper awoke and I was so afraid, the fear a ice knife in my soul, that I would find out soon enough.

Cool air...fresh and wholesome, the best thing I had ever breathed, flooded my lungs and I came back to myself. The sleeper slept, no longer stirring, and the world came back into focus around me.

"Are you alright?" Fatima managed to sound concerned.

"Yes, thank you. That smoke..."

"I see. You must have gotten a good lungful then, sir. That smoke can be quite...potent. It is a special concoction from the Far East called Pig Grass." Soft hands guided me to a wall and I used it for support, doing my best not to fall to my knees.

Potent, yes. What an understatement. *Pig grass, what an ugly name.* "I am fine now." Looking around, I noticed we were in a long, lushly carpeted hallway with doors every fifteen feet or so. Soft light emanated from electric bulbs mounted on the wall behind elegant frosted glass shades shaped like tulips. Brass plates adorned each door bearing room numbers. Considering the distance from the Brown Palace and opulence I'd seen, I reckoned I knew where the Show called home while in Denver.

Smiling, I took Fatima's hand and loomed. Considering that she stood at just at chest height, it was a good loom.

"Dear," I beamed. "Kindly tell me where I can find the manager of this establishment."

She was fast, I'll give her that; she *almost* screamed, but one of my big hands clamped down hard on her mouth while the other crushed her to me. Her fawn eyes grew wide and moist with fright. She felt my strength and did not bother to put up a fight.

"Listen, dear, I do not want to hurt you. Do you understand?"

She nodded against my hand.

"Good girl. I am here to do your employers a dirty and I will need your help to accomplish this. Just information, a teeny, tiny bit of information is all I require and you can go about your merry way. Do you understand?"

More nods.

"Excellent. Now, I am going to remove my hand and you will *not* scream because screaming will be the worst thing you can do, not to mention the last thing." There was no way I would hurt a hair on her head, but she didn't need to know that.

Carefully, slowly, I removed my hand. Tears stared from her eyes. She was crying and I felt like a real shitheel. *Why did she have to cry?*

"They'll kill me," she whispered. "You don't know them, mister. They'll kill you, too."

"I am going to show you why they will not be able to kill me. Do not scream." With my free hand, I removed my spectacles.

Fatima fainted. Luckily, I still had a hold of her.

It took only seconds to revive her and when I did, she began praying in what I could only deduce was Arabic.

"Steady, girl. Steady," I soothed, stroking her hair.

Her eyes couldn't leave mine. "Do not take my soul, Sir Djinn, I beg of you."

"It is not your soul I want, girl, but those of your bosses. Now, tell me where I can find them."

She pointed down the long hallway. "Down there, take a left. At the end of the hall is a lift. Descend one floor and look for room 417. Mr. Ellis and Miss Ophelia should be there." A defiant note crept into the fear in her voice.

"You hate them." Not a question.

"Mr. Ellis is a brutalizer of women. He uses and hits us in places it doesn't show when we are on the move, and Miss Ophelia is Shaitan in the flesh," she spat, hate flaring in her soft brown eyes.

Strong words to describe a woman. Miss Ophelia must have been a piece of work to invoke such strong emotions. Still, it was not in me to kill a woman, no matter how vile, how despicable. *Why do things have to be so complicated?*

My mind must have wandered because I suddenly realized Fatima was speaking to me. "What?"

"I said you can let me go now, mister, I won't tell anyone."

My yellow eyes narrowed, but I let her slip from my grasp. "Fatima, the children that are…acquired, what happens to them?"

She looked away.

I let a little anger into my voice, ashamed I had to use fear as a weapon. "What. Happens. To. Them?"

"Those that are strong stay, others are sold to those who have the means and the weak..." her voice trailed away.

She did not need to finish. Words were unnecessary, only action counted. "Keep your mouth shut, act normal, but if I were you, I would be someplace far away from here."

"You really will stop them? This you can do?"

"How long have you been with them Fatima?"

Perfect teeth worried her luscious lower lip. "Three years now. Since my sixteenth birthday."

Sweet sixteen. A hard thing coalesced inside me. "Yeah, Fatima, I can and I will." My voice was filled with frost and death.

She nodded. "Good." She left in a swirl of multicolored scarves disappearing through the door to the main room.

Time passed in a blur of brightly colored walls and a thin lift barely big enough to suit my bulk and before I knew it, I stood in front of a door marked with the numbers 417.

All was quiet, only the sound of my ragged breathing and the blood rushing in my ears. I put a hand on the glass doorknob and turned.

It opened easily and I was in quick as a wink, gently closing the door behind. What lay before me was a large room with a fine settee and wood and fabric chairs. The floor was hardwood with a Persian style rug beneath a mahogany coffee table. Two doors, both closed, were on either side of the room to my left and right. The silence felt heavy with the possibility of violence.

The right-hand door opened and a woman entered staring behind her. "Come, boy," she groused. "It wasn't that bad, was it? I'm sure you'll get used to it."

Overweight would be a kindly way to put it. Enormously fat was a little more realistic, like a sow stuffed in flouncy green dress that trailed on the floor and a broad brimmed hat trimmed with a mass of feathers. It looked like a stuffed humming bird or two perched in the crown. All in all, she was the embodiment of bad taste and poor color choices.

Had to be Miss Ophelia.

She lay in my grasp before she could turn around and, unlike Fatima, she struggled mightily, but I held her bulk off the floor while she squirmed. It was while I held her off the ground, her high heels drumming a tattoo on my shins that I got an eyeful of what was going on in the other room.

A young boy, a child really, of perhaps six or seven, stood in the center next to a large, four poster bed. He was dressed in a blue flannel blanket that covered his thin shoulders poorly. That was all, nothing else. The blanket was open in front, showing his tiny frame and pale hairless body. Blood dripped down from between his legs as freely as the tears down his cheeks. *Pat, pat, pat*, the crimson droplets splashed and were absorbed into brown wool rug. *Pat, pat, pat.*

What am I looking at?

Then I saw the man. Big, with arms thick with muscle and a barrel chest matted with dense, coarse hair black as Miss Ophelia's evil little soul. Under a prodigious nose lay a thick walrus mustache. Next to him, next to his right knee as he lay on the bed in a contented half-doze, was a bloodstain as large as my fist.

The man was naked.

It hit me...what I saw then. Hit me like a boxer connecting with a vicious uppercut and nausea swelled up within me so hard I almost retched on Miss Ophelia's ridiculous hummingbird hat.

Oh, sweet Lord.

There comes a time when it all becomes too much, when the shock to the system overwhelms and the mind retreats and the monster is let loose. I had no memory of the time before my resurrection, my first memory was one of light and pain and a man recoiling in horror at what he had wrought. I learned anger that day, anger and fear and pain and loss and because I was as new born into the world I had no idea, no words to give meaning to what I felt.

Not like now...there were words aplenty, but none sufficed to describe what surged through me and I had to be what I always was because the monsters I saw needed serious killing in the worst way.

It takes a monster to kill monsters.

"What did you do?" I whispered into Miss Ophelia's ear, hand moving to her throat and gripping tight.

Terror spiced her hushed words. "We have to...so they will get used to it. There are those who come to enjoy it, so it's not so bad."

Snap.

Her neck broke with a crunchy, wet sound and her lifeless body flew through the air neatly flying through the doorway, a good throw, one worthy of a professional baseball pitcher. She flew over the shivering, bleeding boy, to land on the large mattress next to the dozing, naked man, flinging him two feet up and three out to the side. He landed hard, but a thick, woolen rug cushioned his fall somewhat. I ghosted through the door, shutting it quietly behind me.

Turned out I could kill a woman after all.

"What the f—!" was all fat man said before my hands reached his throat and I held him up to eye level. I had already removed my spectacles and secured them in the folds of my canvas coat.

When he met my eyes, he stopped struggling. "Yer da Devil," he choked out.

I shook my head. "No, but you are going meet him real soon." With that, I crushed his throat. He was not worth lingering over; I had more pressing concerns to deal with.

"Boy," I said gently, kneeling and pulling the blanket shut over his naked body. He would need medical attention and soon. "You are going to be alright; you hear me?"

The little boy nodded, tears still streaming down his face and his lower lip began to quiver.

"Shhhh, do not worry, I am going to get you out of here. Get you someplace safe."

Terrible knowledge flooded his eyes. "There ith no place thafe," he lisped.

The loss of innocence in one so young tore at my guts and I fought off tears of my own. "What is your name, boy?"

"Thamuel."

"Samuel. That is a good name. I knew a Samuel once, a real good guy. You going to be a real good guy for me?"

Little Samuel pointed to the bodies with a shaking finger. "You killed them."

"Yes. Yes I did."

"Then I will be a *real* good boy."

"Good. Stay right here, I will be back shortly." I spotted a small settee beneath a covered window and had him lay down. "Close your eyes. Good. Just relax and realize that I will return soon. Very soon."

"It thtill hurts," he sobbed in a strangled voice that broke my heart.

A tear trickled from my eyes. It had been ages since I last cried. "I know, but I am going to get you back to your people."

"I have no people!" he wailed, eyes opening in fright. "They *bought* me."

"From where?"

"The orphanage."

"Here in Denver?"

He nodded.

It seemed that my business in Denver would not be concluded with The Show. I was going to find that orphanage and I would make sure they would never harm, or sell, another child again. "Then you are coming with me."

I was almost to the door when Samuel's voice floated up from behind. "Mithter?"

"Yes, Samuel," I said as I reached the broken doorway to the main room, boots crunching through plaster.

"What'th your name?

"Call me...Uncle."

CHAPTER TWENTY-FIVE

We left Taos that morning, sacrificing a couple of goats because Bilt said a calf or two would not work. It being Thor's Day, and considering the pagan nature of the thunder deity, only goats would do. Picky beings, gods. Not that I would know, mind you.

The first trip back took only twenty minutes or so. This one took over an hour.

We appeared in a verdant field of green dressed in chain mail, carrying swords and crossbows, daggers sheathed at our hips.

It did not take long for us to encounter the locals and to learn we arrived during the Black Death in England, putting the timeline at somewhere in the mid-1300s. The less said about what we encountered the better. We obtained goats quickly and left as quickly as Bilt could cast the spell.

Once again the sunless, cloudless sky and we rode, uncomfortable in our chain mail.

"I think this will take a bit more time, won't it?" said Bilt as he dismounted. "Might as well get comfortable, shall we?"

Despite our clothes turning into chainmail and our weapons reverting to swords and such, our horses remained the same breeds, which led to me believe that only objects reverted to an earlier state. Jed eyed me placidly as I brushed him down, dipping his head every now and again to lip at the verdant grass.

Branch approached, face troubled, the reins to her horse clenched tightly in one hand. "Hey."

"Hey, yourself, Ms. Branch."

"Cecily."

I raised an eyebrow, still brushing Jed. "Nice name." A long pause. "Something tickling at you, Cecily?" Jed had a collection of burrs on his fetlock and I knelt to tease them out of his hair.

Another pause, long enough to grow uncomfortable before Branch said, "I'm sorry."

"For?" Hmmm, Jed did not have horseshoes (I was not a fan), and his hooves looked a mite ragged, in need of a trim and cleaning.

"Calling you an abomination."

Wow, that must have hurt. "That must have hurt."

"You'll never know."

"Forgiven."

She knelt at my side. "Mind telling me how you found the book in the first place?"

I considered for a moment, how much to say, but she earned my trust despite her original misgivings. "What do you know about the siege of Vienna by the Ottomans?"

"Three months in 1683, the Ottomans, led by Suleiman the Magnificent and defended by Nikolas Graf Salm on behalf of the Holy Roman Emperor Leopold I. They were repulsed."

"Good education. That is it in a nutshell. What you do not know is that Suleiman was after the book, which was in Vienna at the time. Thousands of men died to retrieve it and it was there I was...born. As far as I am able to tell, the man I was before was killed by a mortar shell and the book was used to resurrect me."

"You must've been someone important."

"Maybe. Perhaps I was a relative of an important person. I do not know. All I know is that my first memory was one of light, of men shouting in fear and running into the aftermath of a great battle, dead men strewn all about, the ground muddy with blood and offal. I do not know much else. I spent years wandering and eventually made it America in the 19th Century. In the early days of the 20th I was approached by agents of the Vatican..."

• • •

It was midday when the doorbell rang. I'd just finished cleaning a bedpan and I answered the door, a hand towel over my shoulder. I did not expect visitors that day, so I set to greet a stranger.

Not a stranger, but one I knew, a man named Samuel, dressed in snappy new suit, although its somber blackness made him look like an undertaker. No sooner than I recognized him he was in my arms being crushed firmly to my chest.

"Hi, Uncle," he grunted into my shirt.

"Damn, boy, it has been a long time," I whispered. Letting him free, I took a gander. Despite the hard planes and angles of his face, he still looked like the little boy I rescued in Denver. Strong jaw, slightly crooked nose, black hair and deep, almost sad eyes. The horrors of those times still marred his face and would forever. Things always stay with a body, wounds time could never heal. With a start, I realized he was only a couple of inches shorter than me. Children growing provide the measure of passing time. "You look fine."

His smile cut through the harshness of his face. "And you look the same, as ever."

"Not quite," I replied, fingering gray hairs that had started to creep in. "These are new."

"You do age!" he exclaimed.

"Sure. Slowly. How old do I look?"

He gave me a critical once-over. "Hmm...about forty or so."

"Hell, if you met me a hundred years ago you would not think I was day over thirty." I smacked my forehead with the heel of my hand. "Where are my manners, come in, come in."

As I closed the door, his smile performed a slow fade. "I don't want to deceive you with idle chitchat. This isn't a social visit, Uncle."

My heart dropped. Of course not. Samuel was not the type to visit right out of the blue. I sighed and absentmindedly wiped my hands on the towel. "What is it, then?"

Samuel looked around and sat heavily on the couch, removing his fedora and wringing the brim with his long fingers. "What do you know about my job?"

I scratched my head. "You have been doing fine work with the Red Cross." It was his idea to join that distinguished organization. When he graduated from Yale in 1920, it was the first thing he mentioned to me after the ceremony.

"Yes, yes, yes," he said. "It's going well. We have wonderful things in the works. No, I was talking about my other job."

A feeling of unease slithered up my spine and I decided to sit as well. I had hoped the Red Cross occupied the lion's share of his time. I was not a fan of his other line of work. "I know you also work for the government ...a 'think tank' I think they call it."

He nodded, biting his lower lip. "Yes, for the State Department."

"Burning your candle at both ends."

"I can manage."

We sat in silence for a moment, regarding each other steadily and I could see he was nerving himself up for the real reason for his visit. "This is bad, yes?"

Another nod.

Unease gave way to resignation. "How bad, then?"

"What do you know about the German Chancellor, Adolph Hitler?"

"Yes...friends of mine in Munich and Vienna tell me he has appointed Hjalmar Schact, the Minister of Economics as his Plenipotentiary for War. Everyone knows Hitler is gearing up for dustup, but most think it is with Poland and the Czechs. Also heard he is leaning on the Jews something heavy, taking possessions, lands. Bad time for them in Germany."

"Did you know he's into the occult? Magic, sacred artifacts and such?"

Goosebumps flushed across my skin. "You do not say?"

Samuel nodded. "He has a cadre of agents, very small, but very elite, called Die Speziellen. They are composed of highly trained soldiers learned in history and archeology whose sole purpose is locate objects of an occult nature."

Die Speziellen...The Special Ones. Very cute, but that cuteness wore off right quick as I realized what Samuel was about to say.

"He is after the book," I blurted before he could open his mouth.

Samuel nodded. "And the Ark of the Covenant, The Spear of Longinus, the Grail and dozens of others."

"How does he even *know*? The book is possibly the most obscure artifact ever."

"There are theories," said Samuel, shaking his head. "But we know he's got a bug up his ass about it. Our man in Berlin tells us that Die Speziellen is closing in on its location. They've been pouring through old records and maps, burning the midnight oil trying to pinpoint its location."

"Maps of where?"

"Egypt, South America, Mexico, and Austria."

Well...fuck. I rubbed my face and thought furiously for a moment. This was news to me, my contacts in Washington never said a word and I was particularly well informed about foreign events. All part of my bread and butter, as it were.

"You need my help."

Long fingers continued to worry the hat brim, an affectation that used to amuse me. Samuel could never sit still for minute. Even as a young boy he was always on the move, getting into trouble. "Yes, Uncle. You have an idea where it might be and we need you to go on a mission to retrieve it, but you won't be alone. In case you're wondering, I haven't mentioned you by name, only told my superiors I had to travel to San Diego to consult a historian and that I might know someone who can help. If you say yes, you will travel to where it is hidden and hand it over to the Vatican. They can safeguard it forever."

For a brief moment I regretted telling Samuel about the book, about my history. I instantly dismissed such a feeling as petty. If I could not trust this marvelous young man, then I was truly alone in this world. "The Vatican? Give it to a bunch of priests?"

He laughed, a high, clear sound that warmed my heart. "Uncle, the Vatican makes Fort Knox look like a child's sandbox. And it won't be priests who guard it but the *Manus Dei*, their elite group of soldiers who duty is to fight the enemies of mankind. At one point in time they were known as the Knights Templar. The Templars still exist, but now as a separate organization."

This was all too much. Knights and Nazis and a crazed pinhead Austrian who wanted world domination, along with deadly quests and magical artifacts. I was getting too old for this shit.

"I cannot," I sighed. "Elizabeth needs me."

"Uncle, she's nearly a hundred years old! Hire a nurse. Hell, hire two, I'll get the government to foot the bill. We *need* you."

I gave that consideration, knowing that I could milk Washington for a ton of greenbacks, which would go a long way for what I had planned. No...I had other obligations. My face settled into stubborn lines. "No. Sorry Samuel, but you will have to send your own men find the book first, them and those *Manus Dei* Templars or whatever. And even John Carter, Warlord of Mars, I hear he is a firecracker with a blade, but not me. I can give you the location of where I saw it last, but that is it. Elizabeth needs me; I have potential cases to take because I will have change identities and location soon. I am swamped."

He knew the look on my face. He knew there was nothing he could say to alter the situation...my mind was made up. With a sigh, he stood and we hugged. I had let him down, I knew that, but I had bigger obligations to fulfill.

"I'm at the Hotel del Coronado until tomorrow, Room 106," he said sadly, slipping a piece of paper into my hand. "Call or come by if you change your mind."

He left, the door closing on his slumped shoulders and weary countenance. Letting him down hurt more than I thought it would.

Ring-a-ring-ring! The metallic notes bounced off the walls, an irritating peal for attention. Not for the first time I considered installing an intercom.

Up the stairs and down the hall to Elizabeth's bedroom. The door was ajar and I entered to finder her sitting on the edge of the bed in her nightgown, the large brass bell she used to summon me still in her hand.

Mary's granddaughter was in her nineties, but still sat straight and strong, her once-thick hair a thin, gray wisp tied into a bun at the back of her head. Mentally, I smoothed away the crevices and ravines of her face, straightened her nose and added baby fat to her cheeks and saw the sweet nineteen-year-old I'd rescued from the Dead Rabbit's a lifetime ago. No matter how thin her skin had become, no matter how liver-spotted, she was still that precious girl.

"I heard what you said to Samuel," she said simply, a stubborn set to her jaw that I knew so well. "You should go."

"You heard all that?"

"I may be ancient, but I'm not deaf. I heard. You should go."

Usually all I have to do is remove my sunglasses and the bad guys back down right quick, but Elizabeth was made of sterner stuff. I left my sunglasses be and placed my hands on my hips.

"Don't you dare!" she snapped, shaking a wrinkled finger at me. "I'm not a foolish little girl anymore. I'm at the end of my days and, if necessary, can take care of myself. You go on and do what you have to do. That Hitler man is setting to make a miserable time for the world, anyone with even one good eye can see that. Mixing race with religion as if they were the same thing. *Hmph!*"

I stood there, stunned beyond belief at her ferocity. This was the most energy I'd seen her display in years. Her eyes blazed with a passion long thought dead, glittering like jewels and hard as English oak.

After her return home from the clutches of Templeton Reid and the Dead Rabbits, Elizabeth retreated from the world into a landscape of books and education. She became a virtual recluse, hiding in her room with her tomes. Her mother and father were beside themselves with worry and I was long gone, having made myself scarce, so they could not rely on me to help out.

Eventually, Elizabeth emerged and rejoined society, but still kept her distance from others, choosing a solitary existence that excluded adventure and romance. Instead of a life of marriage and children, she chose education, becoming one of the most beloved teachers in Brooklyn Heights.

For forty years she taught, doing her damndest to offer the best education the children of New York could receive and she was good, better than most. Certainly no one surpassed her in dedication.

But her life lacked passion. Not the passion for learning or teaching, but the kind of passion found only in the embrace of a loved one. She had traded a life of possibilities for herself for offering those same possibilities to others and was content to do so.

How do you tell someone they made a mistake if you are not sure that they made one? Thanks to her, kids who might have grown up to be thieves, rapist and murderers became doctors, lawyers and bankers and was that a bad thing? Trade your kids, or possible kids, for other people's children and help make them productive human beings.

I could not help but think what her kids would be like, though. Little girls, little boys, cute as buttons and loved so much the heart would fair burst just looking at them. They would be smart as whips, too, becoming whatever they felt like. Perhaps writing books, horror novels, maybe, where the mindless monster threatens the frightened villagers who respond with torches and pitchforks.

No.

But they would have been pretty kids and I would have watched over them like I watched over poor James's kids and loved them, their doting, caring Uncle who would bring the great gifts on Christmas while their parents gave them the soft presents. The kind of presents kids hated to receive on the holidays because they would be filled with nice button-down shirts and socks and the kids would groan dramatically, but Uncle always handed out the toys because Christmas was about love and giving and nothing was too good for the family.

By God, those kids would have been something.

I had been caring for her as the book of her life reached its final pages. It was no imposition, she required little except her books, newspapers and radio and a bell when she lacked the energy to stand and needed assistance. As for me, I still provided security services to the wealthy and influential and that bit of business was doing quite well, thank you. I had offices all across America and no longer needed to attend all assignments personally, there were plenty of ex-soldiers from the Great War for whom peacetime was a curse. They provided the backbone of my industry, while I took only the choicest assignments, enough for me to keep my identity deeply buried.

"You are not going to let this go, are you?" I asked resignedly.

She shook her head vigorously. "No, Uncle. But it is time, far past time, for you to let me go."

I knew I would not see her again, not in this life, so I gave her one last Christmas present, an early one. I left to do what was asked of me. After all, Christmas is for giving and I steeled my heart, letting her go.

•   •   •

Beefsteak Charlie's was a hole-in-the-wall diner near the waterfront, the kind of place where they served greasy, but flavorful, food and it was the only place in all of San Diego where you could find an honest-to-goodness Philadelphia-style steak sandwich. All the trimmings...cheese, peppers, mushrooms, the works. The owner and cook, Charlie, was from Philly and he declared to all and sundry that the city was *the* finest in the entire US of A. He was six-foot-five and weighted at least 350 pounds of fat-covered muscle and no one *ever* asked him that if Philly was such a hot place, then what the hell was he doing in California?

I was on my third sandwich when Samuel entered the restaurant, two other men in their twenties dressed in somber suits following. Both had solid builds and carried themselves with an easy grace that told me they could handle rough situations. Samuel embraced me and the two men treated me to hard, calloused handshakes. Soldiers at the very least.

"Thanks for call and agreeing to meet," Samuel whispered before releasing me. "This is agent Braun from the Department of the Navy," he introduced the slightly taller man with close-cropped blond hair thinning at the front. As he sat opposite to me at my booth, I pegged him for second-generation German. In fact, he looked like poster boy for Hitler's idea of an Aryan ideal. The other one was introduced as Agent DiCicco. That was it, no further explanation. Looking the man over with his blacker than black hair, fair skin and deep brown eyes, I figured he must be one of the mysterious *Manus Dei*. The Italian surname and small gold crucifix worn on shining chain resting on the vest of his dreary suit were my other clues.

As for me, I kept it casual with gray slacks, a red button-down shirt with gray stripes and comfortable shoes and my ever-present sunglasses. And enough makeup to take the edge of my scars.

The waitress arrived with three coffee cups and saucers, placing them in front of my guests. "Can I get you gents something to eat?"

"Thanks, Marlene," I said with a smile. "They will have three specials and coffee."

Marlene dimpled prettily. "Gotcha, doll."

DiCicco's eyes followed the waitress's swaying rear as she disappeared into the back with the order. Sure acted like a regular joe, not a priest. One point in his favor.

Braun started things off without preamble. "Sam tells me you're the big expert on this Book of Ur thing, a real historian and a tough guy. You also run a security services company. That right, Mac?"

He sounded just enough like a movie mobster to really get under my skin, but I let it slide. "It is what I do."

"You don't look like any historian I've ever met."

I raised an eyebrow. "Really? And what are historians supposed to look like, *Mac*?"

Braun grinned tightly. "They wear tweed jackets with patches at the elbows and smoke pipes and shit. You look like a bruiser."

"Yes, well I left my tweed jacket at the drycleaners, but let me say you look exactly like what I pictured a G-man looks like."

"Devastatingly handsome?"

"Stupid and full of himself."

Samuel closed his eyes and grabbed Braun's arm before he could rise up out of his chair. "Please you two, that's enough.

"If you do not mind, sir," DiCicco said hastily in the flat, neutral accent and precise, clipped speech patterns of someone to whom English is a second language. "Will you kindly remove your sunglasses?" He tossed Braun a hard look. The other man sat there trying to stare a hole in my head.

"No." I shook my head for emphasis. "It is a medical condition; my eyes are very sensitive to light."

His eyes narrowed, but he gave me a terse nod and Braun took over, speaking slowly, evenly. "Sam also tells me you speak fluent German, Italian, French, even Chinese."

I shrugged. "My father's money well spent on an extensive education."

Braun continued as if I never spoke. "He also tells me you have combat training, fighting the Germans in France near twenty years ago. Is that where you got those scars?"

My finger traced the line down my face, no longer purple thanks to makeup, but still obvious. "Yes. German bayonet. The other two were caused by bullet fragments."

"Your medic did a shit job. No offense."

"None taken."

"Anyway, Sam tells me if anyone can find the book, it's you. In fact, you might have an idea where we could get the thing." He kept staring at me with the cold dead eyes of a killer.

I finished my food, biding time, building a good lie. Thankfully, Marlene chose that moment to arrive with three plates filled edge to edge with enormous sandwiches. We thanked her while she poured more coffee for the three and I talked while they greedily stuffed their faces.

Braun ate like his stomach had been eyeing his liver for lunch, while DiCicco proved far more fastidious and neater. That did not stop him from taking a big bite or two. Those Philly sandwiches were *that* good.

Here goes. "There were maybe a handful of texts found that mentioned the book, all have been either lost or destroyed," I said. "No one knows much about it except that it is the possibly the first book ever written. Perhaps around the 14th century B.C.E., and finding it would be like finding out that the first automobile was really built by King Louis XIV."

DiCicco confirmed his identity by saying, "The Vatican has no records of such a tome."

"Of course they do not. Like I said, only a handful of texts ever mentioned the book by name. The rest is oral history. Bad oral history, at that. I am surprised Hitler even *heard* about the thing."

"I can answer that," said DiCicco quietly. "Jan Gunther von Kimmel. An aristocrat from a very old lineage. One of the oldest in all of Germany and a historian and archeologist of repute. He is a professor at the University of Heidelberg and he is the one who informed the Chancellor of the book's existence. They call him Das Arbeitspferd, The Plodder. Perhaps he has one of those rare volumes that makes mention of the book. Be that as it may, he along with a group of Die Speziellen Samuel told you of are on their way right now to Austria to search for the book while other teams have been dispatched to Egypt. If it exists, we have to keep it from Hitler's hands."

Shit. They really might on the right track.

"Surely you do not believe in magic grimoires or ancient artifacts of power." I kept my voice light; skeptical while inside my heart was beating like a triphammer. The Germans must have had an idea where the book lay if they were sending this Plodder guy there and that was scary on a host of levels. How they knew baffled me, but they knew *something*. This changed things.

"It doesn't matter what we believe." Braun stuck a cigarette in his mouth and lit it with a silver lighter. "It could contain recipes for haggis for all I care. Our job is to get the book. Period. End Of Story." He raised an eyebrow in Samuel's direction. "Can he really handle himself, Sam? He looks kinda beat up and long in the tooth."

Samuel's grin was savage. "I've known him almost my entire life." His eyes looked back to the past. "He's capable of things you wouldn't believe."

The two agents looked skeptical, but nodded slowly.

"Okay, old-timer," Braun said as he finished his sandwich, cigarette burning slowly in one hand. "You tell us where to look. Come with us and if we meet Hitler's nancy-boys, you stay behind us. We're tasked with protecting civilians and that include you egghead types."

"Fair enough." He wanted to catch bullets with his teeth, that was okay by me. "Who else is with us?"

DiCicco took that one. "Nobody. It will be easier, not to mention safer, with only three. Less suspicious that way. Braun speaks German, as do I, so blending in shouldn't be difficult."

I crossed my arms over my chest. "There is the matter of my compensation."

Braun jumped in. "Don't be greedy. You will have the thanks of a grateful nation." He stabbed his smoke out in the ashtray almost angrily, as if the thought of the government actually paying me for services rendered was un-American. He should have known better...in America, it's all about who gets paid.

I laughed long enough for them to fidget and scowl. "Yeah, whenever I need to buy groceries, they always take my gratitude in lieu of payment. Next month I am fixing to get a car, maybe the dealership will take kind words and kisses. Besides, I do not think you will be working for free, will you?"

"I can take care of that for you," Samuel said hastily before Braun could retort, sliding a slip of paper across the table. "This is what the government is prepared to offer if you're successful."

Unfolding the paper, I stared at the number scribbled there. A lot of zeros. A *lot*. "That will be fine. When do we leave?"

Braun smiled, a frosty, unpleasant thing. "Now."

"Gentlemen," Samuel said as the two stood. "Let me speak to him alone, please."

They nodded and walked out the door to stand and have a smoke in the parking lot.

Samuel turned his kind eyes to me. "Thanks, Uncle."

I smiled thinly. "Thank Elizabeth, she turned me around. I guess it is the right thing to do, we cannot let that mustache wearing moron grab hold of the book."

He dipped on hand in his suit jacket and removed a small box. "These are for you, developed special by our top minds. Way ahead of their time. They're called contact lenses. They'll change your eye color. I figure blue will let you blend in better. The instructions are in the box along with a second set in case you lose one and they can be worn for hours at a time. Still, bring your sunglasses just in case." He produced another box, larger this time. "This is a special solution to soak them in at night. Be sure to thoroughly rinse them before applying. The full instructions are inside."

Contact lenses. I'd heard of the concept, but never seen it in use. Last I heard the things could only be worn for a maximum of two hours before the eyes began to sting and water.

"Thanks, kid."

"Stay safe, Uncle, and get that damn book."

•　　•　　•

"Well, what happened?" asked Branch. Cecily.

I shrugged. "Went to see the Oracle of Delphi, an old Greek woman with skin like old shoe leather, not the one we visited in Greece, but an earlier version in a different house. She pointed me in the direction of England. Turns out the book was in the possession of a professor of Archeology at Oxford."

"Bilt."

"Bilt. I took the book from him and gave it to the *Manus Dei*. He has been rather raw about it ever since. We worked together again from time to time, although he still carries a grudge."

"Holy shit."

"You kiss your mama with that mouth, Agent Branch?"

About that time we suddenly found ourselves beneath a blanket of stars, the heavens a magnificent display of light above our heads.

Then everything went to shit.

CHAPTER TWENTY-SIX

Denver, November 1904

Samuel's eyes closed and his face went slack. Even though he was in pain, torn from being brutally abused, the kid was exhausted beyond words and would sleep for a time.

My anger proved to be a cold, leaden lump in my belly, freezing my guts solid. No mercy, no compassion, only the dire dread purpose to kill everyone in charge of the Show. It is one thing to dispassionately speak of murderous child molesters, but something else to encounter evidence of their handiwork..

I shut the bedroom door behind me, locking out the grisly scene of little Samuel sound asleep no more than ten feet from the bodies of Miss Ophelia and the mustachioed man. Walking as quietly as I could across the large room, I placed an ear against the far door.

Muffled conversation and music being played on a phonograph. Stephen Foster, if I was not mistaken. The conversation consisted of four or five people. Raucous laughter and belching along with the occasional holler of men cursing each other good-naturedly. No wonder they had not heard the commotion from the bedroom...they were almost loud enough to wake the dead they would soon join.

My boot hit the door, which flew open in a shower of splinters and the *ping* of metal bolts tearing asunder, revealing a good-sized room with a circular table in the center. Five men sat at that table, cards in hand, bottles of dark amber whiskey at their elbows. All were dressed well in suits and waistcoats with jackets slung on the backs of their chairs. A thick haze of smoke from several cigars floated about the room and caused my eyes to water.

They stared, aghast, at my size and the blazing yellow of my eyes and I stared back, stunned by one man, the man facing the door. A man I knew.

He was a bit older, a bit pudgier, but the same air of menace surrounded him like a dark, shimmering cloak, promising violence at every turn. More salt in his hair than before and squint lines seamed his face behind gold spectacles, but it was the same man I met all those years ago. I almost laughed at the irony, for who else could Mr. Ellis be but him?

Ellis Swearengen.

Ellis 'Al' Swearengen.

The cheroot perched between his lips fell unheeded to the table, burning a hole in the cards spread wide there. "You," he whispered, the word conveying more terror than a scream.

Everything became still, the sound of our breathing concealed by the rowdy music blaring from the phonograph. We all stared, by my eyes were for Al alone. The moment stretched like saltwater taffy, lasting for far longer than I thought possible.

Like a shattering glass, the tableau broke when one of the men, a lanky blond in a bowler hat, started to draw, but I was fast and they were not that far away and I was there grabbing the gunman's arm as it came up, the derringer clasped in his fist barking once, the shot going wide and I *pulled* hard, so hard, and muscles tore like tissue paper, fabric ripped, blood spurted splashing my face in a coppery crimson wash and I held the arm up, no longer attached to the man with the bowler hat.

Two shots, both missing me because the men were so frightened, their faces white and eyes round, and I was swinging that arm in great arcs. My yellow eyes felt hot, as if they would explode from my skull and I could see everything and just then a bullet tore through my cheek, shattering teeth on its bloody trip and searing a groove in my tongue before exiting the other cheek in a spray of tissue and enamel. I grinned horribly at the man who shot me, a portly gentleman in a dark brown beard that reached to his belly, and he fell away in a dead faint.

I would live, their bullets could not kill me, but it sure hurt like the blazes and I took my anger out on another shooter who clipped my shoulder with a huge Colt Bisley, my fist slamming down hard on the crown of his head, instantly crushing the bones of his neck. His eyes rolled up white before he collapsed.

Another bullet tore into my lung, the shooter taking his time like a true gunman. Fancy quick draws miss more often than not; ask Wyatt Earp, who once told me that calm nerves and steady motion, not necessarily fast, ensured accuracy. The shooter, another tall man with a ferocious, black mustache, shot again and the bullet passed through my other lung and damn if that didn't *hurt* like a sonofawhore. It also put a hole in my favorite coat, which irritated me to no end. My fist started near the floor and came upward at locomotive speeds in an uppercut that ripped his lower jaw from his skull with a sickening *pop*, my oversized knuckles and hand well able to take the damage. His last shot before my fist completed its damage snagged a chunk out of my left ear and that stung even more than the lung shot.

Warm, aromatic liquid splashed against my coat. Brandy. Very good brandy by the smell. There came a crackly, hissing sound and a flare of light momentarily brighter than the electric bulbs on the ceiling. I turned just in time to see a lucifer land on the brandy-soaked canvas of my coat.

"Burn, motherfucker," barked Swearengen in a voice thick with hate.

And burn I did...with an enormous *whoosh*, my coat was afire, blue flame licking everywhere and I could smell it crisping my hair and I was burning, burning, *burning*.

I shrieked, terror trying to clog my throat as the fire began to eat through my coat.

Burning! I am burning! The alien thought ricocheted off the inside of my skull in a voice that was mine, but not mine. Although I recognized the cadence, the timbre was much deeper with a strange, metallic, overlapping effect as if it echoed instantly and forever.

Then the leviathan woke, that deep dark thing from the far reaches of my soul, the secret giant come to cast the world asunder and I almost knew, I almost *remembered* what happened before, what was before the book and the madman who gave me life as a monster. It rushed up, that leviathan, and with it dread things.

Cold hard metal pressed against my forehead and I glimpsed a barrel of a gun an instant before the hammer struck. White pain blossomed in my skull, eclipsing the agony of burning, along with a sharp report that burst my eardrums. Another report, more pain and I fell, the leviathan receding, taking memory with it down into the depths and I tumbled away into my own private world of pain and burning terror.

• • •

Iron bands around my chest making it hard to breathe and pain like I'd never known ate at my neck. I was uncomfortable, lying on something hard and slick and cold, my buttocks mashed down flat against the unyielding surface.

Slowly, oh so slowly, my lids cracked open. It was dark, but not to my eyes and what I beheld was a pale ceiling light, an ornate circular bowl made of frosted glass with a leaf pattern in cold iron around the edges.

Ugh, my head *hurt*, a shooting pain that sent sparks across my vision and I tried to raise my hands to my skull, but they would not move. The pain originated at the back of my neck where it felt hot and sticky. Blinking rapidly, I tried to move my head, but that was immobile as well and I was working up a good case of pissed off before I realized I was *tied* to that cold, uncomfortable surface.

Swiveling my eyes, I could barely make out the thick chains binding my chest, digging deep into flesh. Dead iron bound my arms and legs as well, links partially cutting off circulation so that my fingers and toes felt like they were wrapped in dense cotton..

No matter how I grunted and strained, the chains would not break, would not budge, would not give me an inch of slack to work with. Finally, I gave up and bellowed my frustration and anger at the circular dome of the ceiling light.

A clicking and scraping reached my ears, then a dull thud. "Let me go!" I thundered. A useless attempt, really, considering somebody went to a lot of trouble to secure me good and proper, but it sure felt good just to scream and curse.

Time moved like molasses in the winter and I had plenty of it to ponder my situation. What happened to Samuel? Was I still in the hotel? All I knew for sure was that Al Swearengen's filthy mitts were all over this and he was not done with me yet. The man was a woman beater, a pimp, no doubt a murderer and other things I had not found out about and he would be back soon, if only to gloat. I had humiliated and embarrassed him in Deadwood and there was no way he would pass up an opportunity to cause me a powerful amount of hurt.

By slow degrees, my butt became numb, then my back, my calves and my shoulder blades, all points of contact with the hard surface I had been strapped to. Along with the numbness came a dryness at the back of my throat that grew and grew, my lips and tongue desiccating to brittle leather. Every attempt at swallowing hurt, like drinking ground glass, but I kept at it, desperate for any moisture. Adding that to the burning, scorched feeling on the back of my neck and I was a pretty miserable sonofabitch.

Click. Harsh, metallic. The overhead grew brighter and I blinked rapidly, momentarily blinded. It took almost a minute for my eyes to adjust.

A man came into view, hovering over me with a huge, shit-eating grin. Thin faced, slightly crooked, tea-stained teeth and a long, straight blade of a nose. He had virtually no lips.

"Good to see you awake, sir," he said softly in a clipped, British dialect. I snorted.

His smile did not waver an iota. "You have an amazing collection of scars. Shoulders, chest, legs and, of course, your face. Your flesh looks to have been crudely stitched and those scars have not whitened with age, remaining a dark purple of a recent injury. Very curious."

"My doctor was not very good. Always in his drink, you know." I licked my parched lips with a dry tongue. "Speaking of drinks, I could sure use one."

His he frowned in mock dismay. "Of course." Seconds later, a flask came into view. "Here you go lad."

"Mind loosening one hand so I can hold it?"

"I am afraid not." The man uncapped the flask and tilted it to my lips. Warm gin flooded my mouth and hit the back of my throat. I tried not to gag, but drops sputtered out from between my lips.

Gin. Why did it have to be gin? The stuff tasted like fermented mule spit mixed with turpentine. How those Brits drank the stuff without burning a hole from throat to crotch was a mystery to me. Still, I was thankful for the nasty stuff, it wet my tongue well enough and cleared my sinuses.

"That is fucking vile," I gagged. "What is next, shepherd's pie and spotted dick?"

A long finger traced the jagged purple scar on my cheek, then drifted to my shoulder. "This one looks as if someone had sewn your arm back on. Poorly at that." The finger traced the wide, pink scar above my knee. "And this, I would swear, is where your leg was reattached. Fascinating." He leaned in close enough that I could smell the gin on his breath. "You are delightfully interesting specimen. Why, the myriad of scars on your chest and stomach tells me you were split open like a rabbit on a spit."

"I am going to kill you, you know that?" I said conversationally.

He laughed, an ugly, sneering sound. "Feisty. I like that. Allow me to introduce myself: I am Dr. Gabriel Talent. I am the proprietor of what you Americans refer to as the Show. May I have your name, sir?"

This was the man, the head that moved the body of the snake. I forgot my burning neck; I forgot the nasty taste of gin on my tongue and the fact that I was bound head to foot with enough chain to crush a lesser man. All I wanted to do was sink my teeth into his face and rip and rend until I drowned in his blood.

I thrashed, or attempted to, but it was no use, the chains kept me tight.

"Do not even try, sir," chuckled Talent. "Those chains can hold a full-grown Brahma bull and the table you are lying on is of solid English oak. There is no escape."

Oak? Hmmm...that gave me an idea.

"Tell me, sir Whatever Your Name Is, I have read Mary Shelley's marvelous book. A classic, of course, but my question is, did you know the woman? Is it *your* story?" He teeth shone, glistening with unnamable emotions and the look in his eyes reminded me a man I once knew who stared too long into the sun. He spent the rest of his days in unblinking madness and that is what I saw in Talent's eyes, that same slightly hysterical insanity.

"I do not know what you are talking about."

"Please, sir. Do not take me for a fool. Mr. Swearengen shot you twice in the head and in both instances the bullets were spit out of your skull in less than a minute. All the while, you were moaning and groaning, speaking in a strange tongue. You are something special, a creature created by man who is immortal and stronger than human!" At my startled look, he laughed that ugly laugh again. "Yes, Mr. Swearengen told me about his encounter with you in Deadwood. He said you have not aged at all."

My lips pressed into a tight, thin line, not wanting to give that shit sack any satisfaction.

"Mr. Swearengen also passed on one tidbit of information I found very, very interesting," Talent continued in a more normal, conversational tone. "He told me of your fear of fire."

I kept my mouth shut.

"I noticed the burn on your neck has not healed. Interesting, is it not?"

This was not going well for me. A drop of sweat rolled down my temple and into my hair.

Cool liquid splashed my chest and arms. A strange, almost fishy smell hit my nostrils, slightly musty. "What the hell?"

Talent grinned even wider. "Hell indeed. It is whale oil, although not of fine quality. However, I suspect it will burn quite well."

No!

Seeing my horror, Talent raised a lucifer, letting me take a close look flammable little stick. One strike and it would catch, setting my chest afire and that thought scared the everloving shit out of me.

"What do you want?" I whispered.

"Answer my question," he said in a voice full of razors and glass.

It's easy to act stoic and brave when safe and snug in your home, a loyal dog at your feet and a snifter of fine brandy at your elbow. Quite another thing entirely when you are staring at your worst fears come to life.

"You-you asked if it was my story, Mary Shelley's *The Modern Prometheus*. No, no it is not. She was inspired by me, but it is not my story."

The lucifer disappeared. "Really? But your eyes! The creature in the story had dull yellow eyes. I will admit that yours are a brilliant yellow, almost glowing, but it cannot be a coincidence."

I shook my head. "It is not. In the book, the creature does have yellow eyes and skin so translucent that its muscles and veins were somewhat visible. When I was...brought into this world, my skin was...clear, but over the years it has thickened and darkened to normal. Only the eyes are the same."

"You knew Mary Shelley, perhaps you told her your story and she used it for her own ends."

"Yes, I knew her." *Mary, my love.* "And I do not give a cuss if I inspired her to write the story. It was her right to do so and I never cared about it at all."

"What about Dr. Frankenstein? Was he real?"

Damn, my neck hurt so much, every beat of my heart pulsing pain to the top of my skull. "No."

"What about your hands and feet? They are rather overlarge."

The pain in my neck, the thought of Mary and her smile, holding her in my arms and knowing I would never do so again finally broke through my terror, splintering it into kindling. "Just kill me and get it over with," I growled. His rapt attention was getting on my tits. I had an itch on my right thigh that was starting to really annoy me something awful.

Talent looked shocked. "Kill you? Why on earth would I do that? Do you have any concept what a distinguishing customer would *pay* for you?"

Oh damn.

"Fuck off," I said angrily.

Scrrrriiitccchhh! Sulfur tickled my nose and the next thing I knew my chest was on *fire*.

Fear clogged my throat as the oil burned and the heat began to build. I knew it would be only be seconds before my flesh started to roast and I almost welcomed it, despite the terror. I wanted the leviathan deep within me to wake and break the bonds of quiescence. I wanted to see what would happen when it was let out to hunt. Perhaps I would die, perhaps I would turn into the kind of monster everyone feared. Perhaps everyone would die.

Samuel. *What about Samuel?*

Would Samuel die?

No.

Instead of screaming my rising terror, I held my jaws shut, locking my fear down deep in my burning chest and closed my eyes.

Oh, God, it hurt so bad.

Relief was a soft blanket. It settled down on the flames, removing the heat before it could mortify the flesh of my chest and arms and damn, did it ever feel good. Talent patted away the rest of the licking tongues of fire until all were extinguished.

He left without a word.

Silence...blessed silence. I'd forgotten what a wonderful it could be and I reveled in it, luxuriated. Finally, I could think again. My neck still throbbed, but my chest was cooling. He had doused me before I could really burn. The bastard just wanted to fuck with me.

Which reminded me...English oak. I ran my numbed fingertips over the wood and felt nothing but a vague pressure against skin. The chains were biting deep and more and more of me was becoming numb.

I wiggled, trying to move my hand. My arms were bound at my sides, but there was small movement I could achieve with my hands and I used it to my best advantage, pressing my fingers against the cool wood.

Taking a deep breath, I *pushed*. Nothing. The oak was too strong and I had no real leverage. Sighing, I made a fist and using only my wrist, I knocked. Hard.

My big knuckles cracked against wood with the sound of a gunshot, so loud in the room. I cringed, waiting for a response. Nothing.

I knocked again. Harder. *Crack!*

The door opened. "What are ya doin'?" shouted a deep voice. A guard, I presumed.

"Can you get me water?" I asked.

"Is that why yer makin' that racket?"

"Yes."

"Fuck ya. Jus' be quiet." *Slam!*

It seemed I irritated my guard. Good.

Crack! Crack! Again and again and the first threads of pain worked their way up my arm as skin split. *Crack!* The wood started to become slick with blood and the guard pounded on the door, yelling at me to shut the fuck up, but I did not. I just kept on knocking and the pain kept coming, then receding as my healing took over and I let it, giving myself respite before continuing my attack on the table. *Crack! Crack!*

Over and over again

"Shut it the fuck down!" my guard yelled through the door.

Again and again, *crack! crack! crack!* Rest, heal and repeat.

Crack! Wooden splinters drove deep into my knuckles as the surface under my hand gave way, splitting and tearing.

The door opened. My guard came into view. It was the man who had fainted during my attack on Swearengen's crew. He still looked plenty scared, but he overcame his fear and socked me a good one across the jaw. Blood flooded my mouth and I just grinned, my teeth red.

"Keep it down!" he screamed, a worm-like vein throbbing on his temple.

My bloodied hand lay flat over the damage I caused and I prayed that he would not look down. It would not take but a moment for him to figure guess my design.

"Fuck you," I growled as his eyes began to roam.

His blue orbs flashed back to mine and flinched a bit at my fierce yellow gaze, but it did not stop him from delivering another good wallop. More blood on my tongue and I think he loosened a couple of teeth.

"Ya keep it down or I'll give ya what for," he yelled before storming off and slamming the door.

I grinned. *Crack!*

It took only three more knocks before my knuckles finally punched through wood and drove even more splinters into my hand. I stopped, waiting for the guard to arrive, to give me another wallop and call for help when he saw the hole I'd just made. One minute, then two. Nothing.

Thank God. My fingers, now healed but still numb due to the chains bound tight around my upper arms and forearms, traced the hole. About as big as a Double Eagle, enough for me to slip two fingers in and begin to worry wood.

In order to escape, I had to break the wood near the chain so I could free an arm, after that it would be over and I find Samuel and Talent. Samuel I would send home. Talent I would send to Hell.

With a terrific wrench, the wood gave, folding down and under, freeing my arm and loosening the chains around my torso. Once my arm was free, I was able to lever the chain from around my forehead, although skin went with the links. Nails of hot pain seared into my skull and pins and needles began to flow around my extremities as the blood returned. I almost fainted with relief.

No time for that, though. All the ruckus alerted the guard who came in to see me slide almost bonelessly off the table.

"Holy shitfire," he whispered. He clumsily drew a Colt from the holster on the outside of his left thigh and fired, shooting a hole in the floor next to my foot in his haste as I unsteadily rose. His second shot took me in the stomach just as I stumbled within reach.

Crunch! His windpipe folded around my knuckles and he fell, choking and gagging.

I looked down, realizing for the first time I was completely naked. Luckily the guard did not need his clothes anymore. After stripping his corpse, I saw that his shirt and waistcoat were too small, but the pants would work, even if they did ride up to mid-calf. Not much in the way of a wardrobe, but it was a damn sight better than letting my pride swing out for everyone to see.

The bronze plaque on the door read 407 and the hallway looked the same as the one I had taken earlier. The guard's colt in hand, I raced down the hall to 417 and burst in at speed, tearing the door from its hinges and reducing it to splinters and surprising Townsey, who was lounging on the settee, smoking a cigar.

Just the man I wanted to see.

As I stood to my full height, pistol cocked, he stared at me in horrified fascination, eyes flicking from my chest to my face.

"Ah, Townsey," I purred, smiling wide enough to make my scars itch. "There you are."

He shook his head. "N-no." The cigar fell from his lips to land on his crotch.

"Yes."

"Oh, please no."

"Oh, yes," I affirmed, advancing slowly.

While his eyes tracked my progress, the cigar hissed and sputtered as a large, wet stain appeared under it, dousing the coal.

"Where's the boy? The one that was in that room?" I pointed to where I killed Ophelia and the mustachioed man.

"Uh, the doc is lookin' at him."

I came nose to nose with the fat man and smelled the fear sweat rolling off him in a foul wave along with the odors of piss and cheap cologne. "Where?"

He gulped. "503. R-room 503. I-I-I didn't have nothing to do with the boy, mister. I'm not like that. That's *sick*."

Townsey was a pig and an opportunist, but did he deserve to die? As I watched him sweat and fart in panic, I realized that while he did not participate in the abuse children, he sure did not stop it, either. He also shilled people who did and that was good enough for me.

His death was quick, a bullet to the brain pan that painted the curtains behind his head in red and pink.

Room 503. Easy enough to find and no one in the halls, only the muffled grunts of people fucking and the occasional bray of a donkey. I was surprised, but it disturbed me too much to investigate. For a moment I worried that the sound of gunshot might alert guards, but realized there was plenty of noise coming from the various rooms, some more alarming than firearms.

As I approached the door, a man exited. He was bald as an egg and wore a Van Dyke beard. There were bloodstains on the cuffs of his black striped white shirt. His eyes caught sight of my feet, then traveled slowly up, taking in the short pants and my bare, scarred torso with its plethora of scars. Before he could react, I had him by the throat and against the wall.

"Is Samuel inside there?" I whispered fiercely, indicating 503 with a tilt of my head. "Blink once for 'yes', twice for 'no'."

He gasped and gargled and I had to put the barrel of the Colt in his mouth to quiet him down. "Answer me!" I hissed.

Blink.

I made sure his watery gray eyes stayed glued to mine. "Will he be alright?"

Blink.

"Is anyone else in there?"

Blink.

"More than one?"

Blink.

"More than two?"

Blink blink.

Two. Good. "You are the doc." Not a question.

He answered anyway. *Blink.*

"Good night." I choked him until he was unconscious and set him gently on the floor and once again, burst through the door.

This suite was similar to Swearengen's on the fourth floor, a big room with two doors, one to the left and one to the right. There is where the similarities ended. The main room had no settee, no tasteful clocks or rugs. It was bare, with white sheets covering the floors and walls, rendering it a stark, sterile white that almost hurt to look at. In the center was a sheet-draped table next to a steel cart containing a myriad of what I could only guess was surgical instruments.

The table was occupied. Fatima hogtied here, naked and shaking, while Talent loomed over her, facing the door. A scalpel was held carefully in his hand and he was in the process of cutting a deep gash in her cheek when I barged in. Before I could stop him, he placed the blade to her throat.

"If I twitch," he said, no longer the picture of a jovial Brit. Evil and malice wafted from like heat from a bonfire. "She dies."

I raised the Colt.

"Ah, ah, ah..." he warned, pressing the blade slightly. Blood flowed from Fatima's perfect skin, scarlet against desert brown.

"Maybe," I said, aiming carefully. "You will not even twitch."

Blam!

The bullet left a round, bloodless hole between Talent's eyes before cratering the back of his skull. He gaped for one, two, three seconds before slowly folding in on himself, the scalpel clattering on the tabletop.

There was not time to rejoice in my marksmanship because two steel-cable arms wrapped around my torso, pinning mine to my sides. A grunt, then I was heaved into the air while the arms tried to squeeze the breath out of my lungs.

Snarling, I rammed my bare foot back, my heel connecting hard with bone, which gave with a *crunch*. My attacker shrieked and let go and I landed nimbly on my feet, turned to a big brute hopping on one foot. He was a monster, almost my size, bald, with coal-black skin and angry eyes. He was easily the most massive man I had ever seen.

God made man, but Sam Colt made all men equal...or so the saying goes. I unceremoniously shot him in the heart and turned back to the room.

Fatima just lay there and I thought she was dead, but upon closer inspection I saw the mottling of bruises around her eyes and the terrible swelling taking over her face. She had been beaten badly, her nose broken, and was only semi-conscious.

I tore strips of sheeting from the table and made a crude bandage, which I placed on the flowing cut on her cheek. Having mended broken noses before, I placed my fingers on either side of that damaged area of her face and straightened it out with a faint *pop*. Talent's jacket made her a fine blanket and I left her to look for Samuel. He was sleeping in the small room to the left, curled up around his knees on a small cot.

Gingerly, I stroked his peaceful forehead, marveling at a child's ability to sleep through the loudest ruckus, but then I noticed a small empty brown bottle on the side table next to the cot. I read the label...laudanum.

The doctor must have used it to ease Samuel's pain and the boy would be out for a while and not even the Rapture would wake him. I picked him up gently and cradled him in my arms. Poor lad, I suspected he would have a lifetime's worth of nightmares.

In the main room, Fatima was sitting on the edge of the table wearing Talent's jacket, which covered her from neck to knee. Her face was swelling to grotesque proportions. She handled herself calmly and with great dignity. One tough lady.

"I did not run fast or soon enough," was all she said before standing, wobbling only slightly. "Thank you for the bandage."

"Let's get out of here."

"What about the rest of them?"

"Them?"

"Talent's people."

My gaze fell to Samuel's peaceful face. "Can the Show go on without Talent?"

She shook her head, her long black hair flowing like water. "No, he was the money and the brains behind everything. Without him it all falls apart."

"Then it is time to go. I have a little boy here to get to safety. Go ahead, take Talent's shoes, or the doc's. It is cold outside and you will need them."

Fatima gazed at Samuel, her face moving painfully. "What a sweet child."

"Yeah," I murmured. "We have to get out of here."

Apparently the sight of bloody, half naked people seemed to be normal circumstances because we made it all the way out the front door. It turned out that the Show current venue proved to be the Cambridge Hotel (the second swankiest place in Denver next to the Brown Palace). We barely elicited a glance from the night manager as we crossed the lobby and I made a mental note to investigate the hotel staff later for their ties to Talent's mobile brothel..

We were almost a full block away when a shot rang out and a bolt of fire set up shop in my left buttock. I fell to one knee, the precious burden of Samuel still in my arms as snarly, nasty voice sounded out from behind.

"Turn around, you fucking unnatural *thing*, so I can see your eyes when you die."

Swearengen. Of course. Cursing my aching ass, I turned my head to see him standing twenty feet away, a godawful huge pistol in one hand and a makeshift torch in the other. Looked like he used a table leg, rags and thick oil. Sighing, I placed Samuel carefully on the cobbles.

Cobbles? Hmmm.

While carefully arranging his body, feeling Swearengen's eyes on me all the while, I ran the fingers of my right hand across the uneven ground, using the little boy to shield it from sight. "What do you plan on doing with the boy?" I said, folding part of the blanket under the boy's head. "The woman?" *Please*, I prayed. *Please let him be a talker.*

"Hurry up there, you cocksucker," he snapped. "I don't need the boy. That kinda game is not the one I run, but the girl, well...she's an earner and she'll keep earning. Now turn your ass around so I can take care of business. It's late and I have..."

I never figured out what else he was going to say, the six-inch cobble I had pried free (with very little effort) flew through the air and hit him straight on the forehead with a wet *crunch*. Swearengen fell backward, skull crushed, his finger spastic on the trigger, sending a shot into the night sky. I did not even have to skin the Colt tucked into my waistband.

Sometimes prayers do get answered.

•   •   •

We did not return Samuel to the orphanage from which he had been sold, but it turned out fine in the end. Fatima grew mighty fond of the lad and he took to her like a duck to water. Thanks to the Riverwoods, she received enough seed money to start her own business...flowers, of all things. The orphanage that sold Samuel became the quite the scene...seems like the director and two of his cronies were so riled up and sorrowful that they all hung themselves.

Pity.

I made sure Fatima and Samuel were on their feet before heading out. From time to time I got mail. Seems Samuel learned his letters just fine.

An interesting note to close the case...three months after the incident in Denver, a prominent local businessman from St. Louis by the name of Melvin Ambrose was found dead. Turns out he'd been gutted, then dumped in the Mississippi for the catfish to eat. Seemed like Mr. Virtanen got to practice knifework after all.

I hoped with that, little Charles Riverwood could rest in peace.

CHAPTER TWENTY-SEVEN

A half-second. That is how much time it took for me to notice that the armor we wore reverted back to modern clothing and that the swords at our hips were once again pistols. In that instant I felt a surge of relief so large that it near overwhelmed me.

Out of the darkness a hand grabbed me by the throat and squeezed mercilessly, the bones of my neck crumbling with a wet crunch. Lightning flashed behind my eyes as my head filled to the brim with unbelievable electric agony and everything below my jawline went away.

I flew through the air and landed in a jumble of limbs, sand in my mouth, the wet snap of bones that I did not feel echoing in my ears. I came to rest a dozen yards away. I could not move my head, but it faced back toward the horses. My uncanny eyes saw what happened next as if during high noon.

It whirled like a dervish, jumped like a spider, fists flailing, knocking Branch to the ground. More bone snapping. Carter stood in a firing stance, 9mm blazing. The creature, the *thing*, staggered, jerked with every round but it kept coming at the agent undeterred by the withering hail of bullets.

It looked to be a blackened and twisted caricature of a man trailing gray ribbons, and it kicked out. Carter flew backward to land several feet away. A backhand connected to Bilt's jaw and gold teeth flew along with a stream of blood and spit. The wizard fell with a soft groan, eyes crossed.

Something shifted sickenly in my neck, the bones starting to realign, small pieces attaching to larger, blood vessels knitting together. God, it hurt so much, every subtle movement a symphony of agony and I could not move my head to look away as the thing kicked our collective asses.

Even though his chest must have been on fire, ribs broken and bruised, Carter managed to grunt his way to his feet as feeling came back in my hands and chest. Teeth gritted, the agent drew a K-bar and staggered toward the creature, who squared off with the grace of a ballerina, hissing and spitting.

"C'mon, you fucking fuck," Carter snarled, the knife slicing through the air. The creature leapt, panther quick but the agent was faster, the K-bar moving almost too fast to see. An arm flashed toward Carter's throat but he was not there to meet it and the monster landed where the agent was standing a moment ago. Minus a hand.

Like a dying spider, the hand lay palm up on sand, fingers twitching spastically and the creature hissed like a steam kettle, the knot of blackness that was its mouth wide open.

Shattered bone clicked together, fusing and suddenly I could feel my feet. A lump of fire burned at the base of my skull, but I ignored the pain and stood unsteadily, boots digging deep into the sand.

Carter whirled and the arm that ended at the wrist suddenly found itself edited at the elbow in a shower of dust particles that hung briefly in the air like dandelion fluff. He tried to dodge the next blow, but it spun him like a top, heels digging into soft sand before falling.

I stood, the last of my neck bones sliding in place as nerves regenerated. I burst into a sprint as the thing knelt to pick up its forearm and reattached it to its elbow. Ten yards and my feet kicked up sand in great showers. Too slow, my neck still not fully healed, but I had to soldier on. Five yards and the thing attached the severed hand to its stump. My arms came up, great hands grasping.

It spun, hands outstretched, my own grabbing at its arms. With a horrid crunch it thrust its fingers into my chest like knives, breaking through bone and digging deep. Pain erupted behind my eyes as blood gushed from my mouth, the things fingers clenching around my lungs and *squeezing*.

In my long life I have been shot, stabbed, burned, dropped from a cliff, hanged and had more broken bones than I can count, but having a monster squeeze both your lungs in its hands really took the taco. As I vomited blood, my vision began to darken around the edges, right before I saw a damn big knife slice downward, twice, *snicker-snack.* And that was the last thing I saw before the lights went out.

•   •   •

Coming to did not hurt. One second absolute nothingness, the next awareness accompanied by a damnable itching in my chest that felt like ants were scurrying about my ribs. It did not make matters any easier to see Carter looking down on me with a shit-eating grin that split his beard wide. "Wakey, wakey, eggs and bakey."

Oh, God, kill me now. I sat up, feeling an uncomfortable tinge in my chest. "What happened."

"The prophecy happened."

"Please, nothing cryptic. I cannot stand it."

"Look to your left."

I did and it took a second for what my eyes beheld to make sense to my brain, like an optical illusion where the sailboat is hidden in a pattern of dots. Scattered about the golden sands were dozens of pieces of what looked like beef jerky wrapped in tattered gray rags. It was the wrapped skull, jaw still silently working, that put the puzzle together. "You have got to be fucking *kidding* me!"

"Yep," said Branch, coming into view, wiping her hands on a small towel. "It's a mummy."

I shook my head. "The Dead, just like the oracle prophesized."

"And a pretty gross one, too," said Branch, stuffing the towel into her saddle bags. "Carter cut its arms off, I took the head. Bilt help scatter the pieces a bit, which were deciding to move about a bit, trying to join back together. It's still...unalive, I guess is the best way to put it."

"How long was I unconscious?"

She shrugged. "Not long. We got to watch your lungs grow back. Even grosser."

"So where are we? And why has everything reverted to normal?" I pointed at the rifle still holstered on Jed.

"We're here," Bilt replied, coming into view. His mouth looked horribly swollen and he spoke as if he had cotton balls tucked in his cheeks. "Our destination. Or close to it. As for your second question, well, Eden doesn't exist in normal space and time, does it? It exists outside our reality, the journey required us travel the soft spots between time to get here, didn't it? I reckon that since we're beyond time and reality as we know it, everything went back to normal." Turning to the agents he said, "Now I have to use some magic to make up for the state my mouth is in, I do. You can thank me now for the healing." He trudged off to do whatever it was that wizards do.

They mumbled their thanks and commenced eating some food. Branch offered me a candy bar which I downed in less than a second.

"Thanks, Cecily," I said around a mouthful of chocolate. My head pounded, so I placed my forehead on my knees and took deep breaths, feeling my newly healed lungs expand and contract, glorying in the sensation. "Where's Eden?" I finally asked.

Carter shrugged. "I guess we'll wait for daylight and find out.?"

Great.

The four of us drank water from our canteens and shared dried fruit (mangoes, apples, and banana chips) while taking our ease. Carter went on burial detail and placed each piece of the mummy at least five yards away from each other. The last to go was the skull and I felt its regard as Carter scooped out a goodly sized hole in the sand and plopped it in. I really did not worry about it reconstituting itself because by the time it did, we would be dead or long gone. I preferred long gone by a mile.

It was kind of nice staring up at a million stars (minus the moon which must have been in its new phase) and taking my ease with people for whom I had become rather fond. Even Carter.

Branch actually pulled up a patch of sand and sat next to me, munching on an energy bar and staring at the stars above. I tried not to be freaked out, but a trickle of unease still teased my spine. As for my other two companions, they kept themselves to themselves, Bilt reading a heavy, leather bound volume of sort and Carter playing a game on his smart phone. I wondered if he had any bars.

When the sun kissed the sky, I wolfed down a couple of energy bars and took a long drink of water. "Where to now, Bilt? I asked.

The tubby wizard gave me a golden smile and held up one of the diamond eyes, spinning slowly in a circle until he pointed away from the emerging sun. "There you go."

Think of the Sahara, then add more sand and make it a bit flatter. That is what the world we trod upon looked like. Sand, sand, and more sand with a heaping helping of sand thrown in for good measure. Despite the fact that it was a desert, the air was cool, the sun bringing the temp up to the mid-seventies. I did not even have to remove my heavy canvas coat.

After what felt like hours and hours of riding I saw a smudge on the horizon, a greenish tinge that told me something grew ahead. I urged Jed into a trot, then a slow canter, which was the fastest he could go considering the terrain. Camels would have been better for that place.

The green haze resolved itself into a stand of trees, albeit like none I had seen before. Palm like bark with jade branches spreading out leaves that reminded me more of ferns waving gently in the soft breeze. Coconut sized fruit with hard yellow rinds dangled from the green branches and I reckoned getting hit by one of those would do your head a dirty.

By the time we reached the trees we realized that they stood atop a ridge where sand gave way to soft, wet soil that led down into a large shallow valley pregnant with green. Trees both familiar and unfamiliar dotted the bowl of the valley carpeted in soft, tall grass so green that it almost hurt to look at, a green that seemed more real, more solid, more *present* than normal, as if our world was a bad photocopy of the abundance below us. A small lake sat in the center of the valley, fed by painfully clear and clean streams.

"Eden," I breathed.

Carter and Branch crossed themselves while Bilt merely gave with a golden smile. We stared for several minutes, trying to drink in the sight that assaulted our eyes with its splendor. Flowers in colors for which I had no name poked up out of the long grass, graceful shapes giving out sweet odors that tantalized...sweet, tangy, smells that never graced our noses in the world from which we came.

"What are you waiting for? Applause?" asked Bilt, urging his mount down the ridge. "We have a book to recover."

"This feels almost...blasphemous," whispered Branch.

I heard her just fine. "Bilt said Eden is open to mankind again, maybe that is what the book is for, to help us find this place."

"Great, now humanity can build trailer parks. Disneyland Eden?"

"That is not going to happen, Branch. We go in, find the book, then Bilt takes us back to where we belong." I grinned. "Easy peasy."

Carter grimaced. "Easy peasey, he says."

"Yes, yes I do."

I urged Jed after Bilt, taking the slope easy so the horse would not stumble. We rode for a bit, the sun crossing the sky throwing our shadows hither and yon, the scent of wildflowers as intoxicating as the finest brandy. Carter and Branch rode with pensive looks, their bodies tight, uncomfortable while Bilt leaned forward like he wanted to race his Thoroughbred at the Kentucky Derby.

Close now, I could feel it in my water, the end of our long journey, close to the book. Somehow, perhaps because I lived because of the book, I could sense it near, an itch at the back of my mind that urged me on.

What would we find? Who would we find? Another monster, perhaps? Something from the dark legends of humankind that struck terror even in the most hardened of us? Those thoughts occupied my mind so much that our arrival at the lake was somewhat of a surprise to me and I could see the two agents reacted the same way.

Water clear as glass stretched out before us, so clear I could see the floor of the lake littered with silt, rocks and vegetation. Multi-colored fish swam lazily, looking as if they swam through air rather than liquid and I wanted nothing more right then than to strip down to my skin and bathe in that crystalline lake.

It was at that point that the air split with the sound of a gunshot and Carter grunted, red blossoming on his chest. He groaned and fell from his bay mare, disappearing into the tall grass.

I spun in the saddle only to feel a blow to the head that barely registered before the lights went out.

"What you're doing is wrong. Flat out wrong."

A pinpoint sting on my forehead brought me fully awake, but I kept my eyes closed, savoring the darkness. I was getting mighty sick of being shot and beaten to death.

"Please, the book belongs to the Church."

Wait, that was Branch. To whom was she speaking?

The voice that answered seemed familiar. "It belongs to the person that can hold it. The Church could've used it to solve the world's problems, instead they chose to store it in the basement. That's a crime in and of itself."

What the hell? I knew that voice, but I could not recall.

"You want to use it for your own gain, not to help humanity."

"Well, I do admit to selfishness, but what's wrong with helping myself as long as I help others? I healed your fellow agent and the Jew is merely unconscious." Footsteps approached and a hard hand gently slapped my face. "As for this one, he's playing possum. Open your eyes, big man."

Oh well. My eyes cracked open to slits and I could see the blue above. No telling how long I was out. I glimpsed a man with a deeply lined, pale face with hair and beard liberally salted. He looked to be about sixty or seventy years old and his features spoke of a life hard lived. "Who are you?" I tried to rise, but a boot to the chest kept my down and I realized that my wrists were bound with leather strips that looked to be part of Jed's reins.

The man smiled down at me. "Don't hurt my feelings, Mr. Fredricks? Or is Vaugh? Vickers? Stein? Or is it Frankson? You've had a slew. We took a trip once, you and I when I was younger. Don't you remember?"

"DiCicco?" *No, it could not be!*

The man smiled. "You remember. This pleases me."

"That's his name?" I turned my head toward Branch who lay nearby, face twisted in disgust. "DiCicco? I know him as Anthony Seppi, my *Primus*."

Everything clicked into place. "You stole the book. You are the head of the *Manus Dei*, the *Primus*. That gave you access."

That grin never faded as he nodded. "Yes, of course. When we recovered it all those years ago, I had to return it to the Vatican, they would have hunted me down relentlessly, but I managed to study it a bit and learn the spells for longevity. I used them to extend my life and the Church attributed it to God's grace. The Vatican has a tendency to trust old men who are useful."

I had to buy time. My bonds felt tight and I knew I would never burst through such thick leather, a more effective binding than handcuffs which I could have snapped easily. "Why?"

He shrugged. "You want me to monologue a bit? The part where the villain gleefully informs the protagonist of his dastardly plans? Why not? You're not going anywhere." He sighed. "I have no plans to kill you, keeping your four prisoner is easy now that I have studied the book for a time. Besides, murder in the Garden would be blasphemous.

"For years I urged His Holinesses to use the book to better mankind, to bring enlightenment to the world. Foster peace, end war...all to no avail. I hatched a plan to steal it and use it for good. Thanks to my initial studies, I learned of your origins as well and knew they would come to you when it went missing. It was simple to use my contacts to alert the Sicarii, the idiots in Jacob's Rule and The Venerable Church of the Unclean Word that it had been stolen and you were to blame. I knew they'd slow you down if not stop you." He shrugged. "Seemed like a good idea at the time."

"I suppose that mummy was yours, then?"

"Of course. The book gave me the spell and I used it."

"Now what?"

DiCicco knelt, pointing a heavy revolver against my forehead. "Now I convince you to join me."

CHAPTER TWENTY-EIGHT

San Francisco, May, 1965

"Whaddaya see, Vic?"

I waited a second before responding, counting those I reckoned were guards for the house I surveilled. "Think this is it, Charlie."

"Good. I hate hanging my ass out here." Charlie Graves spat a stream of tobacco juice off to the side. A good egg, Charlie, fast with a draw and steady as they came even though his habit of tobacco chewing disgusted me to no end.

Thanks to capitalism, the wealth I acquired over the years multiplied to the point where I became a rich man even though I felt no need for money except to use it to keep my identity a secret. California offered diverse cultures and a plethora of strange faces that I did not stick out. Too much.

My investments ensured that I could sell the security business and devote myself full-time to aiding children and runaways. I also started a series of shelters for abused animals, finding them safe homes where they would be treated well. Every now and then I did do a spot of work for the wealthy and influential. Never know when a favor would be needed.

On this particular occasion my contact in the police department alerted me to incidents of disappearing prostitutes, the kind of case the cops had no real interest in solving. Sex workers disappeared with great regularity, but what made this one different was the sheer number. Over a dozen in the last thirty days and needless to say the commissioner did not cotton to finding out more as long as respectable people were left alone. Thinking like that really pissed me off, so I felt more than willing to investigate.

Talk to enough lowlifes and you can figure out what is what quick. People knew that girls went missing from the Tenderloin and a several even witnessed their last Johns they were seen with. The police did not care, except for my man, Harper, who had a soft spot for the ladies.

It did not take long to suss out where the girls went and I collected Charlie, who owed me, to help out. Maybe I was losing my touch, but I felt four hands could do the job better than two.

Most people would not have seen the guards, they had skills, hiding in alleys, one dressed as a bum, but I saw them and knew we had to take them out. I felt no compunction about it seeing as they took part of something dastardly.

"Let us go, Charlie," I whispered, duck walking to the edge of the roof.

"Right behind you, Vic," he replied.

I hung over edge, the alley floor only a couple feet below my boots, then dropped, my knees taking the shock. Charlie joined me a second later. "You take the two on the left, I will take the ones on the right. Quiet now."

"Don't teach your gammy how to suck eggs, Vic."

I grinned. We staggered out of the alley, a pair of drunkards heading home after too much of a good time. Our clothes, rumpled, our hair disheveled and our speech slurred. It usually works. Not this time. These fellows were *that* good.

The first one leapt forward, knife angling for my throat but I leaned back and felt it pass a millimeter from my skin. I grabbed his wrist and squeezed, the bones cracking as I pulled hard, bringing his head down to meet my knee. His nose broke with a loud pop, blood spraying against my jeans. The second man drew his pistol and I wrenched the knife free from the first and threw it underhand at the man. My aim was good and it entered his left eye, plunging in up to the hilt. He gave a soft cry and fell to the curb, bleeding and thrashing. I broke the first man's neck with a savage twist and spun to see Charlie wiping a knife on the shirt of one of the two men he dispatched. His grin was pure mean.

"Remind me never to anger you," I commented blandly.

"Fuckin' right."

No cameras, a point in our favor, but the door looked like someone welded quarter-inch steel plate and painted it brown. We stood to either side of the door so no could see us.

"What now, Vic?"

"Listen, Charlie, I am going to do something here and you have to keep it under your hat. Forever."

"That's a mighty long time, Boss."

"That is why they call it forever."

"You're the boss, Boss." Charlie nodded.

Crouching, I put my shoulder to the door and *heaved*. Now, these guys must have thought quarter-inch steel good enough for safety, but the frame was simple wood and while I could bend steel, breaking wood is a hell of a lot easier. With a loud crack, the frame splintered and the door fell inward with a resounding crash and we rushed in, pistols at the ready.

The first two guards, dressed in black three-piece suits, died before they could draw their weapons. The second two managed to draw, but we shot them before they could fire, crumpling in a welter of blood.

We stood in a large foyer floored in marble, hazed in gun smoke. A woman crouched on the floor dressed in a long, navy blue evening dress with a string of large pearls around her throat. She whimpered as she held a hand in front of her face in an attempt to shield her eyes. "Don't kill me," she whimpered.

Looking around, I saw a door to the left and one straight ahead. "Do not give me a reason to. Where are the women?"

She pointed to the left. "Through there and up the stairs."

I lifted her to her feet. "Come on. After you."

"No!"

"Yes. Do not make me force you." To Charlie, "See if there is a basement or cellar. Bad guys always keep things in the basement."

"A basement, Vic, in California?" he asked incredulously.

"Trust me."

"You got it, Boss."

The woman, older, almost matronly, led the way upstairs to a short hallway with three doors, left, right and straight ahead. "I'm just one of the women those guys used to keep the others in line," she babbled as I stood considering my options. "Which door?"

She pointed to the one straight ahead. My foot met wood and it splintered most satisfactorily, the door slamming open. Shrieks met my ears. The room, small, barely large enough to be considered a decent closet, was crammed with a dozen women of various ages from very young to those in their thirties. They all shared one trait, every one of them looked lovely, almost extraordinarily so. Obviously chosen for their looks.

These women, these poor women, in various stages of undress, looked at me fearfully, one rubbing her bruised cheek where the door hit her. "You can leave now. You are safe."

They did not move, instead they stared fearfully. Not at me.

Pain blossomed suddenly between my shoulder blades, sharp and all-encompassing. I spun, my vision clouding, ripping the knife from my guide's hand, her face a mask of hate. My fist smashed into her nose, spreading it across her cheek along with snot-laden blood. She fell, sobbing and screaming.

"Go!" I shouted.

Half the women stampeded out; the rest still remained staring at me incredulously. "What about our kids?" one asked.

Bang!

Once again I spun, only to see Charlie, smoking pistol in one hand and a look of absolute red rage on his face. "Bitch!" he screamed at my guide, who he had just shot dead.

"What is going on, Charlie?"

"You women, git on outta here, move it! Your children are downstairs."

They left in a hurry until only one remained, a woman lying against the wall. Her eyes stared at a place only the dead could see. Olive skinned and dainty, she looked like a flower just starting to brown along the edges of the petals.

Charlie strode forward and yanked the blade from between my shoulders and I grunted in pain.

"You okay, Vic? Need a hospital?"

"Jesus, that hurts!" I took a deep breath. "Yes, Charlie, I am okay. What the fuck is going on?"

"There was a basement after all, just like you thought." There were tears in his voice. "Kids, Vic, fucking kids. You shoulda seen them. They'd been *brutalized*. These bastards were using them to keep the girls in line. Prolly gonna kill them when they sold their mothers."

"Then I am glad you killed the bitch."

"I wish she'd come back to life so I can kill her again."

I entered the small room and knelt beside the dead prostitute. Her face, so striking in life had become ashy in death and her brown eyes looked so deep, so pure. "I wonder who she was."

"Vic, let's get outta here before the cops come."

"They hardly come to this side of town, Charlie, unless they are looking to line their own pockets. We have time."

Downstairs a lone child, a boy of perhaps seven, stood in the foyer looking at the dead men. He bore a striking resemblance to the dusky woman upstairs. "Hey, little man," I said, kneeling. "What is your name?"

The raw sadness of his gaze washed over me. A bruise colored one eye and he was barefoot. "Stavros," he replied.

I nodded, taking his shoulders gently. "Stavros. That is a good, strong name. Tell me, Stavros, do you have a father? Aunts? Uncles? Any relatives?"

He shook his head. "Just mommy."

Damn. "All right, Stavros. Your mommy cannot be with you now, she is taking a trip to Heaven." My voice thickened with grief. "And she wants me to take care of her good little boy. Do you want to come with me? I can take you someplace safe."

He nodded, tears forming in his big, brown eyes. "Okay, Mister."

I smiled and he did not flinch. Score one point for Stavros. "You can call me Uncle."

CHAPTER TWENTY-NINE

"Join you? Are you crazed?"

"Absolutely not," DiCicco said with all sincerity. "I work to do what you do, to save the innocents of this world. The book will tell us all we need to make it happen. With the grimoire I can cast the necessary spells to bring about real change." DiCicco smiled. "Look at me, I cast the same spell that Methuselah used to extend his life and with the book I can become young again. Think of those who deserve longevity, the good people who can help us make a difference. And that's just the tip of the iceberg."

I could not get over the gall of the man, but I knew I needed time, so I pretended to listen. "All of that directed by you, of course."

DiCicco shrugged. "Why not? I'm devout, principled and care for humanity, much more so than the Church, which exists now only to expand its influence and power. You know that the Church looked the other way when it came to pedophile priests, merely relocating instead of punishing them. That indicates severe rot in the institution. I look upon the world with a purity of vision and the discipline to do what needs to be done. Can the Church say that?"

He was not wrong. The Church in all its history committed atrocities without compunction and violently spread its message across the globe without remorse like Vikings raiding England. The Crusades, for example. But all that power in the hands of one man rubbed me the wrong way. "Think about the old saying...absolute power corrupts absolutely. You think you are the good man now, but what happens when someone does not agree with your methods? There will be millions, billions, who will not want you to 'save' them, so what then? Will you kill them? Rape their minds until they are forced to follow your lead? Or just force them to comply?"

"They will come around."

"How?"

DiCicco snarled. "They will see my grace, bestowed upon me by God. I will be seen as savior, a god."

And bingo was his name-o. "And so it begins. A god, DiCicco, really?"

The *Primus* abruptly stood; face twisted in consternation. "I—I didn't mean that, you tricked me!"

"Did I? Or did I just expose your hypocrisy?"

DiCicco walked away, disappearing into the tall grass only to return in a moment with what looked like an iPad in hand. "Here, if I can't convince you with logic, maybe an appeal to your curiosity will persuade you."

I sighed. *Of course the book is a tablet.* "Persuade away," I said, humoring the man. Out of the corner of my eye I saw movement.

"With this book I was able to discover your origins, who created you, what you are, how you came to be, *who* you are. I know the secret of your immortality and why you feel some deep, dark leviathan lurks in your subconscious." He patted the tablet. "It's all in here."

The words hit me like an electric jolt. For centuries I had wondered about my origins, questions that knocked about my skull like pachinko balls for such a long time I had grown used to the noise. Still, the temptation to give in proved great, so great that I remained silent for a moment to consider my options.

If I am being honest, I was tempted. Imagine being an adopted child, always wondering about your birth parents, the questions you must have, what you would do in order to find that information. It was an itch that begged to be scratched, a maddening sensation that wears down self-control to the point of insanity. I lived with it 24/7, 365 days a year for centuries. Maybe I succumbed to madness long ago and never noticed, a lunatic obsessed with justice against those who would abuse the innocent children of the world, willing to do anything to achieve my goals. My mind went back to the day I accidently killed that child which sparked the genesis of my obsession and led me to the path I trod for all those years.

Maybe madness colored my vision for so long that I no longer made room for a life, companionship. Love. But why choose love when those that came close to your heart withered and died thanks to the slow, relentless march of time? Perhaps it was time for me to focus on myself for a change. Perhaps I really should learn the truth of my existence.

Nah.

"DiCicco," I said softly. "I know who I am. I do not need a book or magical device to tell me that. I am a man. A monster, a long-lived servant for those who are unable to help themselves. Maybe I do not have a soul, but that does not mean I have to act like it at all. It is my belief that if I do not have a soul, maybe I can grow one."

That set him aback in shock, his eyes narrowing. "You arrogant fool, I'm offering you the answers to *everything* you desire. I've read your file, I've worked with you, I know you've been wondering about yourself for centuries and now you have the chance and you throw it in my face like a used dishrag? You're no man, you're an aberration suckling at the teat of the world and if you can't help me fix the world, then perhaps you should just die."

"Everyone dies, DiCicco, I have lived long enough to know that, but I have learned a lot over the years, including something you have obviously forgotten."

"Ha! Which is what, pray tell?"

"Never turn your back on a wizard."

Blue light suddenly surrounded DiCicco's body and he *blazed*, almost eclipsing the sun in brightness. I turned my head away, eyes screwed shut, but the furious light still sent black and orange spots to invade the darkness behind lids. This kept up for what felt like forever until it suddenly stopped and I blinked away tears, eyes adjusting the absence of the blue.

"Yeah, that'll teach the wanker, it will," grumbled Bilt, frowning mightily. As for DiCicco, he lay in the grass, still as a corpse.

"He dead?" I asked.

"Nah, but he'll sleep for a week and wake up wishing he was."

"Good job. Untie me, please."

Instead, Bilt strode toward the fallen *Primus* and picked up the tablet. "Ah, here she is."

"Bilt..."

"Don't give me that look, you big ape. I've been waiting for this since you forced me into this ridiculous journey, I have. Now don't you worry your bloody great head about it, I'll bring us back to the real world. Tied up like a roped calf, that is."

"Bilt..."

"Don't you Bilt me, you! I don't care about nothing but accumulating knowledge. Purely selfish, I am. The spells in here need reading, they *want* someone to use them, they do, and I'm just the lad to give it a bloody go."

"Bilt..." I warned.

Face crimson, he screamed, "What?"

"You are making the same mistake."

From behind the wizard Branch clubbed on the back of his skull with a rock, catching the tablet from his nerveless fingers as he fell.

"What an asshole," she sneered.

I sat up, nodding to my bands. "Do you mind?"

"Oh, of course."

Untied, I checked on Carter who snored like a buzz saw, looking beneath through the hole in his shirt where he had been shot to see nothing but pink, healthy skin and a dime-size scar. *Thank God*. It was then I realized I actually *cared* about the slender asshole. Just goes to show that almost anyone can get under your skin.

"Now what? You think Bilt will take us home now?"

I grinned, pointing to the tablet. "We have the book; we do not need him to do so. It might take practice, but we will get there."

"Did you think this might happen?"

"It crossed my mind." I found Jed and pulled out a King-Sized Payday bar from a saddlebag and began to munch. *That is the ticket right there.* "What I was not counting on was DiCicco. That surprised me and let me tell you, after years and years, very little surprises me these days."

Carter came to after I gave him a couple of light slaps, something he let me know verbally and in great detail how much he did not appreciate it, most of it anatomically impossible and considered illegal in the continental United States. I filed the more colorful euphemisms a way for later use.

Branch trussed DiCicco up like a BDSM enthusiast, even going so far as to gag him with a torn strip from one of her shirts. Cannot say I blamed her, considering the betrayal by her own *Primus* and all. If it was me, I might have used my underwear (I almost replaced that gag with the underwear but I stopped myself at the last second).

"Damn, my head feels like someone's using for a set of bongos," complained Carter. "And my mouth tastes like a goat farm."

"It begs the question...how would you know that?"

"Fuck off."

"Good to see you are feeling well, Carter."

"Fuck off twice."

When Bilt woke, he found himself *sans* shirt, shoes, bound but not gagged. I stood in front of him, staring down as he slowly realized his current situation, which did not please him one bit. "You asshole!"

"Yes, and you are an asshole for trying to steal the book."

"Where're the agents?"

I shrugged. "Sent them off so we can have alone time, sweetheart."

"You're a wanker, you are." Bilt closed his eyes and for a moment I thought he merely tried to come to grips with his situation, but instead he chanted words I did not understand and did not sound like they came from a human throat. Before I could move, my body glowed with the same blue intensity DiCicco's had when Bilt incapacitated him. Swirling with azure energy, I could only stand there as Bilt continued his incantation, the light flowing upon my skin like warm liquid. I felt a sensual sensation tingling throughout my body and memories of Mary's sweating skin next to mine came to the fore, the smell of her, the taste of her perspiration and the sound her breath in my ear. Mary, my poor, lost Mary whose family I guarded for all these years. She gave me purpose; she gave me hope and taught me about love and forgiveness.

I closed my eyes, reveling in the sensation, the memories of Mary and our oh so brief time together. One night of intimacy, but in that one night I lived a lifetime of love and for that night I felt truly happy, content with my lot at last. It was a feeling that eluded me ever since. I held onto that feeling, those memories, let them wash over me, around and through me until I felt near bursting with joy, like my body had become a balloon.

My eyes opened to see the last of the blue light soak into my skin and disappear down the drain of my body. I felt refreshed, better than I had before. In fact, I felt ready to do handstands and cartwheels all the way home. A smile stretched my face and I looked upon Bilt who stared back with what I could only think of as a mixture of terror and amazement. "You...you weren't affected by my spell!" he cried.

I could not help but feel overjoyed and an answer came to me straightaway, right or wrong, it was what I went with. "You use magic Bilt, but I *am* magic and it cannot hurt me unless I want it to." *Good enough explanation as any.* It made me uneasy, but I decided to gag Bilt because I could not trust him to try something that stupid again.

•　　•　　•

Since the sun decided to set for the day, we made camp, not bothering to light a fire as the sky above and its unfamiliar constellations provided enough light for my companions to see by. We stared at the stars and talked until we fell asleep

In the morning, once we snacked, we loaded our captives on our horses and trotted out of the valley, although we stared back for a goodly long time. It is not often that one voluntarily rides away from paradise, but at least we made it there, which is a sight more than most people can say.

EPILOGUE

Needless to say, we made it back. I will not bore you with the sordid details.

Of course, I let Bilt go. He cursed me up a storm, but that is all the cursing he could do since I seemed immune to his magic. I mean, I was bitten by a wolfman and had not grown extra hair on the full moon, so what could he do to me?

I gave the tablet to Carter, of course, who took the first flight to Rome from Denver. Even though he never thawed to me, his handshake turned out to be firm and strong, his gratitude genuine. My eyes itched to see him go, my throat thick with a lump. Had to be the flu or infection, the only explanation I could think of.

As for Branch, after we bid goodbye to Carter at the airport security checkpoint, she took my arm and led me toward the West Terminal exit.

"Are you sure you want to quit?" I asked as we made our way to the parking garage.

She shrugged. "I've been lied to all these years by my *Primus*, DiCicco, and I don't know how to process it yet. I need time. Sure, I know he indoctrinated me with all that abomination bullshit so I would eventually betray you, I get his motivation, but the Church has been the biggest part of my life for as long as I remember. Now...now I feel a little lost. I've never not been part of something bigger than myself."

I thought about that for a minute as we exited the garage and paid for our parking at a booth. The attendant tried not to stare at my scars. I could not blame her. They stood out so against my fair skin, I simply smiled and drove off after receiving my change. "You are so different since we first met."

Her grin lit her face like the sun. "And you're still the same."

"Now that is just mean."

"Seriously, you're a better person than you realize. I know you're haunted by your past, we all are, but you put your efforts doing what's right, which is a hell of a lot better than most."

I shrugged. "So, what about you? What do you want to do?"

Silence reigned for a minutes as she chewed on that. "Perhaps I could throw in with a security expert I know, a man who helps children and the innocent."

My eye brow climbed north and I gave her the old side-eye. "Do you think this security expert will take you on? I think I know who you are talking about and he is picky."

"Oh, I've had a good teacher." Branch grinned. "Besides, recently I've done pretty good work and the guy I worked will provide an excellent recommendation."

"Hmm."

She punched me in the arm. Not too hard. "What do you mean, 'hmm'."

"Well, I have not taken someone under my wing for a while. Not used to it."

"A partner."

"Partner? Now you are aiming a bit too high."

"You need a partner."

"I do not."

"You do. To watch your back."

"No." My tone became adamant.

"Yes." She countered.

"No."

"Yes."

"You are not going to let this go, are you?"

"See, you finally understand."

"I know a good restaurant where we can order fresh-caught halibut."

"Good, I'm *starving*." Branch placed a hand on mine.

Something warm happened in my chest. Not sure what. "Okay, partner."

THE END

ABOUT THE AUTHOR

Mark Everett Stone attended the University of Nebraska in Omaha, majoring in Journalism and minoring in English. He is the author of over ten books, one of which, *The Judas Line*, received a starred review from Publisher's Weekly. He currently resides in Redding, California with his heroically-patient wife, Brandie, their two sons, a cat, a snake and a neurotic dog.

NOTE FROM MARK EVERETT STONE

Word-of-mouth is crucial for any author to succeed. If you enjoyed *The Book of Ur*, please leave a review online—anywhere you are able. Even if it's just a sentence or two. It would make all the difference and would be very much appreciated.

Thanks!
Mark Everett Stone

We hope you enjoyed reading this title from:

www.blackrosewriting.com

Subscribe to our mailing list – *The Rosevine* – and receive **FREE** books, daily deals, and stay current with news about upcoming releases and our hottest authors.
Scan the QR code below to sign up.

Already a subscriber? Please accept a sincere thank you for being a fan of Black Rose Writing authors.

View other Black Rose Writing titles at www.blackrosewriting.com/books and use promo code **PRINT** to receive a **20% discount** when purchasing.